I0757603

BONES IN BLACKBIRD

THE LEGACY OF LUCKY LOGAN

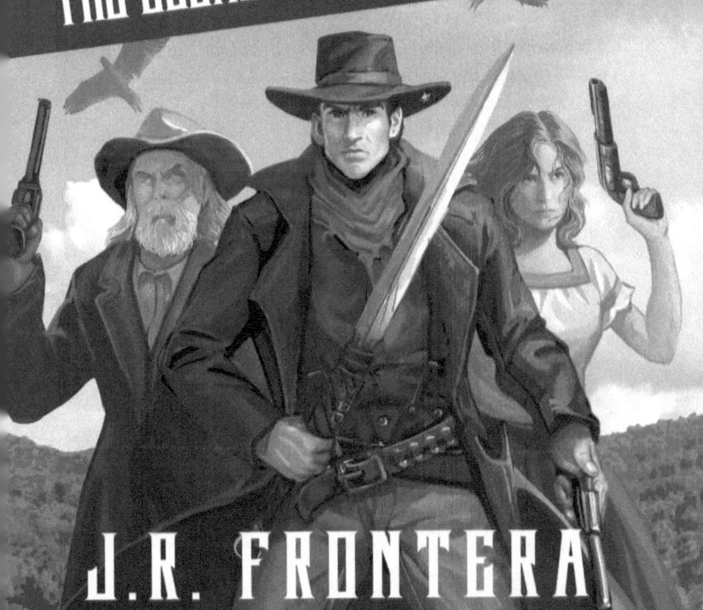

J. R. FRONTERA

Published by
TIN CAN

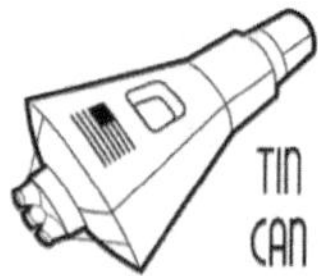

An imprint of Wordwraith Books, LLC
705-B SE Melody Lane #147
Lee's Summit, MO 64063
http://www.wordwraiths.com

This is a work of fiction. Names, characters, places, and incidents are products of the author's imagination. Any resemblance to actual events, organizations, places, or persons, living or dead, is purely coincidental or used fictitiously.

Version 1.0

http://www.jrfrontera.com

Cover art by Duy Phan
Cover typography by J. Caleb Design
Formatting by Charity Chimni
Maps by renflowergrapx and New Horizons

BOOKS BY J.R. FRONTERA

All books available on Amazon.com and most other online retailers, wherever books are sold.

THE LEGACY OF LUCKY LOGAN

(scifi western)

Bargain at Bravebank

Bastard of Blessing

Bones in Blackbird

Demon at Devil's Deep

(and more coming soon)

N'SPACE

(humorous space opera)

Galapalooza

The Starburst Inn

STARSHIP ASS

(humorous space opera)

Of Sporks, Overlords, and Moon Worms

Of Donkeys, Gods, and Space Pirates

Of Donkeys, Dogs, and Rogue Bits

Of Donkeys, Cogs, and Hot Bodies

COMPLETE

For a fully updated book list check out https://jrfronter a.com.

FREE BONUSES ALERT!

Enjoying this series so far and want to go deeper into this world?

Then you might want to head to your computer and check this out...

https://jrfrontera.com/the-lost-and-found/

DEDICATION

For the Poncho Agenda ... outlaws for life!

WORDWRAITH BOOKS
PRESENTS

A NOVEL PRODUCED BY

J.R. FRONTERA
PAT STEVENS
VICKY MEYER
JEAN LOWE CARLSON
MANDI RACKERS

COVER ART BY

DUY PHAN

COVER TYPOGRAPHY BY

J. CALEB DESIGNS

FORMATTING BY

CHARITY CHIMNI

MAPS BY

RENFLOWERGRAPX
NEW HORIZONS

WITH SPECIAL THANKS TO

SYDNEY STOKOE
SARAH TRUMBLEY
BETA READERS

SARAH TRUMBLEY
SYDNEY STOKOE
TAYLOR PARK
E J McKENNA
OBSI
BRAINSTORMING ROUNDTABLE

JAMIE DAVIS
MEDICAL CONSULTANT

MATT CARLSON
FIREARMS CONSULTANT

TOM FARMER
SWORDSMANSHIP CONSULTANT

RANDY AND AUDREY HUGHEY
LATIN CONSULTANTS

AND STARRING
ROGER CLARK
IN THE AUDIO PRODUCTION

THE LEGACY OF LUCKY LOGAN
BOOK 3

WRITTEN BY
J.R. FRONTERA

NORTHERN WILDS
WESTERN TERRITORIES
CENTRAL COMMUNE
KINGDOM OF CANADA
Dakota
Kansas
Iowa
Califia
— rumored
Utah
Purgatory City
Missouri
home
EAST REPUBLIC
Pennsylvania
Valley of Lightning
Arizona
Lesser Texas
Blessing
Akansa
SOUTHERN STATES
Bravebank
Greater Texas
Grave Gulch
Redemption
SOUTHERN WILDS
THE INDEPENDENT AMERICAS

HANG 'EM HIGH

I couldn't see shit wearin' this bonnet.

Made me wonder how the women-folk put up with 'em.

I kept my eyes on the ground, mostly, bent over and holdin' a walkin' stick in my right hand. Partly to complete my disguise, and partly to help balance myself after standin' here fer hours. The crowd had arrived bit by bit over the course of the mornin', but I'd been one of the first ones here. Been here since dawn. Watched the sun come up over the town square … over the gallows. Watched the shadows of those nooses stretch out long across the ground, and then slowly shorten as the day wore on.

The cotton dress I'd donned over my usual clothes was startin' to get awful hot, but there weren't nothin' I could do about that.

The hangin' was set fer noon. And noon was comin' up awful fast now.

The crowd had swelled, all right. Fillin' in around and behind me, men and women and children, and vendors sellin' cakes and rock candy and jerky, and tinctures and whiskey.

I ignored 'em, all of 'em, the spectators and the vendors both. Ran over this plan of mine again and again in my mind, tryin' not to calculate too awful much the odds of gettin' killed in this venture.

I couldn't afford to get myself killed. Not when I

still had to get Ethelyn from Nan. But neither could I have stayed rottin' away in that jail cell back in Bravebank while Holt got hanged. The man was an insufferable, selfish bastard … but damn it all, he'd saved my neck too many times to count in the last eight years.

At least I owed him this. At least I owed him a try.

Sweat slipped down my face and I swiped at it with the back of my left hand, then brushed that hand against my hip, feelin' at the outline of my pistol beneath the skirt of the floral-patterned dress. I'd cut a slit in the fabric there along both holsters, so they could be covered up fer the most part, but still within easy reach fer when I needed 'em quick.

I'd never pulled a job dressed like a woman before, but it'd seemed the only way I was gonna have a chance of gettin' anywhere near this place without bein' recognized or lookin' suspicious. And so far, it was workin'.

Except fer this damned bonnet completely cuttin' off my peripheral vision. It hid my face, sure enough, but the narrowed field of view made me nervous, too.

I took a slow breath in and let it out just as slow. Glanced up to look through the gallows scaffolding, across the square, to where I'd tied my mule Joe and the skinny old mare Seven Knives Sally had gifted me. I'd only barely managed to get Joe back from that livery in Sonoita in time to make it here before the hangin', and as luck would have it, I'd found Holt's horse in the Destry livery last night.

The hostler here was a downright drunk, so it'd been easy enough to sneak the horse out, but I didn't exactly want him tied in the middle of town considerin' the law had been notified of the missin' animal and tack this mornin'.

So I'd left him outside town a ways, along our planned escape route.

If this plan of mine didn't end with both of us dead, I imagined Holt would be mighty sore about havin' to ride that old mare outta here, but then, she'd be carryin' him to freedom, so surely he'd get over it.

I checked my line of sight to my distractions next, tryin' to only minimally turn my head so as to not reveal my very unladylike features to the folk pressin' in close on either side. Didn't want anyone realizin' I weren't no old lady till I was good and ready fer 'em to realize such a thing.

But they were still there, my distractions, three small bundles of dynamite I'd planted in the wee hours of the mornin', wedged up along the rooftops of some of the surroundin' buildings. One above a dentist, one above the bank, one above the post office. Two to my right and one to my left. Fairly easy shots from my vantage point here at the front of the crowd, but I'd have to be fast.

And not miss.

I took another slow breath in attempts to quiet my hummin' nerves.

Too much feelin' threw off yer aim, and I was feelin' an awful lot right now…

A commotion rose up among the crowd to my left, where the jailhouse sat along that side of the square, and I glanced that way to see the lawdogs leadin' Holt out.

My hand tightened around the top of the walkin' stick and I sucked in a breath.

He looked as grumpy as ever, hands bound together in front of him, a decent-sized gash along his left temple bruised and swollen. He was held by a deputy on either side, and had another man in front and behind him.

The crowd parted to allow 'em through to the gallows stairs, but booed and hissed as Holt passed, some shoutin' out that he was a murderer and a monster. A few flung pieces of rotten produce at him, fruit and vegetables that hit him in the chest with a wet smack, splattering a mess everywhere.

I shifted on my feet and clenched my jaw, eyein' my distractions again, memorizin' their locations. Then looked back to Holt to see him spittin' and yellin' insults at the townsfolk, which only earned him more rotten food and vehement invitations to go to Hell.

The sheriff and his deputies tried to settle the crowd some as they took Holt up the stairs, put him over the trap door, and settled the noose around his neck. And then they stepped back, positionin' themselves at the four corners of the stage. They didn't have their guns drawn, but they looked alert, all right.

It was generally known around these parts that Holt Haggerty didn't run with no gang, so they weren't likely expectin' a whole heap of trouble from any outsiders tryin' to save his neck. But it was also generally known that Holt Haggerty *did* often run with at least one other unsavory outlaw.

Me.

They were almost certainly expectin' me, and lookin' out fer me, too.

I tried to keep my head angled away from 'em, so all they'd see was a pretty floral bonnet and not my face while I ran more calculations in my head.

Four of 'em, the noose rope, my three distractions. I was gonna need both pistols. And every shot had to count.

Another man ascended the gallows stairs now. He was dressed in a rather nice suit and held a rolled up piece of paper in his hand. He motioned for the crowd to quiet, and to my surprise, they did. He stepped to the edge of the gallows platform and I dropped my gaze back quick to the dusty ground so he wouldn't notice my features as he scanned the masses spread out before him.

"Good people of Destry," he yelled out, "and all those gathered here from elsewhere in the Territories as witness! Today we will have, at last, the ending of a criminal outlaw who has terrorized our towns for far too long!"

The people cheered. Whooped and hollered.

He motioned them quiet again. "As Mayor of this fine town of Destry, I must commend our Sheriff Bell and his deputies, who apprehended this criminal before he could make off with much of our hard-earned money."

More cheerin' and shoutin' from the crowd.

Holt scowled and grumbled somethin', but it was lost beneath all the ruckus.

The mayor waited till the noise died down some, then continued, "It will be my pleasure to oversee this execution, and I beg all of you here today to remember: crime does not pay."

It was my turn to scowl and grumble then, and I shifted again on my feet, my metal leg whirrin' softly beneath the skirts. Maybe crime didn't pay … but it had kept me fed fer plenty of years now. Fed, and sometimes warm and comfortable, too.

"Now…" the mayor said. He unfurled the rolled paper. "Holt Haggerty, for the crimes of capital murder, assault, robbery, arson…"

That list was gettin' awful long. I wondered if my list were that long these days. Probably.

"… theft, kidnapping…"

Kidnapping? I didn't remember that one. But then, Holt had been an outlaw fer a long time. Certainly longer than just the eight years I'd been runnin' with him.

"… forgery, impersonating an officer of the law…"

All right, I *did* remember that one…

"… selling stolen goods, horse theft, and cattle rustling, I do hereby sentence you to hang by the neck until dead." The mayor gave a little nod of finality and curled up that paper, and another wave of murmurs and excited chatter circled through the gathered crowd.

The mayor squinted upward, to the stretch of blue above. Weren't a cloud in the sky. The merciless sun glared down at us full-bore, directly overhead.

High noon.

Time fer the hangin'. Time fer Holt Haggerty to die.

He looked back to Holt then, a rather smug look of satisfaction crossin' his pinched and sweaty features. "Well?" he asked. "Any last words?"

I risked a glance to Holt myself, lookin' up at him standin' on that gallows stage from beneath the shade of my bonnet, and I slipped my left hand through the cut in the skirt on my left hip to curl my fingers loose around my gun grip. The three middle fingers of that hand had bandages around their ends where Charles Miller had pulled off the fingernails not so long ago. And they were still sore, too. But I'd been practicin' drawin' and shootin' with those sore fingers since I'd escaped the Bravebank jail, till I was comfortable enough with 'em that I could rely on 'em today.

I eased my right hand downward now itself, along the length of the walkin' stick, closer to my right holster.

My heart beat in my throat. Sweat slid down my temples to run down my neck.

Holt glared out at the crowd pressed in on all sides and they hushed as he opened his mouth. "Yeah," he grunted. But then his clear blue gaze found mine, and he paused. Surprise went over his creased, grimy features, then a cautious hope, but he looked away again quick before any of those lawdogs could take an interest in what he might have seen. His face went hard and angry again, and he focused his glare on Destry's mayor. "Yeah," he said again, one corner of his mouth quirkin' into a smirk. "The best-laid schemes of mice and men often go awry, and leave us nothing but grief and pain, fer promised joy."

I rolled my eyes, cursin' him silently, hopin' his bein' cute wouldn't tip off those four armed men up there.

But the mayor only seemed perplexed, then shook his head. "Quoting literature will not gain you any sympathy here, Haggerty. Saying pretty words does not make you a civilized man."

Holt snorted in amusement. "You would know about that personally, wouldn'tcha, Mayor?"

The gathered masses booed at that comment, and shouts to get on with the hangin' already rang through the square.

The mayor agreed with 'em, 'cause he drew himself up straighter at Holt's insult and gestured to the sheriff. The sheriff nodded, pulled the black hood from where he'd had it tucked into his belt, and shook it out as he went to Holt's side.

"Goodbye, Haggerty," he said, and put the hood over Holt's head before Holt could snap anything in return. "And good riddance."

The mayor stepped over to the lever. All he had to do was pull it, and that trap door would swing open under Holt's feet, and he'd take a long drop on a short rope, his neck snappin' like a twig.

Unless I didn't miss.

I took in another slow, deep breath of the hot afternoon. Another trickle of sweat slipped down my face, but I didn't dare wipe it away. Not now. Not this close.

The mayor rested his hand atop the lever and affected a solemn expression. The masses around me went deathly quiet, their anticipation thick as mine, but fer entirely different reasons.

Someone across the square coughed, and a baby started cryin'.

A light breeze stirred, coolin' the sweat on my brow and shiftin' my floral skirts around my ankles.

"May God and the Holy Mother alike have mercy on your soul," the mayor said.

He pulled the lever.

ONE BULLET LEFT

I drew and fired twice before my walkin' stick hit the ground; one bullet fer the noose rope and one bullet fer the dynamite above the dentist's place. Holt grunted as he fell all the way through the trap door and hit the ground hard, and a split second later that dynamite blew a hole in the dentist's roof.

The crack of the explosion washed out over the crowd, many of whom screamed and ducked, many of whom turned tail and fled, pushin' and shovin' each other in their haste to vacate the premises. The mayor hit the floor of the scaffold, hands over his head, and those four armed lawdogs drew fast, too.

But I already had bullets ready fer 'em, firin' at two from my right pistol and two from my left pistol even as I lurched forward to duck beneath the gallows stage. All four of my shots hit home; I saw all four men stagger just before divin' into the shadows underneath 'em.

I went to Holt, who'd managed to push himself up sittin' and lifted his bound hands to yank the hood off his head. I shoved my right pistol back into its holster and grabbed him under one arm, haulin' him to his feet. "Come on," I hissed. "We gotta go."

"Nice dress," he muttered, followin' me out the other side of the scaffoldin' to run toward the horses. "And nice shootin'."

"We ain't out of this yet," I scowled back, and

even as I twisted around to say it, I saw the sheriff up on the gallows put us in his sights.

I'd shot him, all right, but I hadn't killed him. I fired back at him with my left pistol and missed, but made him duck away, anyway. Then I switched my aim and planted a bullet in the dynamite above the bank.

It exploded with another crack, makin' Holt instinctively wince and duck, and keepin' that sheriff laid out flat, and promptin' a fresh wave of screams and shouts from the remainin' townsfolk. The rest of 'em fled fer cover now, terrified and confused, though a few brave souls seemed determined to hold their ground, hands hoverin' above their guns as they searched fer a target amid all the chaos.

We reached our mounts before they spotted us and I hiked up my skirts in a hurry, then fair near leapt up into my saddle, gatherin' the reins quick and tearin' that damned bonnet off my head so I could see proper.

Holt caught his saddle horn in both bound hands and swung up onto that skinny mare just as quick. "The hell is my horse?" he spat.

"Waitin' down the road," I ground out. "Let's just get the hell outta here, yeah?"

"With pleasure, kid."

We ducked as shots rang out behind us, and I pulled Joe around to put a bullet into the man who was shootin' at us.

It was the last in my left pistol's cylinder, so I holstered that one quick and switched hands, movin' the reins to my left and pullin' my right pistol just as that damned sheriff pushed to his feet again on the gallows.

I shot at him same time as he shot at me, and fire seared through my left bicep as his bullet tore through it. I yelled out and swore, but mine got him in the chest and he flung backwards, sprawlin' next to the mayor who was still all hunkered down.

I ground my teeth against the pain in my arm and fired my right pistol one last time, lightin' up my third distraction to punch a hole in the post office roof. Wood splinters rained down into the street, the few folk who were left in the square whippin' around to face the newest noise with a start.

Joe danced sideways under me, chewin' at his bit, but then I kicked him up into a gallop to get shut of this town quick, fer which he didn't need much convincin'. He didn't much like all the explosions and shootin', big ears swivelin' around all over the place and eyes rollin'. Well, he was probably gonna need to get used to that.

But fer now we high-tailed it outta there, and none too soon, neither.

I only had one bullet left. And it'd be mighty hard to reload with all my cartridges hidden under this damned dress.

Hard hoofbeats followed after me and Joe, and I glanced back once over my shoulder to make sure it was Holt.

It was. The noose still hung around his neck, the frayed end of it split by my bullet flappin' in the wind. He was bent low over his borrowed horse's neck, urgin' her on till we were runnin' side by side, flyin' down that road and fast puttin' distance between us and the town of Destry.

I'd kept Holt's gelding tied to a tree a ways off the road a few miles on, and we stopped there only long enough for him to switch mounts. Then we were off again, ponying the mare behind us despite Holt's protests she'd only slow us down, and we kept a hard pace northeast fer as long as the horses could manage.

It reminded me eerily of the time we'd fled Bravebank after murderin' three of Nan's men and makin' that deal with Taggert. The deal that had turned out to be no deal at all.

My fists tightened around my reins at the memory, but I shoved all of that away again soon enough. None of that mattered anymore. It was done. In the past. All I could do now was move forward … and not repeat the same stupid mistakes.

No more makin' deals with anyone but Nine-Fingered Nan directly.

And no more givin' her what she wanted without seein' my sister in-person. In-person, and alive and well.

"Van!"

Holt's bark jolted me outta my stew of rage and I glanced over at him sharply.

"Horses need a rest," he said, noddin' toward his own, all lathered up and blowin' hard. "We should find a place to stop fer awhile."

"Oh. Right." Joe was all lathered, too, and that poor mare was draggin' at the end of her lead. We slowed 'em up and let 'em walk while we looked fer somewhere suitable to hole up, and eventually decided on wanderin' up onto a nearby mountain a ways where the bigger boulders would hide us and we'd have a good view out over the surroundin' land, so we could spot any pursuit comin' long before they reached us.

We dismounted there, and Holt held out his bound wrists. I fished under my skirts fer my knife and cut the thick coils of rope fer him.

He gave a hiss of relief as his hands were freed, then immediately reached up to pull the noose off his neck and toss it away. "That was closer than I ever wanted to be to dyin'," he muttered. Then he glanced up at me, clapped a hand on my shoulder. "Thanks, kid."

I shrugged. "You woulda done the same fer me."

I think.

Maybe the last time we'd seen each other we'd been throwin' fists, and he'd almost drowned me in that horse trough ... coulda drowned me in that horse trough easy enough ... but he hadn't. And anyway, he'd pulled me outta plenty of scrapes before that. Surely he woulda done the same again if I'd been facin' the noose, no matter our recent disagreements.

"Damn right," he said, and he sounded truthful enough.

But maybe he was just feelin' especially appreciative at the moment given his fresh brush with mortality.

"Only maybe not dressed like that."

I scoffed and shook my head, movin' away from his skeptical stare to start unsaddlin' Joe. "Only way I could get close enough to make the shot I did. Figured they'd be expectin' me to come and try to save yer neck. Figured you probably didn't want me to miss splittin' that rope."

He gave a grunt of agreement.

I made to pull the saddle off the mule, but the weight of it made that bullet hole in my left bicep flare somethin' awful, and I spat a curse as I lost my grip, the blanket and saddle both hittin' the ground in a heap.

Holt appeared at my side, hooded blue gaze takin' in the blood spread all down my left sleeve. It stained all the flowers on the dress there a deep, dark red. "You got shot," he stated flatly.

"Just a flesh wound," I managed. "I'll be alright." I hooked my right hand into the gullet of my saddle and pulled it over where I wanted it, then went back to get my blanket out of the dirt and shook it out, draped it over the saddle's cantle.

Holt eyed me the whole way, then went to his own saddle and started rummagin' in his bags fer supplies. "Why don't you let me take a look at it, anyway. Probably needs stitchin'."

"Probably," I conceded. "But we'd better see to our tracks first. And the horses."

Holt turned, frowned at me fer a minute, and then to my surprise, nodded instead of argued. He brought his handful of stuff over to me—whiskey, needle and stitchin' thread, a roll of bandages—and set it down atop a flat boulder to my right. "Fine. I'll see to our tracks. You get things settled here. And take off that godforsaken dress. When I get back I'll stitch you up."

I shrugged again. "All right."

He moved off down the path we'd come up on, grumblin' to himself.

"Holt."

He stopped and turned, quirkin' an eyebrow in question.

I pulled my left pistol, opened the cylinder, and dug out six bullets from under my dress. I loaded 'em, snapped the cylinder closed again, and tossed the gun to him. "You might need that."

He caught it neatly. Hefted it in his hand, then gave it a twirl and stuck it in his waistband. "Just might," he said. Then he went on down the path and disappeared from view, and I turned my attention to the horses.

And to gettin' out of that godforsaken dress.

ANY KIND OF FAMILY

It didn't take him long to return, but I was restless waitin', anyway. I paced back and forth along the little rise we'd stopped along, watchin' the stretch of land below until I finally saw him reappear.

He was alone. And no one followed him that I could see.

Satisfied, I went back to my saddlebags to get us a little somethin' to eat.

And so he wouldn't think I'd been too worried.

He rounded the bend just as I'd pulled out some bread and cheese and jerky. "Hungry?" I asked.

"Sure, some. But you ain't gettin' out of bein' stitched. So sit down and let me look at yer arm."

I sighed but did as he instructed, settlin' cross-legged on the ground and puttin' my back up against another big rock. In truth, it was nice to have a minute to rest. I'd been racin' against the clock ever since managin' to get outta that cell in Bravebank. Hardly had any decent sleep fer days. Now that I'd made it to Destry in time, and not only that, but managed to pull off my one-man rescue with both of us still alive ... well, that reality still seemed to be soakin' in. My body was finally startin' to relax a bit.

At least until Holt started pokin' and proddin' at that wound in my arm.

Then I ground my teeth against the fresh waves of pain.

He rolled up that shirt sleeve far as he could, then dumped some whiskey on the hole in my flesh.

I nearly came right up off the ground at that, swearin' as the bitin' sting went all the way through my arm. But Holt put his other hand against my chest and pushed me back down, holdin' me flat against the rock.

"Easy now," he said. "That's over. It's done. Just gotta stitch it now. Here." He pushed the whiskey bottle into my right hand. "Take a few swigs."

I glared murder at him, but took the bottle and did as he said fer that, too. Then I looked away and focused out on the far horizon, focused on breathin', focused on holdin' tight to that whiskey bottle, while he closed up the hole.

"Looks like it went all the way through," he said as he worked. "And missed the bone."

"Like I said," I ground out. "Just a flesh wound."

"Lucky it weren't worse," he muttered. "But I'll need to close it up on the exit side."

"Do whatever you need to do."

There was silence between us fer awhile, while Holt concentrated on his task and I concentrated on ignorin' the way the pain made me sweat. My left arm and shoulder were awful tender to the touch already, thanks to the treatment I'd suffered at the hands of Charles Miller … thanks to that electrical rod of his. And now this. Another bullet. Another scar.

I switched my attention away from that unpleasant line of thought and instead tried to figure out just what to say to Holt. There were sure a lot of things I wanted to say to him right now. A lot of things I'd considered sayin' to him durin' all the days

I'd been scramblin' to make it here in time to save him.

Things like remindin' him of how he'd almost killed me last time we'd seen each other.

Remindin' him *he'd* been the one to walk away from *me*. Things like tellin' him it'd been a stupid thing fer him to do, to attempt a bank robbery all by himself with me nowhere near by, nevermind the fact he mighta pulled off such a thing once … he shoulda known better than to push his luck.

Weren't that what he was always tellin' me? And then he'd gone and done that himself, and look where it had landed him … right into the noose.

I opened my mouth to say all those things, but then hesitated. And closed it again. All of a sudden I didn't have the energy fer it anymore.

Seemed Holt had somethin' to say himself, though, 'cause that's when he cleared his throat. "So," he started, still stitchin'. "Yer still alive."

"Fer now." I wanted to make the point that so was he, but only 'cause of me, but I swallowed it back. He was surely well enough aware of that. No need to rub it in. Gettin' his praise weren't why I'd rescued him, anyway.

"And … any word from Nine-Fingered Nan?"

I swallowed back the bitter laugh, too. Instead all I said was, "Yeah."

Holt looked to me in surprise, then turned back to the stitchin'. "No shit? Well? What'd she say?"

I considered all the things he'd missed. Considered how all of it had ended. And decided he didn't need to know about most of it. I'd never hear the fuckin' end of it. So I only wet my lips and shook my head. "She said … she said to keep waitin'."

Holt snorted.

"But she gave me this." I set the whiskey bottle aside and reached into my shirt pocket with my right hand, pullin' out the folded piece of paper I'd kept there since Nan had given it to me. "It's a letter. From Ethelyn."

Holt's hands stilled. He glanced to the paper in my fingers.

He didn't have to say nothin' fer me to see the skepticism written all over his grimy features. I gave him a hard glare in return. "Yes," I snapped. "It's her script. You can look at it yerself if you want."

"All right, all right," he relented. "Ease off. I ain't never seen the girl's writin'."

"Well I have. Lots. Mama was a schoolteacher, remember? Made us practice our letters all the damn time—"

"All right, I said." Holt tied off the thread he'd used to close up the exit wound at the back of my bicep and used his teeth to clip it. Then he sat back, exchangin' the thread and needle for the roll of bandages. He tore off a length, wrapped it over the holes a few times, and tied that off, too. "I ain't gonna fight you on that anymore, kid."

I'd kept on glarin' at him as he worked, but my expression softened at that admission of his. What exactly did that mean?

He sighed heavily and settled cross-legged next to me, then reached across my lap to snatch up the whiskey bottle fer himself. He took several heavy swigs before lowerin' it and swipin' the back of his hand across his mouth. "Look. When I was … when I was sittin' in that cell fer all those days, waitin' to die … I realized…" He stopped, shook his head, cleared his throat again. He looked away, squintin' out into the harsh daylight. "Well, I realized I had no one. I used to have the gang, ya know. Grew up with 'em. And they were all bad men, sure, but they was my family, through and through. We were at least loyal to each other, if not to nothin' else. And when all that started to fall apart, I had yer pa at least. We was like brothers, ya understand. Like brothers."

He took another swallow of whiskey, and I dropped my eyes to my hands in my lap and that letter still held between my fingers, rememberin' what part of this story I knew.

Growin' up on that ranch in Kansas, Pa had never said a word about Holt Haggerty. Never said a word about the gang he'd used to run with. Neither had Mama, though she must have known. She must have. Maybe she hadn't truly grasped the whole of Pa's sordid past—I still didn't think I did, even now —but she musta known somethin' about it, surely.

Holt shrugged. "But then that ended, too. And … well, kid … it's good to have family. Any kind of family. Bein' on yer own ain't all it's cracked up to be, especially out here. Most lone folk don't last long, and there's a reason fer that. So … I guess what I'm tryin' to say is … if ya really think yer sister might still be alive out there, and ya really think you might have a chance to get her, then a' course that's what you gotta do. And I'm … I'm sorry fer always bein' such a bastard about it, I guess."

I lifted my eyes to him again in surprise—I didn't think I'd ever heard him apologize fer nothin'—but he was still lookin' out at the shimmerin' horizon. He kept starin' out there, rather resolutely, and swigged more whiskey.

A corner of my mouth quirked. "And if a damn fool uncle of yers really thinks he can get away with robbin' a bank a second time all on his lonesome and ends up gettin' himself arrested and put in the noose, well … you refrain from tellin' him how stupid he is and save his ass, anyway."

Holt scoffed, lookin' at me sideways. "Save his neck, more like." He offered out the whiskey bottle and I took it, helpin' myself to more.

"Thanks fer comin' fer me, though, honestly," he said quietly. "Especially given the situation with Nan and yer sister. I thought fer sure I was a dead man."

I only shook my head. And covered my inability to find proper words by drinkin' yet more whiskey. Had I taken a risk leavin' Bravebank when Nan had instructed me to wait? Maybe. But she'd let me sit fer three weeks before, and I had a good idea she planned to let me sit fer even longer this time, if only 'cause she knew it made me hot under the collar.

But I weren't gonna let her manipulate me like that. Not anymore.

Just like I weren't gonna wait all that time coolin' my heels in a jail cell if I could instead save Holt's life.

Like he'd said, it was good to have family.

Any kind of family.

"Thanks fer stitchin' me up," I managed finally. Then I glanced to that gash on his temple and frowned. "Looks like maybe you shoulda had some stitchin' yerself."

He shrugged and shook his head. "Naw. That'll

be fine." He gestured to the bandaged three middle fingers of my left hand restin' in my lap. "What about that?"

"Uh." I lifted that hand, then winced as the motion lit pain in my bicep. "Nothin'. Ran into an old friend, that's all. It'll be fine."

He eyed me skeptically. "Uh huh." But to my relief, he didn't press further. "Welp," he said abruptly, pushin' to his feet. "We'd best move on. We can eat in the saddle. We'll need to take the long way 'round to Grave Gulch, make sure no one can follow our trail."

"Grave Gulch?" I repeated.

He looked down at me like I'd lost my mind. "Yeah. Where else you think we'd go? Those bastards took my guns *and* my hat … I'm gonna need to get the ones I got stashed back at camp."

Well, that *did* make sense. But Grave Gulch was in the wrong direction fer where I needed to go. "I need to make another stop first."

His gaze narrowed. "Oh yeah? Where at?"

I got to my feet myself and handed him back his whiskey, though there weren't much left of it at this point, then tucked Ethelyn's letter back into my shirt pocket. "I need to pay a visit to the doc."

He frowned, lookin' me over. "I think I did a fine enough job on that—"

"No, not fer that." I lowered my left hand carefully, patted at my thigh. "Fer *this*."

Holt took a step backward. "The metal leg?"

I nodded.

"What, it been botherin' ya?"

"Naw, it's been fine, generally. But it … it *did somethin'*, while you were away. And I don't know how it happened, or how to make it happen again … or how to make it **not** happen again. I need some answers. And preferably sooner rather than later. Woulda gone to see him already, if I hadn't needed to come here fer you."

Holt took another step backward. "Whaddaya mean, it **did somethin'**?"

"I mean it … it **did somethin'**." I tried to make an openin' gesture with my hands, then winced as my newly injured bicep twinged with pain again. "It … it opened up. Had blades comin' outta it, and a pistol in there and everythin'."

Now his eyes went real wide. "A pistol? Inside? A pistol **inside** the leg?"

"Yeah. A pistol inside the leg."

He blinked rapidly and let out a long, low whistle. "Fer Chrissakes, boy, what you been smokin' while I was away?"

I scowled at him. "I ain't been smokin' nothin', damnit. I'm tellin' you, that's what happened. And I'm gonna go talk to the doc about it. Figure I'll pay him a house call. He's got a place just outside of Bravebank. So that's where I'm goin'. If … if you wanna go on to Grave Gulch, you go ahead. I'll meet you there when I'm done with him."

Holt only looked at me fer a long minute more, then he turned away and went toward his saddlebags, chucklin' and shakin' his head. "Oh no, no no. I gotta hear this story. And what the doc has to say about it. See if he tosses you into the insane asylum."

I rolled my eyes and went toward my own stuff, grabbin' the blanket with one hand and walkin' over to Joe to throw it up over his back. "I ain't insane," I insisted. "I'm tellin' you, it happened."

Joe turned his big head toward me, prickin' up his big ears, and nickered softly. He snuffled at my pockets, but I pushed his nose away. That Sonoita hostler had soured him on sugar cubes, and now I was payin' the price. Don't even know why I'd taken the trouble to go all the way up there and get him, anyway. Surely weren't worth the effort.

He nudged me with his nose again.

"Lay off it, would you?" I snapped.

"Don't think the mule believes you, neither," Holt commented.

"Yeah, well, both of you shut it."

Holt only chuckled to himself again, and Joe only kept sniffin' at me fer sweets, but we managed to get saddled up anyway, and I ponied that mare behind me once more as we headed back down the mountain and angled toward Bravebank.

Toward Dr. Balogh's homestead.

HOUSE CALL

It took us another four days to get there, bein' as we took the long way 'round to throw off any pursuit, and paused sometimes to check fer a tail. But we stayed clear of anyone comin' after us, and by the time I spotted the Balogh windmill on the horizon the afternoon of the fourth day, we were fair certain we'd escaped the incident at Destry free and clear.

And by the time the Balogh house came into full view, I was fair certain somethin' was very, very wrong.

We approached from the south, givin' me a clear view of the little garden out back. Last I'd visited, the plants had been thrivin' and green. Now they were shriveled and dead. And the windmill weren't turnin'. The well bucket was overturned a distance from the well wall, and the barn doors were open.

Nothin' moved 'cept dust in the little breeze that cooled my skin.

I pulled Joe to a halt some distance out from the house, and my hand slid down to the iron on my hip.

"Don't look like anyone's home," Holt said.

My mouth went dry, my throat suddenly tight. *Goddamnit, Doc. What did you get yourself into?* "Let's just be careful. Keep your eyes open." I drew my pistol, thumbed back the hammer, and nudged Joe onward.

We circled around toward the front of the house and found the door ajar; the window near it broken.

I tried to swallow, couldn't. My heart dropped into my stomach.

"This don't look promisin'," Holt muttered.

I ignored him, swingin' down from the saddle and headin' quick fer the door in a crouchin' run. I put my back up against the front frame of it and then peered around the corner, searchin' fer any movement inside.

There weren't none. Only shadows and sunlight, stillness and silence.

I put the barrel of my gun up against the door and pushed it open further, slow and careful, then winced as it creaked on stiff hinges.

I paused, waitin' fer anyone to reveal themselves at the noise, but there was nothin'.

Holt came up behind me, holdin' his borrowed pistol low and ready. "Anythin'?" he whispered.

I shook my head, then stepped inside. Into a disaster. The kitchen table and chairs had been overturned, floorboards ripped up, cupboards opened and their contents strewn all over the place. What few upholstered chairs sat in front of the fireplace had been torn up, and the ashes from the hearth itself scattered across the floor.

But there weren't no bodies. No blood. And no bullet holes.

"What the Devil happened here?" Holt breathed.

My heart pulsed in my throat as I moved toward the bedrooms, keepin' my pistol ready. I didn't understand what was goin' on here, but it surely weren't nothin' good. I kept thinkin' of that boy Radley helpin' me out, and of Fanni and Mrs. Balogh, who'd never fully trusted me. But they'd taken me into their home nonetheless. Fed me well and nursed me back to health. I'd always suspected their kindness might get 'em killed someday ... but I'd always hoped I'd be wrong, too.

"Goddamnit, Doc," I hissed. I knew he shouldn't have been flauntin' around that Old World tech ... I eased open the first bedroom door to find it ransacked same as the rest of the house. The bed was a mess, the bureau drawers yanked open, clothes all over the place. The other bedrooms were the same, too, includin' the guest bedroom I'd stayed in. Not even the lace curtains had survived the pillage; they'd been ripped down and tossed to the floor.

But there were no bodies and no blood, and I breathed a little easier as I rejoined Holt in the kitchen.

"Just who was this doctor, anyway?" he asked.

I shrugged. "Just a doctor. Bravebank's doctor." Just a doctor who could attach a metal leg to a person. A metal leg that could sometimes move on its own. A metal leg that could be its very own arsenal, if I could figure out how the hell to work it.

"Well," Holt mused, lookin' over the mess we stood in again, "someone wanted somethin' from him, clearly."

"Clearly."

"But no bodies," he said, echoin' my previous thoughts.

"But lots of their clothes are still here," I noted.

He nodded toward the aging produce strewn out across the wood stove and all over the floor. "And lots of food, too."

"Let's check the barn," I suggested.

We went out the back door nice and careful, past the wilted garden toward the open barn doors. It was dark in there beyond the rectangle of light comin' in through the front, and I paused at the entrance to squint into the blackness. I held my breath and listened, but everythin' was still quiet.

Too quiet.

Weren't no animal sounds comin' outta there. And the wagon was usually parked in the middle of it, in the space the rectangle of sun now illuminated. The space that was empty.

"Wagon's gone," I said quietly.

"And I don't hear no horses," Holt added.

"Mules," I corrected.

"Whatever."

A moan sounded out of the blackness, makin' me and Holt both jump and duck behind the barn walls, one of us on either side of the doorway, bringin' our guns up.

We waited there. Listened.

Another moan. Sounded like a man. Weak. Someone in pain.

"Fuck," I spat, and I dodged around the doorframe and moved into the darkness, strainin' to see after the dazzle of the afternoon sunlight.

"Van!" Holt hissed from behind me, but I paid him no mind, still searchin' fer the source of the voice.

"Hey," I said, feelin' at my belt for my coin pouch, which was also where I kept my matches. "Someone in here? Where are you?"

Another moan, close. To my right.

I could make out a dim shape there, just beyond

the edge of the sunlight. Looked like a person sittin' down. In a chair, maybe. But all hunched over.

The fingers of my left hand finally found the matches amid my coin and pulled 'em out. I holstered my pistol to strike one, held it out toward the guy, and then winced. The flame revealed a man, all right, and he was sittin' in a chair, sure enough, but he'd been tied there. Wrists bound around the back of it and ankles tied to the legs, and he was all hunched over 'cause he seemed barely conscious. His face was a bruised, bloodied mess, both eyes swollen shut and blood runnin' from his mouth where it looked like he'd had several teeth knocked out.

I stepped back out of instinct, even as a flash of terror stabbed through me at thinking it mighta been Dr. Balogh. He was tall and thin like Dr. Balogh, but his face was so disfigured I weren't sure I could have been certain either way.

"Fuckin' hell," I whispered.

The match flame singed my fingertips and I hissed as I shook it out.

"That him?" Holt asked from the doorway. "That the doc?"

"I … I can't tell," I admitted.

"I don't like this, Van. I think we oughta go."

"Yeah…" I murmured. "Yeah." But instead of turnin' to leave, I stepped forward again, pattin' gently at the man's knee. "Hey. Hey, you. You awake? Can you talk? What's yer name? Are … are you…" I struggled to swallow. "You Dr. Balogh?"

"Van…" Holt started.

But he was interrupted by the sound of Joe's bastardized whinny.

I forgot about the bloodied man tied to the chair

in front of me and whipped around, knowin' what the mule's overly social nature must be heraldin'. My frantic gaze met Holt's just as he realized the same thing, his eyes goin' wide.

But it was already too late.

Two silhouettes loomed up behind him just as he started to turn, and one cracked him over the head with a pistol. He went down to his hands and knees with a grunt, and my own gun was outta leather and takin' aim when a sharp voice cracked through the heat like a whip.

"Drop it or he dies, boy."

I registered the gun pointed at Holt's head at the same time I recognized the voice, and my finger stilled a hair's breadth from squeezin' down on my trigger. Instead I opened my hand, let the gun slip down and hang by its trigger guard, and I lifted my left hand too fer good measure, nevermind the fact it made my bicep twinge in protest.

The second shadow moved forward, her tall stature and wide-brimmed hat framed in the barn's doorway.

God-damned Nine-Fingered Nan. And she had one of her pistols trained on me.

"I said drop it."

Reluctantly, I did so.

"Well, well, well, *well*," she drawled then, and I noticed she did not holster her weapon. Nor did her lieutenant take his gun away from the back of Holt's head. "If it ain't Van Delano and the old man Haggerty himself. Imagine seein' you here."

THAT AIN'T A DEAL, THAT'S A GAMBLE

Nine-Fingered Nan walked toward me, her shadow stretchin' out in front of her as she approached, slow and unhurried like she always seemed to be.

Two more of her people appeared in the barn's doorway behind her, and one of 'em went to pick up Holt's pistol—my pistol—from where he'd dropped it in the dirt. They tucked it into their waistband, then stepped back to watch me and Nan, hands loose atop their own gun grips.

Looked like she had three men and one woman with her this time.

I wondered if she ever truly went anywhere alone.

Holt sat back on his heels, grumblin' and rubbin' at the back of his head. His fingers came away bloody.

But my focus went back to Nan as she neared, too close. I tensed, wantin' to step back, to move away, but instead I held my ground and met her cool, steady stare with a glare. I wondered how angry she'd be that I weren't where I was supposed to be right now.

Guess I was gonna find out.

She halted abruptly not three paces from me. "You," she said. "Yer an awful slippery little pup, ain't you? Guess that's probably how you've managed to live this long." She turned a half-step to look back at Holt. "And you. Ain't you supposed to be dead? Thought they was gonna hang you?"

Holt grunted. "Lotsa people was gonna hang me over the years. But I'm still livin', too."

"So I see." Nan turned back to me, pale blue eyes lookin' me over, calculatin'.

I resisted the urge to shift under her scrutiny; tried to figure if I could possibly snatch that pearl-gripped pistol from her hand and shoot her with it.

"That why you were so keen to get outta that cell I put you in?" Nan asked. "Had to go save the old man, eh? Huh. Well, ain't that touchin'? Just warms the heart." She smiled, holstered her pistol, and crossed into the barn's shadow to go to the man in the chair. "And now you're here. How ... *interestin'*."

I watched her warily from my own place in the shadow, but she only took a fistful of the beaten man's hair and pulled his head back to better expose the muddle of his face.

"No, Mr. Delano, this ain't Dr. Balogh," she said. "This is Dr. Wright. He replaced Dr. Balogh when Balogh apparently up and left a month ago. But turns out he's rather good friends with the Baloghs. They even told him where they took off to in such a hurry. Took some convincin' fer him to tell us about it, but ... well, he finally came to his senses." She shook her head and released his hair, and he slumped forward again. "Guess Bravebank's gonna need another new doctor."

My mind raced at this information, tryin' to put the pieces together. Had it been Nan's people who had trashed the house and beaten this Dr. Wright? And for what? Lookin' fer the doc and his family? Fer clues about where they mighta gone? But why?

I remembered Nan's interest in that old lockbox she'd had me steal from Baron Haas, remembered how Professor Morton—Head Curator of the Royal Museum, of all places—had said it was Old World, and my stomach twisted.

She *was* interested in Old World tech, and she musta found out Dr. Balogh knew somethin' about it. Again I got overly conscious of my left leg, possible Old World tech itself, and the seam where the metal rod went into my flesh pulsed.

Nan circled around the back of the man's chair, around behind me, to come up along my right side. She put a hand on my shoulder and leaned in close enough I could smell sweat and horse.

It was all I could do to not recoil. Somehow I managed to stay still, fists balled, starin' straight ahead at Holt, who watched me with the same tightly strung uncertainty I currently felt jumpin' around in my gut.

"I suppose the question now," Nan said slowly, "is what exactly are you doin' here, Delano? You just sprang Haggerty from the noose. Why come here, of all places?"

I swallowed, but said nothin'. My heart beat in my ears.

She leaned heavy on my shoulder, squeezin' with bony fingers. "Nothin' to say? Well, maybe you need some convincin', too." She gestured at her men, and the one behind Holt gave him another whack on the head. He fell forward, but two of 'em grabbed his arms and hauled him back up to his feet, where he staggered, sagged.

"No," I blurted. "No. No need fer convincin'."

"Better start talkin', then," Nan said.

I swallowed again, shook my head. "Weren't … weren't nothin'. Nothin' important. Just payin' a house call on the way back to town, is all. Thought I'd check in on the family."

She smiled thinly. "Ain't that sweet. You friends with the Baloghs too, are ya?"

"No," I said quickly. "Not friends. More like … more like acquaintances, maybe."

"I see. So you thought you'd pay a house call, check up on the family of your *acquaintance* Dr. Balogh, that it?"

I nodded.

"Uh huh. He gave you that leg, didn't he? The metal one."

A lance of alarm went through me at the question, but she didn't give me time to confirm or deny.

"I saw his workshop. It was quite impressive."

A frown flickered across my face despite myself. *Workshop? What workshop?*

"It's all makin' sense now, Delano," she said, and she mercifully released her grip on my shoulder, then gave it a hard clap and I grimaced. "Ya see, we've been watchin' this place fer weeks. Ever since my men first came here in search of the good doctor and found him gone. Watchin' and waitin'. All kinds of folk been showin' up here lately." She moved to stand sideways between me and Holt, who hung dazed between two of her men, and looked to each of us in turn. "We took the time to question each of 'em, a course, and I think the picture is finally startin' to become clear. Lucky fer you, Delano, 'cause that means I ain't gonna throw you right back into a cell. I had a deep, dark one in mind fer you, given your slippery nature, but now … now I think you'll prove more useful here."

I resisted my first instinct, which was to tell her to go to Hell, and instead growled out, "How so?"

That was the point anyway, weren't it? Fer me to play this stupid game of hers. To give her what she wanted so she'd give me my sister. To prove I could make a bargain with me more worth her while than any deal she could make with a foreign merchant. To show her just how stubborn we Delanos could be.

Nine-Fingered Nan grinned at me. "I'm so glad you asked." She turned and went to the woman in the doorway, who handed over a folded newspaper without even bein' asked. Nan brought the newspaper to me, and I took it from her with a frown.

Unfolded it and stepped into the sunlight so I could read it proper.

The headline across the top of the front page said somethin' about thousands of birds fallin' out of the sky … dead. My frown deepened. There weren't no thousands of birds in the desert … but then I realized this hadn't happened here. It had happened near a town called Blackbird, all the way over in Akansa. And the paper was dated about two weeks ago.

I looked back to Nan and shrugged. "So? What's dead birds got to do with anythin'?"

Nan snatched the paper outta my hands. "It ain't about the dead birds, boy. It's about what killed 'em."

Oh. Well I hadn't read that part of it yet. "So what killed 'em, then?"

Now Nan shrugged, and she paced over to poor Dr. Wright again, gazin' down at him with her hands on her hips as she spoke. "Oh, lots of different people have lots of different theories about that. But the one I'm most interested in is the speculation there might be Old World ruins in the area."

Well there it was. Her own admission of her interest in Old World tech. Even still, there was lots that didn't seem to add up quite yet. "In Akansa?" I shook my head. "Never heard reports of any ruins there."

"Yet," Nan said.

Dr. Wright whimpered, and Nan turned on her heel to march back in my direction.

"And yet, accordin' to the doctor here, that's where the Balogh family headed off to in such a hurry. Curious, ain't it? Why would a doctor, a *good* doctor, mind you, suddenly up and leave his homestead and his work to drag his family cross-country in a wagon?"

I only stared at her, havin' no answers.

"It ain't the birds he cares about, I can tell you that," Nan supplied.

"Even if there were ruins there," I said, and I hoped there weren't, 'cause I didn't want nothin' to do with any Old World ruins, "how does that got anythin' to do with the birds?"

Nan arched an eyebrow at me. "Well now, you don't got to concern yerself with that part of it. What I want you to do is go to Blackbird and see if you can't find your *acquaintance* Dr. Balogh. Seems that's where he's gone off to, and I've got a good idea he went 'cause he's got a notion those ruins do exist, and he suspects he knows where. You go there and you find him. Sure he'll be glad to see a friendly face and all. You find him, you find those ruins, and then you send me a telegram back to Bravebank and you tell me exactly where they are, you understand?"

I didn't like the greedy gleam in her eye. Not at all. "What if … what if he ain't there?"

Nan glanced back at the badly beaten Dr. Wright, then turned those pale eyes on me. "Oh, he's there."

"And if there ain't any ruins in Blackbird, after all?"

"Well then." She stepped closer. "Guess that means you ain't got nothin' left to bargain with." She turned away before I could protest, stridin' quick toward the barn door.

So I made my protests to her back. "That ain't fair! I ain't got no control over what may or may not be in that goddamned town! You can't put that on me!"

"Them's my terms, Mr. Delano," she said. "Take 'em or leave 'em."

I took a step after her, but three pistols moved quick to point at my chest and I drew up short. "That's horse shit!" I spat.

Nine-Fingered Nan reached the doorway, paused. "Oh, and one more thing." She spun back to face me, her black skirts flarin' out and then settlin' again around her booted ankles. "Time is of the essence here. I don't hear back from you in two weeks, I'm tellin' that man who wants yer sister he's won the bid, ya hear?"

I risked another step forward, and the three pistols lifted higher. Hammers clicked back. "*Goddamnit* … look. I'll go to Blackbird. I'll find the doc. But you can't make the ruins a part of the deal … that ain't no deal, that's a gamble."

Nan cocked her head to one side. "Then I guess it's a good thing luck runs in yer family, eh, Delano?" She chuckled. "Now you best get goin'. Time's a tickin'."

REST IN PEACE

She left me standin' there, speechless and starin' after her in disbelief.

Her lieutenants followed her out, the two who held Holt dumpin' him to the dusty ground before doin' so.

And then they were gone, all of 'em, and soon enough I heard 'em ride off from the direction of the rear northern corner of the barn. A place Holt and I wouldn'ta been able to see 'em, or their horses, from where we'd come up from the south.

Watchin' and waitin', she'd said.

Fuck me.

Swearin', I reached down to grab my pistol outta the dirt and shoved it back where it belonged. Then I went to Holt, helped him sit.

He winced as he did so, a hand goin' to his head again. "Fuck," he growled.

"You okay?"

"No. Got one helluva fuckin' headache."

"Yeah…" I glanced over toward Dr. Wright. "Least yer still better off than the doctor here."

"Sure. Guess so."

I let him gather himself and stood, lookin' around fer my other pistol before I realized one of those lieutenants had made off with it. "Shit. They took my goddamned gun!"

Holt grunted. "Don't surprise me. No good

sons-a-bitches, all of 'em." He struggled up to his feet and I reached out to steady him as he swayed a bit. "I'm fine. I'll be fine. But we better get on to Grave Gulch now that we're both out weapons."

I nodded.

Behind us, poor Dr. Wright let out another pitiful whimper.

I winced, looked back in his direction. "What should we do with *him*?"

Holt followed my gaze into the darkness, where the shadows mercifully masked the man's horrific injuries. "Put him out of his misery. That'd be the kind thing to do."

I sighed. Didn't much like the thought of it, but he was right.

So I drew my single remainin' iron and went to the man's chair. Now that I took the time to look closer as well as I could in the limited light, I realized the chair he'd been tied to had come from the house. It was one of the kitchen chairs. I hadn't even noticed one was missin' when we'd been inside earlier.

And Dr. Wright was in awful bad shape. Not just his face, but the rest of him, too. Looked like they'd broken both arms, and his legs, too. I hissed a breath through my teeth and shook my head. "Sorry, Mister. Real sorry. But it's gonna be over soon."

I took a step back, and in one shot ended the poor man's pain.

"May he rest in peace," Holt murmured.

After some deliberation, we decided to bury him.

Nevermind the fact we didn't really have time fer such a thing, nor were we in any shape to do it, considerin' the fact I still had that hole in my arm and Holt was still woozy from those knocks on the head.

But we decided to do it, anyway. Mostly 'cause it just seemed wrong to leave him sittin' there tied up when his end had been so miserable. And maybe there was a little part of me that felt obligated in some way, if he were really a friend of the Baloghs. They'd done plenty fer me when they didn't have to, and I feared that somehow, some way, Nan figurin' out what Dr. Balogh knew about Old World tech was maybe because of me. And if that were true, then what had happened to Dr. Wright was also maybe my fault.

I didn't exactly know how, but the notion kept naggin' at me, anyway. Maybe if I buried the man, I could bury that snakin' guilt along with him.

We cut his body free of the chair and dragged him out back of the barn, then some distance further.

And that's when we found those others Nan had mentioned durin' our little chat, and Holt spat a colorful string of profanity.

She'd made a pile of 'em, but certainly hadn't bothered to bury 'em. Looked to be at least four bodies, though it was hard to tell now as the scavengers had come to call; pulled 'em apart and eaten some of 'em. And the flies were nearly as thick as the stench.

"Fer fuck's sake!" Holt ended his tirade at last, but his face had gone awful pale.

I had nothin' to say, myself. I couldn't imagine who these people had been … didn't want to imagine. Other friends? Family, even? Patients come to satisfy a curiosity about why the doc had suddenly vacated his office in town?

Or were they folk of a different nature? Treasure seekers or prospectors after the same ruins as Nan, who'd gotten wind about the doctor's particular hobby? Maybe even scholars like Professor Morton?

The possibilities were wide and varied, but likely none of 'em had deserved what had happened to 'em.

I swallowed back the bile in my throat and looked out across the stretch of desert beyond the pile of dead.

"We can't bury 'em all," Holt said.

"No. Just Dr. Wright." I nodded to the left, toward a big saguaro cactus. "Over there, how about? Seems as good a spot as any."

"Sure. Sure." Holt swiped at the sweat runnin' down his face with a sleeve. "Let's just get this over with and get the hell out of here."

It was near dusk by the time we finally got Dr. Wright properly laid to rest, retrieved our mounts, and left the Balogh homestead behind, both drenched in sweat and exhausted. But we kept our pace swift and rode in silence fer hours, travelin' well into the night before we drew up to make camp.

We made a small fire and ate a quick meal and listened to a band of coyotes yip and yowl in the distance.

I sat cross-legged on my bedroll, starin' hard into

the flames and tryin' best I could to make sense of things. What could Nine-Fingered Nan possibly want with some Old World ruins in Akansa? She certainly didn't need any ancient trinkets fer status or money like the barons of Blessing seemed to like. And why had Dr. Balogh gone there, too? If he'd wanted ruins, why not go to those that had already been discovered, and weren't halfway across the continent?

I couldn't sort it. Couldn't make no sense of it at all, so eventually I gave up. Not like it mattered, anyway. I surely didn't care about any of that old stuff, nor what anyone else wanted to do with it. Didn't even care that Nan wanted some of it fer herself. She could have it all, far as I were concerned, long as she gave me Ethelyn.

Soft snorin' made me look up, across the fire. Holt laid there stretched out, already asleep.

I smiled despite myself and shook my head, then laid out atop my own blankets. Damn it all, but I'd kinda missed the old bastard. He was sure a lot easier to get along with when he weren't complainin' about every damn thing I did. He hadn't even asked me fer more about what Nan had been talkin' about back at the Balogh house. Hadn't said a word about her sayin' she was gonna throw me back in a cell, hadn't asked why I'd been locked up again in the first place, hadn't asked how I'd managed to get free, hadn't wanted to know about why there now seemed to be biddin' on my sister at play.

'Course, maybe all that was 'cause he'd been knocked nearly senseless by that lieutenant.

Maybe he'd mostly missed that entire conversation.

Either way, I weren't gonna argue the outcome. I liked him keepin' quiet.

I dropped my hat onto my belly and then folded my hands under my head, starin' up at the stars and listenin' to those coyotes, and waited fer sleep.

I didn't sleep much, truth be told, my dreams fulla the sight of Dr. Wright's ruined face and that pile of bodies, and my bullet missin' Holt's hangin' rope, so that the last thing I saw before I jerked awake were his feet kickin' the air.

"Nightmare?" Holt asked quietly from somewhere to my right.

I sat up and scrubbed my hands over my face, notin' it was dawn now, the sun stainin' the sky above a deep pink. I took a deep breath of the cool mornin' air. "Yeah."

Holt grunted. His footsteps crunched over in my direction, and then there was a tin cup of coffee under my nose.

I took it gratefully with a nod of thanks. Well, he really *was* feelin' remorseful fer his past behavior, then. Maybe he needed to face the noose more often.

"Those still botherin' ya?" he asked.

"Always," I grumbled.

He'd made breakfast too, turned out: salted pork and beans and biscuits. We ate and saddled up and headed out again with little else said between us. I kept thinkin' about my dreams, and about how the hell I was supposed to find Dr. Balogh in Blackbird, and how I might somehow fulfill Nan's terms only *after* seein' Ethelyn myself if the old hag was expectin' a telegram. That was gonna make things a lot more complicated.

Well, guess I had time to figure it out, considerin' it was gonna be a long journey to get there in the first place.

We were finally comin' up on Grave Gulch three days later, nearin' the hills in which we'd made our semi-permanent camp, when I broached the subject with Holt. I'd been enjoyin' the quiet, sure, but now I wanted some answers.

"You gonna come with?" I asked. "To Blackbird, I mean?"

Holt glanced to me, his face reddened by the sun in the absence of a hat. "Ain't decided just yet."

"What else you figurin' on doin'?"

He shrugged. "Ain't decided that, neither."

I hoped he didn't plan to try and rob any more banks by himself. "Figure I'll supply up at camp. Then head on to the station over in Redemption, Lesser Texas. Given I don't got much time to do all this findin', I'll go by train far as I can, then ride the rest of the way."

Holt nodded. "You even know where Blackbird is?"

"No. Never heard of it. Figure I'll ask the locals once I hit the first station in Akansa."

Holt nodded again. "Good enough plan. You really think there's ruins there? Seems to me if there was, we'd of heard about it by now."

My stomach twisted at his statement, if only 'cause I agreed with him. But I didn't want to consider that possibility at the moment. So I only shrugged. "Guess we'll find out."

We passed the bleached bones of a human skeleton, tied up on sticks planted in the ground to make it look like it was still alive and standin'. The sentinels of Grave Gulch. Meant to warn away those who didn't follow the particular religion of the town's dominant cult.

But Holt and I hardly noticed 'em anymore. We rode on past, our mounts just as oblivious to the bones as we.

"What you gonna do if there ain't any ruins there?" Holt asked suddenly.

I gulped back the defensive swell of frustration, the urge to snap at him. It was a fair enough question, and one I'd possibly have to answer before the end of this errand. But I supposed I already knew the answer, anyway.

If there weren't no ruins, I'd have to figure out where Ethelyn was bein' held myself. And I'd have to figure that out before I broke the news about the ruins to Nan. Somehow. And then I'd have to confront Nan directly, and hope it went better than all the other times I'd tried to confront her. Hope I'd get the draw on her fer once. Hope I could end her before she ended me.

Then I'd have to go get Ethelyn.

I supposed the "*what* would I do" weren't so hard to figure out, after all.

It was the "*how* would I do it" that was the tricky part. And fer that, I had no answers yet.

I opened my mouth, closed it again, and blew out a heavy breath. "One thing at a time, old man."

Why did it seem I was always sayin' that?

We rounded a small rise up in the hills north of Grave Gulch to come upon the cave we'd made our home fer a good long while now.

And we both reined up sharply. My hand dropped down to the pistol at my hip.

A saddled horse was tethered to a bush just outside the cave entrance.

AN UNEXPECTED GUEST

"You expectin' guests?" Holt muttered under his breath.

"Naw. You?"

He shook his head. "You tell anyone about this place?"

This time I went ahead and glared at him. "'Course not. I ain't stupid. What about you?"

"'Course not."

Well, maybe they was just squatters. Happened upon the place accidentally and found it to their likin'. Least we'd found 'em now … hopefully before they'd had a chance to make off with any of our stuff inside. "Stay here," I instructed Holt. "You ain't got no guns. I'll go take a look."

"Be real careful," Holt said as I dismounted.

I didn't bother to reply. 'Course I'd be careful. I pulled my pistol and circled back around the rise we'd just come by, approachin' the cave mouth from the east side—the opposite side we'd originally approached from. I pressed my back up against the rock as I inched toward it, gun at the ready. The clearin' in front of it showed signs of a recent fire, smoke still risin' from the ashes. And there were fresh tracks in the dirt, too.

The horse itself was sturdy and well-built, a bay roan stallion with a shiny black mane and tail. It watched me draw nearer with only mild interest.

I paused at the edge of the cave's entrance and listened, but I didn't hear no one movin' around. Didn't hear no voices. I leaned forward, peeked around the curve of the rock.

Our crates were all still there, stacked just like we'd left 'em toward the back, right at the edge of the natural light. But one of the oil lamps had been lit and set atop 'em, illuminatin' the start of the cave's back chamber.

Still, I didn't see no one back there, and no movement, neither.

Frownin', I stepped inside, though I kept close to the wall and kept alert fer any shift of shadow.

"Stop right there," a woman ordered from somewhere the light didn't reach. And it was pitch black back there. "Don't get any funny ideas. I have you in my sights right this moment." A squealin' whine started up, one that sounded awful familiar. Almost sounded like that big cannon-gun did when it was warmin' up, about to spew a slew of bullets.

I stopped all right, and straightened, leanin' closer to the rock wall, strainin' to see into the blackness.

"Identify yourself," the woman ordered.

She sounded familiar, too. I went through the list of women I knew—women who mighta come here lookin' fer me—but the list was real, real short considerin' none of the possible candidates knew about this place. "Uh ... this is *my* place, lady," I ventured. "If anyone should be identifyin' themselves, it's you. You're the trespasser here. You wanna tell me what yer doin' squattin' at my camp?"

"Van?" The whinin' sound stopped abruptly. Someone shifted back there, and then bootsteps came across the rocky floor. She stepped outta the darkness finally, squintin' at me. And she was holdin' that big cannon-gun, sure enough.

The flash of long, wavy red hair in the lamp light spurred recognition and I lowered my own gun even as my mouth fell open. My mind struggled to comprehend. "Ch-Charlotte?"

Sayin' her name didn't make it make any more sense why she might be standin' in front of me right now. Why she had risked comin' back here after all she'd been through, after all *we'd* been through to get her back to Pennsylvania safely, after all I'd done to warn her about those men Charles Miller had sent after her.

She relaxed, her shoulders droppin' and that big gun tiltin' toward the ground. "Oh good, it *is* you. Hard to see your face properly with the daylight behind you like that. Sorry for … for this." She hefted the gun. "But I had to be sure. Where in the world have you been, anyway? I've been waiting here for *days*."

I just kept starin' at her, my mouth still open.

She sighed, then turned to set the big gun on top of the nearest crate. She glanced to the dusty toes of her boots and cleared her throat, smoothin' at her skirts. "Well? Nothing to say?" Those dark blue eyes of hers lifted again to meet mine, and I managed at last to shut my mouth.

"Uh." There were too many questions. Too many things that didn't make no sense. I tried to sort through to the most important one. "What … what are you doin' here?" I looked her over, looked around the cave, looked back over my shoulder toward her horse. "You all right? Everythin' okay? What's happened?"

She let out a little laugh. "Nothing's happened. I'm fine. I just ... well, truth be told, after everything that happened with Baron Whittaker and all, I found life back in Pennsylvania to be ... no longer satisfactory."

I frowned. What in the hell did that mean? Her family was rich, far as I could tell. And certainly goin' back to an actual home with carin' parents, real beds, and three guaranteed square meals a day was better than wanderin' around out here in the wilds.

"And ... and I was worried, too." Her smile faltered some. "You didn't say much in your telegram ... just that Charles Miller might be after me. And then I didn't hear from you again, and you never answered my other telegrams—or letters—and I feared that perhaps he had gotten ahold of *you*. I couldn't stand not knowing."

I blinked at her and tried to squash down the wrigglin' worm of guilt about not writin' her more. But I hadn't been back to Grave Gulch to check the post since before settin' off on the errand to get that lockbox. If she'd sent me other letters or telegrams, I hadn't even seen 'em yet. "So you ... so you came all the way back out here? Just fer that?" I hissed out a breath and shoved my gun back into the holster. "You shouldn'ta done that. It ain't safe."

She stood straighter, throwin' her shoulders back. "I went to Grave Gulch to check the papers when you didn't show up here. They said Charles Miller was murdered around a month or so ago, and the killer is still unknown and on the loose. I'd assumed that was your doing."

I winced at that statement. Not 'cause I regretted murderin' that bastard, I sure as hell didn't regret that one bit. But because if she'd heard that, she'd probably also heard the part where that whole posse had been murdered, and how they'd determined it musta been me who'd done it. Nevermind that *that* part of it weren't true. "Yeah," I admitted, decidin' not to bring up the posse, just in case she hadn't heard that bit yet. "But that don't mean it's safe around here. There's a new Baron Whittaker now, and he still wants my head fer killin' his pa, and maybe yers too."

"But your telegram said there weren't any bulletins of me up for that," she said, matter-of-factly.

I rolled my eyes. "Yeah, well … we don't know what Miller mighta told the new Baron Whittaker about who killed their pa, do we? And anyway, just 'cause you don't got yer face on any posters don't mean it's safe around here. There are plenty of other folk who'd be plenty happy to rob you. Or kidnap you and sell you off. Again. Or worse." I stepped past her, checkin' over the cave's interior and notin' she'd made herself at home. Some of our crates were open, and she'd helped herself to some of the food stores. As well as re-organized 'em, looked like. And she had a little cook area set up, and a bed roll laid out. I reached down to start rollin' up the blankets of her pallet.

"Hey!"

I ignored her protests. "You need to get out of here. Go on back to Pennsylvania."

"I am most certainly *not* going back to Pennsylvania," she said with a huff, stalkin' over to me. "I came all the way back here to make sure *you* were safe. Since you couldn't bother to send a note and tell me so. And your sister. You never mentioned your sister. Did you get her?" She peered out toward the cave entrance. "Is she here?"

I paused in rollin' up her blankets, my fingers diggin' into the thick wool as my teeth clenched. "No," I growled out. "Not yet. Still workin' on that."

She sobered then, lookin' back to me. "Oh."

"What the blazes is goin' on in here?" Holt yelled, appearin' suddenly at the entrance astride his horse and leadin' Joe and the mare behind him.

Damn. I'd been so surprised to see Charlotte I'd completely forgotten to tell him the coast was clear.

"We got a visitor," I yelled back.

Holt dismounted and strode inside, then stopped short when he saw Charlotte.

I figured I musta looked just as surprised as he looked now when I'd first seen her, too.

Charlotte, fer her part, did not seem surprised to see him. She didn't look happy to see him, neither. "Ah," she said flatly. "It's you."

His clear blue eyes narrowed at her. "And it's you," he said.

"She was just leavin'," I said, and I handed Charlotte her rolled blankets. Then I went to her pack and started pickin' up her various other belongings and stowin' 'em inside.

"Well," she said, "it is certainly good to see you again as well."

Her affronted tone was hard to miss, and another twinge of guilt hit me. I straightened, one of her small iron skillets in-hand. "It ain't … it ain't that I ain't glad to see you. It's just that it ain't safe, like I said. And if somethin' happened to you while you were here 'cause of me … well, I got enough to deal with tryin' to get my sister back, understand? I don't want to have to worry about you too, is all."

Charlotte turned to face me, holdin' her roll of blankets to her chest. She wore one of her nice dresses again, like that purple one she'd bought in Peridot the day I'd seen her last, only this one was a pale blue that set off the red of her hair. "You don't have to worry about me," she said evenly. "I can take care of myself. Came all this way alone just fine, didn't I? And found your camp again, too. I had to make sure the Whittakers hadn't caught up to you. Or Charles Miller. And to see if you'd managed to free your sister."

I stuffed the skillet into her pack. "And just what did you figure you'd do if the Whittakers or Miller *had* gotten ahold of me?" I ventured, not botherin' to mention that they had, indeed, gotten ahold of me, and that I'd only barely escaped alive, but she'd missed that part. "You came here by yourself? What good would that have done?"

Her eyes narrowed. "My father is lobbying for a special organization back in the Republic as we speak. Ever since I was first kidnapped. And after I returned and told him everything that had happened, and after he received the telephone call about Miller sending men all the way back east after me, even though I'd escaped once already … he nearly has Congress convinced to approve it."

Holt gave a rather loud snort of amusement. "Congress? Lady, ain't no one out here give a damn about what yer Congress says. Pardon the language, but it's the truth."

She spun a half-step to face him with a glare. "If

Congress approves its formation, they'll move to work jointly with the Commune's Council, too. It won't just be the Republic's Congress involved. It'll be the Republic *and* the Commune, working together to clean up the Territories."

Holt and I both barked laughter at that idea.

But I swallowed mine back as she turned her blazin' blue glare on me. "Er ... okay," I relented. "All right. But I still don't see how an organization that don't exist yet would help you here and now, bein' that you came all by yerself."

She straightened her shoulders again and tilted her chin up defiantly. "My father has already started recruiting men himself. To form a private organization until the larger, federal one is approved. If needed, I could simply call upon them to help. He could have them here within days."

I lifted my brows. "That wouldn't do you no good if a person grabbed you again though, would it? You'd never get a chance to send word fer 'em. You shoulda brought 'em with you from the start."

Her defiant gaze softened, and her eyes dropped toward her boots again. "Well ... I didn't want them to know where I was going just yet. Didn't want father to know, either. He is insufferably controlling. He never would have allowed it."

I sent an alarmed look over her shoulder to Holt, who shook his head. Then I pulled my stare back to her. "Yer father don't even know yer here?"

She shook her head. "No. But my chambermaid knows. She and I are rather close. I left her a note with my whereabouts. Told her if I did not return within a certain time, she should give it to my father."

"Charlotte…" I found it hard to find the words without spittin' out a slew of profanities. "He's gonna be worried sick about you. Probably thinks you got snatched again. Probably organizin' those men to go out lookin' fer you right now!"

She pursed her lips, marchin' forward to grab her pack away from me. She threw the blankets down on top of it and started tyin' 'em on. "He won't. At least not yet. I told him I was leaving. I just didn't tell him where."

I only watched her, thinkin' about how worried her family must be, and she finished tyin' on the blankets and hefted the pack up and onto her shoulder.

"And anyway," she went on, "I'm a grown woman. I can make my own decisions about where I go, thank you very much."

Well, maybe that were true, but she *had* just admitted to not tellin' her father exactly where she'd headed off to, fer the express reason he wouldn'ta allowed her to go. Which sounded to me like maybe she couldn't act on her decisions as a grown woman as much as she might have liked.

But I decided not to mention any of that. Instead all I said was, "Well you can take the train back east from Redemption. Just so happens that's where we're headed, too. We'll take you there."

A FOOL'S ERRAND

"What about your sister?" Charlotte asked as I turned away from her to start gatherin' my own supplies outta crates. "Does Nan still have her? Did you find out where she is?"

Just as well I weren't facin' her no more, 'cause all her questions made me grimace. I focused on openin' one crate after the other, findin' myself another pistol—my last spare—and several more cases of bullets. "No," I said. "I mean … yes, Nan still has her." I rolled open the cylinder of the new pistol and started loadin' it. "But no … I ain't figured out where she is, yet. No one's been too keen to talk on that." I snapped the loaded cylinder closed, gave the new pistol a few experimental turns, then tucked it into my empty holster.

Across the way, Holt was rummagin' in some crates himself. He pulled out one of his other hats and shoved it onto his head, then withdrew another gunbelt, fittin' it around his hips.

And I scowled at what he pulled out of that crate next. A familiar bundle wrapped in oilcloth and tied with leather thongs. I preferred to keep that thing buried away, just like Pa had preferred it … Holt preferred to try and pawn it off on me at least once a year, no matter that I kept tellin' him no.

He took the chance now, too, lookin' up at me with a raised brow at the same time as he lifted the package. I could read the expression on his face clear as day: *Might as well take this one now … no use lettin' a perfectly good gun go to waste.*

But I narrowed my gaze and shook my head, makin' a point of pattin' the pistol I'd just settled into the holster at my hip.

He rolled his eyes and muttered somethin' I couldn't hear, but made no further arguments fer the time bein', to my relief. Instead, he just nestled the thing back into its place in the crate and resumed fishin' out his own replacement weapons.

Charlotte watched us both, one to the other.

I saw a frown pass over her face, but then turned back to my supplies as her gaze shifted in my direction.

"Then where are you going now?" she asked simply.

"To Redemption, like I said."

"All right, I mean *why?*"

I paused in pullin' out more stores of food and sighed heavily. I glanced over my shoulder to Holt, caught him watchin' me. But when my eyes met his, he only shrugged. He was gonna stay out of it, then. Had no opinion on if I should tell Charlotte about this newest errand or not. I didn't much want to tell her about it, myself.

Didn't want to chance her tellin' me it was a fool's errand.

I still expected Holt's good nature about the whole thing to end eventually, and I didn't need no one else tellin' me I was crazy fer doin' this. I already knew that well enough.

"Do you think she might be there?" Charlotte pressed at my silence. "Your sister?"

I resumed takin' stock of flour, cornmeal, lard, dried fruit, salted meat, and coffee. "I'm … I'm makin' a trade," I said finally. "With Nine-Fingered Nan. I'm helpin' her find somethin', and then she's gonna give me my sister."

I waited fer Holt to say somethin', to go on about how Nan would never give me Ethelyn, or about how she was only fuckin' with me, but he said nothin'. Just kept his attention on readyin' his own spare pair of pistols.

Well, I was sure his grumblin' would return soon enough. And anyway, I was beginnin' to believe him. I'd do this one last errand fer Nan, sure … but she weren't gettin' what she wanted outta me this time without me gettin' Ethelyn first. I'd make certain of that.

Somehow.

"Really?" Charlotte asked. She didn't sound convinced, neither. "And what she's looking for is in Redemption?"

"No. What she's looking for is in Blackbird, Akansa." I stuffed what food I'd chosen into another pack. "But we're gettin' on the train in Redemption, same as you. Well, *I'll* be gettin' on the train, anyway. Not sure about Holt."

He straightened from the crate he searched through, lookin' more himself now with his hat and two guns perched on his hips again. "I'll go," he said, then shrugged. "Might as well. Don't figure I got anywhere else I need to be."

A strange sorta relief filtered through me at his words. It was always nice to have another gun in the fight. I gave him a nod. "All right, then. Guess we're all gettin' on the train in Redemption." I looked back to Charlotte as I cinched up my pack. "You'd better be sure you got all your belongings. We're on a tight schedule; be leavin' this afternoon."

But she didn't move, only frowned. "*Blackbird,* Akansa?"

"Yeah…"

"The place where all the birds died?"

I blinked. "Er … yeah. You know about that?"

"Everyone knows about that."

Holt and I glanced to each other. *We* hadn't known about that. Not till Nan had shoved that paper into my hands. But then, Holt had been locked in a jail cell awaitin' his own hangin' and I'd been pushin' hard to get there in time to save him. Neither of us had been payin' much attention to anythin' happenin' elsewhere.

"It's happened before, you know," Charlotte said.

"What's happened before?"

"This kind of die-off. Around Blackbird. There's some old texts that mention it. And tales the local tribes still tell about it."

I grunted, swingin' my pack up over my right shoulder. "Those texts and tales say anythin' about it bein' related to Old World stuff?"

Charlotte shrugged under the weight of her own pack. "Not particularly. They mostly attribute it to the actions of gods or goddesses. Or some beings called the Guardians."

"And how exactly do you know all this?" Holt demanded.

Charlotte fixed him with a witherin' look. "I like to read. You should try it sometime. Might find it enlightening."

He glowered at her, but I cleared my throat

loudly before their bickerin' could escalate further. "We should best be goin'."

Alas, neither of 'em moved fer the exit. "What could Nine-Fingered Nan possibly want from Blackbird?" Charlotte mused.

"Maybe somethin' that ain't there," I admitted. "But she didn't give me a lot of time to search fer it, so we'd best be gettin' a move on, like I said." I reached out toward her with my left hand and gestured at her bag. "Here. Lemme take that fer you."

She arched an eyebrow, lookin' me over skeptically. Her gaze lingered on the bandages wrapped around my left bicep and the three middle fingers of my left hand. "You're hurt. Again."

I scoffed. "Yeah. That happens a lot. I'll be all right. Don't mean I can't carry yer pack out fer you."

She hesitated fer a moment more, then sighed and handed it over.

The weight of it made my arm protest somethin' awful, all right, but I bit back the grunt of pain and hefted it onto my left shoulder, then headed fer the horses.

We loaded up, takin' all the extra canteens and usin' Sally's skinny mare like a pack horse, then headed out again, leavin' Grave Gulch behind as we followed the Gila River southeast. We'd keep to the river till afternoon tomorrow, then strike out across the desert fer another day before meetin' back up with it again. And after that it'd be another three days across the open before we reached Redemption.

That leg of the ride concerned me most; especially now with Charlotte along.

There was a little minin' settlement in the middle of those three days we could stop over at, I supposed, but I'd heard tales it weren't the most civilized of places. Still, I didn't think we had any choice **but** to stop there, given it was the only guaranteed waterin' hole in that three-day stretch of desert.

And it weren't ever wise to pass up guaranteed water.

I tossed another glance to Charlotte as I brooded over such thoughts.

Turned out her skirts weren't skirts at all, but rather wide-legged pants so she could easily ride astride the saddle. Clever. She'd braided her long red hair, donned a straw hat, and buckled a gunbelt around her waist equipped with a sixgun.

It gave me some reassurance to see her with a weapon, and it made me think of her wieldin' that big cannon-gun the night we'd burned down the Whittaker estate. But we'd left that thing behind, too, put it back into the crate she'd dug it out of. I figured the pistol would be easier to manage, and easier to travel with. Least she hadn't come out here unprepared, seemed like. I wondered then how she'd crossed that desert from Redemption to get out here in the first place. Wondered if she'd done that ride all by her lonesome, or if maybe she'd hired a stagecoach. I hoped she'd hired a stagecoach; though if she hadn't, there was clearly a lot more I had to learn about Ms. Charlotte Harrison from Pennsylvania.

We rode mostly in silence through the afternoon into the evenin', though I had the naggin' feelin' both Charlotte and Holt had things to say. Hell, I had things to say, too, but I weren't exactly sure how to say any of 'em just yet. So I kept my silence, kept my focus on the trail ahead and Joe's big ears floppin' around in front of me.

We camped near the bank of the river just as the sun sank low behind the mountains in the distance. The water ran black as ink in the fadin' light, and Charlotte and I set about carin' fer the horses while Holt wandered a ways in search of more tinder fer the fire. He didn't have to go far; this area was littered with the dry, brittle skeletons of dead cacti and brush.

Even still, soon as he was only a vague silhouette against the horizon, Charlotte dumped her saddle to the ground and turned to me. "He do that to you?"

Her sudden speakin' startled me, and I nearly dropped my own saddle. Somehow I managed to set it down semi-gracefully, then straightened with a frown. "Huh?"

"That." She waved toward my left bicep, where the bandage showed through the hole in my sleeve, then jerked her chin in Holt's direction. "He actually shoot you for hiding his money like you thought he might?"

It took me a long minute to process what she were sayin'. Then I remembered that the last time I'd seen her, Holt had nearly shot me fer wantin' to take the money he'd stolen from Blessing's bank to Nan. Only Charlotte had knocked him out before he could do so, and then I'd tied him up and taken the money, anyway. And at the time, I'd thought he might shoot me once he woke up and freed himself, sure.

But all of that seemed so long ago now. So much

had happened since then. "Oh," I said finally. "No. No, not Holt. Someone else did that. He *was* awful put-out about it, but he didn't shoot me fer it." Punched me in the face, yeah. And nearly choked me out. But he hadn't shot me. He'd even come with me afterward to—we'd thought—confront Nine-Fingered Nan and get Ethelyn.

Instead it had only been Nan's man Taggert, double-crossin' her, and some poor nameless girl who'd somehow gotten caught up in all of it.

Memories of that dark-haired woman flashed through my mind again; memories of how she'd looked at me while she was dyin', blood gurglin' up between her lips. She'd died, and fer nothin'. Fer some cruel bastard's entertainment.

I swallowed hard and turned away from Charlotte before she could see any of the anger that welled up, hot and sudden. I focused instead on unpackin' Sally's mare, tryin' to breathe through it.

A light touch on my right arm a minute later made me jump and whirl around, nearly beltin' out a yell before I realized it was only Charlotte, come up close all silent-like.

She rocked backward as I whipped around quick to face her, eyes goin' real wide. "Oh, I'm sorry. I didn't … didn't mean to startle you. I only wanted to say … I brought your pistol back." She drew the gun on her hip and offered it out to me, and in the dusk's weak remainin' light, I saw it was indeed my gun.

The one I'd lent her when I'd sent her home to Pennsylvania.

I swallowed back my racin' heart, tryin' to cover up how much that touch of hers had alarmed me. Guess I weren't used to folk sneakin' up on me like that. At least, not any friendly folk. I pushed her hand and the gun back toward her. "No. You keep it. I don't need it."

"I brought my own gun," she said, shovin' it at me again. "It's yours. You should have it back. I don't need it, either."

She had it nearly pressed into my chest. I folded both my hands around it, around her hand that held it, and gently lowered it. "Charlotte…" But then I forgot what I was gonna say, distracted by the feel of her warm skin beneath my palms, a sharp contrast to the cool, smooth steel of the gun.

She only looked up at me, waitin' to hear what I was gonna say, and I realized abruptly how close she was standin', too. When had she got so close? She watched me, eyes searchin' my face, and made no move to pull either her hand or the gun from my grip.

"Charlotte," I tried again, and wet my lips. *Damn it all, Delano, focus.* I lifted my gaze away from her, cast it over to the bony horse that stood beside me. "Keep it. Please." There. That's what I'd been meanin' to say. I pushed it back at her again, and let go of it. Let go of her. Then turned resolutely to resume unloadin' the mare.

She stood there beside me fer another long minute, but I kept myself busy. Made my hands forget the feel of hers by rubbin' 'em across coarse blankets and scratchy twine and rough canvas.

"All right," she said finally, and then she sighed softly and settled my pistol back into her holster, steppin' away to go about readyin' the fire.

I drew a deep breath, exhaled slow and quiet.

Holt returned then with an armful of dead

branches and withered cacti. He set the lot of it down next to where Charlotte crouched with the flint in-hand, and his hooded gaze swept over our makeshift campsite. "The hell you two been doin' this whole time? Get with it or we'll be eatin' dinner at midnight!"

I gave him a scowl, but picked up the pace, anyway.

The rest of our night passed quiet and uneventful, and the next day's ridin', too.

It weren't till the second night I spotted trouble.

COPPERWELL CAMP

It was the silhouette of a rider against the horizon, fer just a second.

Or ... I *thought* it was.

We'd just settled ourselves into camp fer the night, and there was only the barest thread of light left in the sky. But we was in the flat of the desert now, with nothin' substantial around us fer miles and miles. The mountains were off to the north and east, and the river, too. A few scraggly plants and spiny cacti littered the flat, of course, but it weren't enough to hide a person.

I put a hand on Charlotte's arm as she pulled the tinder box from her pack. "Wait," I said quietly. "No fire."

"What is it?"

I shook my head, starin' hard into the distance where I swore I'd seen the person. But there was nothin' there now. I kept searchin' the horizon, strainin' to see any movement, any sign of another rider.

Holt stepped up beside me, gun already drawn, squintin' off in the same direction. "See somethin'?" he asked.

"Thought so." I cursed the fadin' light, cursed our lack of caution over the last day. We hadn't bothered to check our trail or cover our tracks, figurin' no one had tailed us to Grave Gulch, so we musta been free and clear when leavin' there.

But then, Holt and I both had our faces printed on plenty of posters around here. Someone coulda been after us for a whole multitude of reasons, not least of which was me recently rescuin' Holt from the noose.

"There hasn't been another soul out here all day," Charlotte whispered from the other side of me. She was also peerin' out into the dark now. "Or yesterday."

"Yeah…" And it was true. We'd been alone fer the whole of the journey so far. And in the daylight we could see mighty far across that flat stretch of desert.

Still, that didn't mean someone couldn't've ridden up durin' dusk, while we were preoccupied with our supplies and the horses. It also didn't mean the rider was hostile, if they *were* out there. But I didn't much want to take any chances.

Even if now there seemed to be no sign of 'em.

"Coulda been a deer," Holt ventured.

"No," I snapped. "It was a person. A rider. Hat 'n all."

Holt frowned. "Well, if they were out there, I don't see 'em now."

"Let's take watches," I said. "And no fire tonight. Just to be safe."

"You think … they might mean us harm?" Charlotte asked.

After what she'd been through out here, I was surprised to hear her wonder such a thing.

Holt snorted in amusement. "Missus, we got all kindsa people after—"

I jabbed him in the side with my elbow.

He side-stepped away from me, rubbin' at his ribs and givin' me a look. But at least it seemed he'd caught my meanin'. "I mean, we got all kindsa bad people out here in the Territories. It's always better to assume they wanna rob and kill ya than to assume they're friendly."

Charlotte looked deeply concerned about that statement. Guess her talk of her father's organization cleanin' up the Territories had been mostly focused on Nine-Fingered Nan's operations and those barons of Blessing. Guess she hadn't figured the individuals out here could be just as dangerous sometimes.

"I'll take first watch," I said. "You two get some sleep."

"I'll take second watch," Holt said.

"And I'll take third," Charlotte offered.

"No," Holt and I said in unison.

"There's no need," I said as she opened her mouth to protest. "The two of us is more than enough to cover a night, and there's no use in you missin' out on sleep too if it ain't necessary."

She crossed her arms and tilted her head to one side, fixin' me with a challengin' glare I could only just barely see in the swiftly growin' dark. "Exactly. There's no need for you two to miss more sleep than you need when there are three of us here. We all take equal parts watch and we all get more sleep because of it."

Holt stepped up to put in his two cents. "We'll be alright on less sleep. We're used to it. Won't be no trouble fer us to take over while you get some quality rest—"

"Don't you go on putting up that selfless act on

my account," Charlotte snapped, turnin' on him. "It doesn't become you, and I know better. You were ready to shoot Van over that money you stole—money he needed to free his sister!" She rounded on me before Holt could bluster out an objection to her assessment. "I didn't come out here to be coddled or treated like some fragile flower. I've had a whole lifetime of that, and I am quite through with it, thank you. I survived six months in the mines at Whittaker's ruins, remember? How much sleep do you think I got during that time? Huh? How much food or water? How many displays of human decency?" She shoved the tinder box rather violently back into her pack. "Not a lot. I will be just fine. And I will take third watch, or we'll be parting ways just as soon as the sun comes up. Understand?"

I considered her points, shiftin' on my feet. They were fair good ones, in truth. And I already knew she could shoot well enough. I glanced sideways at Holt, but he'd only got that grumpy look across his face again. So I nodded. Shrugged. "All right, fine. Fine. You take third watch."

"Thank you. That wasn't so hard now, was it?"

But she didn't give me time to answer that question. She only grabbed up her pack and marched off a ways to lay out her bedroll.

Holt muttered under his breath and holstered his pistol, then clapped me on the shoulder. "Keep yer eyes open, kid. And wake me if yer even the slightest bit suspicious." He dropped his voice so Charlotte couldn't hear. "I ain't got no plans to go back to that noose."

I nodded, and he went off to get settled fer sleep, too.

We didn't talk the rest of the evenin', and in fact Charlotte acted like me and Holt weren't even there. I tried my best to leave her be, to not spend overly long watchin' the dim shape of her huddled under her blankets after she fell asleep.

I tried to keep my eyes sweepin' the horizon instead, searchin' far as I could see in the silvery light of the full moon, lookin' fer distant fires and listenin' fer hoofbeats or voices.

But I saw nothin' out of the ordinary, and heard nothin', neither. And after awhile I began to wonder if maybe I'd just been seein' things.

Maybe I'd spent too many years an outlaw now, always on the run, suspicious of everyone, even Holt most times.

Maybe.

The night passed without incident, and even though I kept scannin' that horizon fer the whole of the next day, we never saw another rider. There was a stagecoach near midday goin' west, and we nodded greetings to the drivers and passengers and their armed escorts as we passed by each other, but those were the only other travelers we saw along the trail.

I was grateful neither Holt nor Charlotte bothered to bring up the fact that maybe I'd been mistaken about what I'd seen. And grateful too that both of 'em seemed still just as alert as me in watchin' fer anyone followin' us.

Maybe I'd been wrong … maybe it'd just been a deer, after all. But an abundance of caution weren't never a bad thing, anyway, and we'd let our guard slip too much before. I didn't want it to happen again.

We came up on the mining camp of Copperwell in the late afternoon, the warped, agin' wood of its few buildings risin' up outta the shimmerin' desert flat like a mirage. Necessity had made it more than just a mining camp, I supposed, bein' as it was one of the only settlements out here in this wide open stretch of nothin', but it weren't quite a town, neither.

It had one hotel, two saloons, a corral for the horses, and water. And that was all we needed.

Big canvas tents were pitched all around the outskirts of the camp, encirclin' the hotel and the saloons. We rode through 'em, and I saw various other wares fer sale in some of the larger ones. We declined the invites of the vendors to peruse their goods, hot and weary and only wantin' some time to rest outta the saddle.

We dropped the horses off with the hostler first; paid fer 'em all to get some grain, and wandered over to the hotel to book our own rooms.

There was another disagreement there when Charlotte tried to pay fer all three, and then Holt and I tried to pay fer hers, and it escalated till I thought maybe the hotel proprietor might throw us all out. So we finally agreed to each pay fer our own, and Charlotte and I asked after baths, then looked expectantly to Holt, who was puttin' off a mighty powerful smell himself.

He grumbled about it, but begrudgingly slid over his coin fer the same.

The bathhouse was a separate building, and at

least there was no argument about lettin' Charlotte go first. Bein' as she was a lady, and this camp was real scarce on women, I paced outside the door while she washed up to ensure none of the locals got any lewd ideas. When she'd finished, she emerged dressed in a fresh set of clothes, damp hair fallin' around her shoulders and smellin' of chamomile soap.

I walked her back to her room and saw her inside before I headed back down to wash up myself. It didn't take long. Copperwell's baths weren't so much *baths* as basins of tepid water you could scrub yerself with and dunk yer head into.

Still, it was somethin', and it felt good to rid myself of the crust of sweat and dust that had caked up after too many long days of ridin' hard. Made me think of Sally's baths, though … made me *miss* Sally's baths. Hot water, good whiskey … Nora and Nettie.

Shit.

I splashed more of Copperwell's water over my head, tryin' to bring myself back to the present. Back to the grimy little minin' camp instead of the boomin' river oasis of Blessing.

I toweled off, dressed again, and took advantage of the provided shavin' materials to purge myself of the lengthy stubble along my jaw. My hair was gettin' awful shaggy too; would need a cut soon. But that would have to wait. Copperwell didn't have no proper barber.

I stepped out into the early evenin' feelin' like a new man. Nevermind the fact this was a grimy little minin' camp. It beat the open desert any day.

Or at least, it beat the open desert long as it didn't harbor anyone tryin' to kill or collect me.

I wandered the streets a bit while I waited fer Holt to scrub up, and as the sun kept droppin' toward the west, the miners slowly started comin' back from their labors, and the tents and the places between the buildings gradually filled up.

The hotel had a restaurant, and some of the big tents offered food as well. And then, of course, there were the saloons. The place went from bein' all silent and still upon our arrival to gettin' awful loud and rowdy the closer it got to dusk.

Normally I wouldn'ta minded such a thing, woulda preferred it, in truth, since rowdy crowds were easy to get lost in. But tonight it made me a mite twitchy.

Maybe it was 'cause of that disappearin' rider I swore I'd seen the night before.

Or maybe it was just 'cause of Charlotte bein' here, too.

Either way, I kept my senses on high alert and my hands near my guns, and made my way back toward the hotel to collect the rest of my party fer supper.

CAN'T FIGHT YER NATURE

We ate at the hotel, bein' that it held the least number of locals and was therefore the quietest part of camp. Weren't much of a fare offered there, but I hadn't had much of a proper meal since I'd left the Bravebank jail, so I was more than happy fer somethin' other than hard biscuits and beans.

We sat at an old rickety table, the three of us, spoonin' up bowls of a cowboy stew made mostly of beef innards and topped with crumbled cornbread. Helped ourselves to some whiskey, too.

I sat in the chair facin' the front door of the establishment and lookin' out the big front windows, keepin' an eye out fer any trouble. Holt sat at the opposite side of the table, keepin' an eye on the back door.

And Charlotte sat next to me, mostly watchin' the other hotel guests—of which there was only two — as she downed her stew with as much gusto as any man.

The competin' piano music from the two saloons banged out across the main street—the only street— and filtered into our eatin' space, punctuated by hoots and hollers from men who'd already drank too much and the occasional angry yell from a man who'd just lost at cards or dice.

Charlotte finished her stew and pushed her empty bowl away.

I'd finished mine a little while ago; had sat back in my chair and crossed my arms, put a boot up onto the empty chair across from me, and been broodin' over all the noise outside while I waited fer her and Holt to finish.

"I want to go with you to Blackbird," she said abruptly.

I came up straight in my chair at that, my boot thumpin' back down to the floor as I twisted to face her. "What?"

Holt gave a little laugh into a heapin' spoonful of his third bowl. "Don't think so, Missus."

She glared across at him. "And why not?"

"'Cause we don't know exactly what we'll find in Blackbird," I answered fer him. "Or who. Could be dangerous."

"You don't say?" She turned sideways in her chair to face me and one eyebrow arched high. Despite the hat she'd been wearin' while ridin', the sun had pinkened her fair skin and darkened her freckles. She'd left her hair down since her bath to dry, and it framed her face now in wild waves as she stared me down. "I seem to recall being involved in dangerous situations before. Let me think … how did that turn out?" She feigned concentration, bitin' her lip.

I opened my mouth to head her off, knowin' she musta been referrin' to the night we'd burned down the Whittaker estate, but she answered herself before I could get a word out.

"Oh that's right. I believe I was *not* the one to get knocked out and tied to a chair."

I shifted on the chair I sat on now, uncomfortable with that memory and with the volume of her voice. I glanced over at the other two older men takin' their supper here, but they didn't seem interested in our conversation. Still, I motioned fer her to keep it quiet. Didn't want to chance her yellin' out the Whittaker name when there was still that ridiculous bounty out fer me over that.

To my relief, she did drop her voice, but she didn't ease up on blastin' me. She leaned toward me, instead. "I seem to recall being the one to finish that job, and the one who saved you from a lot more suffering. Not to mention saved your life. So if you don't want me along, you'll need a better excuse than that."

Holt snorted another laugh into his stew. "She's got a point there, kid."

I turned away from her glare as unexpected heat rose into my face, focusin' instead on my empty stew bowl. I drummed my fingers against the table-top restlessly and tried to find the words that might express my reservations about her company without soundin' downright impolite. "If you would have stuck to our *plan*," I hissed, "and not been so hell-bent on revenge, that night mighta gone a lot differently."

Holt almost choked on his food. "Now where have I heard that said before?"

I glowered at him. It *did* sound an awful lot like what he was always sayin' to me … but that didn't make it any less the truth.

"I had a chance to end that bastard," Charlotte growled through her teeth. "I couldn't just leave without trying. Or without freeing everyone I possibly could. Not after what I'd seen. You would have done the same. I know you would have."

"He sure woulda," Holt muttered.

I glared harder at him and shifted again in my seat, knowin' that was probably true, too. Still, he really weren't helpin' my case here. "Yeah, well … well…" It weren't that I didn't *want* her along … alright, no, it *were* that I didn't want her along … but not fer the reasons she suspected, I reckoned.

"Yer family," I muttered finally. "They'll be worried sick. Might send those fellas yer pa hired out lookin' fer you."

She straightened in her chair. "My family will be worried about me just as much as they might worry about their prize stallion becoming injured and no longer able to breed."

Such an analogy was about the last thing I'd expected her to say, and I was caught not havin' the faintest idea how to reply.

Same as Holt, it seemed, as fer once he had nothin' to say, neither. But he dropped his spoon into his bowl, and his face twisted up like he was tryin' to make sense of her statement.

"Incidentally, their prize stallion is the horse I brought along for this journey." She sounded awful proud of herself. Fer a second, a half-smile pulled at her lips. But then her expression hardened again, and bein' as she'd struck me and Holt both speechless fer the moment, she elaborated. "Yes. That's right. I am the only daughter of six children, and the youngest. My parents have always seen me as a prize to shape and polish and offer out as a match to whoever might best serve *their* interests … to whoever might extend the most advantageous arrangement in exchange for my hand in marriage. But now…" She dropped her eyes to the scuffed, sticky tabletop and her empty stew bowl. Huffed a sigh and slumped.

"Now, after my six months in captivity, it seems I'm *damaged goods*. No longer suitable for any kind of match that might meet their previous hopes, or meet their highest standards." She gave a little shrug, studyin' her hands. "Only two places that might take me now, they say. Mr. Wellington—who is very, *very* much older than me, mind you—or the convent. So needless to say…" Her dark blue eyes flicked up to meet mine. "That is why I did not tell my father where I was going. And that is why I have no interest in going back to Pennsylvania. And why I wish to accompany you to Blackbird. Do you understand now?"

I sat there fer another long minute in silence, tryin' to digest this new information. I glanced to Holt, but he was only frownin' down into his food.

Damaged goods? How did they figure that, I wondered? And how could they say that about their own daughter? One who'd survived things plenty of others hadn't, and who'd managed to bring some good out of her harrowin' experience, too. Anger stirred in the pit of my stomach.

"And anyway," Charlotte said into the continued silence, "my parents are deeply grateful to you for your help in freeing me, you know. All of my family feels they owe you a debt they can never repay for getting me home safely, so that they might still have a chance to leverage me for some advantage or another. I'm sure it would put all their minds at ease to know I have you for a *chaperone*, no matter where we go."

I didn't like how she emphasized that word. I weren't fit to be anyone's chaperone, let alone hers. I had a hard enough time keepin' myself outta trouble

—and alive—I surely didn't want to be responsible fer no one else.

Holt chuckled, apparently findin' that idea downright amusin'.

I supposed all those bulletins with my face on 'em hadn't found their way out to the East Republic yet. Maybe they never would. But if she or her family had any idea of even half the things I'd done in my life, they'd change their opinions of me right quick, I was sure of it.

"Charlotte..." I said again. "I just don't think it's a good idea fer you to—"

"Then let me put it a different way." She stood from her chair abruptly. "I am not going back to Pennsylvania. I've had enough of everyone else always deciding what I will or will not do, or where I can or cannot go. First my parents, then Nan's people, then the baron ... and when I returned home again I realized it might have certainly been more comfortable, but it wasn't all that different to being held by Baron Whittaker. And that..." She huffed a breath and shook her head. "I'm not living like that. Not anymore. So this is it, Mr. Delano. I'm going to do *something*, with or without you. I'll go to Blackbird to see what's there, because I've read about it and it's *interesting*," she shot a glare to Holt before bringin' that hard blue gaze back to me, "and maybe I'll even decide to live there, just because I feel like it. Or I'll go to Blackbird to help you look for whatever you need to find for Nan to get your sister back. You helped me get my revenge on Whittaker, I'd be more than happy to help you get your sister. But you just decide which you prefer."

I blinked up at her, tryin' to sort the implications of everythin' she'd just said.

"I suppose you have until Redemption to make up your mind. Now, if you'll excuse me, I think I'll retire for the night. The current company has exhausted me." She made to leave, then paused and turned back; grabbed the whiskey bottle off the table and took it with her.

"Hey now!" Holt protested, but she paid him no mind.

"Charlotte," I tried, but she didn't listen to me, neither.

She only marched on across the restaurant to the door that crossed into the hotel lobby and the stairway that led up to the rooms, went through, and disappeared.

I released a growl of frustration, turnin' back to my empty stew bowl.

Holt finally finished his third helpin' and pushed his own bowl away, swipin' the back of his hand across his mouth, and then his hand across his pants. "You sure know how to pick 'em," he muttered.

I pushed away my sudden disgust at his lack of table manners and growled at him, too. "I didn't pick no one." And I hadn't. Charlotte Harrison had burst into my room at the Seven Knives Saloon by chance. She'd been in trouble, needed help. So I'd helped her. It was just as simple as that.

Just as complicated as that.

"Y'know," Holt said, "it may not be so bad to have her along, now that I think about it."

I doubted that. "Oh yeah? How so?"

He shrugged, diggin' out a toothpick from his

shirt pocket to pick at his teeth. "She seems pretty good in a fight."

"She knocked you over the head."

"Yeah, that's what I'm sayin'." One of his hands went up to touch gingerly at the spot she'd whacked him, even though that had been months ago. A spot I figured was still sore after Nan's lieutenants had more recently given him a good knock there, too. "And she did a fine job of it. Knocked me out cold. Seemed she did a fair enough job doctorin' ya up, too, after what that baron did to ya. And she said it herself, she *did* save yer life."

"Yeah," I admitted. "Sure." I wished she hadn't taken the whiskey with her. My glass was empty, and I coulda used more of it. "But just how was you plannin' to pay fer the train into Akansa, huh? I sure don't got enough left over to cover fer three of us plus our mounts. I barely had enough fer this meal. I gave all my money to Nan. And I got a notion you don't got that kinda money on you, neither."

As I'd expected, it seemed he'd already spent most of his share of that Blessing money. Least, I hadn't seen much of it left when we'd been gatherin' supplies at Grave Gulch.

And the way he chewed on that toothpick now, starin' down into his bowl, told me I'd guessed right. He only shrugged again. Then cast his eyes around the room before leanin' forward, over the table, and keepin' his voice low. "Figured we'd find some … *generous* folk along the way who might be inclined to help us out."

"Uh huh." Of course that was his plan. But then, it had been my plan, too. Up until Charlotte had showed up at our camp. Up until she'd insisted on comin' with us to Blackbird. "That's a problem then, ain't it?"

Holt lifted his bushy brows, echoin' my question from earlier. "Eh? How so?"

I leaned forward over the table, too, and tilted my head in the direction Charlotte had disappeared. "You really want to do somethin' like that with her around?"

"Ha!"

His bark of laughter startled me, but he leaned back in his chair, tipped it back on its two rear legs briefly before lettin' it thump back to the floorboards. "Kid…" he paused, composed himself, and lowered his voice again. "You already got her involved in plenty of other things, remember? Bank robbery, arson, theft, *murder.*"

I squirmed in my chair and gestured fer him to shut it, even though I was fair certain no one could hear anythin' he was sayin' above the ruckus comin' from outside.

"And I don't remember you bein' so concerned about her innocence at that juncture," Holt went on, ignorin' my discomfort. "She was perfectly happy to engage in those activities, weren't she? And it sure sounds to me like she all but stole away that horse she's been ridin'. So why not include her in our future engagements? Might be kinda nice to have a woman on board, ya know? Imagine the marks she could—"

"No," I snapped, and it came out harsher than I'd intended. "We ain't gettin' her involved, Holt."

He drew back a bit at my tone, those heavy brows of his drawin' down to hood his glare. "Well why the hell not?"

"Because," I hissed, "she only took part in those other *engagements* to get free of the baron. And to help me get Ethelyn back. She didn't come back here to lead a life of crime, Holt."

He grunted. "Sounded to me like she don't know what she came back here fer, really. She just said she's gonna do *somethin'*. How do you know a life of crime weren't on her list of possibilities?"

I narrowed my eyes at him. "Her father is tryin' to start a whole organization to come out here and clean up, fer fuck's sake. We can't ask her to get involved in any of our ... our *business* ... shouldn't even think it."

Holt crossed his arms and chewed harder on his toothpick. "Fine. What then? You gonna set her loose? Let her go off on her noble crusade all by her lonesome and probably end up right back in some baron's harem?"

I scowled; swiped up my whiskey glass. But it was still empty, so I scowled some more and slammed it back to the table, probably a little too hard. "No."

"Well then? I'm all ears, kid."

"I ... I dunno." I didn't want to cut her loose, no. And I didn't want her comin' with us to Blackbird, neither. I wanted her to get on the damn train and go home. To Pennsylvania. To the Republic. To her family with their gates and guards where I could at least be mostly certain she'd stay safe. "But we're gonna have to find a different way to afford that train, at least. I don't wanna have to take advantage of any *generous* folk while she's around."

"I see." Holt sat there starin' at me, passin' his

toothpick from one side of his mouth to the other, arms still crossed.

I ignored his scrutiny and eyed my empty glass again. Decided I was gonna buy another bottle, my dwindlin' coin be damned. I'd just pushed my chair back from the table in order to go get it when Holt spoke again.

"It ain't really about her at all, is it?"

"The fuck is that supposed to mean?"

He leaned forward and squinted at me from under his hat, unfoldin' one arm to jab his index finger down on the table as he made his point. "It's about *you*."

"Huh?"

"You don't want her to see what kinda man you really are."

I pressed my palms flat against the table and pushed to my feet, glarin' down at him. "Yeah? And what kinda man is that?"

He mimicked my movements, puttin' his hands flat against the table to stand eye-to-eye with me. He leaned close, his clear blue gaze holdin' mine evenly. "Yer a fuckin' outlaw, Van," he whispered. "A criminal. A thief and a murderer. That's why you don't want her to come, ain't it? You don't want her to figure that out, 'cause apparently she ain't put it together yet?" He let out a low whistle and shook his head. "Good luck, kid. Ya can't fight yer nature."

"Oh it's my nature now, is it?" I bit off. "That ain't what you said back in Bravebank when you were wantin' me to pull another bank job with you. You were all afraid I was gonna go straight … or did you forget that already?"

Holt snorted. "If ya ever manage to get yer sister,

sure. Sure, I do think you'd give honest livin' a try, fer her sake if nothin' else … *after* you find her. But before that…" He clucked his tongue and shook his head. "Before that … well kid, I ain't sure there's anythin' you *wouldn't* do, if ya needed to."

"If I *needed to* bein' the key factor here, Holt."

"Like you *needed* to cut up Lloyd Renneker?"

I ground my teeth at the reminder of that deed. "He was reluctant to talk."

"Seems you mighta enjoyed it a little, though. Or maybe a lot."

"He deserved it," I growled.

"Everyone deserves somethin', kid. Includin' you and me. So like I said … ya can't fight yer nature."

"It ain't my nature," I snapped. "Might be yers, but it ain't mine."

Holt straightened and lifted one bushy eyebrow. "Guess we'll see about that, won't we?"

"Guess we will."

He held my stare fer another minute, then finally blew out a breath and plucked that toothpick from between his teeth; flicked it off across the room. "All right. I'll leave you to yer self-righteous nonsense, then. I'm gonna go find me a game of cards. Maybe I can win us enough fer that train trip, eh?" He winked and gave my right arm a playful punch.

It landed just below the scars from Baron Whittaker and I clenched my teeth against the wince.

He turned and ambled away, unconcerned.

But I glared at his back until he stepped through the front door and left the establishment, and then I grumbled a good long string of profanity and went to get more whiskey.

Maybe I were an outlaw, but bein' such a thing had never been my first choice.

It weren't my nature.

Didn't matter that a whole stack of wanted posters might say otherwise. Didn't matter that my pa was once one of the worst to terrorize half the continent. Didn't matter what Holt said now.

It weren't.

And I was gonna drown the sharp edges of doubt needlin' at my mind in whiskey, so help me God.

TIME TO GO

I drowned those doubts, all right.

And most my sense. Sat there and downed almost a whole bottle of whiskey all by my lonesome, watchin' the front door and the street outside through those windows as the sky grew darker and the lamps grew brighter.

The two older fellas who'd been havin' supper in the restaurant with us finished their meals and left, and over time a few other folk wandered in and ate and wandered out again.

I sat there till the hotel proprietor came along and told me he was closin' up and I had to go. He suggested one of the saloons, said they'd be open all night.

So I grabbed up that almost-empty bottle of whiskey and stumbled out the door and into the night. The cool air hit me and sobered me up a bit, and I eyed those two saloons. One was clearly a fancier establishment than the other: had two floors and a balcony where the other had only one floor and a canvas roof.

But neither seemed much to my taste this evenin'. I surely didn't wanna gamble, seein' as I was already awful low on money and was generally shit at it, anyway. And there was a part of me that suspected I shouldn't drink more than my current bottle, neither. At least, not if I wanted to make the ride tomorrow in any good time.

The piano music was bangin' away, the noise of general merry-makin' spillin' out into the street along with several drunk patrons. But I didn't hear Holt shoutin', and there hadn't yet been any shootin', so I figured he was farin' well enough at his cards.

That bein' the case, I pivoted in the street to go right back to the hotel. Lurched through the front doors and gave the man at the desk a nod as I started up the stairs. Had they always been so damned creaky?

I found the door to my room, but paused with my hand on the knob.

Charlotte had rented the next room over. And there was a flicker of light shinin' beneath the door.

It was awful late. What was she doin' still awake?

Curious, I stepped over to her door, instead. Hesitated. Took a breath. Took another swig of whiskey. And rapped my knuckles lightly on the wood.

There was a moment's pause before she answered. "Yes? Who is it?"

I started to lean my left shoulder against the wall, then grimaced as the bullet hole in my bicep made itself known and straightened again. "It's me. It's Van."

Another pause. Then, "What do you want?"

I grimaced again, this time from the coolness in her tone. "I … I just wanted to, uh … be sure you were all right in there?"

"I'm quite well, thank you."

"Do you … need anythin'?"

"No. I'm fine, thank you."

I sighed and closed my eyes, leaned my forehead against the door so that my hat slid backwards and nearly fell off. "All right." A buncha other words clogged my throat. Words like, *Would you open the door? Can I come in? Can we talk about what I meant to say earlier...*

But none of those words came out, despite the fact my mouth opened.

"Are you drunk, Mr. Delano?"

The question surprised me, and I shut my mouth and pulled myself back from the door. Had I slurred that badly? "No," I said. But then I realized just how much this hallway seemed to sway. "Maybe."

Footsteps came across the floor and I stepped back as my heart jumped, my awareness sharpenin' when the door opened at last.

But it only opened a crack. And Charlotte stood there, lookin' up at me. Her hair was down, fallin' over her shoulders, and she wore the white blouse with the blue trim and blue skirt she'd been wearin' before, too. She looked me over, as if searchin' fer somethin', then brought her eyes back to my face. "You think it's wise to so heavily imbibe before a two-day ride across the desert?" she asked.

That weren't what I'd been expectin' her to say at all. But I shrugged. "I dunno. Try not to do much thinkin'. That's what this is fer." I brought up the whiskey bottle.

Her eyes widened at the sight of it. "Did you drink all of that by yourself?"

I squinted down at her, then squinted at the bottle. Was that a bad thing? "Maybe," I said.

She rolled her eyes and shook her head. "It's late,

Mr. Delano. We have a long ride ahead of us tomorrow. Go to bed. Get some rest. And no more whiskey." She reached through the crack in the door and wrested the bottle from my grip. "You've clearly had enough."

"But—"

She shut the door in my face, nearly closin' my nose in it. "Good night, Mr. Delano," she called through it, and I heard the sound of her latchin' it. Then the sound of her footsteps movin' away.

I sighed again, saggin' against her door. But I still couldn't quite get myself to say those other words. I understood her sentiments, her desire to help and, given what she'd said about how her parents treated her, why she wouldn't be so eager to head back home. And I hadn't meant to upset her with my reluctance to have her company. But damn it all … I was gonna get Ethelyn free, no matter what I had to do to do it.

And I weren't sure just what I was gonna have to do in Blackbird.

It could get ugly. Could get bad.

And if it did … Holt was right. I didn't want Charlotte to see it.

Didn't want her to see what I might have to do.

Didn't want her to think I was that kinda man.

"G'night," I muttered into the door. It was all I could muster. Then I pushed myself away and straightened my hat; staggered down to my own room to get some rest like she'd said.

She was right, anyway. We had a long ride ahead of us still. And I was tired, sure enough. And lookin' forward to a real mattress. I locked my door behind me, threw myself down across the bed, and fell asleep wearin' my boots and my belts.

A gunshot jolted me awake.

Fer a second I thought it might have been a dream, but then there was shoutin' and sounds of a scuffle. Somewhere close.

Another gunshot split the night, and the second one finally got through the fog of sleep and whiskey. I scrambled off the bed, got my boots tangled in the sheets and fell hard. I swore, crawled free of 'em, and pushed up to my feet, gropin' fer my right pistol.

I remembered now. We were in Copperwell, in the hotel, and I'd drank too much whiskey. Again. I stumbled sideways as the room tilted, but then caught the wall to steady myself. Through the window I saw the moon, fat and full but duller now … as the first brush of dawn lit the far horizon. The camp had fallen all quiet and still again.

Except fer whatever was goin' on outside now.

My first thought was that Holt had gotten into trouble. Maybe the cards hadn't gone his way, after all. Or maybe they *had* gone his way, a little too well fer someone else's likin'.

I ran to the window once I'd regained my balance and peered down at the street below. There were fellas fightin' there, all right. One looked dead, sprawled out in the dirt. But there were four more of 'em, and it looked like three against one. The fella gettin' beat on didn't look like Holt, though. His hat and duster were the wrong color, and his figure too tall and slim to be the old man.

Also, this guy looked like he knew how to fight.

Not that Holt couldn't hold his own in a scuffle, but this fella was doin' a decent job of fendin' off three other folk who clearly wanted him dead. I wondered why they didn't just try to shoot him, but then I noticed the pistols lyin' in the street. And the longer I watched, the more I realized every time a fella would try and grab fer his gun, the middle fella managed to thwart their efforts somehow.

Well, looked like he certainly had the situation handled. And anyway, if it weren't Holt, it weren't none of my business. I holstered my pistol and turned away from the window to head fer the door of my room, only weavin' a little as the world was still spinnin'.

This camp may not have had a sheriff, a jailhouse, or a gallows … but any time folk got murdered in a place, Holt and I made sure to clear out. Murder made townsfolk start askin' a lot of questions, especially of outsiders. Made 'em jumpy. Suspicious. And prone to lynching.

Camps like Copperwell weren't no different.

I yanked open my door to find Holt already on the other side of it, about to knock.

"Time to go," he said.

"Yeah."

"Don't forget yer hat."

"Shit." I crossed back to the bed to retrieve it, shovin' it down on my head as Holt went to rap on Charlotte's door. I rejoined him just as she pulled it open a crack to peer through groggily.

"What's the matter? What's happening?"

"We gotta go," I said.

Worry replaced the vague sleepiness of her features. "What? Why? Did you…" She glanced to our guns, then over her shoulder toward the window behind her. "That wasn't *you* shooting, was it?"

"No," I assured her. "Not us."

"But someone did get murdered," Holt said. "And murder is a messy business. We don't wanna be around when the hammer drops over this little incident."

"Why?" she asked again. "We didn't have anything to do with it!"

"Just trust us." I stepped forward, put a hand against her door and pushed it open wider. "We've had experience with this a time or two. It's better if we leave now. Get yer things."

She looked like she might argue fer a space, but then she only sighed and nodded, scrubbin' her hands over her face. "All right. Give me a minute." She left the doorway to move into the room; started gatherin' up the stuff from the bedside table and the bureau, to include our first bottle of whiskey, which was still mostly full.

"Fast as you can," Holt prodded.

He was gettin' restless already, but so was I. The longer we stayed here, the greater the chance we'd get stuck here till the murder investigation concluded.

"Yes, yes," she hissed. "I understand the need for urgency. What about you two? No things to pack?"

"I didn't bring nothin'," Holt said.

"I left my things with my saddle," I said.

Charlotte sighed. "Of course you did." She

tossed a brush into her pack and cinched it up, then threw it over her shoulder. "Ready. Let's go."

We went. Down the hall and down those creaky stairs, but then we turned to go out the back door of the restaurant, bein' as that fight was happenin' outside the hotel's front doors, and we surely didn't want to get involved.

The camp had roused a bit now, the gunfire havin' been a rather insistent wake-up call, and the continuin' sounds of the tussle drawin' an increasin' number of folk out of their tents to see just what the hell was goin' on.

Holt, Charlotte, and I ignored the flow of people headed fer the center of the camp and instead made our way to its outskirts, to the corral and our horses. We caught our four mounts, pulled our saddles outta the barn, and tacked up in record time. I double-checked all the canteens, makin' sure they were full.

They were.

We'd made sure to do that yesterday, shortly after arrivin'. Never knew when you might need to leave a place in a hurry, and this camp was the last chance fer guaranteed water till Redemption.

Satisfied on that account, I wedged my boot into the stirrup and was about to mount up when a voice spoke outta the pre-dawn gloom.

"Hold up there, Delano."

I froze. It was a man, but it weren't Holt who had said that.

"Ah ah," the voice said. "You too, Haggerty. Hands up where I can see 'em, both of you. *All* of you."

LAWFUL BUSINESS

Somethin' hot lit in me at his mention of *all* of us.

He had no right to include Charlotte in this. Whatever *this* was.

"Hands *up*, Delano. *Now.*"

I pulled my boot from my stirrup and hissed a breath through my teeth as I complied, holdin' my hands shoulder-high as I slowly turned around.

And I didn't like at all who I found there, standin' a few paces away with both guns drawn: one pointed at me and one pointed at Holt.

Least he didn't have nothin' aimed at Charlotte.

Duster. That fuckin' bounty hunter from Sonoita. His well-tailored clothes were streaked with dirt, his lip bloodied, and he had a cut on his left temple. That had been him in that tussle outside of the hotel, I was sure of it.

What I weren't sure of was how he'd managed to get free of those other three men and get over here without the camp residents noticin'.

I hadn't any idea how he'd managed to find me here, neither, though I certainly wondered then if it mighta been him I'd seen so briefly against the horizon the other night. But if it had been, why hadn't he made a move earlier? Why had he waited till we'd reached a camp, with plenty of other people around? Woulda been far easier on him to take me in the open desert.

"Who are you?" Charlotte demanded. She stood next to her horse, but they were both behind me and Joe, and I wondered if Duster could see the gunbelt she wore from his vantage point.

Didn't much matter either way though. I didn't think she was fast enough to get a good shot at him, especially not with me and Joe in the way. And I prayed she wouldn't try. I didn't want to get shot, neither by her nor Duster … and I really didn't want *him* to shoot at her. I had a good feelin' he wouldn't miss.

"Howdy, ma'am," Duster said, and bein' that his two hands were currently occupied, he nodded in her direction in lieu of tippin' his hat. "Pleasure to make your acquaintance. The name is Dustin Barrett. But around here, most people just call me Duster."

His good manners raised my hackles and I gritted my teeth.

"Van, you know this fella?" Holt asked. He was off to my right, next to his gelding with his hands up same as me. I could see him calculatin' though, tryin' to figure if we had any chance if we drew against this man called Duster.

"More or less," I said. And I didn't think we had a chance, at least not with our hands up and guns still in leather, so I gave Holt an incremental shake of my head, warnin' him not to try it.

Duster smiled. "More or less," he agreed.

"And what business do you have with us, then, Mr. Barrett?" Charlotte asked pointedly. "Especially that would require you to point your weapons at my friends here?"

Duster's smile widened.

There was a commotion buildin' in the center of camp, and I wished he woulda picked better timin' fer this. If we didn't get outta this place soon, we might very well *all* end up lynched.

"Your friends?" he drawled. "I beg your pardon, ma'am, but you seem like much too sensible of a woman to call these two no-good outlaws your friends."

"I don't think you know much about me, Mr. Barrett," Charlotte answered coolly. "Or about these two men here. So I would appreciate it if you would lower those pistols. These men are escorting me cross country, and we have a long way to travel today. I'd like to get going."

"That's right, *Dustin*," I said. The commotion in camp was gettin' louder, and comin' our direction. "Seems you've caused quite a ruckus here. Probably best we be movin' on. Quick as possible. Maybe we can resume this business another time, yeah?" I took a step backward, toward Joe.

"We'll be gettin' out of here quick-like, all right," Duster agreed. "But you'll be comin' with me, Delano." He glanced toward Holt, then Charlotte. "And if you come quiet, I'll even let your friends go. Even as temptin' as it is to get two-for-one." He grinned toward Holt, who only scowled at him and spit into the dirt.

"Mr. Delano isn't going anywhere," Charlotte said evenly. "Am I correct in assuming you are a duly appointed warrant officer, Mr. Barrett?"

Duster's grin vanished, and his gaze sharpened as his eyes focused on Charlotte again. "That's correct, ma'am. Maybe you weren't aware, but these two men you've hired are worth quite a lot of money. This one especially." His right gun extended toward me. "Like I said, both no-good outlaws, wanted for various crimes across the Territories. It's my sworn duty to bring them to justice."

I wished he'd shut up already. I really didn't want him gettin' any more specific about my various crimes. And that crowd was comin' awful close now … I wanted to be well away from here by the time they got here.

"Yes, yes," Charlotte said, seemingly as impatient as me. "And you're based out of where? The Commune? The Republic?"

Duster straightened, his pistols lowerin' just a bit. "The Commune. Council-appointed. Out of Abilene, Kansas, to be exact."

A jolt went through me at the mention of that town. I was familiar enough with that place. Had a lot of memories there … a lot of memories I hadn't bothered to remember fer a lot of years.

"I see," Charlotte said. "Well then you've probably heard of my father, Senator John Henry Harrison out of Pennsylvania? And I can assure you, he will be *most* put out if you were to rob me of my escorts at this juncture."

I blinked; glanced again to Holt, but he looked as surprised as me. A senator? A fuckin' *senator* was her father?

Duster, too, seemed at a loss. His pistols lowered further, his brow creasin' with his frown.

"There he is!" came a shout, and I winced.

Well, they'd found us now.

"Hands up, Mister!" another man ordered, and I figured they musta been talkin' to Duster, since the rest of us already had our hands up. "Drop yer guns or we'll shoot!"

I shifted my gaze over Duster's shoulder, where the mob of miners were comin' down the main street at us, and most of 'em held weapons of some sort, everythin' from rifles and pistols to pickaxes and pitchforks.

Duster's shoulders sagged and he let out a long, heavy sigh.

"Shoulda just let us be on our way," I muttered.

He shot me a glare, but then he fixed a friendly, pleasant expression on his face and lifted his hands, letting his twin pistols hang off his index fingers. "Now, now, folks," he called out.

"Take it easy. I assure you, I'm on lawful business here."

"Murderin' a man don't seem too awful lawful to me!" someone shouted.

Duster looked straight at me when he answered. "What if that murdered man was a dangerous criminal, huh? You want that kind of person in your camp? I did you a favor."

"Yer gonna need to come with us, Mister," another miner spoke up, an elderly gentleman with rumpled white hair. "Surrender yer guns peacefully and come over to the saloon with us and we'll get everythin' sorted out."

The bounty hunter slowly turned around to face the crowd, who were pressin' up close now, fannin' out to gradually surround us, and our window of opportunity fer escape was fast closin' with that circle.

"Now look," Duster said, facin' down a good number of guns, and it was nice to have 'em not pointed at me fer once. "I can assure you, I was well within my rights to shoot that man. I didn't murder those other three, did I? Go on and check … they're all still breathin'. Trust me, they didn't want the same for me. They were trying to murder *me*. Now, if you'll excuse me, I have pressin' business to attend to. *Lawful* business, as I said. Just so happens I'm a duly appointed warrant officer, and these folks here are wanted by the law in several states and territories."

There was that title again. And the folk of Copperwell camp looked befuddled by it. But Duster nodded his head back toward me and Holt and Charlotte and I tensed as all those eyes shifted to us.

There was still a small openin' in the crowd to the north, and I looked to Holt to see if he were just as ready to spring as me.

He gave a barely perceptible nod.

"I've been after one of them for awhile now," Duster told that millin' mob. "So I'd appreciate it if you'd let me collect him, and then I'll be on my way. Outta your hair. And we can forget all of this unpleasantness."

I twisted to look back at Charlotte. She didn't seem as confident as she'd sounded just a minute ago, her face pale, eyes wide, and the reins of her horse gripped white-knuckled in one of her raised hands.

She met my questionin' gaze and lifted an eyebrow.

I tried to indicate our narrow escape path with only my eyes, but it were hard to tell if she understood what I was tryin' to say or not.

Well, guess she'd figure it out soon enough. I

needed Duster to stop talkin'. With my luck, he'd convince these miners of his lawfulness, after all, and they'd *help* him round me up.

"Whaddaya mean?" someone shouted then from the back of the crowd. "You sayin' yer a … a bounty hunter?"

"That's right," Duster said. "I am, indeed. Licensed and everything. Here, let me show you. Take it easy, now. I'm just gonna get my paperwork, understand?"

He bent down, slow and careful, and set his pistols on the ground. Then he straightened and, just as slow and careful, reached into his inside jacket pocket.

I didn't give a damn what he was gettin', whether it was his paperwork or another gun to put some of these miners outta their misery. It was the opportunity I'd been waitin' fer, so I spun around and flung myself up into my saddle … then almost went off the other side as all that whiskey from the night before made the world tilt again.

I kicked my heels into Joe's sides even as I pulled myself back upright, twistin' my fingers into his stiff mane. He took off like a shot, nearly unseatin' me again, and galloped straight at the little space where the surroundin' folk were sparsest. But those few folk got out of his way quick, leapin' sideways with angry shouts as he barreled past.

Holt followed in a flash, and Charlotte after him, and we left Duster the bounty hunter swearin' and shoutin' in the middle of a mess of confused camp residents.

INTO REDEMPTION

We ran at a flat gallop as long as we dared to push the horses, moved in a zig-zag pattern and sometimes circled back around again to both confuse the tracks and check to see if we had anyone comin' after us.

But we finally had to slow our mad race across the desert, the horses lathered and winded and the sun now a fat, shimmerin' medallion of orange above the eastern horizon. So far, we hadn't seen no one else out here, no one followin', but that didn't mean they wouldn't be comin' eventually.

"Wh-what was all that?" Charlotte blurted breathlessly as soon as we'd slowed. Her eyes were bright from all the adrenaline and her straw hat had come loose, hangin' behind her from its tie. She dropped her reins to grab it with both hands and shove it back on her head, then attempted to smooth wavy red locks from her face.

"A hasty exit," Holt muttered. He was glarin' at me.

"No, not *that*," Charlotte spat. She waved wildly at the desert around us. "I mean all that weaving and circling! Are you still drunk? We could have made a lot more distance if you hadn't spent so much time wandering all over the place!"

"Helps make our tracks harder to follow," Holt said.

"And gives us a better look at anyone who might be wantin' to follow," I said.

Charlotte's eyes narrowed, and she looked from me to Holt and back again.

I prodded Joe onward a little faster, as much wantin' to put distance between us and Copperwell as wantin' to get out from under her suspicious stare. She was probably wonderin' why and how we knew so many tricks fer losin' people who might wanna come after us. And that, I had no inclination to explain.

"*Shit!*" Holt hissed suddenly, with enough vehemence that I reined up sharply to face him.

"What?"

"We left the goddamned mare!"

I looked over our little party with a start only to find he was right: in our rush to get outta that camp, we'd neglected to bring along Sally's skinny old mare, who had, consequently, been loaded up with nearly half our supplies. I opened my mouth to curse our idiocy … then remembered Charlotte's company and closed it again, settlin' fer a frustrated growl instead.

"Well…" Charlotte said after a moment, "she probably would have just slowed us down, anyway."

"Yeah," Holt growled, "'cept she was holdin' about half our water. And we got two more days till we reach Redemption!"

I shook my head, grittin' my teeth. It weren't an ideal situation, not at all.

But bein' taken back to the new Baron Whittaker by the bounty hunter Duster woulda been *less* ideal, certainly.

"We'll have to be careful," I said. "Ration what we do got."

"Ya think?" Holt snapped.

I tossed him a glare. "What's crawled up yer hump now?"

"I'll tell ya what." He threw his reins down over his saddle horn. "Havin' a bounty hunter all over our ass, that's what. And a *licensed* one, at that!"

I shrugged. The licensed ones were the professionals, sure; the ones folk like me and Holt needed to watch out fer most … but it weren't like we hadn't been hunted by plenty of fortune-seekers before. "He ain't after you. He's after *me*. And those miners'll keep him busy fer awhile sortin' out that murder, and we'll push on quick-like to Redemption and lose him on the train. He might know we're goin' there, but no way he'll guess our next stop. Too many possibilities out of Redemption. It'll take him months to check each one. Should be easy to stay ahead of him from there."

Holt sat still in his saddle and only looked at me, steady and unblinkin'. Like he didn't believe anythin' I'd just said. "I've lived a lot more years than you, kid. Got a lot longer list of deeds that might get those bounty hunters after me. And I just—" He paused and glanced to Charlotte, then looked back to me. "Well, we just had that incident in Destry, didn't we? So why don't ya tell me why this *licensed* bounty hunter is so keen to bring *you* in, but let *me* go? What'd I miss? What kinda bounty could that possibly be, and what in the hell did you do to deserve it?"

I hesitated. Nudged Joe onward again, and the other two followed me, keepin' pace to either side. I supposed at least Charlotte knew about this particular misdeed, so there weren't no real harm in tellin' Holt. He'd been a part of it, too, after all. In a way. So I let out a long, heavy sigh. "Remember good ol' Baron Whittaker?"

"Sure."

"Charlotte and I wrecked his estate, right? Freed all those slaves of his? And then ... well, and then Charlotte murdered him."

A frown creased Holt's grimy, sweaty features, and his clear blue gaze flicked over to the girl. "Charlotte?"

She nodded, but said nothin', her own gaze fixed straight ahead.

"How's that translate to that bounty hunter comin' after *you*, then?" Holt asked.

"The Whittaker family wanted to find those responsible ... they already knew who Charlotte was." I glanced to her from the corner of my eye, but she only kept starin' ahead. "But they didn't know who *I* was. They had a sketch made up of my face ... I dunno who coulda given 'em my description. I guess ... I guess one of the slaves who was there that night, is all I can figure. Maybe one was loyal to the Whittakers, or maybe one was convinced in some other horrible way to give me up. But somehow, they got pretty close to my face with that sketch, and noted my metal leg, and made the bounty fer me bein' delivered alive an amount that's made my life miserable ever since."

Holt grunted. "But there ain't no bounty fer the girl?"

I shook my head. "Far as I understand it, they were fairly confident they could track her down themselves, without help from other folk like bounty hunters." I remembered Miller's thugs havin' found Charlotte's home, remembered what he'd said he would do to her, and bile rose in my throat.

They'd gotten damn close to doin' just that, too.

Then I remembered what he'd done to me, and I swallowed and curled my left hand into a loose fist to hide those three fingers with missin' fingernails. I still kept 'em bandaged most times, but at least the nailbeds had hardened now, and they'd stopped bein' so sore and sticky.

We rode in stony silence fer a minute, till Holt said, "How much?"

"How much what?"

"How much is the bounty?"

"A lot."

"Van."

"What?" I turned my head to meet his glare and shrugged again. "What does it matter? You gonna collect it yerself?"

His glare turned into witherin' disgust. "Course not."

"Then it don't much matter, does it?"

"If I'm gonna be ridin' with ya, then I'd like to know what to expect fer the rest of our journey. So yeah, it matters. The lady here deserves to know, too. Maybe she'll change her mind about wantin' to come to Blackbird with us if it means she's gonna be chased outta every town we try to lay our heads in. How much we talkin' here, Van?"

I hesitated again. I glanced over to Charlotte once more only to find her lookin' at me now, an eyebrow quirked.

"He does raise a good point," she said. "I doubt

it will deter me from going to Blackbird, but perhaps it will prevent future surprises, yes?"

"I doubt it," I grumbled. Not with the way my luck tended to run, anyway.

"Well at least … maybe I could find a monetary way to dissuade these bounty hunters from their quest," Charlotte offered. "As I mentioned when we first met, my family *is* quite wealthy."

I tried to mask a wince, wishin' she hadn't announced that in front of Holt. Maybe he weren't eager to collect on *my* bounty, but I wouldn't put it past him to try and weasel some of Charlotte's money off her. "Nah," I said quick, before Holt could speak. He'd sat up straighter in his saddle already. "No need to get your family involved. Anyway, you already said you don't want nothin' to do with 'em anymore."

"I never said I would get my family involved."

"Then how did you plan to get that money?"

Charlotte looked away from me abruptly, fixin' her eyes on the flat of the desert that stretched before us. And I could swear it weren't just the sun and risin' heat that made her cheeks flush pink. "I … I have some of my own, you know. Brought it with me."

I looked her over up and down again, and then over her pack, strapped to the back of her saddle, and her saddlebags. "And how would I know that if you never told me?"

She straightened her shoulders. "Well. Now you know."

"Guess I do."

"So," Holt said from the other side of me, "how much?"

I kept silent fer a spell, mullin' over if it might really be better to tell 'em or not. They'd probably find out themselves sooner or later, though. Or see the poster with their own eyes on some wall somewhere. So at last I heaved another sigh and had out with it. "Fifty thousand."

Holt yanked his gelding to a halt. ***Fifty thousand goddamned dollars?!***

His voice echoed across the flat and I winced again, motionin' fer him to quiet down as I turned Joe around to face him.

"Van!" Charlotte gasped. She brought her stallion up alongside my mule, her face gone as pale as Holt's had gone red.

"You ain't never gonna get rid of that Mr. Barrett at that price," Holt hissed. "Nor anyone else in the whole expanse of the goddamned Territories!"

"Yeah," I muttered. "That's exactly what the Whittaker family hoped fer." That's what Charles Miller had planned on. And his plan had nearly worked several times over now. Nearly.

Holt spluttered, but it seemed he'd lost all his coherent words.

Charlotte reached over to put a hand on my arm. "Van, that's not fair. I ... I was the one who murdered the baron. They should be hunting me, not you."

"I still did plenty of damage to that estate," I offered.

She shook her head. "Not enough to warrant that kind of price." She looked back the way we'd come, back toward Copperwell camp, and worry furrowed her brow.

"If he gets free of that mob..." Holt looked back

that way, too. Then he faced front again, and I could tell by the hardenin' of his expression he'd thought of a plan. "We could lead him into a trap," he said. "Ambush him. Get rid of him fer good."

Charlotte looked from one of us to the other. "You mean … kill him?"

"Yeah," Holt said.

"I don't know…" Charlotte said, and she shifted uncomfortably in her saddle. "Murdering a licensed warrant officer is … well, that might get the Council's attention. And not in a good way."

"More so than murderin' a metal baron?" Holt quipped.

The pink came back to Charlotte's cheeks as her mouth set into a firm line. "Yes. Much more so than that. And anyway, Baron Whittaker deserved what happened to him."

Both of Holt's bushy brows raised at that, and he looked pointedly at me with blue eyes gleamin'. "Ya don't say?" He was talkin' to Charlotte, but his look said somethin' else. Callin' to mind our argument from just the night before, and what I'd told him about Lloyd Renneker. He went on as I scowled and shook my head, shiftin' in my own saddle now, dislikin' many implications of this conversation. "Maybe this Mr. Barrett deserves it, too," Holt suggested. "After all, we don't really know him, do we?"

Despite Charlotte's misgivings, I considered the notion. Glanced out across the expanse of dust and cacti runnin' east to west and south far as the eye could see, and the distant mountains that cradled the river snakin' north of us. There was no place to hide out here. And little nearby rock to hide our tracks. The wind might cover 'em up eventually, or we could take the time to confuse 'em, but this particular stretch of desert weren't especially suited to ambushes.

"We'd have to go north to find a suitable place," I said. "To the mountains and the river."

Now it were Holt who shrugged. "We'd have shelter, at least. And water. And the water would attract game, too. Probably eat and drink better than we have in days."

I wet my cracked lips, or tried to, already thirsty. And the world felt all wobbly on account of that whiskey, my head achin' now, too. Havin' a camp by the river fer a few days didn't sound too awful bad right now, in truth, and neither did gettin' that bloodhound of a bounty hunter off my back fer good…

But Nan had only given me two weeks to find those damned ruins, if they even existed … I surely didn't have time to be hidin' out fer days hopin' that Duster fella would walk into our trap. The journey to Blackbird alone would take half that time, and that was *if* we didn't have no more setbacks or delays.

So instead of agreein' with the old man, I shook my head. "We can't. Don't got that kinda time. Nan expects to hear from me in two weeks, remember? And it's already been six days."

His mouth pressed into a thin line of disapproval.

In answer, I only prodded Joe back into motion and kept goin' southeast, acutely aware of Charlotte's hand slidin' off my arm as I did so. "We'll make it," I said, forcin' all the confidence I could muster into my tone, though it was more fer Charlotte's benefit than Holt's. "We got a head start. We'll keep up the pace, push on hard, sleep in shifts and forego any fires. Only gotta stay clear of him fer two more days."

Charlotte trailed after me, sayin' nothin' about my plan, which I hoped meant she found it credible enough.

Holt followed after us eventually, too, although he kept mutterin' under his breath. He clearly did not find my plan credible enough, but there weren't nothin' fer it except to keep on toward Redemption.

We'd need to quicken our pace, though, and stay alert.

And if I did happen to see that bounty hunter again between now and Redemption, I was gonna put a bullet in him.

The next two days were a hot, miserable drag. We baked under the sun, movin' as fast as we dared, but still not fast enough for my likin'. I kept watch fer another silhouette on the horizon, day and night, but we never saw one.

The horses had little to forage out here and less grain, thanks to the loss of our pack horse, and we sacrificed a good portion of our water to 'em, preferrin' they stay in good condition in order to deliver us to relief in Redemption more quickly.

We had little to eat ourselves, bein' as we'd abandoned the notion of nighttime fires ... or at least, we had little to eat that was very palatable. But we made do. The second afternoon we happened upon a rattlesnake, so we made a quick, small fire in the daylight to cook it up fer some real meat.

But then we moved on again.

Through it all, we hardly spoke, wantin' to conserve our energy—and our spit.

And through it all, Charlotte never complained once.

Not sure why I kept expectin' her to. Like she'd been keen to remind me and Holt, she'd endured far worse durin' her six months at the Whittaker estate. Surely she could handle this desert ride, even with fewer supplies than we mighta preferred. But I guess the fact she'd been raised an easterner and come from a wealthy family—with a Senator fer a father, of all things—had stuck in my mind, and my expectations of her kept tryin' to align with all my previous experiences with such people.

We plodded into the bustlin' town of Redemption, Lesser Texas at dusk on the second day and went straight to the nearest water trough. We were plum spent and so were the horses, all of us covered again in layers of sweat and dust. Our canteens were dry, our food supplies nearly gone, but we'd stayed ahead of that bounty hunter and survived the ride, and that was all that mattered. We let the horses drink while I took stock of the shops that lined this particular street.

The sun was fallin' quick into the west, brushin' that horizon in shades of purple, pink and orange. Yellow squares of light shone out all down the lane as the shops lit their inside lanterns, and the music from numerous saloons spilled out into the evenin', minglin' with the smells of horse manure, fire smoke, sawdust and smeltin' iron, and whatever happened to be cookin' at all the various establishments.

My stomach growled. But there were several things needin' to be done before I could see to that, and some of 'em needed to be done before the stores closed fer the night.

Too bad we were runnin' so low on money.

I glanced to Charlotte. She was slumped in her saddle, lookin' as exhausted as I felt. She'd braided her hair as usual, but long strands of it had come loose throughout the day and fallen across her face and down her neck, curly and damp with sweat.

And a surge of anger welled in me at seein' her in such a state. Anger at Duster fer havin' accosted us at Copperwell, forcin' us to push harder than I woulda liked over the last two days. Anger at Charlotte herself fer leavin' the safety and comfort of her own home to come out here. Anger at myself fer not bein' more insistent that she go on back home … fer bein' the reason that bounty hunter was after us … fer ever gettin' her involved with my predicament in the first place.

She shouldn't have to endure this. Any of this.

I pulled my gaze away from her as she started to turn her head and silently cursed myself fer all of it. "I'll get us rooms fer the night," I croaked, then cleared my throat. Days in the heat with little water had withered my voice.

"I'll go with you," Charlotte said immediately, pullin' her stallion from the trough.

"No," I snapped, then checked my tone when her eyes widened. "No," I repeated, gentle this time. "You and Holt should go by the general store. Replenish our food stores before it closes up fer the night. We'll want to be on the first train outta here in the mornin'. Won't give us much time fer shoppin' then. We should do it now."

She studied me fer a minute, like she might be weighin' my points to determine their true value.

I didn't miss the displeased glare Holt sent me, neither. He saw through my reasonin', anyway, even if Charlotte hadn't quite worked it out yet.

I wanted him gettin' those supplies honestly this time, and if he had Charlotte along, he'd be forced to do it that way. No matter that it'd probably cost him the rest of his coin. We'd figure out how to fix that later.

"All right," she said at last. "Fine."

"Think you can handle that?" I asked Holt.

He straightened indignantly in his saddle and pulled his gelding away from the trough, too. "Sure. I can handle that."

"Good. Then I'll secure stalls fer the horses and rooms fer us. Meet me back at..." I scanned the multitude of signs that spanned the length of the street in the swiftly fadin' daylight till I found one that seemed suitable. "Meet me back at the Ownby Boarding House."

"Sure," Holt said, and then he nodded at Charlotte, and the two of 'em headed off.

I headed off myself, toward the boardin' house. Looked like an okay establishment; well-built and well cared fer, but lackin' the kinda finesse to it that would suggest we couldn't afford it. So I hitched Joe up in front of it and went inside. Got us three rooms and ordered us food and whiskey, and then *I* was outta coin.

Weren't sure exactly how we'd get on that train

tomorrow ... guess we'd have to figure that out later, too.

Night had come full-on and I was just startin' to get worried when Holt and Charlotte finally appeared, and I let out a breath of relief as they made their way over to my table.

"Everythin' go all right?" I waved at the place's proprietor, and he nodded, then gestured fer a young lady I guessed were his daughter from their vague resemblance, and she slipped into the back to grab our food.

"Sure," Holt said. He pulled out a chair fer Charlotte, then one fer himself.

I raised my brows at the old man. Hadn't known he possessed any manners.

"Yes," Charlotte said, droppin' down into the seat with a thankful sigh. "Fine. We should have enough to last us several more days in the saddle."

"Bein' as we don't exactly know how far the train can take us toward Blackbird, yet," Holt added.

"Good. Good."

The young lady emerged from the back, balancin' three heapin' plates, and set 'em down one in front of each of us. Beef and onions, carrots and potatoes, cornbread. She swiped her hands on her apron and smiled at us. "I'll be right back with your whiskey."

She disappeared again.

The three of us fell to eatin' without much talkin', tired and hungry as we were, and when the young woman returned with our bottle of whiskey and three glasses, we helped ourselves to that, too. When we'd finished our meal, I volunteered to take the horses to the livery. Urged Holt and Charlotte to go ahead and retire fer the night, since we'd need an early start the next day.

To my surprise, neither of 'em argued. Not even Holt. The heat and dehydration musta drained him more than I'd suspected.

We all said our good nights, and I made sure the both of 'em had retired to their rooms, and Charlotte had locked hers, before I headed back out to get the horses. I'd take 'em to the livery, sure.

But then I was gonna look around Redemption some more, see if I couldn't find us some … *charitable donations*.

GOOD SAMARITAN

Robbin' folk in the middle of a town was always tricky.

Drunks made the easiest targets, of course, but they also tended to carry little coin, considerin' they'd already spent most of it on their drink, or sometimes other vices.

The best time to rob a person in the middle of a town was in the evenin', when they'd finished their daily work and had gathered up what money they had before headin' out to the saloon or the brothel fer the night. If you could catch 'em before they spent it, you could get awful lucky sometimes.

But I'd already missed that opportunity. All of Redemption's folks were already wherever they wanted to be fer the night. In their homes, in the saloons, in the brothels. Already spendin' that money.

Fer awhile I just walked the streets, observin' people, considerin' my options. Redemption was a fair-sized town, and it had its share of the wealthier population. Robbin' rich folk had a better pay-off, but it was also riskier. Rich folk tended to get real mad about bein' robbed. And they had the money and the influence to convince the law to do somethin' about it. And sometimes they held long-standin' grudges.

And sometimes they posted a fifty-thousand dollar bounty fer you and made yer life miserable.

I sighed and pulled up the collar of my duster against possibly bein' recognized fer want of that particular sum of money.

I angled toward an electric sign that proclaimed the presence of a stage theater and movie house. Wealthier folk liked to go to those places, I knew. Liked to think it gave 'em culture, or somethin'. Whatever that meant. Least, that's what Mama had always told me.

Not that we hadn't gone to such shows a time or two as a family, ourselves.

I lingered around the establishment until whatever show that had been playin' ended, and folks started pourin' outta the place. They were all talkin' excitedly and looked in awful high spirits. Well, someone's night was about to have a bad turn.

But they'd get over it. Coulda been worse. They coulda had a sister bein' held by Nine-Fingered Nan. Coulda had to have their leg sawed off. Coulda had a whole buncha shady individuals wantin' to take off the metal replacement, too. Coulda had a licensed bounty hunter after 'em.

I scanned quick over the departin' crowd, tryin' to decide on the best target, until a mighty familiar figure over at the other corner of the building caught my eye.

And it was right about that time he recognized me, too.

I straightened from where I'd leaned against the front wall of the establishment. "*Holt?!*"

"*Van?!*" he hissed back. "The hell are you doin' here? Thought you went to put up the horses!"

"I did!" I crossed over to him, excusin' my way through the rest of the people exitin' the theater to plant myself right in front of him, crossin' my arms. "And I thought *you* said you were gonna get some sleep?"

"Ha! Fat chance of that. Came to take some air."

I squinted at him. "We're an awful long way from that boardin' house."

He squinted back at me. "And an awful long way from the livery, too."

I blew out a breath and uncrossed my arms, puttin' my hands instead on the tops of my guns. That was a fair point, but I weren't sure I should tell him my real purpose here. I glanced back toward the dispersin' crowd. If I didn't go quick, decide on someone to follow, I was gonna miss my chance…

"Unbelievable," Holt muttered, bringin' my focus back to him.

"What's unbelievable?"

"Yer out here lookin' fer donations, ain't you?"

"I just—"

"After all that nonsense you spouted off the other day about it not bein' yer nature—"

"It ain't," I snapped. "It ain't my nature, it's *necessary*." I jabbed a finger into his chest with the last word.

He knocked my hand away.

"We gotta get on that train tomorrow," I hissed, mindful of the people who still meandered by occasionally. "And we're outta money."

"Yeah," Holt said, also keepin' his voice low now, "that's what I been sayin'. But you had to go and get up on yer High Horse, didn't ya? You said we had to do it honest."

"Yeah, well…" I shifted on my feet, lookin' again to the stragglers that were left now, wanderin' away into the dark. "Turns out we don't got time fer that."

"Ya don't say?"

I didn't much appreciate his scathin' tone and shot him a glare.

"So?" he prompted. "We gonna do this or not? You pick a target yet?"

"Naw," I grumbled. "Saw yer ugly mug and stopped lookin'."

He scoffed. "Good thing I'm here, then. I got someone in mind."

Again, I turned to look about the front of the place, which had now almost entirely emptied. "And where, exactly, would this person be?"

Holt smiled beneath his scraggly gray beard and slapped a hand to my shoulder. "Just follow me, kid." He stepped around me and headed off with a rather confident stride, so I followed, all right.

It became clear just who he'd selected soon enough. We caught up to 'em as they walked leisurely arm-in-arm, a young couple, finely dressed. Probably married only a few weeks, judgin' by the blush that graced the woman's cheeks and the stupid grin plastered across the man's face.

They turned a corner to head toward the numerous residences built just outside the town proper, and I saw the glint of a pocket watch at his breast, and a fat ring on her left hand. Not to mention the pearls around her neck, and her earrings. And whatever money they happened to have on 'em, of course.

They were a good pick. A real good pick.

I moved to Holt's side, gave him a nudge. "Good Samaritan?" I whispered.

He looked to me in surprise, then grinned and nodded. He darted off down the next alley to our left to get ahead of our couple and pick a good spot in another alley, and I kept followin' 'em. It was a ploy we'd engaged in many times over our years together.

Holt played the victim; a poor, hapless old man, and I played the bad guy, preyin' on the weak. Acted like I was robbin' him just as our real target passed by. It only worked on a certain type of people, of course, but that certain type would *always* intervene, sure enough.

They'd rush right into the alley to save the poor old man, and then we'd rob 'em blind.

This young couple … well, they sure looked like just the type of folk who'd rush to Holt's aid, all right.

And as it turned out, they were.

We got back to Ownby's Boarding House before midnight with more than enough cash to cover our three seats and three stalls on the train, plus a fair amount of jewelry to sell, too, fer more cash or maybe fer trade … once we found a proper place to sell or trade 'em.

That couple had been awful put-out, a course, but mostly they'd just seemed genuinely shocked and horrified that their noble effort to prevent an injustice had backfired so spectacularly as to leave 'em without all of their hard-earned cash, one of their wedding gifts, and two of their family heirlooms.

Well, they were awful young still. They'd figure it out eventually.

We'd tied 'em real good and gagged 'em and left 'em in a spot no one would find 'em fer a good long while. Long enough fer us to get outta town. But not long enough to cause 'em any real bodily harm.

And so, Holt and I went to bed that night feelin' awful proud of ourselves. We hadn't had a robbery go so quiet and smooth fer a good long while.

I shut myself in my room almost whistlin'. Hung up my hat and my gunbelts, set my boots by the end of the bed, and crawled under the covers. Couldn't remember the last time I'd laid down fer sleep feelin' so content.

Oh wait. That's right. There was that night at the Seven Knives Saloon, after Nora and Nettie had given me their very particular attentions fer hours on end and taken everythin' outta me.

But aside from that night, it'd been a long, long while, certainly.

I slipped just as easily into sleep this night … only sleep didn't treat me so gentle.

The nightmares came again strong as ever.

I snapped awake with the echo of my own yell still in my ears, adrenaline tinglin' in my limbs. Took me a minute to come out of it, realize where I was, and the soft light of dawn comin' through the crack in the curtain was a welcome relief.

Meant I didn't have to go back there. Back to those damned nightmares.

Couldn't even remember which one this had been. Mama and Pa's murder? My frantic search fer Ethelyn? Findin' her dead? That poor nameless girl lookin' up at me while she died in my arms? Or maybe it had been Charles Miller again with his pliers and knives and brandin' irons.

I shuddered, exhaled, and sagged back onto the mattress, skin damp with sweat.

Well, none of that mattered now. I was awake again, and with no time to entertain any of those horrors. I fumbled at the night table beside me till my fingers found the stolen pocket watch. I grabbed it, flipped it open, checked the time.

Oh good. Train station should be open by now. And we had plenty of time fer breakfast, gettin' the horses, and gettin' to the platform to buy our tickets before the train itself arrived.

I scrubbed a hand over my face and clambered out of bed. Put myself back together slowly, feelin' more tired than I woulda liked thanks to those awful dreams. I stopped in front of the small mirror above the vanity to tidy myself up a bit, but there weren't too much I could do without another bath and a shave and maybe a laundry service. Maybe I shoulda took advantage of those things while we were here.

Funny how the regular presence of a woman seemed to constantly remind me of how rough I looked.

Scowlin' and shakin' my head, I gave up.

I went to Charlotte's room first, hopin' to have at least a few minutes with her before Holt brought down the mood, as he was invariably known to do.

I rapped on her door, then swore and belatedly tucked in my wayward shirt-tail.

But she didn't answer.

I knocked again, waited.

Still no answer.

I shifted on my feet, glanced both ways down the empty hall. Maybe she was just especially exhausted from our two-day ride. So I knocked again, hard and forceful this time, loud enough to wake her, but hopefully not loud enough to wake anyone else in the nearby rooms. "Charlotte? You awake in there?"

Silence. No murmured voices in reply. No footsteps across the floor. Nothin'.

Concern tightened in my belly. I knocked one more time, rattlin' the door in its frame. "Charlotte? You all right?"

The door to my left yanked open and a thin, disheveled man dressed only in his union suit stepped out, glarin' at me through heavy lidded, waterin' eyes. "Hey!" he slurred. "The hell is goin' on out here? Folk tryin' ta sleep!"

The door behind me opened then, too. Holt's room.

I didn't even turn around as I heard him step out into the hall. "What is it?" he asked, and I could tell by the strain in his voice he was ready fer trouble. Probably already had his guns on and his hand ready, too.

But I didn't answer him, or the man to my left. Instead I dropped my own hand down to rest lightly on the grip of my right pistol, set my left shoulder against Charlotte's door with a wince, and tried the knob.

To my surprise, the door swung open freely, and I nearly pitched face-first onto the floor as I stumbled through it. I'd expected it to be locked.

It had not been locked.

I righted myself and took in the room at a glance, the concern in my belly hardenin' into dread. Not only had the door not been locked…

Charlotte was gone.

GONE MISSIN'

Fer a good long minute I just stood there starin' at the empty bed, my breath stuck in my throat as my mind raced through all the terrible possibilities of where she mighta gone or what mighta happened to her.

I hardly heard Holt step in behind me, hardly saw him come up beside me, hard gaze sweepin' the room.

"Huh," he said. "She's gone."

The bed was neatly made, sheets tucked into crisp corners and everythin'. Weren't a trace of any of her stuff anywhere. The window was closed, the curtains opened to let in the soft mornin' light.

Sure didn't look like someone had grabbed her, anyway. No signs of a struggle, none of her belongings left behind.

"Well. That'll sure make our train trip cheaper," Holt stated. Then he turned and ambled back out into the hall, apologizin' to the man next door and lettin' him know there weren't no trouble. There was more murmured conversation, and then the sound of the neighborin' door shuttin' again.

But I still just stood there, strugglin' to understand.

Had she … had she just left? On her own? Of her own free will?

Why? And … and where would she go? Was it

'cause of me? Was it 'cause I'd snapped at her last night? 'Cause I hadn't let her come with me to the livery? 'Cause we'd made such a fuss when she'd first said she wanted to come with us to Blackbird? Would she have gone there by herself, then? Without us?

"Van?"

I startled and turned around to see Holt in the doorway.

He arched an eyebrow and jerked his chin in the direction of the stairs at the end of the hall. "You comin'? I want some decent grub before we get stuck inside a train fer days."

I blinked. Frowned. Looked back over my shoulder to peer at the empty room one last time. But there was just nothin'. Nothin' out of the ordinary. Nothin' that might tell me where she'd gone, or why. Not even a note. I sighed and pulled off my hat to run my fingers through my hair, then resettled it back on my head. "Sure. Yeah. I'm comin'."

Holt gave a snort as I left the room and pulled the door shut again behind me. "Are you ... are you *sulkin'*?"

"What? No."

"Uh huh. That why you look like a god-damned kicked puppy?"

I growled as I pushed my hat a little lower on my head, a little forward to shade my face a bit more as we headed fer the stairs. "Don't know what yer talkin' about," I muttered. "Don't like the thought of her out there on her own, is all. You should know that."

"Oh I think I know that, all right."

I glared at him, and we started down the stairs.

"She's already been nabbed once. And that was all the way over in Pennsylvania! You'd think she'd know better than to go wandering off all by her lonesome, especially around here."

"You'd think," Holt agreed, but I got the sense he was patronizin' me. He went on again before I could make a rebuke. "Just look at it this way, kid. Now we don't gotta worry about how we do things, right? Remember how you were all worked up about hidin' our business? Now we don't gotta fret about it. Good riddance, I say."

"You were the one who said she might be good in a fight," I pointed out.

We reached the main floor and the common room, set with multiple tables and already startin' to fill with people takin' breakfast. And yet it lacked the presence of any red-haired women as much as the room upstairs had. Another wave of concern twisted at my gut. If only she had at least said *where* she might be goin'…

Holt waved at the man behind the desk across the way, and he gave a nod in acknowledgement. Then the old man turned to me. "Yeah, sure. I did say she might be good in a fight. But you made it clear you wouldn't be lettin' her do any fightin'." He dropped his voice. "Or any robbin' or murderin'." He raised his voice again. "So what's the use, then? And if she can't be useful, then her takin' off is good riddance. That's all I'm sayin'."

I only grumbled at him, havin' no good argument to the contrary. He was right. Right about all of it. Charlotte bein' gone *would* make things a whole lot easier, especially once we got to Blackbird.

Too bad all his good reasonin' weren't makin' me feel no better about it.

He picked a table, and we sat, and the same young lady as the night before brought us coffee, heapin' bowls of porridge, boiled eggs and a plate of dried fruit. Holt dug into his, but I found myself without much of an appetite. So I mostly just picked at mine, managed a few bites, and then a familiar figure stepped through the boarding house front door.

I shot to my feet so fast I bumped the table, and Holt swore as his coffee sloshed out into his porridge.

"Charlotte!" I barked.

She looked my direction in surprise, then smiled as she recognized us and made her way to our table. "Oh good, you're awake. I was about to come up and rouse you."

She wore an outfit I hadn't yet seen on this trip, and I wondered where she'd been stashin' it. It was cream-colored and clean, all except the rim of her flared ridin' pants, anyway, which were caked in dirt same as her boots. The top was a fitted jacket, and a purple silk neckerchief—scarf—was bunched at her neck. She looked like she'd had a wash herself, all shiny and clean, and she'd wrapped her long hair into a coiled bun, donned her straw hat again, and wore that gunbelt with my old pistol smart around her hips.

I stared at her. "I ... you, uh ... you..."

"You left," Holt said flatly. "Gave us quite a fright, young lady."

I managed to pull my gaze away from Charlotte long enough to squint down dubiously at him. He kept eatin', not payin' any attention to either me or Charlotte and surely not lookin' concerned in the least about her brief disappearance.

She, too, eyed him skeptically. "Oh my, really?"

"Well, ya sure gave *one* of us a fright," he grumbled into his porridge.

I cleared my throat as Charlotte looked back to me with a frown. "I was just, uh … concerned," I managed. "You know … you might still have people out there lookin' fer you, Miller's men, maybe … or someone else, even, and I thought … I mean I didn't want … I think it's better if none of us wander off alone." I spit the last of it out all at once, frustrated by the sudden difficulty of findin' the right words.

She lifted her eyebrows. "Oh? *None* of us should wander off alone?" She gave me a pointed look, then shifted it to Holt, but he was focused on his food.

Warmth rose into my cheeks as I realized she was probably seein' right through to my real meanin', but I stuck by my claim. "None of us. Not after what happened at Copperwell."

"Ah." Her dark blue eyes came back to me. "I see." Whether or not she believed me now, she let it go, to my relief. "Well, as you can plainly see, I am perfectly fine. The morning has been productive, but uneventful. I only went to freshen up and purchase our train tickets—"

"*What?*" I blurted the word in unison with Holt.

She had his full attention now. He dropped his spoon into his bowl and sat back in his chair, starin' up wide-eyed at her.

Charlotte looked at the both of us like maybe we'd gone crazy. "Whatever is the matter with that?

Aren't we taking the train to Blackbird? Wasn't that the plan?"

"You shouldn't have paid our passage," I said, and I grabbed immediately for the little pouch on my belt that held all my coin. And that stolen pocket watch. And that stolen ring. "Here. I'll pay you back fer mine."

"No," Charlotte said. "Absolutely not. It's a long trip, and not cheap, especially with our mounts. Do you think I came out here without funds for supplies or travel? Or for anything else I might need? I've got plenty to cover it, just let me do you this kindness."

"No," Holt and I both said in unison again.

Charlotte seemed awful put-out, then. An expression came over her face that reminded me somewhat of the way she'd looked the night she'd ended Baron Whittaker, her glare bright and fierce as she raked it across me and Holt both. "This is precisely why I left early this morning," she hissed. "So I needn't have this argument yet again. I will not take your money, either of you. If you put it on that table, that's where it will stay. Now, I'm going to have some breakfast. I suggest you finish yours. The train leaves promptly at eight twenty-two."

With that, she spun sharply on her heel and left us—again—choosin' an entirely different table to sit at.

I watched after her with my hand still searchin' in my belt pouch ... but I gave up shortly after with a sigh. Least she weren't wanderin' around the Territories somewhere by herself. Least she hadn't left us entirely. And that bein' the case, I didn't need her any more upset with me than she was already.

"Ain't right," Holt muttered, sittin' forward in

his seat to resume his meal. "Her spendin' all that money on the likes of us. That woman is almost as stubborn as you."

I snorted. "Maybe." I took my seat back and picked up my spoon again. I watched Charlotte from the corner of my eye as she received her food and coffee, half of me wantin' to go over there to try and make amends. But maybe I'd wait till she didn't look quite so angry.

She *had* burned out Baron Whittaker's eyes, after all. And burned up his genitals. And then shot him point-blank. And she'd knocked Holt out cold, as well, when she'd thought the old man was gonna shoot me.

Yeah, I'd just wait. Few more minutes wouldn't hurt nothin'....

"Hey," Holt said suddenly. "How much money you think she's got on her, anyway?"

I switched my gaze back to him quick and fixed him with the most serious look I could muster. "No," I said, and it came out dead serious. "Absolutely not."

He lifted his hands, porridge drippin' off his spoon to spatter the table. "All right, all right. Don't get yer dander up. Was just curious, is all. But how much you think her family is really worth?"

"Holt. You lift even one coin off her and I swear to the Holy Mother you'll regret me savin' yer neck."

He grinned, then chuckled and shook his head. "Careful, boy. That kinda talk can get ya into trouble."

I shrugged. "I don't mind trouble. Me and trouble get along just fine."

That got a bark of laughter outta him. "Do ya now?"

"Sure."

"Uh huh." He chuckled again and let out a low whistle. "Sure, kid. Sure. Like I said, just curious, is all. Just curious." He went back to his porridge, scrapin' out what was left of it, actin' like our conversation hadn't happened at all.

I glared at him fer a good long while more, till I was certain he'd got the notion of robbin' Charlotte or her family outta his head. Then, finally, I relaxed and tucked into my own food at last.

Too bad it was cold now.

BETTER SAFE THAN DEAD

Eight twenty-two came sooner than I'd expected.

We passed the rest of breakfast, the journey to the livery, the fetchin' of our horses, and the ride to the station in a stiff silence that itched at me good as a swarm of sand flies. But I weren't sure exactly how to fix it, so I just stayed silent, hunched in my saddle and broodin' over how we'd even ended up in this state.

We got to the train platform just as the thing itself pulled up, hissin' and steamin' and blowin' its whistle fit to make all the horses nervous. But we coaxed 'em up to it, showed the conductor our honest-bought tickets, and he pointed us in the direction of the livestock car. So we moseyed on down that way, dismounted, showed our tickets again, and handed our mounts off to the handlers.

Charlotte spoke to them at length, insistin' our animals be treated with utmost care, makin' sure that was clearly understood, and handin' over some extra money to ensure complete comprehension.

Holt and I stuck close by in the meantime, both watchin' the bustle of the platform with wary interest. We didn't travel much by train, neither of us. Didn't have much use fer it, most times. And truth be told, I didn't much like it.

Didn't much like all these people runnin' about here, neither. Good place fer pick-pockets. Hard to keep track of all the faces to try and note which ones might be familiar or not.

Or friendly or not.

My scannin' gaze stuck suddenly on the hulkin' shadow of a man standin' at one corner of the station building. He leaned his shoulder casually against the wall, and his ankles were crossed and his chin dipped low like he didn't have a care in the world, but there was somethin' about him I didn't like.

Maybe it were the fact I couldn't see his face beneath the lowered brim of his hat. Maybe it were the way he was all tucked into the shadows of the building and the awning that covered all the benches fer waitin' passengers. Maybe it were the fact he weren't sittin', but nor was he involved in any other business like all the rest of the people on the platform currently.

He was only standin' there. Loose and still—too still, thumbs tucked into his gunbelt.

A crawlin' sensation rippled up my arms, like he was somehow watchin' me without watchin', and my right hand went down to my gun. I brushed the grip fer reassurance, kept my palm there restin' lightly.

Better safe than dead.

I glanced to Holt, but he was lookin' out in the other direction.

So I squinted back at the shadowed man, and entertained the idea of goin' over to confront him. If he were just a fella mindin' his own business, no harm would come of it. But if he were a man after me fer that fifty thousand dollars—or any multitude of other reasons—it'd be better to put a bullet in him now.

Except … except there were an awful lot of witnesses here, if it did happen to come to that.

"Shit," I muttered.

A commotion at the train car behind me made me tense and turn, only to find it was Charlotte's stallion causin' the ruckus. Holt's gelding and my mule had boarded easily enough, but the roan was none too happy about this situation. He pinned his ears and danced away from the handler, eyes goin' wide as the man tried to lead him up the ramp.

The handler held tight to the reins as the stallion reared up a little, and I swore more under my breath. This was just what we needed. A damn horse causin' a scene, drawin' all kinds of attention…

"Hey," Charlotte said sharply, and I thought she was talkin' to the man tryin' to lead her horse before I realized her glare was fixed on her mount, instead. She stalked over to him and took the reins back from the pale-faced handler, then turned to the horse and pointed a finger at him like he were a child instead of a thousand-pound animal. "You stop that," she scolded. "This is no time for that nonsense. Behave yourself!"

The roan blew at her loudly, still dancin' and throwin' his head. But his ears had come up now instead of bein' pinned flat-back, and swiveled around as if he were tryin' to take in the whole platform at once.

Charlotte turned to the man still waitin' beside the ramp. "Why don't you show me what stall you want him in? I'll take him."

The man nodded wordlessly. He looked relieved. I didn't blame him.

An angry stallion weren't nothin' you wanted to mess with.

They all disappeared inside the train car, the roan followin' Charlotte up into the dim interior with hardly a hesitation.

I took that chance to turn back and check on that shadowy man I didn't much like. But he was still just standin' there. He hadn't moved at all. Hadn't looked up at the commotion.

Maybe he weren't here fer me. Maybe he weren't a threat at all.

Maybe he were just a real tired fella who'd fallen asleep standin' up.

Maybe I was startin' to get just as jumpy as Holt.

I shook my head and followed up the ramp after Charlotte and her horse just to keep an eye on things, but paused in the doorway to stay out of the way as they got the roan settled.

Charlotte untacked him, urged him into the little stall, and patted his neck as he snorted again. "There, there, now, Sugar. You'll be all right." She pulled another handful of dollars from her belt pouch for the man who stood watchin' her, bewildered. "For the trouble," she told him. "He can be a little bull-headed, but he's not mean-spirited. Now, like I said, I want exceptional care for him and the others in my party, you understand? I trust you can see to that?"

The man took the money in one grubby hand and nodded. "Sure thing, ma'am."

I watched him close through narrowed eyes, but he seemed honest enough. Didn't seem to have the twitchy nature common to most unsavory types.

And so, our mounts all taken care of, Charlotte

and I descended the ramp and rejoined with Holt to make our way back to the passenger cars and get our own selves similarly settled fer the journey.

I kept my hand light on my pistol grip, once again tossin' a glance to that sleepy shadowed man as we passed him by, separated by at least twenty yards and plenty of busy folk. Still, he didn't stir. Didn't so much as twitch.

Some of the tension in my knotted shoulders relaxed. I caught up to Charlotte's side just as Holt was askin', "You really name that beast of yers Sugar, or is that just yer chosen term of endearment?"

She scoffed. "That's his name. And he's hardly a beast."

"Coulda fooled me," I commented.

"What kinda name is *Sugar* for a *stallion*, any-way?" Holt said.

Charlotte's eyes narrowed as she turned to glare at him. "It's a mighty fine name, thank you very much. For a mighty fine steed. He really is sweet as sugar most the time. The train has him upset, that's all."

Holt grunted. "The train has me upset, too. Never much liked bein' stuck fer hours in a little tin can."

Charlotte and I both ignored his grumblin', as we'd reached the conductor once more. We flashed those tickets a third time, and he ushered us pleasantly on board.

I let Charlotte and Holt climb the stairs first and went up last myself. A prickle at the back of my neck made me turn just as I topped 'em; a naggin' feelin' to take one last look across the platform. Just to be sure.

A habit honed by years of livin' as an outlaw now, and sharpened by the outstandin' presence of that fifty thousand dollar bounty on my head.

My eyes went first toward that shadowed man leanin' against the wall. Another habit.

Only he weren't there no more.

He was gone.

My fingers tightened around the railin' that encircled the back of the train car, my heart jumpin'. I searched the millin' crowd below me frantically, but saw no one there that resembled him.

He'd vanished.

I hardly noticed our walk through the various cars toward our seats, preoccupied by thoughts of that suspicious, shadowed fella, and by checkin' every face we passed to see if they looked familiar.

But I didn't see anyone recognizable on the train; didn't even see anyone who resembled the fella from outside. Fer some reason that didn't make me feel no better, and I was still distracted by the time we reached our berths.

"Here we are," Charlotte said. She'd stopped outside a pair of wooden slidin' doors. "I'll take this one. You two have the next two down the way, next door." She nodded her head to the right, further toward the front of the train.

Holt let out a low whistle, lookin' over the doors we stood in front of and then over at the next two sets of doors. "Three? You got us each our own space?"

Charlotte shrugged. "Sure. Seemed the most comfortable option." She slid open one of her doors to reveal the chamber on the other side, and the sight of it finally made me forget my frettin'.

I'd never seen a train space like it, that was fer certain.

Of course, on the rare occasions I happened to travel by train, I always picked the cheap seats. The hard wooden benches in the back. Never could afford anythin' better than that. Certainly never anythin' like this.

It was spectacular.

Plushly furnished, the walls wood-paneled, with an upholstered chair and a small table tucked in underneath a luxurious-looking bunk draped with thick bedsheets, and a window framed in floral-patterned curtains. It even had electric lights.

Charlotte cleared her throat and I blinked, comin' outta my stupor to look to her in question.

"You boys want to get settled?" she prompted. "The train will be pulling out soon and they'll want everyone seated."

"Oh," I said. "Right."

As if emphasizin' her point, the steam engine gave a long, loud blow of its whistle.

I moved to take the compartment next to hers, and Holt took the one next to mine, mutterin' under his breath. A pair of finely dressed folk squeezed past us in the corridor as we reached our respective doors, and I couldn't help but notice the way they wrinkled their noses as they passed.

Well. We probably coulda used another wash, sure.

And I bet we stood out like sore thumbs here,

too, and not just because of our smell. Our clothes were sweat-stained, covered in dust, and clearly not new. A stark contrast to their own sparklin' clean tweed suits.

They probably wondered how in the hell we'd managed to find our way up here.

Suddenly self-conscious, I stepped quickly into my compartment and slid the doors shut behind me. At least these fancy berths offered a lot of privacy. We'd be safe enough from pryin' eyes and contemptuous looks enclosed in these here spaces. And the doors even locked, too.

I locked mine now and heaved a sigh of relief, sinkin' down into the chair and finally allowin' myself to relax.

The hard part of this journey was over with, now. This train would speed us along across the country and get us to Akansa in no time. Then I just had to find Blackbird, find Dr. Balogh, find those ruins, and then figure out what exactly I was gonna do with that information.

What exactly I was gonna do with Nine-Fingered Nan.

I leaned back in that soft chair and tipped my hat down over my face. Well, I had two whole days stuck in this damned tin can, like Holt had said.

Surely I could think of somethin' by then.

HUNTED

Turned out it only took one day trapped in that little tin can to make me restless as a caged circus tiger. I walked through the cars a bit, tryin' to settle myself, till the other passengers started givin' me suspicious side-eye and one of the train employees told me I really needed to sit down as I was makin' folk nervous.

Guess I probably did look more like someone who might rob 'em rather than just another traveler. So then I occupied myself by takin' little walks each time we stopped at a station. And in-between stops, sometimes I found a game of cards or dice in the lounge car. We took lunch and then dinner in the fancy kitchen car set aside fer the wealthy folk with the private berths.

Wealthy folk like we was pretendin' to be at the moment.

I had to admit, it was better than the jerky and bread I usually brought with me.

After dinner, Charlotte gave me one of her books and told me to read to soothe my mind, but I couldn't seem to focus on the words. There was too much botherin' me still. Too much left unknown and uncertain.

So I gave up. Shut the book and set it aside and went back to that kitchen car. They had a bar there. A bar that served up plenty of whiskey.

If there was anythin' that could soothe my mind of its many concerns, it'd be whiskey.

The rhythmic noise of the train coastin' along the tracks, the slight sway of the car, the dim nighttime scenery blurrin' by outside the windows … it was all kinda mesmerizin'. I sat there on one cushioned bench fer who knew how long, just watchin' the land outside slide gradually from brown and barren into one more green and fulla trees, swayin' along with the motion of the car, helped along somewhat by the three-fourths bottle of whiskey I'd drank by then.

To my surprise, Holt hadn't wandered in here yet. But he'd been deep into a game of poker last I'd seen him, and he was a hard man to get away from his cards even on his bad days.

And Charlotte … well of course Charlotte weren't in here drinkin' herself stupid. She was still shut up in her little private room, probably readin' like a proper lady would. Or maybe doin' somethin' else they liked to do. Somethin' productive.

That left me here on my bench, all by my lonesome.

Just me and my whiskey.

Well, I supposed there were a few other fellas here, sure, leanin' on the bar and makin' small talk with each other. But none of 'em paid me any mind except fer tossin' me one of those contemptuous looks now and then.

I ignored 'em. Weren't nothin' I weren't used to.

It was real, real late by the time I roused myself from that mesmerizin' view to finally head back to my little room. Figured I should probably sleep some tonight. And I was far enough along into the bottle now I thought that might be possible.

And so I staggered outta the kitchen car and down the narrow corridors of those sleeper cars till my weary, blurred vision found my own little hidey hole. I slid the door open, but then paused in confusion.

It was dark in there. The only light came from what shone through the doorway from the corridor I stood in. My shadow stretched out long in the middle of the rectangle of light, and I stood there frownin', sure I'd left the lamp on.

Maybe the damn thing had burnt out while I'd been gone.

Grumblin', I crossed the small space to the opposite wall where the light had been screwed into place next to the window. My fingers fumbled fer the chain, except then I noticed those floral curtains had been pulled shut.

I might not have been sure about the light, but I was damn sure about the curtains, even in my inebriated state. I'd left 'em open.

I straightened; pulled the chain fer the light even as I set the mostly empty whiskey bottle down onto the table and swept my hand back fer my right pistol.

The light didn't come on. My foggy mind had barely registered that fact when a brush of sound came from behind me and I whirled, pullin' my piece, just as the door to my room shut.

Plunged into abrupt darkness, I didn't see the fist

that came down onto my right wrist and jarred my pistol outta my grip. Then there was another fist that drove into my gut. I doubled over with a grunt only to get a crack in the chin that sent me staggerin' back into that table seein' stars.

The whiskey bottle rolled off onto the carpeted floor and I followed soon after it, strugglin' to re-gather my wits. I groped fer my left pistol, but hands on the back of my duster hauled me up to my feet, and I got slammed face-first up against the back wall, up against that curtained window, and my right arm got twisted brutally behind my back till a cry wrenched outta me. Felt like my shoulder was about to come outta the socket.

"All right, all right, take it easy," I ground through my teeth. "What the fuck do you want?"

The man holdin' me to the wall and nearly pullin' off my arm grunted. His free hand went to my left hip and relieved me of my second pistol. I heard it thump to the carpet, too. "Just you, De-lano," he said. "You're worth enough all on your own."

I ground my teeth. Goddamned bounty hunters.

"You're an awful popular fella these days, ain't you?" he said, and I realized he sounded awful famil-iar. "Keep havin' to wade through a line of folk just to get at you, seems like. So here's what's gonna hap-pen. You're gonna come with me, nice and quiet." I heard the clink of manacles as he pulled 'em from his belt. "We're gonna go have a seat in the mail car, and we're gonna get off at the next stop." He cuffed my right wrist, grabbed my left arm and wrenched it behind my back too. "And you ain't gonna cause any trouble at all, now, are ya?"

I opened my mouth to tell him there wasn't a chance of that in Hell, braced myself to push back off the wall into him, but before I could either speak or act, the door to my little room slid open forcefully, jarrin' on its hinges, and another shadow loomed in the resultin' splash of light.

The click of a hammer pulled back punctuated the sharp order, "Don't you move or I'll blow a hole right through you."

The bounty hunter and I both froze.

Charlotte. But my relief was short-lived, realizin' if she blew a hole through him, she'd blow a hole right through me, too. Surely she knew that.

Surely the bounty hunter also knew that.

Nevertheless, her intrusion gave him pause. I felt his weight shift from leanin' on me, presumably to look back at her and judge the true nature of what threat she might pose, but both his hands had been preoccupied with cuffin' me. He didn't have a weapon ready to point back at her.

He cleared his throat. "Good evenin', ma'am. Apologies if I woke you. But I think you'd rather not get involved in this. Like I told you before, it's all lawful business, and discharging a firearm, especially toward a warrant officer while he's trying to conduct that lawful business, on a train full of innocent folk no less, won't be taken well by local law, I can tell you that."

Warrant office—fuckin' hell. No wonder he sounded familiar.

It was that goddamned bloodhound of a bounty hunter Duster. Dustin Barrett.

Fuck me.

How in the hell he'd managed to squirrel away

from Copperwell so quick after committin' murder, or track us across all that open desert without bein' spotted, or get on board this train along with us unnoticed was beyond me.

But none of that mattered now. All that mattered was how I was gonna manage to get away from him this time, trapped on a movin' train cuttin' through the middle of nowhere. A train fulla innocent folk, just like he'd said.

There were lots of witnesses here. Lots of people who could turn on us quick.

Fuck.

"And like I told *you* before, Mr. Barrett," Charlotte said coolly, "I have hired these men on business. For the time being, at least, they are under my protection … and that of my father."

Duster gave a little laugh. "Ma'am, that's not exactly how this works. I don't think you understand what this man stands accused of—"

I planted a boot against the wall in front of me and shoved myself backwards, crashin' into him hard and knockin' him off balance. We both went down to the floor, me landin' on top of him, and I heard the air go out of him with an *oof*. His grip on my arms loosened; I yanked out of his hold and rolled off him, jumped to my feet—stumbled a bit thanks to the whiskey and that crack on my chin—and searched frantically fer a gun.

The nearest one was the pistol held outstretched in Charlotte's hands. My pistol. The one I'd given her. She still held it toward the bounty hunter, who was scramblin' to his feet now himself, but her eyes were on me. Her mouth opened like she were about to tell me somethin', and I realized abruptly she was still in her nightgown.

I'd never seen her in a night dress before.

Duster lurched up standin' behind me and the motion in my peripheral view pulled me from my momentary distraction. I snatched the gun from Charlotte's hands and darted past her out into the narrow hall.

"Van!" she blurted.

But I paid her no mind, chargin' away from her and headin' fer the car's back door.

Duster came after me, as I'd known he would; I heard Charlotte's alarmed gasp as he musta shoved past her.

"Mr. Barrett, I demand you stop this pursuit immediately!" she yelled out after us, but the bounty hunter didn't pay her any more mind than I had. He did not stop his pursuit, didn't even slow it. His runnin' boots thumped quick on the carpet behind me, gainin' fast.

He was taller than me, and had a longer stride.

Not to mention hadn't downed a whole bottle of whiskey just recently.

I couldn't outrun him fer long.

I shouldered through the car's back door, jumped the gap to the next car, and shoved the pistol into my holster so I could climb up on the railin' and then jump to grab hold of the edge of the roof. My left bicep strongly protested as I hauled myself up, and I hoped I hadn't just pulled out all of Holt's stitches. The pain pulsed from the bullet hole now, sharp and angry. I gritted my teeth and tried to ignore it.

Duster burst through the door behind me, but I

weren't quite quick enough in my climb, and he saw my boots disappear up top.

So he started up after me.

"*Shit*." I shoved back to my feet and staggered again, this time not just 'cause of the whiskey, but 'cause of the swayin' train and the fierce wind that came with such a vehicle hurtlin' unhindered down a track in the middle of nowhere.

I suddenly questioned the wisdom of my decision to come up here. There were fewer obstacles in my path and fewer witnesses, sure … but that also meant there were fewer obstacles fer Duster, and fewer witnesses to anythin' *he* might do, too.

'Cept then I remembered I had the high ground here.

So I braced my feet against the push of the wind and leveled my pistol at his head just as it appeared over his scrabblin' hands at the lip of the roof.

The manacles he hadn't quite managed to get on me dangled from my right wrist, and even though the rest of the world was all a bit wobbly, my hand was steady.

I glared down at him as he paused his climb. "Think real careful about how you want this to go down, bounty hunter."

He glared back up at me. "I could say the same to you, Delano."

"'Cept I ain't the one with a gun pointed at my face."

He smiled, gave a tilt of his chin in acknowledgement. "No. But like I told the lady, shootin' a licensed warrant officer won't reflect well on you with the local law. With any law anywhere, matter of fact."

I scoffed. Had to shout to be heard above the rushin' wind. "You seen all my posters, Mister. You think me shootin' another peace officer is gonna make any difference to the opinion of any law about me? I hardly think so. Shot a sheriff down in Destry just about two weeks back, even. I surely won't blink over shootin' you just the same." I thumbed my hammer back to make my point more clear.

Truth be told, most days I woulda shot him already. Woulda ended him without even thinkin' about it, and thrown his body off the train.

Why didn't I just shoot him now? My finger twitched on the trigger, but didn't pull.

All I kept thinkin' was how he'd been willin' to let that Sonoita sheriff give me a trial. I'd been locked up, easy pickin's fer a bounty hunter to make off with, and worth fifty thousand dollars … and Duster had been willin' to chance sacrificin' that kinda money. Fer what? Respect fer his friend? Respect fer what Sheriff Longley was tryin' to do out here in the Territories? Respect fer the law?

Charlotte burst through the back door of the car we'd just come out of, still in her night dress, red hair whippin' wild around her face, and jolted me abruptly from my contemplations. She had another pistol, one of those I'd dropped back in my room.

I was about to yell out at her to go back inside, to stay outta this, not wantin' to chance her gettin' a poster of her own, but Duster took advantage of my eyes comin' off him and hooked a hand around my left ankle.

That was my metal ankle, so I didn't feel his hand grab me, but I sure felt it when he yanked my leg out from under me. I crashed to the roof, my pistol firin' as it jarred, but the bullet went wide. I landed on my back with a grunt, and then that bastard of a bounty hunter leveraged himself up onto the roof quick as a cat and pounced on me just as I was tryin' to roll back to my feet.

Charlotte shouted somethin', but I couldn't understand her.

I was too preoccupied with wrestlin' the man sittin' on top of me. I twisted under him and brought my gun hard across his face.

He sagged sideways, givin' me space to press the barrel of my pistol right up to his heart.

I didn't have time to fire; his left fist smashed into my right wrist hard enough to make my hand go numb. The gun went flyin'. It skittered away across the roof, disappeared over the edge.

"Fuckin' hell," I spat.

"God damnit, Delano," he growled, takin' two fistfuls of the front of my duster, "you are *really* starting to piss me off."

I grinned up at him. "That's what I'm good fer."

He cocked a fist back, presumably meant to knock me unconscious and shut me up fer awhile, but a shot rang out instead and the bounty hunter yelled as a spray of blood painted the left shoulder of his jacket.

The hand that woulda landed in my face went instead to cover the wound. Just a graze, looked like, but I'm sure it still hurt like hell.

I didn't waste time feelin' sorry fer him. I hit him good in the chin like he'd done to me earlier and shoved him off while he was reelin'. Then I jumped to my feet and whirled toward Charlotte, who'd climbed up here herself now, damnit. "Go back inside!" I snapped at her. "You don't want this on you."

I didn't wait fer her to reply or to argue, but took off again across the roof, aimin' fer the back of the train. Weren't entirely sure what my plan was … didn't exactly have a plan at all, I supposed, I only knew I didn't want Charlotte involved in any of it.

Thumpin' bootsteps came after me again soon enough, too heavy to be hers with her bare feet and her night dress.

So Duster was up again and on the chase.

Fine. Long as he weren't payin' no attention to Charlotte fer nickin' him in the shoulder. Long as she didn't follow after us, too.

I came up quick on the end of this car; made the leap over the gap onto the roof of the next car.

And stumbled as the train made a curve around a rock bluff.

I hit my knees closer to the roof's edge than I woulda liked; got a dizzyin' view of the ground blurrin' by below, but then I was up and runnin' again.

And Duster right behind me.

NO TICKET

Someone fired.

I ducked, but I couldn't tell if it was the bounty hunter or Charlotte shootin'.

Out here, the train's wheels clatterin' along the tracks was especially loud, and the damn wind whistlin' past didn't help things none, neither.

But I didn't slow, just kept on runnin', jumpin' from car to car.

Two more shots barked from behind, but I weren't too worried about 'em aimin' at me. At least, not aimin' fer a mortal wound.

Charlotte wouldn't be the one shootin' at me, clearly, and if Mr. Dustin Barret wanted that fifty thousand dollars, he was gonna have to get me to the Whittakers alive. At least that poster had been very explicit about that condition.

Else he probably woulda shot me back in my room when he'd got the jump on me, and I'd already be dead.

But if he thought I was gonna make takin' me alive easy on him, well, he was sorely mistaken.

I made another jump onto the next car, but only barely made it across. That whiskey was takin' its toll, and all this runnin' and jumpin'. My lungs and legs burned, muscles weakenin' as they tired out.

Goddamn, I didn't remember this train bein' so long.

But I was almost to the end of it now. Then I was gonna throw that Duster bastard over the side of it and be done with him. Quick and clean. And none of those innocent folk below would ever have to know anything about it…

"Delano!" Duster roared. "I swear to God, the more you make me chase you, the more hurt I'm gonna lay on you once I get ahold of you!"

"Too bad you need me alive fer that money," I called over my shoulder.

"Don't mean I can't shoot you plenty of places that won't kill you," he snarled back.

A bullet pinged off the train roof to my left, makin' me swear and jerk sideways, then stumble again.

Almost fell off the train my own damn self before I regained my balance and continued my run. If only I had any guns left to shoot back at him…

The memory of the one tucked away inside my metal leg came to me then, and I shuddered at all the other memories that came along with it. If only I could figure out how I'd managed to make the leg open … I tried to will it open, now, runnin' along that train roof, tried to picture myself murderin' Duster just like I'd intended to murder Charles Miller at the time my leg had weaponized.

But nothin' happened. It stayed just as it always was, a regular collection of rods and gears, and I scowled.

Just as well, I supposed. Weren't sure how I'd get to all those weapons anyway, bein' as I was actually wearin' pants at the moment. And it surely weren't worth shuckin' those right now to try and figure it out.

I jumped yet another gap between cars—but in my current weary state I didn't quite make the distance. My boots missed the next roof and I flailed as I fell, only barely catchin' hold of the edge.

But my left arm was havin' none of this, and the bullet hole in my bicep spiked agony all the way up into my shoulder as I struggled to pull myself up. I hissed a curse as my grip slipped and I hit the deck below, anyway.

I was too slow to get up, breathin' hard and the world still rockin' from the train and the whiskey.

Duster dropped down next to me.

"All right," I panted, usin' the rail to haul myself back to my feet. "All right. Maybe we can talk about this—"

He decked me hard in the face.

I went backwards into the train car's door with the force of it, stumbled through it, right into the aisle between the rows of hard wooden benches.

The cheap seats.

The folk sittin' in 'em gasped at my rather forceful entrance into their space, some of 'em startled from their uncomfortable slumber.

But I used the momentum to turn and keep on goin', staggerin' down the aisle and noddin' pleasantly to people as I passed 'em, despite my now-throbbin' head and the fact I tasted blood. "Howdy, folks."

They stared at me wide-eyed and murmurs circled in my wake, around Duster, who stalked after me.

But he was movin' a lot slower now, too. I suspected he didn't want to cause a scene, neither. Maybe he'd managed to get outta Copperwell awful fast after his murder there, but it had cost him his prize that mornin', anyway.

Surely he didn't want that to happen again here.

So we both only walked quick down that aisle, stayin' as quiet and non-threatenin' as we could manage, and I made it to the back door and went through it, but stepped to the side and pulled my knife instead of tryin' to make the roof again or go through the next car.

We'd almost reached the caboose now, the mail car, and everyone knew the mail car carried a few armed gents nearby or inside to guard the enclosed valuables. I didn't want to get anywhere near those gents. Not fer this business.

I moved soon as Duster stepped through that doorway himself, aimin' a stab at his heart.

He was quick as a goddamned snake, blockin' the downward arc of my knife with his left forearm and drivin' his right fist into my gut again. I doubled over his arm as all the air went outta me, but even as I choked, tryin' to breathe again, I saw the glint of his right pistol's grip.

So close.

I snatched it fast with my left hand and straightened, spinnin' it on my index finger to land it properly in my palm, but he'd felt me pull it and was already movin' sideways as I fired.

The bullet that shoulda gone through his face instead splintered a chunk outta the back corner of the car we'd just come out of. Some of the folk inside screamed.

I ignored 'em, adjustin' my aim in an instant; saw the bounty hunter draw his second pistol at the same time he stepped toward me, and I didn't wait to see if maybe he'd go ahead and shoot me, and all that money be damned.

I fired again.

It weren't my best shot, not by far, but it tore through his chest high on the right side and made him stagger back with a cry. I braced my own self against the deck's railin' with my right hand and gave him a good solid kick in the chest with my metal foot.

He careened backward, hit the rail on the other side and then went over it, and disappeared into that blurrin' landscape.

I slumped, tryin' to get my air back, my grip on the railin' the only thing holdin' me up. I looked down to the gun in my left hand. It was a nice one. Well, he'd owed me a pistol anyway. I holstered it and limped to the opposite side of the narrow deck to lean over the rail and look back along the tracks.

We'd already left him far behind, the train movin' at such a speed that even if the fall hadn't killed him, he'd of never been able to catch onto it by the time it was already gone. A horse couldn'ta even caught up to this train at this speed. But he didn't have no horse, neither.

Injured the way he was, stuck in the middle of nowhere with no horse and no supplies ... well, I didn't put his odds of survival at too awful good.

And that was just fine with me.

I pushed away from the rail to turn back to the car fulla folk in the cheap seats. And realized they were all starin' horrified at me. That back door stood wide open, givin' 'em all a good, clear view of what I'd done to Mr. Dustin Barrett.

I straightened with a wince and cleared my

throat. Tucked my right hand casually behind my back so maybe they wouldn't notice the manacles hangin' off that wrist. Tried to look unconcerned as I jerked my chin back in the direction of where the bounty hunter had disappeared along the tracks. And said the first thing that came to mind. "No ticket."

Their eyes grew wider. They looked from one to the other in a moment of shocked silence, and then all frantically scrambled to produce their own tickets, which they held up and waved about fer my benefit.

I blinked. Hadn't expected that to work.

But since it had, I made a show of glancin' over all of 'em as I ambled slowly back through the car, down the aisle between the seats. Now that the rush of the chase and the fight was over, all the hurt settled in and made itself at home. My left arm throbbed somethin' awful around that bullet wound, my chin and my middle were sore, and he'd split my lip with that last punch.

I swiped at the blood on my chin with a sleeve, nearly at the opposite door when Charlotte came through it and stopped me up short.

She halted abruptly herself, wild eyes lookin' me over before searchin' around the rest of the car. She gripped one of my pistols in her right hand, still wore her night dress and had no shoes, and her long hair was loose and wind-whipped, tangled and fallin' every which way, makin' her look more like a degenerate than a lady.

The people behind us gasped and murmured again at her appearance and I grimaced, takin' her shoulder to gently turn her around and usher her out of their view. I shut the door behind us and shrugged carefully outta my duster.

"Where is he?" she asked. "Where's Mr. Barrett?"

I swallowed. Shook my head as I settled my duster over her own shoulders and tugged it tight around her. "He's, uh … he won't bother us anymore."

She stepped back from me with a start. "Did you kill him?!"

"No," I blurted before thinkin'. But then as she fixed me with a certainly skeptical look, I doubled down. "No. Only convinced him that maybe chasin' me weren't the wisest of decisions." Well, it weren't exactly a lie. I *hadn't* killed him. Directly.

Guess that was probably the real reason why I hadn't blown a hole through his skull when I'd had the chance up on the roof: Charlotte.

She was sure complicatin' things, all right. If not fer her, I coulda taken care of Mr. Barrett with a whole lot less effort. And a whole lot fewer bruises.

Her dark blue gaze narrowed up at me now, but I only reached out and lightly pried the pistol from her grip, slippin' it back into my other holster. Then I put an arm around her again and ushered her onward, back toward our berths.

"Do I need to speak to him further myself?" she asked.

"No. No, I think he got the message clear enough." I resisted the urge to look back over my shoulder, over the rail. That bounty hunter would be miles back by now. I opened the next door fer Charlotte, waved her through.

In truth I woulda rather not had both of us paradin' down the center aisle between curious and suspicious folk in our current state, but there was nothin' much to be done fer it. I weren't gonna take Charlotte back the whole way on the roof, and anyway, I didn't think I had the energy to climb up there again myself.

She held my duster close around herself as we went, and we made the rest of the walk to our rooms in silence.

"However did you end up like this?" Charlotte asked suddenly, softly.

I jolted from broodin' over my tussle with Mr. Dustin Barrett—over the fact I'd let him get the jump on me so good—to look at her with a start.

We sat in her room now, with its workin' electrical lamp, and I'd shucked my shirt so she could look at that hole in my bicep. I'd pulled out Holt's stitches in all the excitement, all right. But it'd been long enough now they looked about ready to come out anyway, so she was pullin' the rest of 'em free fer me and cleanin' it all up, and I had a fresh bottle of whiskey clutched in my right hand to dull the angry fire of the process.

We'd already picked the lock on those manacles and set 'em aside, so I'd been starin' into the steady shine of that lamp and tryin' to distract myself from the uncomfortableness of the scrubbin'.

And from the fact Charlotte was leanin' so close.

But her question surprised me enough to make me forget all that. I frowned at her. "I had a run-in with a particularly determined bounty hunter who is particularly good at huntin' people. And also particularly good at throwin' punches." I ran my tongue gingerly over the fresh split in my bottom lip and then winced. My head was achin', too.

She glanced up from her work on my arm, then pursed her lips and shook her head. Her red hair was still an awful mess, but she'd shed my well-worn duster now for a velvet house robe instead. Another garment I hadn't yet seen on our trip. And she'd pulled all these medical supplies from her pack, too. Made me wonder what else she might have hidden away in there.

"No," she chided. "I mean how did you end up like *this*." Her eyes flicked downward toward the mostly healed wound in my bicep. "Living like this. Getting shot at so much. Having men like Mr. Barrett after you. Having to be on the run so often. Always looking over your shoulder … barely having a thing to call your own." She raised her eyes to mine again, and then her gaze wandered over my face, also bruised and bloodied thanks to Mr. Barrett, and to the scars over the rest of me.

Scars from Baron Whittaker's crowbar. Scars from Mr. Miller's electrical rod. A few others here and there from various jobs, scuffles, and barfights. And that weren't countin' the stripes on my back, neither. Those from Mr. Fisher when I'd been accused of stealin' his wife's fine silver.

I shifted on the plush armchair at that memory, at the familiar stab of bitter anger that always came with it, and shrugged. "Just do what I gotta do to survive," I muttered, and I weren't entirely sure then if I was really talkin' to her or myself. "Till I find Ethelyn."

Charlotte sat quiet fer a minute, seemingly contemplatin', but then she went back to those stitches. "That man you travel with—"

"Holt?"

"Yes. Holt. He's not your father."

I gave a snort and shook my head. "No. No he is not."

"So how did you end up with a man like him? You don't seem very much alike. I know he didn't really want to help me back in Blessing. And he would have kept all that money for himself. And I certainly know if he had been the one tied to that chair being tortured at Baron Whittaker's place, he would have let the baron kill all those slaves if it meant less pain for himself."

I tightened my grip on that whiskey bottle, knowin' it was probably true.

"He would have given me up right away, too. And probably told Whittaker where to find the doctor who made that leg."

Also probably true, unfortunately, so I said nothin'.

"But *you* didn't," Charlotte said, and she paused in her work again to sit back on her stool. "All along the way across the country, after those bandits kidnapped me, sometimes I was able to yell for help. And yet ... no one lifted a finger to aid me. You were the first person who seemed to care at all in a long time ... and then you even seemed to care about those strangers you didn't even know. So how in the world did you end up traveling with a man like Holt, living a life like … like *this*?" She gestured at my sorry state.

I almost wanted to laugh. But it weren't funny, really. And the laugh stuck in my throat and then choked into somethin' that felt more like a sob, anyway, so I only ended up drinkin' more whiskey. "Dunno," I said finally. "Just bad luck, I guess."

Or good luck, dependin' on which way you looked at it. If not fer Holt findin' me, and carin' enough about the son of his once-best-friend to spring me, I woulda hanged at sixteen. Though whether or not the last eight years had been better than bein' dead … well, sometimes I couldn't be sure.

Charlotte was quiet fer another long moment, long enough that the silence started to make me itchy. But then she asked, "Do you ever … do you ever get tired of it? Of living like this?"

The question drew a long, quiet breath outta me that I made sure she couldn't hear over the sound of the train coastin' down the tracks, and I shrugged again. "Don't think about it much, I suppose."

And I didn't. Least, not anymore. No use lamentin' a fact I couldn't change.

"What about … *after* you free your sister? What will you do then?"

My frown came back.

Charlotte just sat there on her stool in her velvet house robe, watchin' me like she'd just asked the most innocent question in the world.

So I gulped more whiskey and turned to stare out the window at the darkened scenery streakin' by. Truth be told, I'd never much entertained the idea of a life after findin' Ethelyn. Weren't ever sure I'd even live long enough to find her in the first place.

And now that I knew Nine-Fingered Nan had her, I was even less certain of that. And even more certain of the fact that if I did live long enough to find her, and free her, I'd die doin' it.

"Don't know," was all I said. It came out rough, so I cleared my throat. "Guess we'll see."

Charlotte did not seem especially pleased with my lack of specificity regardin' my future. She sighed, then resumed her attentions on my arm. She gave one final tug on the last piece of thread, and then I was free of those stitches. She wrapped a fresh bandage around her fine work before packin' up all her supplies. "I suppose at least you have a purpose in life," she said at last. "A drive. A function. As for myself … admittedly, I'm feeling rather lost. I don't … I don't have anything for myself, like you have with trying to free your sister. When I realized I didn't want any of what my parents had planned for my future … that I'd had quite enough of being controlled by others … well, I had hoped that maybe I could at least help you, if you still needed it. I thought maybe I could help you like you had helped me."

I looked back at her at this confession.

"This is … this is all rather overwhelming," her gaze wandered to the bullet hole in my arm again, "but at least it's a choice. At least it's a choice I can make for myself. Although I'm not entirely sure how helpful I've managed to be up to this point."

I looked around at her plush accommodations … accommodations Holt and I would have never sprung fer ourselves, and then glanced pointedly at my freshly bandaged arm. Maybe she *was* complicatin' things, sure, but she'd also been useful a time or two. "You do a fine job of doctorin', I can tell you that. Better'n Holt. And … and you're pretty good in a fight, too."

A faint trace of a smile pulled at her lips. "Only thanks to my eldest brother. He taught me many things he was not supposed to. Things not becoming of a lady." She sobered suddenly, and her gaze shifted away.

On impulse, I reached my left hand out to cover the top of hers. I understood that feelin' of bein' lost well enough. Had felt it myself fer years, back when I'd thought Ethelyn had perished along with my cousin in Colorado.

And I wished then that I could help Charlotte somehow … give her her own purpose. And preferably one that didn't involve Nine-Fingered Nan, or any kinda personal vendetta that would likely get her killed.

Maybe … maybe after. After Ethelyn was free and Nan was dealt with, if I happened to still be livin', maybe then it might be somethin' I could entertain…

Charlotte cleared her throat and stood abruptly, pullin' her hand out from under mine. "Sometimes it seems like you might be trying to die on purpose, you know," she murmured.

I blinked at her abrupt change in subject, her abrupt movement, tried to pull myself back from darin' to think about a future. And scoffed. "Not hardly. If that's what I was tryin' to do, well … I'd be dead already. Woulda let our friend Duster take me just now, if that were the case. Nah." I drank more whiskey, straight from the bottle. "Dyin's easy out here. It's stayin' alive that's the hard part."

"Hmmph. Well." She moved across the small space to stuff the medical supplies back into her pack. Then she straightened, smoothed at her velvet robe, and plucked my shirt from where I'd tossed it over the top of the small table. She handed it out to me, and I took it in my left hand with only a little wince. "After we get your sister, if you should want a different sort of life—one quite a bit less hazardous to your health—I'm certain my family could use a man of your caliber on their estate."

I almost spit the whiskey I'd just swigged.

"I may not have particularly enjoyed my life there, but just because I will not be returning doesn't mean *you* couldn't find gainful employment there. Or … or once I find a place to finally settle myself, I would be more than happy to welcome you there, also. I could use the help, I'm sure. You and your sister both," she finished, ignorin' my wheezin' and coughin'.

I glanced up at her through waterin' eyes and tried to recover my air around the whiskey I'd sucked down the wrong pipe. "Charlotte," I croaked, but then I stopped myself. I'd been about to tell her that her family would be far more inclined to see me hanged than offer me room and board at their estate, once they realized I weren't exactly the caliber of man they'd expected.

Maybe my deeds hadn't circulated to the Republic yet. But they would, in time. After long enough of me runnin' free, escapin' the law, escapin' justice … it'd all catch up to me eventually. It always did.

Pa had always told me that. Course at the time I'd thought he'd meant it more in a figurative sense, warnin' me away from potentially wanderin' down a bad path. Didn't realize he was referrin' to his own personal sins till long after, after he and Mama were dead. After Holt had found me and filled me in on what parts of Pa's past I'd never known about.

Until then, I'd never suspected.

I wondered if Charlotte suspected anythin' of me now. My stomach twisted at the thought, though I couldn't be sure if I hoped she was entirely innocent of suspicion, or if I hoped she had some inklin' so as not to be entirely disappointed later.

I shook my head and swallowed back the bitterness that rose in my throat. "Charlotte ... I ... I couldn't do that."

She tilted her head to one side. "Why not? Wouldn't it be better? For you and her both. You could have a roof over your head, a real bed, three square meals a day, a paycheck." She paused. "And more than one shirt."

I grunted, wet my lips. "I have more than one shirt." I had two, to be exact.

"Oh. Well ... maybe you should put on another one for now, then. We'll have that one laundered." She nodded to the one still in my hands.

I dropped my eyes down to it as well and then winced at its condition. That woulda been a good idea, sure. Except... "Er. My other one is still with all my other stuff. With the mule. In the livestock car."

"Oh." She sighed. "No matter then. But would you at least consider my offer? Please?"

I gave a sigh myself. Let the whiskey bottle sit on

the table so I could scrub that hand over the un-bruised part of my face and rake it through my shaggy hair. It was long enough now it was startin' to curl. Had those waves to it, like Mama's hair. Reluctantly, I nodded. "Sure. Fine."

She seemed to relax a little at that, even smiled. "Thank you. That's all I'm asking. Just consider it."

"Yeah. All right." But I wouldn't. I couldn't. I couldn't do that to her. Or to her family. Or to myself. Even just her mention of all those things, all those things I couldn't have—not now, and probably not ever—had dredged up a wash of that old, sour anger.

That kinda life had been taken from me the night Mama and Pa were killed.

And I'd gone and destroyed my chances fer it in the future by runnin' with Holt fer so long. By agreein' to aid him in so many nefarious exploits. By bein' so hell-bent on findin' my sister I'd gone and done some truly terrible things.

"Well." I shook myself outta that dark place and pushed stiffly to my feet. "We'd best turn in. Get some sleep. Thank you fer … patchin' me up. Again. And fer comin' over to see what all the ruckus was about in the first place. Might not have got out of that scuffle otherwise."

She gave a nod, grabbed the whiskey bottle from the table and took a long swig herself.

I lifted a brow, wonderin' if my influence was startin' to rub off on her, then wonderin' if I found that upsettin' or amusin'. I couldn't quite decide.

She offered the bottle back to me. "Let's just hope that's the last time I patch you up for a good long while, yes?"

I took my hat from where I'd set it on the arm of the chair and settled it back on my head, then took the whiskey. "Yeah. Let's hope."

But I didn't even have time to drink to that sentiment before a commotion erupted in the hall outside. And it sounded like … singin'.

DAY NINE

Charlotte and I looked to each other in confusion, and I set the whiskey bottle down again to rest my hand light on that fancy pistol of Duster's as I went to Charlotte's door, my shirt still clutched in my other hand.

I hooked one finger in the door handle and slid it open a crack to peer out, even as the singin' got closer, and louder, and I was fair sure I recognized the voice.

Sure enough, bout that time, Holt came into view in the corridor. He weaved back and forth in the narrow space, and if it weren't fer the walls on either side of him, I weren't sure he'd have been able to stay standin'. But he seemed in real high spirits, grinnin' ear to ear, face flushed with alcohol, and beltin' out snatches of every song I'd ever heard him sing in no sensical order whatsoever.

Damn fool old man was drunk as a skunk.

And he was too loud. Much too loud.

Especially considerin' my recent encounter with Mr. Barrett. Now was the time fer us to be layin' low, unheard and unseen 'til we could get far away from all the people on this train, especially those folk back in that car of cheap seats who'd seen me knock a man over the rail.

"*Holt!*" I hissed. "The hell are you doin'? You

wanna get everyone on this train angry at us? Keep it down, would ya?"

He stopped singin', paused in the hall leanin' against the outside wall, and looked up at me in surprise, like he'd just realized I was there, standin' halfway out of Charlotte's room. He blinked at me. "Eh? Van? Van! There ya are! I've been tryin' ta find ya … gotta tell ya … I jus' *owned* these fancy boys at poker, I did!" Thought his grin would split his face in half, and his blue eyes twinkled with more merriment than I figured I'd ever seen outta him. He wheezed a laugh. "Ya won't *believe* the winnin's I took in—we're gonna be livin' high on the hog, we are!"

I motioned frantically fer him to lower his voice. "Holt! Come on now, keep it down. Folk tryin' to sleep around here."

Charlotte stepped up next to me at the door to observe the spectacle herself. The arm of her velvet robe brushed against the bare skin of my left elbow. Absently, I noted it really *was* as soft as it looked.

"Pffft. Sleep. Who needs it?" Holt waved a hand dismissively and stumbled toward us. "I gotta tell you about this game! I had a streak goin', let me tell ya. Those boys ain't seen nothin' like it—"

He stopped abruptly again when he realized Charlotte was there. He stared at her fer a minute like he'd forgotten who she was, and then he looked back to me and seemed to really see me fer the first time, too. He squinted, his boisterous story forgotten. "Hey. What happened to yer face?"

I sighed, but before I could tell him we'd talk about that later, his eyes went rapidly over the rest of me, then between me and Charlotte. His expression changed from confusion to comprehension, and his bushy eyebrows rose high. "Ahhhhh. **Sleep.** Hah! Sure, sure, I see how it is. You two got some *business* to take care of, do ya?"

"What?"

"No need to be coy about it, I seen the way you two look at each other. I understand. I been there too, ya know. A long time ago, sure, but I know how it goes—"

My face flamed as I suddenly realized what he was goin' on about and instinctively I stepped away from Charlotte, out into the hall. "That ain't what this is about," I snapped, frantically hopin' to shut him up before he went on and said somethin' even more embarrassin'. "I pulled out those stitches and she was fixin' 'em."

He lurched off the wall and held up his hands, swayin' in place. "All right, sure, whatever you say."

I shook out my shirt with a snap and shrugged into it. "I was just leavin'. To go to bed. Which is just what you should do, damn fool. 'Fore you bring a whole train-load of angry people down on us." To illustrate my point, I stalked over to him and caught a fistful of his coat, pullin' him over toward his own door.

He stumbled along beside me, chucklin' under his breath despite my less-than-hospitable treatment. "All right, yeah. Let's go to bed. I'll tell you about my game tomorrow. And you can tell me what happened to yer face." He dropped his voice down into a harsh whisper as I pulled his door open. "And about how things went with the lady." He winked, but I only grumbled at him and shoved him into his room like it mighta been a jail cell.

I wished it was. I wished I could lock him in there now so I could be sure he wouldn't cause no more trouble … or say no more stupid things.

"Good night, you old bastard," I growled, and then I shut the door on him. But I could still hear him laughin' to himself on the other side. Scowlin', I turned to head to my own room and caught sight of Charlotte still standin' in the doorway to hers.

She had her hands clasped together tight, and a visible flush pinked her cheeks even in the soft hallway lights. She looked mortified.

Well, so was I. Could still feel my ears burnin'. So all I managed was a nod in her direction as I fumbled at openin' my door. "Night," I muttered.

She nodded in return, her gaze droppin' from mine quick. "Good night," she whispered, and then she slipped from sight and shut her door, and I heard the click as she locked it.

That's when I realized that other bottle of whiskey was still in there.

I swore as I stepped into my darkened berth. Well, I weren't goin' back fer it now. Not after bein' humiliated like that.

Damnable nosy old man. He'd ruined everythin'.

The next day's journey passed blessedly uneventfully.

Holt slept off his drink most the day, which was certainly fine by me. Charlotte and I took breakfast together, both of us refusin' to acknowledge Holt's comments from the night before, and to my relief, the awkward stiffness of our conversation gradually eased.

I didn't pace the train between meals this time, and I only stepped off briefly at our first stop in Akansa to ask after the location of Blackbird and its nearest station, at which point I was told we'd want to get off at Arkopolis and ride north into Blackbird from there.

The rest of the time we stayed shut up in our rooms, not wantin' to risk any chance encounters, or remind anyone of what they mighta seen in the middle of the night last night.

When Holt finally did rouse from his slumber I cornered him while he was in the dinin' car, filled him in on my encounter with Mr. Barrett, but left out the details I didn't want him blurtin' to Charlotte durin' his next drunken episode. Even still, his eyes went wide at my story and he set down his mug of coffee, his plate of half-eaten eggs forgotten.

"Damn, kid. All that happen while I was playin' cards?"

I nodded.

He squinted at me, then glanced around the car where we sat. He leaned forward over the little table. "You *sure* you didn't kill him? The lady ain't here; you can tell me if you did."

"I didn't."

He grunted and sat back in his chair. "Just find it hard to believe a man like him would give up on such a bounty so easily."

I scoffed and shook my head. "I never said it was easy."

"Guess not." He picked up his coffee mug again and watched me over the rim of it. "Can't help but notice that shiny new pistol on yer hip, though. That one of his? He just *give* it to you, then? A token of yer new-found friendship, was it?"

He sipped innocently at his coffee while I growled at him. "He owed me one."

Holt snorted and shook his head. Set his mug down again to return to his eggs with a shrug. "All right. If you say you got him taken care of then I believe ya. Just as long as I don't gotta worry about him showin' up outta nowhere and pointin' a pistol in my face no more."

"You don't."

"Good. Good fer you, kid. Now … let me tell you about that game of cards!"

He did, in great detail, but since I had nothin' else to do I let him go on at length. To my surprise he'd played the whole thing honest; a true rarity when it came to Holt Haggerty's poker playin'. Maybe it'd only been 'cause he'd been so drunk he hadn't trusted himself to cheat in a way that wouldn't get him noticed. Or maybe it was only 'cause we were stuck on this damned train fer a whole nother day, makin' it far more difficult to effect a quick exit should any suspicions be aroused.

But the long and short of it was that Holt had gained us quite a bit more coin. And that was never a bad thing.

By the time we disembarked fer good at the town of Arkopolis, I was both feelin' better and worse about the rest of this errand. Better in that Holt and I now had a fair bit of cash saved up between the two of us so we wouldn't have to rely on Charlotte no more in that regard. Useful fer any more supplies we might need … or fer makin' bribes, which I suspected we might also need.

And worse in that we'd already spent more than one whole week of the two Nan had given me to find Dr. Balogh and those possibly non-existant ruins just travelin'. And we wouldn't get to Blackbird until tomorrow.

Day nine. Day nine, and I hadn't even set foot in Blackbird yet. Not only that, but I still didn't know how I was gonna manage to not send that telegram without seein' Ethelyn first. Didn't even have any ideas.

My fingers brushed Ethelyn's folded letter, tucked into the breast pocket of my shirt, as we waited fer our mounts. Then, once we had 'em and got tacked up—and Charlotte finished her thorough investigation of Sugar's health and well-bein'—we mounted up and headed straight outta town, wastin' no time on pleasantries.

I'd never been to Arkopolis. Never been to Akansa, in fact, despite havin' grown up in the Commune myself. Maybe, if we hadn't been in such a damned hurry, I woulda taken a few days to familiarize myself with the place.

But we didn't have the time. So I settled myself with sight-seein' from the saddle as we went at a steady pace down cobbled streets toward the single bridge that spanned a wide, sluggish river.

And despite the fact we were clearly on the outskirts of the town proper … I could tell without doubt Arkopolis was the biggest town I'd yet set foot into. Could almost be called a city, even. Most of its buildings were stone and brick, and sat in fat clusters toward the town center. But things were busy even out here.

The train station itself was near the riverbank, and there was a big wharf on the bank, too, not far from the station. Several boats were moored there; looked like maybe some smaller fishin' vessels, and some bigger ones probably fulla furs or ores or precious metals. And there was one big flat one fulla logs. Warehouses stretched far into the distance, big wagons pulled by draft horses hauled goods back and forth, and it all reeked of fish.

Charlotte and I were preoccupied by all the activity, but Holt rode on through it as if he'd seen it all countless times before.

He probably had. He'd told me the gang he and Pa had rode with once had taken its origin in the south. Then they'd gradually moved north and west, pillagin' from place to place to avoid the law. Surely they'd been through here at some point.

A chill crept over me at that thought, as our horse's hooves thumped across the thick wooden planks of the bridge, and the slow, muddy water of the river churned beneath us, and we left the sprawl of Arkopolis behind.

Had Pa himself crossed this bridge once? Ridin' alongside Holt just like I was now? Only with a lot of other bad men alongside him, too, I suspected, accordin' to Holt's stories. And the worst of them in the lead: Paul Johnson. A man eventually known as Kill 'Em All Paul.

Holt didn't often share details of the jobs he and Pa had helped orchestrate under the leadership of Paul Johnson, but I often wondered just how bad they got. A man didn't get a name like *Kill 'Em All Paul* fer nothin'.

In all his years before havin' a family and that ranch in Kansas … what had Pa *really* done?

What had Holt done?

"Ya can't fight yer nature."

Holt's words from a few nights ago floated back to me, along with the memories of some of the worst things I'd done myself in years past. Robberies gone wrong, innocent people killed. Lawmen along the way, tryin' to protect those innocents, gunned down like I'd done to that sheriff in Destry. Plenty of honorable men, too, men like Mr. Dustin Barrett, laid in the ground now 'cause of me. Then there was Nan's man Lloyd Renneker, who I'd cut on till he was near unrecognizable and then bled out like a swine.

Well, he hadn't been innocent, nor honorable, and certainly no decent kinda man … but maybe he hadn't deserved such an end, anyway. Maybe.

Suddenly I didn't like this bridge much. Or the lazy expanse of dark river stretchin' out below. Or the busy bustle of Arkopolis behind us.

I pressed my heels to Joe's sides and he picked up his pace. "Come on," I snapped to Holt and Charlotte as he passed 'em by, "we're wastin' time."

GUARDIAN ANGELS

The town of Blackbird was chaos.

So much chaos the town itself couldn't contain it all. It started miles out along the road, where we joined a slow throng of folk movin' toward the settlement, and passed wagon after wagon and camp after camp of more folk who'd established themselves alongside the rutted path.

All kinds of folk.

Prospectors, miners, traders, loggers, and tradesmen of all sorts. Several groups of Natives. Sometimes a clergyman here and there, some with a cluster of followers around 'em and some alone. There were families, too … lots of families. Even a handful of travelin' actors, their wagon painted in bright colors.

And, as we drew closer to the town itself, a few certain … *unsettled* individuals made themselves known. Yellin' out to those of us who passed to beware the temptations of the machines, fer they were the work of the Devil, and that path led straight to Hell. Or that the Old World itself weren't even real and had never existed at all, and we'd all been sold on one big lie. Or that the Great Awakening was comin', whatever that was, and we should all cleanse ourselves in preparation fer the return of the Guardians.

One fella had even dressed himself up like a

crow. Or some kinda black bird, anyway. Put black feathers all over himself and everythin', and he ran up to us screechin' and hollerin' and carryin' on about how his eyes had been opened to the Truth so relentlessly and enthusiastically that I had to pull back my duster and put a hand on my gun to finally scare him off.

Then he went on down the road to bother the next people in line.

"Afraid there's no more room in town," another man said as we ambled by his tent.

When I glanced down to him, I noted his black garb—thankfully devoid of feathers—and the stiff white collar. Another clergyman, then. He spread his hands as my eyes met his, indicatin' his bubblin' stew pot and full tent. Looked like he'd already collected plenty of lost sheep, wearily and warily huddled around the food or sprawled out on blankets.

"You are welcome to join us, if you wish," he said.

I shook my head. "No thanks."

"Are you certain? Room and board in Blackbird is booked up for months."

"Good thing we ain't lookin' fer room or board, then," I muttered, and I kicked Joe into a trot to squeeze past the folks trudgin' along in front of us.

Charlotte and Holt followed after me, and I heard Charlotte thank the man politely fer his offer as she went by.

We may not have needed room and board, no, as we had plenty of our own supplies, but hearin' such news put me on edge, anyway. And seein' the state of the town itself as we finally reached it only darkened my mood further.

I'd never seen so many people wedged into one place in my life. Blackbird weren't a big town to begin with, maybe not even the size of Bravebank, but its streets were less streets now and more rivers of people.

And the noise … so much talkin' and shoutin' all at once, mixed with all the regular sounds of a bustlin' town, which Blackbird had apparently become abruptly and unexpectedly. I guessed it musta had somethin' to do with all those birds dyin'. Although why so many people might be so interested in such a thing, I couldn't fathom.

They were sure makin' my life awful miserable right now, though, and I didn't much appreciate that given my urgent business. I stuck close to Charlotte as we waded through the crowds, aware that she painted the picture of an easy mark even if she weren't, and looked a good one at that with the well-made cut of that cream-colored outfit and the way she carried herself in the saddle.

Least her stallion seemed just as put out by the masses as me; more than once he pinned his ears and bared his teeth at a person who ventured too close, sendin' 'em shyin' away quick. My mule and Holt's gelding, on the other hand, could have cared less about the press of bodies. They shouldered on through like the people weren't nothin' more than long grass.

"How in the hell we supposed to find that doctor of yers in this mess?" Holt called back to me, twistin' in his saddle. He was currently leadin' the way through this nightmarish fray.

I shrugged, scowlin' heavily. "How in the fuck should I know?" Then I winced, rememberin' Charlotte was right beside me. Mama woulda slapped me good fer swearin' like that in front of a lady. But I guess she weren't around no more. And I guess Sally had been right about me. Sometimes—most times—it was all too easy to forget my manners, given the company I most often kept these days.

I raked my gaze across the building fronts along Main Street. We'd about reached the center of town now, and it was near noon. Periodic clouds scudded across the sun, sendin' periodic shadows over all of us below, but they did little to relieve the muggy heat of midday.

It weren't nearly as hot as the desert, but I'd forgot how swampy the air got around here. Like it was tryin' to drown you just by breathin'. My shirt stuck against my skin, and sweat pooled beneath my hat rim and dripped down my temples.

My eyes stopped on the nearest saloon. I weren't sure if Dr. Balogh was the kinda man to frequent a saloon, but then, there weren't many types of men who didn't, and anyway, the saloons were always the best place to get information no matter where you went.

Whiskey loosened lips, and barkeeps tended to hear a whole lot, whether they were meant to or not.

"Start with a saloon," I yelled back at Holt.

He swiveled in his saddle, takin' in the street like I had just done. "Which one?"

"Just pick one!"

"All right." He shrugged and pulled his gelding left, aimin' fer the closest establishment, a place called Ace in the Hole.

I hoped it'd be my Ace in the Hole, all right.

It was as packed as any other place along Main

Street, with all its hitchin' rails in front full up. We milled about there fer a space, tryin' to find a place to fit our mounts, and shoutin' from out front of the store next door drew my attention.

There was a lot of shoutin' goin' on up and down the street, of course, and most of it had blended into just noise. But this particular shoutin' was different. First off, it sounded awful distressed. And secondly, it included a woman's voice.

I pulled Joe to a halt and switched my gaze from lookin' fer a hitchin' rail to lookin' at the little knot of people who seemed to be havin' a disagreement. There were three men, all rough-lookin' and obviously drunk, and they surrounded a small family. The husband had his hands up, tryin' to dissuade the other three gentlemen from violence, but his lip was already bloodied. The wife clutched two small children to her; one in her arms and one clingin' to her skirts.

Passersby had given them some space, wary of the situation, yet scurryin' on by with hardly a second glance. No one wanted to get involved.

I didn't blame 'em. That was usually my rule, too.

Usually.

I swung down off Joe and went straight in their direction.

"Van…" Holt started from behind me, but he didn't try too awful hard. His protests turned into swearin', and then in my peripheral vision I saw him dismount and head after me.

In all my years of ridin' with Holt, I'd had one rule. We never bothered families.

Couldn't very well abide others botherin' families, neither.

So I walked right up to those rough-lookin' men and flicked back my duster to rest my hands light and casual on my gun grips. The worn, familiar one of my own on my left and the worn, strange one of Duster's on my right. "Afternoon, gentlemen," I announced loudly. When they all turned to face me in surprise, I tipped my hat to the woman. "Ma'am." Then I switched my gaze to the nearest ruffian. "There some kinda problem here?"

He sneered at me, and I couldn't help but notice his two friends step closer.

I also noticed, to my great dismay, that Charlotte had followed Holt in followin' me. She came to stand to my left, and the glare she fixed on those three men made me think of the night she'd burned off Baron Whittaker's balls.

Almost without thinkin' I raised my left arm, as if holdin' her off, like she might whip out that sixgun on her hip and gun down all three of 'em right then.

Well. I had no doubt she was at least entertainin' that idea. I was entertainin' that idea myself. But we couldn't very well do such a thing in the middle of the busy thoroughfare in broad daylight. And I preferred not to do such a thing in front of kids, neither.

"Damn right there's a problem!" the man nearest us snarled. "But I don't see how it's any of yer business … so why don't you just move on along?"

I shook my head. "'Fraid I can't do that."

He straightened, though he swayed in place, and squinted at me through watery eyes. "Oh no? You *sure* you wanna get involved in another man's *private* business?" He twitched back his coat, too.

"Now look fellas," the husband spoke up, glancin' between all of us. "There's no need for this. Please. Come on, now."

"He's right," I said to the man starin' me down. "There ain't no need fer this."

"You don't even know what this is about," he snapped back.

"No need. I see you and yer friends harassin' a family—a family with young kids to boot—and I see the lady cryin'," I nodded toward the wife, who had tears streaked down her cheeks, "and I don't got the best manners myself, I admit … but I know that ain't right, no matter what quarrel you mighta got here. So." I shrugged. "You got yer friends and I got mine. But I ain't gonna let you bother this family no more, nor lay another hand on any of 'em. We ain't goin' nowhere. You just decide how you wanna continue this."

A silence stretched between us, and the man I watched glanced from me to Holt to Charlotte, and then to his two friends, then back to the family they'd been hasslin'.

"We're all just trying to make a living here, fellas." The husband tried talkin' sense again, though I guessed that's also what he'd been tryin' to do when he'd got hit in the face. Some men just didn't respond to talkin' sense. "I bought that jackhammer fair and square, Mister. Now Robbie's gone off to get the sheriff … so I figure you got two choices. You can leave it be, go on about your day, and I'm sure more equipment will be arriving in due time and you can get what you need then.

Or you can stay, and we'll talk out this grievance with the sheriff, and you can see which of us the law agrees with. We can see what the sheriff thinks of you and your friends assaulting me and my family for nothing more than being in front of you in line!"

Over to my right, Holt shifted on his feet; shot me a look.

I didn't particularly want to come face-to-face with a strange town's sheriff, neither, nevermind that we hadn't done nothin' wrong here yet.

The nearest drunk's lip twitched at the husband's claim. "You think yer boy'll find the sheriff in any good time in this mess?" He forgot his guns, lifted his arms dramatically as he looked around at all the people flowin' past. Then he threw back his head and guffawed, and his two friends chuckled, too. "Fat chance of that! Whooeee!" He finally stopped laughin' and slapped his knee. "Boy probably got his own self lost by now! By the time he finds his way back here, sheriff or not, we'll have got what we want from you and be long gone, that's fer sure."

"Somebody call for the sheriff?"

We all startled at the nearness of the dusky voice, turned in surprise to see a woman with golden brown skin sittin' astride a tall black horse, and I let my duster fall back quick over my guns at the sight of the star on her chest.

A boy of about twelve or so sat behind her, arms wrapped around her waist.

Must have been Robbie. So he'd found the sheriff in this mess, after all. He reminded me a little of Radley, and my stomach turned at the thought of the Balogh family bein' a part of this mess, too. And at the thought of Dr. Balogh's propensity fer foolish kindness.

Given the current state of this town, the doc and his family had probably already been fleeced fer everythin' they owned.

"Yeah," I said, shakin' off my worries fer the Baloghs and figurin' it best to make it clear real fast I weren't one of the aggressors here. "Seems these gentlemen have some kind of disagreement. And certain parties," I glared at the nearest drunkard, "seemed like they were near to violence."

"They attacked my pa," the boy said sullenly from behind the sheriff.

"That so?" She fixed a deadly glare on the three men surroundin' that family. She was alone, didn't have no deputies with her as back-up, but there was a mean-looking sawed-off strapped to her thigh and she had the look about her of someone who was far past tired of folk causin' trouble.

Their bravado deflated beneath her glower, but their leader tried to splutter one last excuse. "This greedy little dirt-grubbin' maggot bought the last jackhammer! And we *need* that equipment fer our prospectin' venture!"

"I told you," the husband snapped, "it's first-come, first served! That's how a queue works! Ain't you ever bought anything honest from a store before? Good God, man!"

The drunk straightened his shoulders and growled. "You callin' me a thief ya no good—"

"Enough!" the sheriff barked. She pulled her sawed-off free of its holster and reined her horse right into the middle of our little group, so that we all had to step back some. But to my relief, her ire was still focused on those other three gentlemen, instead of on me and mine. "Look here, fellas. I am sick and tired of this petty bickering. And my jail is full-up. So in the interest of efficiency and my well of patience currently running bone-dry, I'll give you till the count of three to get out of my sight or I'm gonna put all three of you in the ground. No jail-time, no trial, no noose, just dead. You understand?"

"But—"

"One."

The fella's two friends skedaddled like quail startled from a bush, disappearin' into the passin' crowd without even a backward glance fer their stalwart leader.

"But he's the one who—"

"Two." She pulled back her twin hammers.

The man spat curses and back-pedaled quick. Never seen a man move so fast, in fact. "Yer just lucky I respect the law, Mister!" he yelled back over his shoulder, glarin' at the husband. Then he cast his mean eyes toward me. "And you! Keep meddlin' in other people's business and just see where you end up!"

"Three," the sheriff said. She leveled her gun at him, though he must have known same as me she weren't gonna take a shot with him so near to so many other folk now.

Still, it had the desired effect. He made a little squeak of alarm and dodged into the general public after his friends, disappearin' quick from sight, all right. The rest of us watched after him fer a good long minute anyway … to be sure he weren't gonna change his mind and come back shootin'.

When that didn't happen, the sheriff hissed a sigh and holstered her weapon. Then she turned in her saddle to help the boy Robbie slide down off her horse.

"You done good, son," the man said, touslin' the boy's hair. He looked up to the sheriff. "Thank you for coming. I know you must be busy," he glanced around at the swarmin' streets, "but we wouldn't have asked after you if I hadn't truly feared for the safety of my family."

"Mmmhmm." She adjusted her hat atop a thick mane of glossy black spirals. "You got a permit for that equipment, then?"

The man shifted on his feet, glanced to his wife. "Well … we were going that way to obtain one when we were confronted by those lowlifes."

The sheriff nodded. "Uh-huh. See that you get one before you operate that jackhammer. This ain't a free-for-all, despite what it looks like."

"Yes, ma'am. Of course, ma'am."

I started to back away from 'em, myself. Now that the threat had passed, we had no more business here. And I woulda preferred not to draw the notice of—

"And you."

I froze, goin' rigid. Blackbird's sheriff stared down at me from atop her horse. Holt sent me a cuttin' glare; Charlotte seemed completely at ease. But of course she did. She didn't have wanted posters of her face up all over the Territories. And she hadn't been facin' the noose just near on two weeks ago, neither. I swallowed, but tipped my hat to the lawwoman. "Sheriff."

She passed a hard gaze between all of us. "Fancy yourselves some kinda guardian angels, do you?"

Well, that was better than her accusin' us of bein' murderers and thieves. But I shifted on my feet regardless under her scrutiny and shrugged. "Just don't like seein' small men pickin' on families, is all."

"We didn't mean to over-step, Sheriff," Charlotte offered. "But I'm sure your resources are stretched thin. We couldn't just walk on by and let that family get robbed."

The sheriff arched one eyebrow and looked out over Main Street. "And yet hundreds of other folk could have," she commented. She heaved another sigh and then swung down off her horse, wavin' a farewell to the family as they went on about their business before turnin' back to us and askin' abruptly, "How would you three feel about being deputized?"

"Er…"

It was absolutely the last thing I thought I'd ever be asked, and I hadn't the faintest idea how to answer. I looked to Holt, but he only stood slack-jawed and wide-eyed, gapin' at the woman. Charlotte, too, seemed surprised, but she held her composure a lot better than Holt. When my eyes met hers, she shrugged.

"I…" I tried to think of somethin' to say. Acceptin' might put us in this sheriff's good graces. Might offer us some kind of protection from other law around these parts. But it also might put us in greater contact with other law around these parts, and I weren't keen fer greater contact with any law in any context, as a rule. Not to mention we hadn't come here to help keep law and order … we'd come here to find Dr. Balogh and maybe some Old World ruins. "We, uh … well we…"

"Congratulations, then," the sheriff said, slappin' me on the shoulder right above that bullet wound so I grimaced. She extended her hand and I took it, still feelin' numb as she shook mine heartily enough to jar my teeth together. "Sheriff Madeleine Reeves. Welcome to Blackbird. Pleased to meet you. Don't got any stars for you, I'm afraid. Fresh outta those. But I'll have some paperwork drawn up for you to keep on your person. For proof, should anyone doubt your claims."

"Uh…" She let go my hand and shook Charlotte's next, just as enthusiastically, and then Holt's, too. The old man looked like he'd got gut-shot, still speechless.

"Anyway. Let me buy you a drink. Come on now." She caught up her horse's reins and led him toward the Ace in the Hole saloon.

Charlotte, Holt and I gathered up our wayward mounts just the same and followed after her wordlessly, and she led us around the back of the joint where things were mildly less crowded. We found a stack of lumber there suitable fer keepin' horses put, looped reins over boards, and headed fer the saloon's rear door.

I glanced back at Charlotte's stallion as we went. "You sure he'll behave himself out here alone?"

She rolled her eyes. "Of course he will."

"You sure this is such a great idea?" Holt muttered at my other side, and he sent an almost imperceptible nod toward Sheriff Madeleine Reeves.

I shook my head, keepin' my voice low. "No. No I am not. But maybe she can answer some of our questions."

And hopefully she won't be askin' too many of her own...

BONES IN BLACKBIRD

We found ourselves crowded at the end of a crowded oaken bar, in the midst of a crowded Ace in the Hole saloon. It was rowdy and loud, and there were three men behind the bar servin' up drinks, but they could still hardly keep up.

One of 'em glanced at us four as we wedged ourselves into a space, a space that grew bigger as some of the fellas at the bar saw the sheriff's star and made room … or just plain took their leave. The barkeep who had spotted us did a double-take at the star, himself, then came our way.

He was a small, slight fella with greased hair and a thin moustache, and he looked as haggard and weary as the sheriff herself. He shook his head. "Sorry, Sheriff. Well's about run dry around here."

She shrugged. "Just give us a round of whatever you've got left."

He pursed his lips. "You sure? All I got is the … er, well … the 'shine, but not the good stuff. Afraid it's better for lightin' fires than drinkin'. Can't promise it won't make you blind."

"Don't much care at this point, Eaton."

"All right, then." He slid us four shot glasses and pulled a grimy stoneware shoulder jug from beneath the bar. He uncorked it, then sloshed some into each glass, nowhere near as graceful about it as Sally had been with that high quality whiskey of hers.

"Just leave the jug," Sheriff Reeves said.

The barkeep hesitated, but then shrugged himself and stuck the cork back in the top of it. He set the whole jug at the sheriff's elbow. "Suit yourself."

"We're celebrating, Eaton," she said, and picked up her glass.

Charlotte, Holt, and I echoed her motion. The smell of the stuff made my eyes water. *God damn.* Weren't exactly lookin' forward to drinkin' it, but I knew better than to refuse it, too.

Eaton leaned on the bartop. "Oh? That so? Watchu celebratin'?"

"More deputies!" Reeves lifted her glass. "These three. Newly appointed." She gestured at us with her drink-free hand. "Deputy ... er..." Her dark brown eyes fixed on me. "Deputy...?"

"Lynd," I blurted. "Van DerLynd."

She dipped her chin in acknowledgement and raised her glass even higher. "Deputy DerLynd ... Deputy...?"

Now she was lookin' at Holt, and he straightened from his slouch on the bar and cleared his throat. "Henry Jones," he said.

I really hoped Charlotte understood what we were doin' here.

When the sheriff looked her way, Charlotte offered a smile and gave her real name ... though at least she said nothin' about Holt and mine's bein' fake.

"Good," Sheriff Reeves said. "All right, then." She turned back to the barkeep Eaton. "Meet Deputy DerLynd, Deputy Jones, and Deputy Harrison. They'll have paperwork by the end of today, but go on and spread the word best you can, would ya?"

"Sure thing, Sheriff."

She turned back to us, holdin' forth her glass. "To your new appointments!" Then she tossed the stuff back.

The three of us raised our glasses, too, and I took a breath and sucked it down myself.

It lit things on fire, all right. All my insides, all at once, burnin' down my throat and up my nose. I coughed despite myself, blinkin' back tears.

Charlotte and Holt didn't fare no better than me, but the sheriff herself hardly seemed fazed. She poured us all another round.

"Congratulations, folks," Eaton said. He was smilin' now under his little moustache. Probably amused by the effects of that swill on us outsiders. But he sobered up soon enough. "It's a noble thing you're doin'. Sheriff needs all the help she can get." He nodded out toward the rowdy floor of his saloon. "As you can probably tell by the current state of this place."

"Is all of this—" Charlotte started, but then she paused to cough and clear her throat, likely still feelin' the effects of that 'shine down her gullet. I know I still was. She took a breath and tried again. "Is all of this because of those birds dying?"

"Something like that," Sheriff Reeves said.

"Mostly," Eaton agreed. "Folk wanna come see it for themselves. Or they think it's some kind of Divine Providence. Or a sign from the Devil. Or they think it's got somethin' to do with the Old World and they've come to seek their fortunes. Or to try and study it."

That made me think of Professor Morton and Her Royal Majesty the Queen of Canada, who'd also been keen on acquirin' that lockbox I'd given over to Nan. I wondered if they'd heard news of this happenstance in Blackbird that far north, and if they had, if the Queen would send another emissary. I hoped not. The professor had left me to die … either from the desert or by the noose … and I didn't want to meet any other folk like him, certainly.

"Had half a mind to throw our newspaper editor in jail," Sheriff Reeves muttered. "That blasted article he wrote—and sent to every other goddamned town on the continent, too, seems like—got everyone all riled up. Brought the whole country to our doorstep, seems like." She threw back her second shot.

I only stared down into mine.

"We can't keep up," Eaton admitted. "I'm fair near outta drink, and food, too. Everywhere else all over town is the same. General store is plum cleaned out, all our equipment's been bought up…"

The sheriff grunted as she poured herself a third shot.

Brave woman.

"I've sent some riders out to Jefferson, to request aid from the Council," she said. "Hoping they can send in the army, maybe, and some wagon-loads of supplies."

"And let's hope we get an answer quick," Eaton added. "Otherwise I don't know what we're gonna do. There ain't enough game left around here to keep feedin' all these people, especially not after the die-off. Folk are already gettin' mean enough with what shortages we got now. Hate to see it get worse."

Charlotte frowned, leanin' over the bar on her elbows.

I kept my eye on the host of other men in this

place, some of whom were leerin' at her from across the room in ways I didn't much like. I turned to stand sideways, facin' Charlotte and the sheriff and Holt, and let my duster fall back again to show that fancy gun on my hip. As much as I woulda liked puttin' 'em in their place right off, we didn't really have time fer all of that. So I hoped us standin' here with the sheriff herself and the reminder of my weapon might be enough to discourage any ideas of untoward behavior.

"Wait," Charlotte was sayin', "what do you mean there's not enough game? Because of over-hunting with all these people in the area? Or … or do you mean other animals died too, besides the birds?"

The barkeep shook his head. "It weren't just the birds, ma'am. Deputy. It was everythin'."

My wanderin' glare snapped back to him at that answer, alarm grippin' my gut.

"*Everything*?" Charlotte repeated.

Eaton nodded gravely. "Everythin'. Birds, deer, rabbits, foxes … even people. Plants and trees fared all right, I suppose, but anythin' else livin' within that place seems to have just dropped dead where they stood. Or flew, as it happened."

Holt whispered somethin' I couldn't hear and sucked down his second shot of 'shine.

Myself, I tried to wet my lips with somethin' other than 'shine and swallowed. "That place? What place, exactly?"

"You didn't read that bastard editor's article, then?" Sheriff Reeves chuckled and grinned at me. "I think you might be the only one on this whole continent!"

I shifted on my feet and shrugged. "Didn't manage to read all of it, no…"

"Well…" Eaton began, and then he leaned an elbow on the bar, too, like he was tellin' us a secret. Though by the sound of it, the location of this strange occurrence weren't secret at all. "The start of it is about an hour's ride out west of town. Far as we can tell, folk and animals all dropped dead in about a three-mile radius, but that's the closest it got to us. Praise be to God and the Mother that's as far as it went."

"And no one knows what caused it?" Charlotte asked. She managed to look deeply disturbed and intensely curious at the same time. I could fair near see her tryin' to work out the puzzle herself, even now, sortin' through information and tryin' to figure where all the pieces fit together. I supposed those books she'd read about this kind of incident hadn't mentioned such details.

And I supposed I only cared about those pieces fittin' together if they led me to some Old World ruins. Or to Dr. Balogh and his family.

"No one knows." The sheriff shook her head. "We thought at first it might be some kind of plague."

"But plagues don't usually stay within an area only a few miles wide," Eaton said.

"And no one else has died since," Sheriff Reeves added. Then she paused, shrugged. "Well. No one's died of *mysterious causes* since."

"What about that area now?" I asked. "People and animals still droppin' dead there?" Much as I loathed the idea … I had a good sense we were gonna need to go there and have a poke around ourselves. And that was gonna prove difficult if somethin' unexplained was still killin' things.

But the barkeep and the sheriff shook their heads in unison.

"Oh no." It was Sheriff Reeves who answered this time. "If only. But no. Place is safe as can be now, it seems. It's been swarmed with all kinds of folk over the last three weeks or so, like Eaton said. Religious pilgrims, those that fancy themselves removers of evil, prospectors, miners, fortune-seekers, academic types of many interests ... you name it, those folk have been there. And aside from them sometimes murdering each other in fits of jealous rage or some kinda disagreement or another ... they've all managed to stay alive."

I frowned heavily at this news and stared back down into my little glass of 'shine. All of this sounded like one big goddamned nightmare. A nightmare I didn't want no part of.

The sheriff heaved a sigh and fixed her gaze on the three of us once more. One corner of her mouth quirked into a wry smile. "So. It seems you've picked a very fine time to visit my very fine town, don't it? Tell me then, if you didn't even read that whole article about the birds ... what business brings *you* here? Come to see the circus in general? Or are you maybe some of those treasure hunters?"

Holt didn't even hear her question, I don't think. He stared past the barkeep's shoulder to the empty shelves behind, lookin' downright pale and unsettled, like maybe he'd seen a ghost. Charlotte furrowed her brow and chewed at her lip and turned her own glass of 'shine around in circles.

Guess that left me to answer, then. I decided to

start with the part of our journey here that would seem the most regular and friendly, and not with the part where I planned to find some Old World ruins for a notorious outlaw. "We're, uh … we're actually just lookin' fer someone. A friend who came up here 'bout a month or so back. Thought we'd join up with him, see how he was gettin' on."

Charlotte looked up to me sharply at that, frownin'.

And a jolt of alarm went through me at realizin' I'd never told her about Dr. Balogh and his family, neither. Here we were usin' fake names and talkin' about a fella she'd never heard mentioned before … and it was too late to clue her in.

I hoped she wouldn't ask no questions that might make Sheriff Reeves suspicious. Hoped she'd keep on playin' along as best she could.

To my relief, the sheriff missed Charlotte's brief puzzled look, too busy quirkin' an eyebrow at me. "Oh yeah? Well good luck finding him in this mess." She tossed a glance over the full interior of the saloon.

"Yeah," I grumbled. "Was gonna start here, actually. In the saloons, I mean. Ask around. He's a doctor … a medical doctor, and a foreigner. Got a thick accent. Name's Balogh."

The sheriff straightened from the bar, and the barkeep Eaton, who'd been driftin' off to see to other customers, stepped back our way quick. "Balogh?" he repeated.

"Yeah. He woulda had a family with him, too. Wife, daughter, son—"

"You friends with that nutter?" Eaton squawked.

I turned to face the bar square at his reaction,

forgettin' all the men I'd been keepin' eyes on fer makin' lewd looks at Charlotte, hope and relief both shootin' through me. "You've seen him?"

Eaton scoffed. "Seen him? Yeah. I'd say. He came through town before all this nonsense began, tryin' to get us all to pick up and move. The whole town! He wanted the whole town abandoned! Ravin' lunatic, is what he is."

"Eaton," the sheriff chided.

"Well it's the truth," the barkeep muttered.

"B-before?" I asked, strugglin' to make sense of this. "He came through *before* the birds all died?"

"Yeah." Eaton pulled the towel off his shoulder and grabbed up a glass from under his bar, wipin' at it furiously like he needed an outlet fer his sudden frustration. "Maybe two weeks before. Came through and told us all to leave. Said it weren't safe."

"Well," Sheriff Reeves put in, "it almost wasn't. That circle of death is sure closer than I'd like, I'll tell you that. Blackbird coulda been nothing more than just a lot of bones, like the rest of the woods..."

Eaton scoffed again, scrubbin' harder at the glass.

"He knew that was going to happen?" Charlotte asked before I could venture the question myself. "Is that why he was telling everyone to leave?"

The sheriff shrugged. "Who knows. He was never very specific about why it wasn't safe here. Which is why no one believed him. I, uh ... well. I locked him up for a night for disturbing the peace. He still didn't settle down, so I told him he and his family needed to leave town by the end of that day or they'd be getting an armed escort to the nearest train station."

I bit back the swell of frustration and the string

of curses that came with it and exhaled a long breath, instead. "So he's … he's gone then?"

The lawwoman nodded. "He is. I'm sorry. He all but got ran out of town."

"And good riddance," Eaton muttered.

"I'm sorry," Sheriff Reeves said again. "But your friend wasn't very popular around here."

"Uh huh." Well. I supposed a part of me was relieved that Dr. Balogh and his family had managed to avoid all the unpleasantness and danger of the current overcrowded nature of Blackbird. But his absence sure did make things more difficult, too. I drummed my fingers against the bartop, tryin' to figure exactly what to do now.

"Did he mention where he might be going?" Charlotte spoke up. She seemed to be playin' along just fine, all right. "When he left town? Or did he talk about any other places he might be interested in, or that were also unsafe?"

"Not that I know of," the sheriff said. "He just seemed awful concerned about this area. Of course, after the … the *incident* … myself and some others went out looking for him. I wanted to ask him some very specific questions at that point, you understand. To see what he'd really known, if anything, about the occurrence before it'd happened. See if maybe he'd even caused it, somehow. But we couldn't find him. Not a trace."

My stomach twisted at this news and I swallowed.

"Heard him and some of our local nutters whisperin' together a time or two," Eaton offered. "Talkin' about the Oracle and those strange Seers."

"The … Oracle?" Charlotte asked. Her gaze suddenly sharpened. "The Natives of this area have old legends that mention such a person ... are they ... are they real?"

Holt muttered somethin' else and reached fer the jug of 'shine, pourin' himself some more.

I watched him through narrowed eyes, but he wouldn't look at me. Only threw back his third shot and then turned away from the bar, amblin' over toward the poker tables. I wanted to yell out after him to get back here, that this weren't no time fer cards, that I didn't like the sound of this no more than he did, but the barkeep Eaton answered Charlotte's question before I could open my mouth and drew my attention back to the conversation at hand.

"Yeah," he was sayin'. "Not sure what those legends might say about an Oracle, but the one we got around here is real enough. Far as flesh and blood goes, anyway. Crazy old coot lives out in the woods. With some other strange folk, too. They ain't exactly a cult ... ain't exactly a religion ... but they ain't exactly normal, either. They don't usually bother no one, though. We leave each other alone for the most part."

"For the most part," Sheriff Reeves agreed. "'Cept for recently. They don't much like all these strangers wrecking their woods. I've tried to keep the prospecting and mining operations under control, but ... well." She waved her hand around at the crowded saloon once more. "Like I said, I don't have the resources to keep up. That's why I've been hiring more deputies wherever I can. Why I just hired you three." She flashed Charlotte and I a brilliant smile, looking happy enough with our appointments that I felt guilty we wouldn't actually be of any help to her.

"Er, right," I muttered. "So Dr. Balogh ... he seemed interested in these strange folk livin' out in the woods?"

Eaton shrugged. "Ain't exactly sure how *interested* he mighta been in them ... but he was talkin' about them a time or two with some other locals, certainly. I do know that. I figured with his nonsensical ravin' he was goin' on about, he'd get along with those crazies just fine."

"But if they all live in the woods," Charlotte said then, "were they killed by the ... the *incident*?"

For that answer the barkeep deferred to the sheriff, lookin' to her with his eyebrows raised in question.

She shook her head again. "Not all of them. Some of them, sure. But most of them, no."

"But if something killed everything in that three-mile radius," Charlotte mused, "then how did they...?"

Sheriff Reeves turned to face Charlotte square, leanin' one elbow on the bar. "Not all of them live within that specific area. And those that do that survived ... well ... they don't much like to talk to outsiders. And frankly, we don't much like to talk to them, neither. I did track a few of them down, sure, after the incident, for questioning, like I wanted to do for your friend. What few I could manage to catch weren't keen on talking. Mostly they just babbled nonsense." She sighed and dropped her gaze down to her glass, contemplating it, seemed like.

I contemplated mine, too, my mind all tangled up with too many things that didn't make no sense.

"Look," the sheriff said, turnin' back toward me, "I don't know what happened to your friend. I do know he left town and took his wagon out into those woods, along the road to the west. Right toward that circle of death. Now, like I said … I didn't find no trace of him or his wagon out there. Never found his body or any of his family's … it's possible he rode on through the area before the incident occurred."

"Or not," Eaton murmured.

The sheriff and I both glared at him and he took a step back, holdin' up his hands.

"There's a lot of ground to cover out there, is all I'm sayin'," he protested.

"Those Seers out there might have seen him pass through," the sheriff continued. "Or the Oracle—" she paused, pursed her lips, sighed, "—*Ms. Dorcas Higgins*—might know something, since the rest of them kinda look to her as their unofficial leader. But if I were you … I'd just let it be. Between those unpredictable woods folk, these greedy new arrivals and maybe even some of Nine-Fingered Nan's men lurking around—"

Charlotte and I looked to each other in alarm at precisely the same time.

"Wait, what?" I blurted.

"Nine-Fingered Nan," Eaton said, driftin' back our way again. "You heard of her, ain't you?"

"Yeah," I managed to strangle out. "Course I've heard of her."

The sheriff gave a nod. "I got word a few weeks ago from a friend down in Bravebank—that's where she's got her base of operations set up for the time being, seems like—and he said he'd heard some of her crew talking about coming up here. Warned me to be ready for trouble. Guess the old outlaw herself saw that blasted article in the papers and took some kind of interest."

My whole body felt numb again. "Yeah," I muttered.

"Course I've had my hands full of trouble anyway ever since the incident itself," Sheriff Reeves went on. "If any of Nan's people *are* here, they haven't announced themselves yet. Or they've just blended in with the rest of the trouble-makers."

"And let's hope it stays that way," Eaton added. "Last thing we need around here is havin' to deal with Nine-Fingered Nan and her outfit."

"Yeah…" I muttered again.

Sheriff Reeves shook her head and picked up her little glass of 'shine, raisin' it in the slow, somber way you did when toastin' to someone's farewell. "Like I said. I'm sorry. But I think your friend and his family are goners."

I watched her down yet another shot of that 'shine and tried to ignore the sick churnin' in my gut at the finality in her words. At the news from her friend, which I was pretty sure meant I might not have been the only one here in Blackbird on Nan's business right now. Tried to ignore the restless urgency crawlin' all over my nerves and makin' it nearly impossible to stand still.

I didn't have time fer this nonsense. Didn't have time to save Dr. Balogh from himself, if he weren't dead already. But then, Nan had only really wanted the location of those ruins, if there were any. And if some folk thought Old World ruins might have caused such an incident of death like Nan had said —nevermind the fact that seemed quite impossible to me—then if there *were* any ruins, they'd probably be somewhere within that circle of death.

We were gonna have to go there, all right. Go and search around those woods and see if any of those eager academics or treasure hunters had found anything yet.

And maybe ask questions of those Seers and that Oracle woman, too. If we could find 'em. And if we could get 'em to talk.

God damnit.

Finally, at long last, I picked up my own second shot of 'shine and tossed it back. I coughed again as it flared down my throat, spread warmth slow through my insides. "Well," I said when I'd recovered myself. "Guess you'd better tell me where I can find this Oracle."

A CRUMB TO FOLLOW

We headed out immediately, as we had no time to spare.

Especially not if we were gonna have to go on some wild goose chase.

I pulled Holt away from his broody observation of, not a poker game as I'd expected, but a woman sittin' at a back table readin' cards fer one fella after another. From the snatches of their conversations I could hear, sounded like they were all wantin' her to tell 'em how fortunate they might be in their recent quest fer treasure.

Fer a second—just a second—I entertained the notion of sittin' down there myself. Maybe the cards could point me in the direction of Dr. Balogh and his family. Or toward some Old World ruins like Nan wanted. Or maybe give me some inklin' of how I was supposed to deal with Nan and free Ethelyn without endin' up dead.

But the line was long. And we didn't have time to wait. And anyway, I weren't even sure if I believed in all that stuff. So instead I only tugged Holt away from his watchin', sent solid glares around to all the men still showin' far too much interest in Charlotte as I ushered her out, and we left Sheriff Reeves to her drink and Eaton the barkeep to his rowdy saloon.

We headed outta town to the west, along the rutted path the sheriff had assured us would lead right into the heart of the area affected by *the incident*. She'd been less sure of the location of any so-called Seers or that so-called Oracle woman, but she'd recounted all the rumors fer us anyway in the hopes they might guide us in the right direction.

My mood had considerably soured in the wake of our discussion with Blackbird's sheriff, bein' as I was becomin' increasingly certain I weren't gonna find what Nan wanted. And if I didn't … well. I needed to get my hands on one of Nan's crew who might know where she was keepin' Ethelyn. I wondered if Sheriff Jennings back in Bravebank might know, even.

He'd refused to discuss Nan's business with me before, sure. And he sure didn't much like me. But after I'd brought Nan that lockbox, and he'd found out she was holdin' my sister, and she'd ordered him to lock me up fer a good long while … well, he'd softened up toward me a bit after that.

And he mighta even been the one to help orchestrate my escape from his jailhouse, too.

Couldn't prove it, necessarily, no. But the circumstances didn't quite add up, otherwise.

Which meant I'd only gotten out with enough time to save Holt because of him.

And if that were the case, I owed him one. Holt and I both did, in fact. If he were now inclined to share with me specifics of Nan's business, I'd be certain to repay him in kind.

If he were still reluctant, though…

I shifted in my saddle, watchin' Joe's long ears swivel in front of me as we moved at a brisk walk beneath the dappled shade of so many trees.

Well, I was runnin' outta time quick, in more

ways than one. And I'd done worse to better men than Sheriff Jennings. I was gonna have to make him talk, one way or another.

Charlotte rode up beside me and cleared her throat, startlin' me from my broodin'. "So. This man we supposedly came up here to find, Dr. Balogh ... I thought at first he was just a ruse you made up to avoid telling Sheriff Reeves our true purpose here, but it seems he's real enough. Does he have some-thing to do with what Nan wants from you, then?"

I sighed. But there weren't no use in not tellin' her about the doc now, I supposed. "In a manner of speakin'. She's got some kinda interest in him, I think. He's the one who ... who, ah, who gave me the metal leg."

Charlotte's eyebrows lifted clear into her hat brim. "And now he's here? In Blackbird? And he came *before* the incident and was telling everyone to leave before anything ever happened? That can't be a coincidence..."

I shrugged. "I mean, it *could* be..." But I doubted it. Not with the way Nine-Fingered Nan was actin' back at his homestead.

Charlotte shook her head. "If he has the knowl-edge to make a leg like yours, integrate it with a living body ... then he comes up here..." She looked to me suddenly with eyes bright and blazin'. "Maybe these die-offs really *do* have something to do with the Old World..."

I didn't much like that thought, even if it meant I was more likely to find what Nan wanted. Neither did I like the thought of the metal currently fused with my bones bein' somethin' Old World, itself...

"We oughta ride on through here, Van," Holt muttered abruptly from behind us. "This place is cursed. Don't like the feel of it."

I rolled my eyes. First Charlotte leapin' into disturbin' theories and now Holt with his incessant suspicion. But in truth, it were high past time fer him to start complainin' about somethin', so I supposed I shoulda expected it. Couldn't believe we'd got this far without his grumblin', really. "We'll ride wherever those ruins might be, Holt," I said. "If we ride on through, then we ride on through. If we don't … well then we don't."

He scowled somethin' under his breath. Probably callin' me names. Things like **bull-headed idiot** and **stubborn sonuvabitch**. But not like he hadn't called me those things plenty of times before. "We oughta go back to Grave Gulch," he finally said loud enough fer me to hear.

I shook my head. "I ain't goin' all the way back to Grave Gulch after we just got here. And not without seein' what's what around here." I turned in my saddle to look back at him. "And anyway, you knew why I was comin' here and you seemed fine with it, then. Why you suddenly so spooked?"

He looked at me steadily from beneath the shade of his hat. Then shrugged. "Birds dyin' off is one thing. *Everything* dyin' off is an entirely different thing. And I never agreed to go lookin' fer that Oracle woman or any of the rest of her flock. Those people ain't right in the head, Van. Don't want nothin' to do with 'em."

"I'm sure there's a perfectly reasonable explanation for what happened here," Charlotte offered.

While I appreciated her calm, given the circumstances, I weren't sure myself if that were true. I couldn't fathom a *perfectly reasonable* reason for every livin' thing within a three-mile radius to suddenly drop dead. But I didn't say that aloud. Didn't want to give Holt any more reason to be suspicious.

And anyway, I was still stuck on the phrasin' of the last thing he'd said. I reined Joe to a halt in the middle of the narrow road and turned him around to face Holt. "Wait. You had dealin's with those Seer folk before?"

He pulled his gelding to a stop, too, but his flat stare at me didn't waver. It was a long time till he answered, though. Long enough I opened my mouth to repeat my question when he finally spoke. "Yeah." It came out hesitant, reluctant. "Long time ago. With yer pa."

I straightened in my saddle. Well that was somethin'. Curiosity and unease both pricked at my insides. I cleared my throat. "And Paul?"

Holt shook his head once. "Nope. Just me and yer pa."

Charlotte brought her stallion around to stand beside my mule again, lookin' between us. She didn't know about my pa. Or that he'd once ridden with Kill 'Em All Paul Johnson. Growin' up in the Republic, she might not have even ever heard of Kill 'Em All Paul.

And I was gonna try to keep it that way fer as long as I could manage.

"Think you can remember where you found 'em?" I asked.

Holt grunted. "Doubt it. Like I said, it was a

long time ago. But even if I did, I wouldn't go there. I'm tellin' you, Van. Those people ain't right."

Frustration at his reluctance welled and I stepped Joe a little closer to his gelding, preparin' to tell him just how I felt about his superstitious nonsense. But I'd only just opened my mouth when a horrific mechanical ruckus erupted from the woods off to my left, and all our horses started, and what birds had come back to this area after escaping death took flight.

"Blazin' Hell!" Holt spat, wrestlin' his gelding back under control. "What is that?!"

Charlotte kept her restless stallion prancin' in circles as he pinned his ears and chomped at his bit, but only shook her head and yelled out, "Sounds like mining equipment."

Minin'.... Good. Maybe they'd found somethin'. Maybe they'd have some answers.

I turned Joe toward the noise, though he was none too happy about it, and spurred him off the road and into the woods.

Holt and Charlotte followed me, though I got the sense the old man, at least, shared the same opinion about this venture as my mule.

We waded through the underbrush fer a ways, climbed a rise littered with large boulders, and then I could see the source of the noise itself.

It was a machine, all right. A big monster of one, lookin' almost like a livin' creature as it squatted over the ground. It had four big legs for support, jointed at intervals to make it adjustable in height, I reckoned, and in the middle of those legs was a round, bulky body. A big drill poked out from the bottom of that body, raisin' steam as it chewed into the rocky ground below it, and a man standin' next to it dumped buckets of water down into the ever-widenin' hole.

He had a wagon fitted with a big water tank, looked kinda like a fire wagon, and harnessed to four horses, and he filled bucket after bucket from the tank to dump down that hole he was drillin'.

It made an awful ruckus, that drill grindin' through all that rock, but I urged Joe up close to the machine anyway until the man realized he had visitors and startled, droppin' the bucket he'd just picked up and dartin' fer the shotgun he had propped up against the wagon wheel.

His machine was so goddamned loud he didn't hear me draw, and he was so intent on reachin' fer his own weapon he didn't *see* me draw, neither. Couldn't even hardly hear the report of Duster's pistol as I fired, but the man saw the bullet splinter a sideboard of his wagon clear enough, and then another pinged into his shotgun and knocked it into the carpet of old leaves coverin' the ground, and he jerked backward with his hands raised.

He turned toward us, eyes frantic, and yelled somethin'.

But I couldn't hear him over all the racket of the drill.

"What?" I belted out myself. I kept the pistol trained on him, but I gestured with my other hand toward my ear, then shook my head and pointed at his machine. "Turn that thing off!"

He nodded. Lifted his hands higher and scrambled over to the thing, then, givin' me one more cautious look, grabbed hold of a lever on the side of it and cranked it downward.

Gradually the drill wound down until it finally stopped, and we were all plunged into a blissful quiet.

I breathed a sigh of relief.

The man by the machine raised his hands again. He was awful thin, his shirt tied around his waist and his dirt-smeared skin slick with sweat. His hair was all matted to his forehead and he looked real, real worried. "What … what do you want?" he blurted. "I ain't worth your time. I ain't got nothing left, understand?"

I glanced to his machine, then to the wagon and its four sturdy horses. "Looks to me like you got a whole lot."

He shook his head. "It ain't mine. None of it. I only operate it. For Mr. Jenkins of the South Pacific Railroad."

I frowned, my gun arm lowerin' some.

"You steal any of his equipment and you'll have to answer to him," the man warned.

"I ain't gonna steal yer stuff. *His* stuff." I holstered my pistol—Duster's pistol—and swung down off Joe. "You runnin' all this yerself?"

He lowered his hands slowly, uncertainly, eyein' me warily as I approached. "Yeah. For now. There were more of us, but…" He shrugged. "We got robbed awhile back. Two of the others got kilt in the tussle. Then three of the others tried to steal from Mr. Jenkins themselves. I stopped one of 'em … the other two ran off. Ain't seen 'em since."

I grunted. Stepped close to the machine and leaned over the lip of the hole to peer down into it.

Then glanced back to him. "You a loyal company man then, Mister?"

He shrugged again. "I dunno. I just know it ain't smart to double-cross Mr. Jenkins. And I'd like to stay alive and get paid. That's all."

"Understandable."

"What do you want?" he repeated. "Look, I'm sorry, but I ain't got nothing to spare. So if you ain't gonna rob me … well then I got work to do. No offense, Mister."

He added that last part hastily, eyes twitchin' down to my guns.

I sighed. "I just got a few questions, is all. You answer 'em fer me right quick and we'll be on our way, no fuss."

His eyes narrowed. "You've already been askin' questions, Mister. You got more questions?"

"Seems I do."

"Yeah? What kinda questions?"

I glanced toward the hole he'd made in the rock again. "You find somethin' down there?"

His narrowed gaze turned hard. "I don't know. Maybe."

"You drillin' through rock fer the fun of it, then?"

He scoffed, shifted impatiently on his feet, sparin' a look over my shoulder at Holt and Charlotte before lookin' back to me. "That's why I'm drilling, Mister. To see if there *might* be something down there. But I ain't sure yet. When I get deeper, then I might be sure."

"But you *suspect* there's somethin' down there? In this particular spot, yeah? That's why yer drillin' here instead of anywhere else?"

He shifted around again restlessly, clearly unhappy with my questions. "Sure. I guess. Look, all I know is Mr. Jenkin's fancy metal detector found something around here somewhere. Could be ore. Could be Old World remnants. Could just be some old rusted parts from a broken down wagon that's rotted away. All I know is I gotta investigate every damn beep of that thing, so that's what I'm doing. All right?"

"But you ain't found anythin' here fer sure?"

"No. Ain't found nothing nowhere yet. Least not anything Mr. Jenkins would want."

"Nothin' Old World?"

He shook his head.

I stared him down fer a good long while, frustration wellin' fresh again at bein' confronted with another dead end. He fidgeted under my glare, so I stepped forward quick, shoved him up against one of the legs of his machine, and drew that fancy pistol to press into his ribs.

He squawked in alarm, hands flyin' up, and I heard Charlotte bark my name from behind me.

Fer a second my anger faltered, but then I remembered what else was at stake here. And it was a lot more than just Charlotte's opinion of what kinda man I was. So I kept my gun jabbed into that man's side and my left hand pushed into his chest, holdin' him up against the machine, and I ignored Holt and Charlotte both. "You wanna stay alive and get paid?" I growled at him.

He swallowed, nodded vigorously.

"Then you better not be lyin' to me. You *sure* you ain't found nothin' Old World around here? Anywhere?"

This time he shook his head vigorously. "No, I ain't found nothin'. I swear!"

"I realize you might think I'd take it from you, if you had somethin', especially given the fact I'm standin' here right now with a gun in yer ribs," I stuck it in a little harder and he winced, "but that ain't what I'm here fer. I'm just tryin' to gather some information, understand?"

"Sure," he blurted. "Sure."

"And I need to be sure you ain't tellin' me no lies. I find the near prospect of dyin' often tends to refresh a person's memory. So?" I pulled my hammer back. "Is it workin'? Anythin' comin' back to you that you mighta previously forgot to mention?"

"No! No, I swear, Mister. I been out here weeks and ain't seen so much as a scrap from the Old World I swear it!"

"Van…" Charlotte tried again.

"How about anyone else?" I asked the man. "You heard of anyone else findin' anything around here?"

He seemed relieved to get the focus off of himself. "T-there was one, I think. Name of Billy Thorn. Heard he found a few trinkets buried and rusted-out … the usual kinda stuff."

My heart leapt. It was a start, anyway. "Where? Where'd he find these things?"

The man shrugged bony shoulders. "Maybe a mile or so further west. B-But Billy … but Billy disappeared. No one knows where he went. You ask me, I think the Seers got him. They've been sabotaging my equipment every chance they get. And his was the only claim I know of that came up with anything remotely valuable. He wouldn't just up and leave it."

I scowled. I surely didn't want no more mysteries added to this whole circumstance, but Mr. Thorn's claim was still the best lead I'd had yet, so I pressed on. "All right, then, Mister. You just give me yer best directions to this Billy Thorn's spot and we'll be on our way."

"You—you sure you wanna go there, Mister? Lotsa people been tryin' to move in on his claim, I heard, but strange stuff keeps happenin' there. Keeps scarin' people off. People keep sayin' that place is haunted. Maybe by Billy himself, if he's dead. Or it's just cursed."

"What kinda strange stuff?" Holt asked abruptly.

The man glanced over at him. "Things going missing. Stuff moving that shouldn't be moving. Fires not burning, whispers in the trees. That kinda thing."

"Uh huh," Holt said. "See, Van, what'd I tell ya?"

I gritted my teeth and leaned a little more weight against the hand I had splayed across the skinny man's chest. "Just tell me where it is, would you?"

He swallowed again. "All—all right, take it easy. You wanna go there, that's your business. I won't stop you."

"*I* ain't goin' there," Holt grumbled.

"Could you also tell us if you've seen a man and his family pass through here?" Charlotte asked. "Would have been a few weeks back. There're foreigners, and they would have had a wagon and two children, a boy and a girl."

Now the man looked toward her, and he frowned. "Missus, I seen a lot of families pass through here, and several of 'em foreigners. You're gonna have to be more specific."

"Name's Balogh," I said, and my heart picked up pace as I waited fer his answer. I hadn't even been thinkin' of the doc and his family, truth be told, too intent on findin' what Nan wanted now that I maybe had a little crumb to follow, and I didn't much like the snake of guilt and shame and self-loathin' that slithered through my gut at that realization. "He's tall and thin, mustached, wears spectacles. His wife's got long brown hair, looks a hardworkin' woman. And his daughter is about my age. His son is maybe ten or twelve. Ring any bells?"

The man frowned. "Not particularly. But like I said, a lot of people come through here. And I don't always see 'em all, you know."

"Sure," I growled. "Well if you do happen to see someone like that come through, tell 'em an old friend is lookin' fer 'em, and to come find me at Billy Thorn's claim."

He blinked. "You planning on staying there awhile?"

"I dunno. Maybe. But that's where he can start, if you see him."

"All right…"

"Now, you were gonna tell me exactly where that claim was, yeah?"

He wet his lips and cleared his throat. "Don't know that I got much of a choice."

"Not if you wanna stay alive in order to keep gettin' paid," I agreed.

He sighed, his chest risin' and fallin' under my hand. "Just remember what I told ya 'bout the curse and all. One of you—all of you—ends up dead, or missing, and I ain't gonna be responsible, you understand?"

My patience was wearin' real, real thin and my next words came out through gritted teeth. "You don't tell me where that place is right now and *you'll* be the one endin' up dead, Mister."

"Okay, *okay*! Fer Chrissakes, I was getting to that…"

He gave us directions, and I warned him if they proved to be faulty I'd be comin' right back to pay him another visit, but he insisted he was tellin' the truth. So I let him go, went back to Joe and mounted up, though I kept my pistol bared and ready, just in case he decided to try and teach me a lesson with his shotgun fer pushin' him around.

But he didn't.

He only stood there next to his machine and glared at all of us.

I gave him a smile and touched the brim of my hat. "Much obliged, Mister. Good luck to you."

He only scowled in answer, so I urged Joe off to the west and scowled myself when the mule nickered to the wagon horses as we passed. But we kept on goin', past the wagon with the water tank, past the big machine with its big drill, and made our way deeper into the woods.

Deeper into that circle of death.

Despite Holt's claim he weren't gonna go to the place Billy Thorn had disappeared, he trailed along behind me. And Charlotte, too.

Over the noise of all our horses steppin' through underbrush and years' worth of fallen leaves, I could hear him grumblin'.

But Charlotte said nothin'.

I chanced a glance back over my shoulder at the

two of 'em and found 'em both glarin' at me, though I suspected each fer very different reasons.

My own scowl deepened as I turned quick again to the front and set my jaw, then urged Joe onward a little faster. We went at a trot through all those trees, and I did my best to ignore the twin glares of disapproval borin' into my back.

BACK TO DAYLIGHT

We found the spot easily enough, as it was obviously marked by the dark mouth of a cave in one particularly steep hillside. The cave itself was shaded by a large rock shelf juttin' outward from the hill, and the space beneath that shelter had been cleared out pretty good, leavin' a nice, flat, open area.

There were signs of people comin' through all around the clearin', all right: underbrush trampled and broken, mats of half-rotted leaves overturned by the tread of many hooves. Looked like Billy Thorn had left a lot of his things behind, too. He'd fashioned a table out of some rough-cut branches and a chair to go along with it. There were tools strewn out along the top of the table, includin' a magnifyin' glass, but whatever he'd been lookin' at seemed to have disappeared along with him.

His bedroll was set back under the overhang of rock, and the remains of a campfire were there, too. Despite the other fella's claim that fires wouldn't burn here, the logs piled up were blackened. So they'd burned at some point, it seemed.

Charlotte and I walked the horses around the perimeter, takin' in the scene. Holt had stopped a ways back, decidin' that was close enough fer him, and there hadn't been nothin' I could say to convince him to come any closer. So I'd given up.

Let him stay there, then, with his irrational fears. Weren't no matter to me.

But as Charlotte and I slowly circled around that clearin', I noticed the things hangin' in the trees that surrounded it.

Skulls.

Looked like cats, maybe. Bobcats. And foxes or coyotes. Maybe some opossums. And birds … lots of little birds, and some bigger birds, too—hawks and the like. They'd been tied together in groups of two to six with strips of rawhide or dried sinew and hung from the lower branches, and some were decorated with ribbons or beads or feathers.

I wondered who had put them there. The strange forest people called the Seers? Or maybe it had been Billy Thorn himself? Maybe he'd thought doin' such a thing would scare off anyone lookin' to steal from him. Or maybe he'd just gone plum crazy and run off to join those forest people himself, and nothin' ill had befallen him at all.

Well. So many empty eye-sockets starin' down at me from those trees weren't exactly the most pleasant sensation, but the colorful beads and rib-bons that adorned 'em didn't exactly lend the most ominous air to 'em, neither. And anyway, havin' had our camp in Grave Gulch fer so long now, I was mighty used to bein' stared at by the long dead.

Weren't so sure about how Charlotte might feel about all these bones, though.

I glanced to her, but she weren't payin' any atten-tion to 'em. Instead, she maneuvered her stallion toward a younger tree and dismounted, then looped her reins around the trunk.

I weren't sure if she'd even seen the skulls yet. I decided not to mention 'em, fer now.

I followed her motions; dismounted and tied Joe to a tree. Then I trudged over to the clearin' where Charlotte was already pokin' around.

"You didn't have to threaten that poor man," she commented as I joined her.

I scowled and kicked at the campfire's logs, stirrin' up a little cloud of ash. But it had gone cold long ago. "I don't got time to be diplomatic," I growled. "I'm runnin' outta time. Nan don't hear from me soon, she's gonna sell my sister. I need answers … and I need 'em quick."

She was lookin' at me now instead of at Billy Thorn's abandoned claim, but I didn't want to face her just then. Didn't want to see her disapproval … or her pity. So I turned away from her and paced over to the entrance of the cave, searchin' fer any other clues maybe left there.

"What happened?" Charlotte asked. "After I left from Peridot? You'd said you were going to go meet Nine-Fingered Nan with all that money and buy your sister back…"

"Yeah." Anger swelled hot and strong enough to choke off the rest of my words. I paused at the mouth of the cave and stared hard into its pitch blackness, as if it had any answers. As if it could tell me why I'd been such a fuckin' fool.

"But … that didn't happen?"

"No," I spat.

"Something … went wrong?"

She asked it gently, delicately, as if fully aware of how much such a simple question could sting. But sting it did. Still. I scrubbed a hand over my face.

"Yeah." Little over a full week now of travelin' together and I'd managed to avoid explainin' this. But I supposed I couldn't avoid it forever. Not if she was gonna insist on accompanyin' us fer the rest of this venture, especially. "Nan and I were both double-crossed by a traitor in her gang," I managed, though I kept my gaze locked on the impenetrable blackness of the cave. "The deal I'd made before for Ethelyn had never been a deal with Nine-Fingered Nan. Once I figured that out … I did go back to Nan. With all that money. And offered it to her for my sister."

Charlotte's boots sounded on the rock as she stepped closer. "And?"

"And…" I ran a hand over my mouth, careful of the tender spot on my bottom lip where Duster's fist had split it. Felt sharp stubble along my jaw and sighed heavily. "And … Nan upped the price fer my sister. Considerably."

There was a moment of silence. Then Charlotte ventured, "But she didn't murder you."

A snort of a laugh escaped despite myself. "No. No she didn't."

"And she didn't decide to sell *you* off, either."

"Not exactly." Though near enough. She *had* threatened to turn me over to the Whittakers if I failed to bring her that lockbox. I swallowed, curled my left fingers with their bandaged tips loosely into a fist.

Seemed she just kept sendin' me off on errands she was sure would get me killed, instead.

The memory of the old hag's maddenin' smirk as she'd departed the Bravebank jailhouse after orderin' me locked up still haunted my sleep. I'd never wanted to put a bullet into someone as badly as I wanted to put a bullet into Nine-Fingered Nan. And I had a good sense she knew that. Had a good sense she would have liked to see me try. Again.

I wondered if she'd put me down if I did. Or if she'd only keep toyin' with me. Shoot me in the other leg, maybe. Or in the arm. Or perhaps she'd try to take off my trigger finger, too. "She enjoys pullin' my strings too much to kill me, I reckon," I muttered. "Or to sell me off. At least fer now."

"So she sent you here to find something she wants. And then she'll trade you that for your sister?"

"So she says."

"You don't believe her?"

"Not anymore." I moved a little further into the cave, restless with the anger this conversation had stirred up inside. The cooler underground air was a welcome relief from the still, muggy heat of the woods.

"If you don't think she's going to make the trade for your sister, then why try so hard to find the thing she wants?"

I turned to face her with a glare, but mostly only 'cause it was a question I'd been askin' myself since we'd headed out from Grave Gulch. "I need to stall her. Delay her sellin' off Ethelyn. If I can find what she wants, maybe I can bait a trap with it. Somehow." It was the best plan I had so far, despite not bein' much of one.

"And what if you don't find it?"

"Well then…" I weren't sure I should tell Charlotte that part of it. But she was lookin' at me now with such a worried, concerned expression I couldn't bring myself to give her the same answer I'd given Holt. I cleared my throat. "Then I'm gonna lie and tell her I *did* find it. And then hope to God I can find Ethelyn myself before she realizes I played her."

I left out the part where I was gonna bleed Bravebank dry to find Ethelyn if I had to.

"And what about Dr. Balogh?"

I let out a breath and turned away from her again, hooked my thumbs into my belts, and shook my head. "Things would be easier if I could find him, I think. Nan thinks he came up here fer the same thing she wants. She thinks he knows where it is. And maybe he does. Or maybe he did. But maybe he's dead now. In any event, he's gone, one way or another. So I guess he ain't gonna be of any help."

A thread of worry weaseled into my gut at the thought of the doc and his family and what could have possibly happened to 'em, but I refused to dwell on it. I had my own problems to deal with here. Plenty of my own goddamned problems.

"What is it exactly she wants, then?" Charlotte asked, followin' me into the cave.

She studied the walls like I was doin' … but I was only doin' it to look busy. To keep myself from pacin' a hole in the floor, or from goin' back to that fella with the drill to beat more answers out of him.

"She wants ruins," I said. "Old World ruins. She thinks there's some out here, and she wants me to find 'em fer her."

Charlotte laughed abruptly, and the sound bounced back into the cave and then echoed out again.

I turned to face her, surprised at her reaction, and more surprised by the fact her laughin' didn't seem to prick at my simmerin' anger like I woulda expected it to. Instead, it was almost a welcome relief. I'd never heard her laugh like that; full and unrestrained. Never seen her throw back her head and smile like she was doin' now, but it seemed to somehow bring a light into all the darkness I'd been feelin' lately, bright and fleetin', and I wished I could hear her laugh more often.

Preferably about somethin' genuinely funny.

She finally wrestled her amusement under control and shook her head, spreadin' her arms out to the sides. "And just how exactly does she think that's possible? Sometimes it takes teams of professional archeologists a *lifetime* to successfully locate any ruins, or else they're found by regular folk purely by chance!"

I shrugged, nodded. "I suspect she don't think it's possible. At least, not in the timeframe she's given me. Unless I could find the doc. If he really does know where some ruins might be around here like she thinks he does, and I could find him … then maybe it'd be possible. But otherwise…" I trailed off, shiftin' to look down into the depths of the cave's darkness again.

Otherwise, Charlotte was right. The chances of me findin' any ruins that hadn't already been accounted fer weren't good. Weren't good at all.

Charlotte followed my gaze. "Well," she said, steppin' closer, "if that Billy Thorn found anything Old World around here, he almost certainly found it in there."

"Almost certainly," I agreed. Too bad whatever he'd found had vanished along with him. I wondered if he might actually still be down in that cave. Lost, maybe. Or trapped. My stomach turned. Truth be told, I didn't really feel so much inclined to head in there after him. Even if it were the best lead I had on the existence of any ruins, and the best chance I had at findin' anythin' else Old World to entice Nan with into a place where I might have a chance to murder her.

Charlotte took another step closer and put a hand on my arm, then sighed heavily. "Guess we'd better take a look."

"Yeah. Guess we'd better."

Charlotte pulled a bulky, square-shaped box from one of her packs, and it weren't until she flipped a switch on the side of it and a beam of light flared out one end of it that I realized it was some kind of battery powered spotlight.

It was bigger and heavier than I would have ideally liked to have taken explorin' through an unknown underground space, but I surely liked the idea of havin' it to see by a lot more than just my puny matches or a candle.

I hadn't thought to bring a lantern with me. And there weren't none of those left here at Billy's camp, neither.

I pulled a roll of twine I kept in my pack fer tyin' various things and knotted the end of it around the tree closest to the edge of the clearin'. When Charlotte looked to me in question, I explained to her there weren't no way in Hell I was goin' into that cave without a guide-rope to get us back out.

"We don't even know how deep it is," she said.

I shrugged. "It was deep enough fer Billy to find somethin' in, weren't it?"

She thought on that fer a minute, but conceded the point.

Then I made sure I had all my matches in my belt pouch, and all of Charlotte's matches, too, just in case that battery light of hers burned out. And then with me unrollin' the twine behind us, and Charlotte blazin' the way ahead with her spotlight, we made our way carefully into the depths.

The cave was deep, all right.

And we weren't the only ones who'd been along this way recently.

There were boot-prints in the soft silt that had gathered in some of the rock depressions. And moccasin prints. And the prints of unshod people, and plenty of paw-prints, too. Now and then we found a circle of ash where someone had made a fire, the nearby cave walls blackened with soot.

"Stay close," I whispered to Charlotte, and I switched the twine to my left hand so my right could be ready to draw. It was only just occurrin' to me that some of the people who'd come after Billy Thorn's treasure might still be in here.

In answer, Charlotte moved close enough to bump elbows. I noted she was keepin' her right hand free, too. Part of me wanted to draw her even closer than that, put an arm around her shoulders or waist, maybe, but that weren't very practical in the close confines of a cave, and with both of us maybe needin' to pull iron at some point, so I resisted the urge.

We moved onward, explorin' every bit of the

cave we could get to as best we could. The main mouth of it was fairly wide, but it quickly narrowed and split, then opened again into a few smaller chambers linked by small tunnels. When we hit a dead-end we doubled back again, and we found more signs of people and animals prowlin' about even in the deepest parts ... but we didn't find Billy Thorn.

Or anyone else still lurkin' about.

Or any Old World trinkets.

Water dripped slowly off stalactites and the walls glistened in Charlotte's light, and we found some places where it looked like Billy had been excavatin' ... him or someone else, anyway. It was a whole lot more organized than that other fella's blunt drillin', but nothin' of interest had been left behind.

We'd been in here hours, seemed like, and I was almost cold now from my sweat dryin' in the chill air. Frustration tightened my chest and clogged my throat at findin' nothin', *again*, and the rock walls that engulfed us only seemed to pull in closer and closer with every minute that passed.

Felt like I couldn't breathe; my attempts to gulp air sent clouds of vapor curlin' around my head, and I gripped at what remained of my ball of twine in my left hand hard enough to send little flares of pain shockin' up from my bandaged fingers.

I turned on my heel, away from the wall I'd been starin' at—from yet another dead end—from yet more nothin'—and started windin' up the line of twine as I followed it back toward the cave entrance. "Come on," I spat at Charlotte. "There ain't nothin' here."

Her light swayed as she hurried to catch up, but

I kept my pace brisk enough she nearly had to jog to stay next to me. I wanted out of this goddamned place. I'd had enough of its oppressive darkness, its deafenin' silence, its suffocatin' closeness.

"Well…" Charlotte asked from beside me, "what now?"

I shook my head. Stepped around a cluster of stalagmites. "Now I guess I got more questions fer our friend with the drill."

She said nothin' fer a time, and I expected her to suggest I do somethin' else, instead. But after a while she only said, "Maybe you can be more diplomatic this time."

"Maybe." But I had no intention of bein' more diplomatic this time. In fact I had every intention of puttin' the fear of God into the man. Whatever would get him to tell me everything he knew about everyone in these woods, that's what I was gonna do. If I had to interrogate every single person diggin' around in this area to get what I needed, I'd do it.

Maybe I could even use my new status as a deputy to make all my questionin' *official*.

"Maybe you can just tell Nan the ruins are here," Charlotte suggested suddenly. "It seems a reasonable enough place."

"Maybe." I turned sideways to slide through an especially narrow passage, the rock scrapin' at my chest and back fer several feet, and my feelin' of bein' squeezed and suffocated only intensified. I hardly waited fer Charlotte to come through after me with the light before settin' off again, windin' the twine fast as I could, more anxious than ever to get back to daylight.

I wondered if Nan would believe me, if I told

her such a thing. She'd told me once I shoulda known better than to lie to her, when I'd claimed to know nothin' about the bank robbery in Blessing, but I couldn't see how she'd know if I was lyin' or not in this instance.

Wouldn't be no wanted posters out fer me because I'd looked around a cave or asked a few questions of folk. And she was several states and half a Territory away. If I sent her a telegram and told her the ruins were here, would she ask fer some kinda proof? And what kinda proof could she possibly want? What kinda proof could I possibly send her, bein' as we were currently so far removed from each other?

She hadn't mentioned anything about that—about needin' any kinda proof fer anything I found. She'd only said to find the doc, and follow him to the ruins, and then send her that location.

But the doc weren't here no more, and there didn't seem to be no ruins, neither.

Would she expect me to send her a lie? Would she have planned fer that?

Tryin' to account fer all these uncertainties was makin' my head hurt. And tryin' to guess at what Nan might be expectin' or not expectin' from me was near impossible. Any time I'd ever thought I'd had her figured out before, I'd been wrong. And the first time my misjudgment had nearly got me killed.

My left thigh twinged where the metal rod buried into the flesh, like the false leg could tell I was once more lamentin' the loss of my natural one.

I was so involved in my ruminations on what to do about Nine-Fingered Nan and her impossible request of me that I hardly noticed the air gradually warmin', gradually buildin' in humidity. It weren't till Charlotte's light spilled out into the clearin' and splashed against the trunks of so many trees that I realized we'd finally reached the surface again, and we'd been in the cave so long that the sun had already set.

I paused there to close my eyes and draw in a few deep breaths of the open air.

Joe nickered at us.

The night sounds here were nearly overwhelmin'; cicadas and crickets and even the familiar song of some tree frogs singin' a thunderous chorus I hadn't heard since I'd left the plains and trees of the Commune fer the desert of the Territories years ago. Fer a minute I went back to all those summer nights at our ranch in Kansas, when we'd been a family together, worried only about gettin' through the next winter.

Before any of this nightmare had started.

"Van!" Charlotte cried.

My eyes snapped open as she grabbed my arm and I was already pullin', the alarm in her voice sparkin' the instinct without me even havin' to think.

I found a target illuminated by her spotlight, directly in front of us at the edge of the clearin'. But my finger stilled on the trigger as my mind finally registered the multitude of nocked arrows already pointed at us ... as Charlotte swept the light around in a panic, and I realized we were entirely surrounded.

THE DEEPER YOU GO

I lowered my gun slowly at the same time I lifted my other hand, hopin' to show these folks I didn't intend to harm 'em so long as they didn't try to harm us.

Charlotte's light stopped on the figure directly in front of us again, the only one who didn't have a visible weapon, and who was clearly the leader of this outfit. She was an old woman, thick and weathered, her gray hair plaited into two long braids that hung over her shoulders. She had a necklace of bird skulls and wore a cloak of black fur with a standin' collar of black feathers that framed her head.

Despite the fact Charlotte had the spotlight trained square on her, she didn't squint. Her eyes were milky white.

Blind, then.

Except she seemed to be starin' right at us.

"Hey ... hey, now," I croaked, and I slid my pistol back down nice and slow into its holster. A quick glance at the rest of those who surrounded us showed mostly clothes made outta rough-sewn shirts and trousers of cotton or canvas, with some furs and skins here and there. Nearly all their weapons were bows, spears, or knives, but there were more than a few guns, too.

There were several tribes of Natives in this area, sure, and yet these people didn't seem to quite match up with what I knew of those tribes. These musta been some of those forest people Sheriff Reeves had mentioned.

The Seers.

I remembered what the man with the drill had said about 'em sabotagin' his equipment every chance they got and swallowed. Charlotte's hand still gripped at my arm, clutchin' hard enough to almost hurt. But at least she hadn't gone fer her own weapon.

Didn't want these folk to fill us fulla arrows un-necessarily.

"Easy," I urged, and I turned my gaze back to the blind woman. "Easy there. We ain't no fortune-seek-ers, all right? Ain't miners or prospectors … we're just lookin' fer a friend." I didn't think it wise at the moment to tell 'em we were essentially just like everyone else out here tearin' up their woods: ulti-mately, I wanted those Old World ruins, too.

Just fer different reasons than most.

The woman said nothin'. None of 'em did. They hardly even moved. Just stood there and stared at us.

My heart crawled into my throat as the silence stretched, until finally I tried again. "Look … like I said … we're just lookin' fer a friend. If you'll kindly let us pass, let us get to our mounts … we'll just be on our way. Get out of your hair. You'll never even know we were here. How does that sound?"

As if to convince her—as if she could see me—I tossed the ball of twine to the ground. My right hand lifted away from my gun grip. "All right?" I prodded.

Her lips pursed, the first motion she'd made since we'd emerged from the cave only to find her waitin', and I braced myself to maybe have to draw again and go down in a storm of arrows.

But all she said was, "You have a poisoned soul, young man."

I blinked, frowned, and looked around the clearin' like maybe she was talkin' to someone else.

Charlotte's grip on my arm loosened a bit, and she shifted on her feet, tossin' me a confused look.

But I surely didn't have no answers, so I only shrugged.

"Though not as dark as your father's," the woman said, and I snapped my attention back to her quick. "He has paid his price now, I see. It is just as I foretold."

Murmurs of agreement circled through her followers at her statement, but I was still strugglin' to sort out just what exactly she was goin' on about. Her mention of my father had made me think of Pa, of course, and how he'd met his end. My heart pulsed in my ears now as I recalled what Holt had said just earlier today about him and Pa havin' dealings with these Seers before.

She could have known my father, sure, but how could she have known who I was now? Without bein' able to see my face, and without me havin' introduced myself?

That ... that was impossible.

Surely she was only spoutin' nonsense, like Sheriff Reeves had said these people were inclined to do. Makin' generalizations that could possibly apply to a wide variety of folk…

But even still, those milky white eyes were fixed on me like she could see just fine, and I didn't like at all the cold unease that crept across my skin at bein' held under that unwaverin' gaze.

"Your price is still to be determined," she said. "The deeper you go, the steeper the price. Surely your father told you that?"

You reap what you sow, and it's time for the harvest…

So Charles Miller had said … I suddenly felt like I couldn't breathe again.

"Van," Charlotte hissed, "what is she talking about?"

I shook my head, but I couldn't get any words out. She couldn't know who I was … she couldn't even *see*…

"You have a great darkness ahead of you," the old woman said, "and a poisoned soul may not survive it. You should look to yourself before you lose yourself. If that darkness swallows you…" She shook her head slowly, gravely. "You will not return from it."

"What does that mean?" Charlotte finally demanded, steppin' forward.

It was my turn to grab her arm now, as the rows of bows on either side of us lifted, the arrows drawn back a little further.

The old woman turned her clouded gaze to Charlotte. "It is only a warning," she said simply. "A favor to a loving father who realized he had lost his way too late."

My throat and the backs of my eyes burned with an unexpected rage toward this strange and cryptic woman … or maybe … maybe the rage was fer my pa, who hadn't seen fit to tell his family of his former life … who hadn't bothered to warn us what his past might bring down on all the rest of us … who'd seemed to willingly welcome death that night, who had maybe even given himself over without a fight to a fate prescribed long before by a blind woman who liked to babble nonsense.

"Enough," I rasped, and it was all I could do to keep that rage in check. I struggled to even out my tone, but I did nothin' to hide the glare I bored into the side of that old woman's face. "Enough of this. I don't know what yer goin' on about, but all we want is to be movin' on, understand? If you'll just let us retrieve our mounts—"

"I know what you seek, Van Delano," she said sharply, and her use of my name sent me rockin' back a step.

I swallowed all the rest of what I was gonna say, the rage abruptly doused by a shock of alarm. *How?* How could she have possibly—

"I have seen your role in the Great Awakening, and I know you walk with one of the Old Ones, else I would rid our woods of your poison right now. You have not come here seeking atonement or forgiveness as your father once did … you have come here only seeking to destroy, and that is something we cannot abide."

"I—I didn't come to destroy nothin'," I protested. So at least she weren't right about *every-thing.* "I told you, we only came to find—"

"You cannot lie to me, Van Delano. As I said, I know what you seek here. And you will not find it without first being Judged."

"Sounds like yer doin' plenty of judgin' already," I growled. I'd been about to say we were only lookin' fer Dr. Balogh. Which weren't exactly the whole truth, but it *was* partially the truth. And anyway, the fact I hadn't come here to destroy nothin' was the full truth, no matter what this crazy old woman thought.

"I do not Judge," she said. "Only the Guardians Judge." She lifted her hands abruptly, palms upward, and flames blazed to life at the remains of Billy's campfire.

Charlotte yelped in surprise and I spat a curse as I pulled her around behind me, and we both staggered backward away from the heat and the brightness now radiatin' from the center of the clearin'.

The old woman stepped forward, closer to the fire. The orange glow of it lit up her heavily wrinkled features, glowed against the whites of her eyes, shone against her collar of black feathers.

I searched frantically around the circle of her followers, tryin' to see if there was a place we could barrel through, tryin' to calculate if we could shoot our way out of this without also goin' down ourselves, but they were clustered in tight and all watchin' us real, real close.

The old woman stepped closer, and Charlotte and I stepped backward again.

"Van…" Charlotte whispered. She was lookin' over her shoulder.

I could hardly hear her over the rushin' in my ears, the poundin' of my own heart against my ribs, but I followed her terrified gaze and found more of those Seers had moved in around behind us to cut off access to the cave, so that our backs were already almost up against the points of their arrows.

Charlotte's spotlight flickered, then went dark.

The fire in the middle roared high, high enough to illuminate some of the trees around us, and those skulls hangin' from the branches caught my eye again. I swear they'd been facin' the other way when we'd rode in … I swear they had … but now they were all facin' toward us, starin' down at us with those empty eye sockets.

Fuckin' hell. We should have listened to Holt.

We never should have come here.

I wondered if he had any idea what was happenin' over here, or if he was sound asleep already. I wondered if he *did* have some inklin' that we were in trouble, if he'd bother to help us out, considerin' the situation.

I wondered if there was really anything he could do to aid us, anyway, as one man against all these armed folk.

As one man against … against whatever this woman was.

I cursed myself fer not listenin' to him, fer so easily passin' off his worries, and then I forced myself to step forward again, toward the fire. It was nearly the size of a full-on bonfire now, unnaturally large fer the few logs that fed it … but the heat it gave off felt natural enough, searin' my skin as I faced off across from the old woman.

"Van?" Charlotte hissed from behind me. "What are you doing?"

My instincts screamed at me to run, but we had nowhere to run to. The only thing left to do here was face her, so I held my ground despite the fear that pulsed through my blood, despite my heart tryin' to choke me as I spoke. "All right," I said, slow and even. "Fine. You wanna judge me, you go ahead and judge me. But why don't you just let her go?" I pointed back at Charlotte. "She ain't got nothin' to do with this. She only came along to help outta the goodness of her heart … you say I'm the one with a poisoned soul, huh? Well then she's the opposite of that. She don't need any judgin' … why don't you just let her go on her way?"

Charlotte stepped up next to me quick. "You want to judge him, you can judge me, too."

Goddamnit. I turned a glare on her. "Charlotte—"

"We've all got poisoned souls, lady," Charlotte said, completely ignorin' my protests. "Maybe some worse than others, sure, but we've all got something we don't like inside ourselves, things we've done we'd rather forget … even you, I'm willing to bet. So why don't you drop this pretentious façade and let's all just go our separate ways, no hard feelings."

The blind old woman turned her sightless eyes to Charlotte. "You are lost, girl. Decide what you want and find your own path. Following does not become you."

Before Charlotte or I could make any sense of that, one of the woman's gnarled hands tucked into a fold of her buckskin tunic and emerged clutchin' somethin'. "I do not Judge," she said again. "Only the Guardians Judge." She threw whatever she was holdin' into the fire and a great column of smoke billowed up and outward almost immediately, obscurin' her from my view.

I reeled backward as it clouded around me and coughed. It was potent, whatever it was; it stung my eyes and my throat and I tried not to breathe it in, pullin' my bandana up over my nose and mouth. I turned to Charlotte to make sure she'd done the same thing, but I could hardly see her through the dark, swirlin' haze. She'd dropped her bulky spotlight, now useless, and her hands were up by her mouth.

I thought I could make out her scarf pressed up over her nose; tried to move closer to see better, but I couldn't seem to walk a straight line. The ground felt like it was rockin'. Swayin' like I mighta been aboard a boat instead of on solid land. I stumbled, tripped, and hit my knees.

My eyes watered, vision blurrin'.

I heard the old woman dronin' on, her voice washin' over me warped and muffled. Sounded like I was underwater. Felt like I was underwater. Felt like I was swimmin' through a thick, soupy murk.

"Only the Enlightened may enter the Temple," she said.

Or, I thought that's what she said. It was hard to be sure. Hard to understand her, and even harder to make sense outta her ramblin'.

"If the Guardians judge you worthy, if you are Cleansed, you may gain what you seek. If the Guardians deem you unfit, as they did Mr. Thorn before you ... you shall be cast into Exile, and wander lost in the In-Between until you perish."

The ... the what? I was gettin' real tired of her nonsense. I lurched to my feet and stumbled toward her. My vision had gone all wobbly and bright, all the colors somehow more vivid and pulsin' in time with my heart. A chant had started from somewhere, surroundin' me and strangely soothin' ... like some kinda lullaby.

I couldn't see all those people with their arrows anymore.

All I saw now was the fire and the little sparks of

its embers, floatin' around me like fireflies. And the woman. The old blind woman who must of have been the Oracle. She stood facin' me and spread her wings.

Wings?

I stopped my advance toward her. Swayed in place, hardly able to keep my feet, and stared at her.

She had wings, all right. Great big black ones instead of arms, and now she had the head of a crow, too. She looked right at me with her beady crow eyes, no longer blind.

"*You stink of death, Van Delano,*" the crow hissed. "*You smell of murder.*"

The big black wings stretched, folded toward me, and I yelled out as they engulfed me, plunging me into darkness. I tried to fight my way out of them, tried to push 'em off, claw 'em away, but my hands found nothin' to grab onto.

I groped fer my gun—Duster's gun—pulled it. I could hardly lift it. It felt like a stone … heavy and unwieldy, clumsy in my grip. It was wet. Confused, I glanced down and found it covered in blood.

I dropped it quick, but the blood was already all over my hand … both hands. And as I gawked down at 'em, tryin' to figure where all that blood had come from, a little circle of red appeared on my shirt, right over my heart. I watched with detached fascination as the circle grew gradually bigger, until the blood soaked my shirtfront. I touched it gingerly, but there was no pain.

At first.

The darkness that enveloped me flashed into a brilliant light, so bright and hot I cried out and threw my arm up over my face, staggerin' away from it.

It … it was our house. In Kansas. Burnin'. Burnin' like it had that night those men had come fer Pa, and Mama had begged me to take Ethelyn and run. Hide. And I had, I'd done it fer her, and they'd murdered her, too. By the time I'd got back, it was too late.

The pain hit then, comin' with the wave of grief like a sledgehammer to my chest. I choked, gasped, hit my hands and knees in the dirt. Clutched at my blood-soaked shirt.

A shape darted in front of me. A shadow across the intense light of the blazin' fire.

Through my swimmin' vision, I saw it make a beeline fer the small stretch of trees clustered at the back of our family's acreage.

Ethelyn. I knew it was her. Knew it in my bones.

I had to follow her … had to go after her. Had to find her *now*. If I let her go now, I'd lose her forever.

So I shoved back to my feet, grittin' my teeth against the hooks of agony that pulled at my ribs with every breath, and followed her. The pain got worse with every step, but somehow I kept goin'. By the time I stumbled beneath the branches of those trees, a vice squeezed at my chest so tight I could hardly draw breath. Black edged my vision, and yet I pushed on.

"Ethelyn," I whispered. "Ethelyn … I'm here. I'm here…"

And then, suddenly and without a sound, she stood in front of me. My ten-year-old sister, with her dark hair disheveled and her jade-colored eyes fulla tears. She glared up at me, lookin' furious.

"Ethelyn…"

I don't know where she'd got the gun, but she pointed it at me now, and it was much too big fer her. She had to hold it with both hands, and it trembled as she tried to hold it steady.

"Ethelyn—"

She shot me.

Fresh pain exploded through my chest. At such close range the force of the bullet punchin' into me sent me sprawlin'. And then I stared up into the branches of cottonwood trees. And I watched spots of black and the sparks of embers float by. And I tasted blood.

Ethelyn came to stand over me. Mama and Pa joined her, and they all stared down at me like I was some stranger.

I opened my mouth, but only blood came out. I couldn't speak. Couldn't breathe. Couldn't even writhe around with the pain shockin' all through me now. My body was heavy and numb.

"What have you done?" Mama whispered.

I couldn't tell if she was talkin' to me fer … well, all the things I'd done since this night, or Ethelyn, fer shootin' her own brother.

"The deeper you go, the steeper the price," Pa said.

I glared at him, twitchin' in my efforts to get up. My fists clenched handfuls of old, wet leaves. I wished I could get the words out. I wished I could tell him I knew the kinda person he'd been now. I knew what he'd done, I knew how deep he'd gone, and he'd gone deeper than any of the rest of us. He had no right to be here now talkin' down at me.

All of this was 'cause of him. He'd started this. He'd started all of this…

"One so stained cannot be Cleansed without consequence."

That was a different voice. It reverberated in my head. I couldn't tell where it was comin' from.

Mama, Pa, and Ethelyn vanished into plumes of black smoke all at once, and my heart jumped at their sudden absence, at havin' 'em yanked away from me yet again. I scrabbled at their last remainin' smoky wisps, but they dissolved away even as I clutched at 'em.

Another voice cried out then. Somewhere far away. Not mine, but one I recognized.

She sounded in trouble.

I rolled onto my side, gaspin' and spittin' blood. Clutched more fistfuls of leaves as I tried to haul myself toward her. "Char—Charlotte?" I'd tried to yell it, but it came out almost soundless. I just didn't have the breath to speak.

Everything had gone dark again. I laid in a vast void of nothin', though I could feel a solid ground beneath me, still smell the sharp, sweet scent of rottin' vegetation. The slow rockin' of the world turned into a sickenin' spinnin', and then I was holdin' onto all those leaves tryin' to anchor myself. Tryin' to make it stop.

But it didn't stop.

It just kept spinnin' and spinnin', faster and faster, pinnin' me flat, until finally, at last, that blackness swept over my mind, too, and I fell into a blissful unawareness.

THE ORACLE

I woke to a chill, a splittin' headache and a sick feelin' in my gut. The nausea lurched up my throat and I rolled quick onto my side to vomit into leaves. Then I groaned and rolled the other way, away from my mess, and tried to blink my blurry vision clear.

There were leaves … a lotta leaves. A whole carpet of 'em. And trees … a lotta trees. With underbrush fillin' up most the space beneath 'em, and the dim light of dawn givin' me just enough light to see by. Birds chirped cheerily, a few flittin' above me from branch to branch.

Birds.

Then I remembered, and I came full awake with a gasp and sat up quick, hands goin' to my chest. It was whole. Unbloodied.

And shirtless.

With a start, I realized I had no clothes on at all. Well, that explained the chill. The days mighta still been warm enough around here, but the nights were quick to cool off. I'd been passed out in the middle of nowhere in this forest buck-naked, and there were strange white markings painted all over my body. And the bandages around the bullet wound in my left bicep and those around my three left fingers were fresh and new. Swearin', I scrubbed at the lines of paint over my left forearm. If I tried hard enough, I could smear it. It weren't permanent, at least, but it was gonna take a good long bath to get rid of it, looked like.

I gave up on the markings and rubbed my hands over my face, tryin' to get my bearings. I didn't recognize where I was. Certainly I weren't near Billy Thorn's claim anymore. A quick look around showed no signs of our horses, or any of my things, or Charlotte. Or Holt.

Shit.

I scrambled up to my feet fer a better vantage point to survey the area and swayed a little. I felt woozy. Weak and stiff. And strange to be standin' there naked with my metal leg in full view again. Maybe there weren't no one here at the moment to see it ... but those Seer folk musta discovered it at some point.

I hadn't drawn these markings myself.

Or ... I didn't think I had. I didn't remember doin' it, anyway. Of course, I didn't remember **them** doin' it, neither. It unnerved me to think they mighta stripped me and painted me and I'd not the faintest idea they'd been doin' it.

I shuddered at the thought. But at least they hadn't strapped me to a table to torture me. And they hadn't sawed off my metal leg fer themselves. They'd only dumped me naked in the middle of nowhere, it seemed. Still not a scenario I was particularly happy with ... but this one I had a chance of rectifyin'. And gettin' outta it shouldn't require the weaponization of my false leg, neither.

I hoped. Especially since I hadn't figured out how I'd done that in the first place.

There was a small creek that snaked through the trees to my right, flowin' around a few more of those big, lichen-covered rocks and fallin' off a little shelf to make a miniature waterfall. Ferns grew in abundance around here, and if it weren't fer my current predicament and the urgency of the errand that had brought me out here in the first place, it mighta been a pretty, peaceful spot.

To my left was another of those steep hills so common in this area, with several rock shelves layered within it draped with grapevines and tangles of wild rose.

The sound of shiftin' leaves and brush to my right jerked my attention that way again and I crouched instinctively, suddenly severely lamentin' my lack of weapons. Or clothes.

I didn't see nothin' there, though. Or no one. Just that creek and those big rocks and all those ferns.

The sound came again, and then around the curve of one of the rocks I caught a glimpse of wavy red hair. My heart jumped. "Charlotte!"

There was a brief pause, and then her head peeked out over the top of the boulder. Leaves clung to her disheveled hair, and she squinted at me. "Van?"

Belatedly, I remembered my naked state and dropped a hand down to cover myself, duckin' a bit lower behind the cluster of bushes I currently crouched behind. From what I could see of her, she'd been painted with the strange white markings, too, drawn in patterns over her face.

I suspected my face probably looked the same then. "Are you all right?"

She frowned, looked around at the woods same as I had done. "I … I think so. Got a bad headache."

"Yeah. Me too."

"Where are our things?"

"I got no idea."

"Where are we?"

"Don't know that neither."

She sucked in a deep breath and let it out slow, then closed her eyes and rubbed at her temples.

"You sure you're all right?" My right hand absently drifted back to my chest, feelin' at the place Ethelyn's bullet had slammed into me. But the skin was unbroken. And I could breathe just fine now, no pain.

Hallucinations. Damn strong ones, too. So vivid.

Charlotte had had her own, I was sure of it. I'd heard her yellin' just before I'd passed out.

"Yes." She opened her eyes and dropped her hands. "Just a headache. The rest of me seems fine. But I would much prefer to be properly dressed right now, of course. And to have the rest of our things."

Dressed. Sure. That woulda been nice.

I couldn't see any of her except her head above that rock, but I supposed she musta been naked, too, then. I shifted my eyes away from her. Didn't want her to think I was the kinda man who might take advantage of such a situation. "You stay here," I instructed. "I'll go see if I can figure out where we are … see if I can find our things."

"Naked?"

I gave a grunt and shrugged. "Well … what else are we gonna do? We won't get nowhere just waitin' here."

She didn't seem to like this idea none, but she knew I was right. There was nothin' else to be done fer it. We couldn't just sit around and hope our stuff would re-appear. "All … all right," she relented at last. "Just … be careful."

"Yeah. I'll do my best." I supposed at least anyone I might happen to come across wouldn't have nothin' to steal off me. I stood from my crouch and kept my back to Charlotte, aimin' fer some semblance of modesty as propriety might demand, or at least fer as much modesty as could be managed in this situation, and tried to ignore the flush of heat in my neck.

If I were gonna be naked with Charlotte, I woulda preferred it be under much different circumstances. Our ridiculous situation now was just all kinds of awkward and unfortunate.

I faced that steep hill with its rocks and its rose bushes, but I certainly weren't goin' up that with nothin' to protect my skin from those thorns. So I decided to go around, instead.

The dawn had brightened now, makin' directions more clear.

And revealin' more of those skulls hung in the low branches. All starin' down at me in uniform.

I muttered curses and turned my back to 'em, tryin' to focus on a plan instead of on how their sightless gaze made my skin crawl now.

Over the rise was east, and the creek went that way, too. I'd try that way first.

Only I didn't even get to start out before people appeared at the top of the hill, and lined up all down the sides of it. Seers, by the looks of their mismatched clothes, and front and center of 'em, starin' down at me with her unseeing eyes, was that old woman.

I stepped backward with a growl, coverin' myself

with my hands again. "So this is what you do to people? Drug 'em and steal everything they've got?"

She ignored my questions and my scathin' tone. "Give thanks, Van Delano. For you have awoken, and with your mind intact. The Guardians have passed their Judgement. You have been given another chance. Both of you."

Three of her followers stepped forward then, two men and one woman. They came carefully down the rise. The woman carried a stack of clothing, with my hat set on top. One of the men had my boots in one hand and Charlotte's in the other hand. And the second man carried a wooden tray set with food. As he got closer, I saw it was baked fish, eggs, peaches, and carved wooden cups fulla drink.

The woman with our clothes stopped next to me first, but I kept my eyes on the old one at the top of the hill. Only after her younger follower had set some folded garments—and my hat—at my feet and moved on toward Charlotte did I glance down at what she'd left.

I snatched up my hat, stuck it back on my head, and noticed the clothes beneath it were not my clothes. They were the rough-sewn, patchwork type like some of the other Seers wore. I scowled, grabbed the shirt, and shook it at the old woman as if she could see me. "These ain't my clothes. Where did you put *my* clothes?"

"My dear child, you have been Cleansed," she stated flatly. "And your clothes as well. They were burned."

Charlotte's noise of dismay from behind me echoed the twistin' in my own chest. "*B-burned!?*

You can't just—you can't just go around burnin' people's things!"

The man with our boots set mine down next to me, then caught my arm as I made to move forward up the hill. I swung around without even thinkin' and cracked a fist into his jaw, sendin' him staggerin' back.

"Van!" Charlotte blurted.

There were arrows and guns out again and aimed at us in a flash, but the old woman held up a hand and kept 'em from firin' even as I realized maybe that hadn't been the wisest thing to do.

But I held my ground unwaverin', fists clenched as I glared up at her and growled, "Tell yer people to keep their hands off me."

Her lips pressed into a hard line. "Only those clothes you wore during your Judgement were burned. The rest of your possessions are quite safe. They will be here for you when you return."

"Return?" I had so many other questions, so many issues with the things she was sayin', it was hard to decide which to bring up first. I was mostly stuck on the fact I'd had Ethelyn's letter folded up in my shirt's pocket. If that shirt had been burned, then the letter had gone with it. I spluttered fer a minute, angry at the gall of these people and at a loss fer what to do about it.

Angry that they'd subjected Charlotte and I both to their nightmarish so-called Judgement, then stripped us naked and marked us and dumped us out here, wherever this was, and now had burned things that belonged to *us*. *Important* things.

"Nothing important was lost to you," the Oracle said abruptly, once again effectively dampenin' my mountin' anger with her disturbin' ability to read my thoughts. "Items of true value were preserved and placed with the rest of your things. You have lost nothing … but you have gained everything. You have seen what future awaits you upon your current path … and you have been given the chance to choose a different one. A chance sought by many, but offered to very few. Do not waste this opportunity."

The man I'd punched in the face was rubbin' at his jaw with his free hand and glared at me as he made his way toward Charlotte to hand off her shoes. Then he made a wide circle around me on his way back to the others.

I glanced down to the shirt in my hand. The letter … did she mean they'd rescued the letter?

"Now," the old woman continued, as if all of this was perfectly normal, "you will have breakfast. And then, if you wish, you may enter the Temple."

What *Temple*? What the hell was she on about? Grumblin', I shrugged into the provided shirt, buttoned it, and then reached down fer the trousers. Well, they weren't mine, but they were better than goin' around naked. "I don't know nothin' about any temple," I snapped at her. "Like I told you, we were only lookin' fer a friend."

The man with the tray of food reached me just as I'd finished makin' myself decent, and he handed me a plate and a cup.

I had half a mind to throw it right back in his face, and yet there were things about these people— or the old woman, at least—I still didn't quite understand. And there was a part of me that didn't want to risk makin' her too awful angry. Not to mention all those weapons now currently aimed at us.

I weren't entirely sure of what she might be capable of, and I didn't exactly want to find out. So I took the plate and only glared at the man as he scurried off toward Charlotte's rock.

"You were *not* only looking for a friend," the Oracle stated dryly from atop her hill. "You were seeking the Temple. But as it happens, your friend already resides within."

That made me turn back around toward her quick. "What?"

"What temple?" Charlotte asked.

"The Temple of the Old Ones," the woman said. She spread her arms. "It is beneath us even now. Your friend has been chosen as the Messenger. The one who will bring the Great Awakening. He resides within the Temple now, conducting his work."

I twisted to look over my shoulder at Charlotte, to see if maybe she was makin' any sense outta any of this. The heavy frown on her face told me all I needed to know. She'd finished donnin' a pair of borrowed clothes as well now, rough and drab compared to the cream-colored number she'd been wearin' before. She set her plate down on the rock she'd been hidin' behind.

"You will find him there," the Oracle went on. "Perhaps. The Guardians have given you passage for now, but they will be watching. See that you do not squander their trust."

She was makin' my headache worse. "All right, lady, look." I bent to put my plate and cup on the ground, then straightened. "How about you just point us in the direction of our things? And tell us which way it is we started from, so we can get back to our other friend, too. And then we'll just be movin' on, leave you folk to your business."

To my surprise, she smiled.

The three followers of hers who had brought us our things clambered halfway up the rise to one of the rock outcroppings all overgrown and grabbed at the tangle of grapevines and thorn bushes. They hauled the plants to one side to reveal a small, dark hole.

Almost looked like a burrow of some kind.

"Here is what you seek, Van Delano," the Oracle said. "Enter or do not enter, but this will be your only chance. If you turn away now, we will not bring you here again."

What in the fuck did that mean? I stared at the small round hole in the hillside, hardly big enough for me to squeeze through, I reckoned. My chest tightened at just the thought of attemptin' it and I swallowed.

Footsteps through the leaves behind me heralded Charlotte's approach, and she came to stand next to me. "You called it the Temple of the Old Ones. Do you mean *that*," she pointed at the burrow, "leads to an Old World find?"

The woman called the Oracle dropped her arms back to her sides, and her smile broadened. But all she said was, "It leads to what you want, my dear girl."

An Old World find... My breathin' quickened at the thought of maybe actually findin' Old World ruins. Findin' ruins none of those other treasure-hunters had discovered yet. That maybe no one had discovered yet. Except fer these strange forest people, anyway, and I didn't think they had any real good idea of what they'd found.

If that's what this really was.

I had no way to know fer sure. And I still weren't convinced that blind old woman even actually knew what it was I was lookin' fer in the first place, or that she was referrin' to Dr. Balogh specifically when mentionin' my "friend". This could have been some kinda trap. Or another delusion from unstable people … a possibly deadly delusion. They'd get me to wedge myself through that hole and I'd get trapped in some cave till I died a slow death of starvation. Or they'd seal me in that little place under the hill, buried alive, and I'd suffocate.

My mouth went dry, though I tried to wet my lips, anyway.

Charlotte stepped closer, touched her hand to my arm. "That could be it," she whispered. "Old World remnants, under this hill."

"Yeah," I murmured back. "Or our graves."

"Well we have to at least look!" She stepped forward before I could make any argument to the contrary and once again addressed the Oracle. "Seeing as you took our things … would you happen to have any matches on you? Or a torch of some kind? So we may … see our way … to the Temple?"

The old woman gave a nod. "We will provide you with light."

"And my guns," I blurted.

All eyes turned toward me and I shifted on bare feet. Hadn't put my boots back on yet. But I took a step forward then, too. "If I'm gonna go crawlin' around in a dark hole, I'd prefer to have my weapons back. You *do* have 'em, don't you?"

She took a stretch of time to answer, just long enough fer an edge of panic to start creepin' into my thoughts. But then she said, "Yes. Your guns are safe."

"Well good. That's good then." I stuck my hands on my hips … my empty hips … tapped my fingers there restlessly. These borrowed clothes were itchy and a little too big. I wanted my own stuff back. All of it. "I'd like 'em back, then," I repeated, when no one made a move to possibly go and retrieve 'em. "My guns. I'd like 'em back. Before we go into the … er, Temple, and all. Please."

The old woman tilted her chin up and looked down her nose at me. I swear it was like she weren't blind at all. "You may have light. You might have need of that. But you will have no need of weapons in the Temple."

I glared up at her, anger warmin' in my blood again. "I'd like 'em back, anyhow."

"You may have your pistols back … or you may enter the Temple. Not both."

I tensed, glancin' over her row of followers. There were quite a lot of 'em, and they were quite well-armed, themselves. I didn't have much chance of gettin' my way here.

"I'm sure it will be all right," Charlotte said to me. Then she turned to the old woman. "You said you'll return our things to us afterward, yes?"

"Yes," the old woman agreed. "If you return, your possessions will be waiting for you."

"*If?*" I repeated, and I sent Charlotte a pointed look.

She ignored me. I hoped her ignorin' my concerns wouldn't turn out as disastrous as me ignorin' Holt's concerns had.

"Let's just go have a quick look, then." She went toward the hole in the hill.

"Wait, Charlotte…" I started after her, remembered I didn't have any shoes, and went back to pull on my boots real fast. Then went after her again. "We don't know what's in there."

She stopped to turn toward me, and I was struck by the enthusiasm in her expression, the brightness of her deep blue gaze. "Only one way to find out, isn't there?"

"What if it ain't safe?"

"Then I will inform you of such a thing when I get inside."

I blinked at her.

"You stay here," she elaborated. "I'll go have a quick look, then let you know if it's safe or not." She started to turn away again, but I caught her elbow and pulled her back around.

"I ain't lettin' you go in there first!"

She squared her shoulders. "Why ever not?"

"Because…" Because if I let her go in there first, and somethin' happened to her, I'd have yet another face to haunt my nightmares. And those were gettin' awful crowded these days. *Goddamnit.* I looked back to that little hole and my stomach turned. This was not what I'd wanted. Not at all. There had better be Old World *somethin'* through there … or this Oracle woman and her band of lunatics were gonna regret all of this when I got back out.

If I got back out.

"Because that ain't right, that's why," I finally

spat. "I'll … I'll go." I gave Charlotte's arm a squeeze. "Then you can follow me, if it's safe."

Charlotte pursed her lips, but the Oracle spoke before she could.

"As I said, the Temple is safe enough. You will have no need of weapons."

I scoffed. "Yeah, well, you'll excuse me if I don't exactly take yer word fer it, given what you've put us through so far. You said you had some kinda light?"

"Indeed." The woman gestured with one hand, and two of her people came forward, each holding a thick stick bound with strips of green and dry bark and dried grasses on one end.

Wonderful. So we'd be crawlin' through a hole with only a crude torch fer light, then. And no way to find our way back out of whatever we were goin' into. Just wonderful.

"But first," the Oracle said, and she pointed to our abandoned plates. "You will eat."

ONLY NIGHTMARES

I surely didn't wanna eat. I didn't wanna take anything from that old woman or any of her people. Weren't sure what it would do to me, fer one thing. Didn't trust that they wouldn't try to drug me again. And I didn't wanna waste any more time, fer another thing.

Nevermind that my stomach was growlin' somethin' awful at the moment, and doubly so when one of those men went and got my plate and my cup and brought it right to me again.

Charlotte didn't seem keen on takin' the time fer a meal, neither, but as had been the case since we'd first run into this band of forest folk … it didn't seem we had much choice in the matter.

So we both took our food and settled down on whatever seat we could find—myself on a rock and Charlotte on a fallen tree—and we ate quick as we could manage, watchin' each other the whole time.

Not sure what we were watchin' for. Signs of a poison, maybe, or bein' drugged again. Or maybe I was just tryin' to be sure Charlotte didn't finish first and make a beeline fer that hole before I could stop her.

I also didn't like how the Oracle woman and all her followers just stood there and watched us eat. They didn't say a word, hardly even moved, just stood there and watched us.

Made me feel like some kinda exotic animal on display at one of those travelin' circus shows, and it only made me try and eat faster. The food itself weren't too awful, though, and the queasiness in my stomach and weakness in my muscles seemed to fade as I ate. To my surprise, the drink was honey wine instead of water. And that made me think of Holt.

"We got another friend, you know," I said, settin' aside my cup to wipe my hands on my borrowed pants. "Traveled here with him. An older fella. Gray hair and a gray beard. Left him a ways back from that cave you first found us at. You happen to see him anywhere around here?"

The Oracle gave another smile, but this one was tight-lipped. "Yes. We know of your friend."

"Oh good. You might want to ... bring him here. I think he would have an interest in this Temple as well."

The old woman shook her head. "I am afraid not. He has not undergone the Judgement, or the Cleansing."

I regarded her silently fer a minute. "What, you didn't throw stuff into his fire, too?"

She folded her hands into her sleeves. "He does not search for what you search for, Van Delano. He refused to be Judged. And refused to be Cleansed. Therefore, he may not enter the Temple."

I frowned at her, wonderin' how exactly a person could refuse to be judged when that *judgement* entailed her throwin' stuff into a fire unannounced. But all I asked was, "Well where is he then?"

"He is where you left him."

"Does he know you abducted us? Does he know where we are now?"

"He has been made aware you are on your own journey, for now."

That made my frown deepen. I remembered how unsettled he had seemed when we'd first been discussin' these Seers. If he knew they'd gotten ahold of me and Charlotte now … would he even stick around to see what became of us? Or would he give us up fer lost and head outta here … back to Grave Gulch, maybe? Would he bother tryin' to track us down? To save us from these people, should things go sideways once we crawled into that hole?

Of all those scenarios, I figured the first was probably most likely.

But then … I *had* just saved his neck from the noose, quite literally. Maybe he'd feel he owed me more than usual. Maybe that would lend him enough resolve to stand up to these folks. If he caught 'em by surprise, he might have a chance at downin' most of 'em before they could return fire.

But of course, that would depend on him findin' us here in the first place. And bein' that I hadn't the faintest idea of where exactly we were … I weren't sure how possible that might be.

"It's all right," Charlotte said from across the way, and I jolted outta my contemplations. "It will be easier without him, anyway. And faster with just the two of us."

I narrowed my eyes at her. I'd always suspected she didn't have a great likin' fer Holt Haggerty, but I didn't much like her passin' him off so easily, neither.

She set her nearly empty plate aside and stood, and I was quick to follow her actions. I held out a hand and gestured fer one of the torches before she could. "All right. Fine. We'll go in, then. But if we don't come out … if *I* don't come out … and he's still around, would you just tell him…" I stopped, hesitated. Took the torch that was offered and let the guy light it with a match. Well, I couldn't tell these people what I really wanted to say to Holt in that case. So I only sighed. "Just tell him I said thanks. Fer comin' all this way with me."

The Oracle gave a nod.

And then, as I saw Charlotte take the second torch, I moved quick toward that damned hole. The vegetation was pulled back again so I could get to it. But everything in me balked at the notion of goin' in there.

I didn't much like tight places.

And this was the smallest place I'd ever considered crawlin' into, fer sure. I stood there and stared at it while my goddamned heart went all flighty, and my breath came hard and fast, and I kept clenchin' and unclenchin' my free hand.

Charlotte came to stand behind me, and the expectation rollin' off her was nearly a physical thing. Clearly *she* had no qualms about tight places, it seemed.

"Wait here," I told her, though it came out as a croak. I cleared my throat and tried again. "Wait here. And I'll let you know if it's safe once I get through."

"I'll just come after you," she said.

"Then we might both be stuck in there. Just wait fer a space first, all right?"

She rolled her eyes. "All right. Fine. Are you going to go then or not?"

"Yeah," I growled. "Yeah, I'm gonna go." *Goddamnit.* I faced the hole again, inhaled deeply, and lowered down to crawl into it. The smell of earth was nearly overwhelmin', and that fear of bein' buried alive rose up sharp and powerful as I slid my head and shoulders through, holdin' the torch out in front.

I had to belly-crawl, the space was so small. The walls on either side nearly touched my shoulders, the ceilin' scraped against the top of my hat, and I had the thought then that if I *had* had my guns on me, the grips mighta got caught and I might not have been able to fit through here at all.

I kept my eyes on the torch, on the flame itself, used it as a focus point to keep my mind off the tightness in my chest, off the nearly crushin' grip of panic as I slithered deeper and deeper into darkness.

Deeper and deeper underground.

What little light filtered in around me from the openin' I'd left behind suddenly darkened, and for a second I froze, the panic clutchin' like a vice and cuttin' off my air.

But then I heard the sounds of another person shufflin' along the packed dirt, heard Charlotte's periodic grunts as she pulled herself through the cramped space after me, and my breath came out in an explosive exhale. Followed by a string of muttered curses.

"Goddamnit, I told you to wait fer a space!" I hissed. But there weren't nothin' I could do about it now. I couldn't even turn back to look at her.

"I did."

"You did not! I only just started in! Did you even wait till my boots were out of sight?"

"There's no way I'm letting you get out of sight, Mister. No way I'm letting you go into this alone.

Now go on." I felt her hand tap the side of my boot. "Why'd you stop?"

"Go on back out." I knew she wouldn't do it, but I had to try anyway. "I don't want us both trapped in here."

"We're not going to get trapped."

"You don't know that."

"And you don't know that we *will* get trapped, either. Now will you just get a move on, already?" She tapped my boot again.

I ground my teeth, already feelin' plenty trapped. Trapped now between her and the rest of this tunnel, wherever it went. The air was thick and soupy, or at least it felt that way to me, and sweat beaded on my forehead and upper lip. Damp earth pressed into my forearms and my belly. The torch guttered.

I swallowed hard and concentrated all my bein' on movin' forward. Crawled, bit by bit, squashin' the well of terror by allowin' myself to hope this would eventually lead us to some real Old World ruins.

To hope the crazy old Oracle and her followers weren't talkin' complete nonsense, despite what other horrors they'd delivered upon us beforehand.

To hope that it might be exactly what Nine-Fingered Nan wanted, and that it would be the last thing I'd need to free my sister.

The flame at the end of my stick lit only a short way ahead, and all it kept illuminatin' was more tunnel. The dirt eventually gave way to damp rock, the light from the entrance we'd started from gradually fadin'. Until at last there was only darkness around us, and only my flame to lead us.

We were movin' at a downhill slant, though, and just when I thought the mountin' panic in me might shatter my tenuous hold on it, I realized my hat didn't scrape the ceilin' no more. And the walls were a little further away from my shoulders.

The tunnel was gettin' a little wider. Finally. And slantin' downward at a steeper angle.

I inhaled a slow, deep breath. Maybe this really would turn out all right, after all.

Except then my arms and my chest fell away into nothin', and in my flailin' around tryin' to catch myself, I dropped the torch. It fell, spinnin', before clatterin' to hard ground some distance below.

My hands scrabbled at smooth rock, but there weren't nothin' good to hang onto, and my weight had already shifted too far forward to stop myself.

Guess I was goin' in after it.

My stomach lurched as I plummeted, and I tried to tuck and roll mid-air so at least I wouldn't land on my head. It sorta worked.

"Van!"

Charlotte's cry echoed out from above just before I landed hard on my back with a grunt, and everything went black.

The smell of damp earth and stone coupled with the faint aroma of an unfamiliar soap drifted into my consciousness, followed by the sensation of a hand pattin' at my cheek. And somethin' soft under my back, and somethin' ticklin' my forehead. And there was whisperin', too, though I couldn't make out the words.

I mumbled, shifted, lifted my left hand to swipe at the thing ticklin' me.

The whispers turned into words. "You're awake! Oh thank the Mother! Are you all right? Is anything broken?"

That was a good question. I took a minute to think about it. To take note of how the rest of me felt. I moved each limb carefully, experimentally, but all seemed in good workin' order. Even the metal one. My shoulders were a little sore, and my headache was worse again … but aside from that, I seemed more or less whole. "All … all good," I croaked. I'd been winded by the fall; only just now fully regainin' my air.

I pulled my eyes open and stared directly up into Charlotte's face.

She was real close, leanin' over me. The torch's weak glow threw patterns of light and shadow across her features, and the ends of her hair still tickled at my forehead. I realized she'd pulled me halfway up into her lap in her efforts to rouse me. She had one arm around under my head, almost cradlin' me, and her other hand had been the one pattin' my cheek.

"Good," she whispered, smilin' down at me. "Good. You gave me quite a scare there, Mister." She stroked my cheek absently, and I lifted my hand again to sweep aside the curtain of red hair ticklin' my forehead. It was silky in my fist.

I figured I should probably say somethin' then, or maybe make attempts to get up and resume our search for Old World ruins … but I rather liked my current position, in truth.

Alas, the moment came to an abrupt end when Charlotte pushed me off her lap and stood.

Confused and displeased by her sudden departure, I laid there on the cold, hard ground fer another long minute and stared up into blackness.

She went to retrieve my discarded torch and paced a distance to my left.

Well, at least this place was a good deal larger than that tunnel had been, then. Maybe this was where we'd be trapped to die a slow death. I watched her maneuver carefully over uneven ground to study the left-most wall in her torch-light and sighed. Supposed it was some small mercy I wouldn't have to die alone.

She went a few steps to her right and lifted the torch to reveal the rungs of a wooden ladder.

Oh. Well. Maybe we wouldn't have to die down here, after all.

I groaned and rolled over onto my side at last, then pushed myself up sittin'. I scrubbed at my face and groped around fer my hat, which I finally found and put back where it belonged.

"After you discovered this … hole," Charlotte said, "I realized there was a ladder leading down here. It wasn't easy to get onto, of course, given the tight space of that tunnel. But it made for a much more graceful decent than the one you managed."

"Yeah. Imagine that's so." I struggled up to my feet with a wince, sore and with my head still poundin'. "You got that other torch somewhere?"

"Yes. Should be right there next to you. Although I thought it probably best to conserve the fuel. We're not sure how long we'll be down here, after all."

"Right." Smart thinkin'. But I bent down and felt around fer the second torch, anyway. Just so I could have it in-hand as soon as we might need it. I picked it up just as Charlotte made her way back over to me.

"If you're feeling up for it, we should explore this chamber. See if there's anything here, or if there's more to this cavern."

I nodded, then swept out an arm. "Sure. After you. Unless you'd rather I lead?"

She paused to regard me fer a second, eyes sweepin' me over and lips pursed. "Maybe not after that fall you just took. Don't want you dropping down any more holes."

I grumbled as she resumed her walk past the ladder, fell in to step close behind her. "Don't want you droppin' down no holes, neither."

"Trust me, I'm watching for them."

"See that you do."

We followed the perimeter of the chamber we were in, but found only regular rock formations you might find in any cave … and some peculiar piles of rubble. Mostly more rock, but broken up into pieces. A few shaped stones were tossed in here and there, and some heavily rusted iron-work.

Charlotte bent to study the iron pieces, but I didn't bother. They didn't look Old World, and my patience was startin' to wear thin again. How long were we supposed to wander around down here in the dark?

"This don't look like no Temple to me," I growled as Charlotte finally satisfied her curiosity and stood. "Looks like just another cave. Same as all the rest."

She shrugged. "Maybe. But these piles of rock

had to come from somewhere." She lifted our single torch high, peerin' at the walls closest to us, clearly tryin' to illuminate the ceilin', too. But it was too high. "This chamber might not be natural."

"Still don't look like no Temple."

"Well … the Oracle's people might have a different definition than you about what constitutes a Temple."

"Think they might have a different definition than me about a lot of things," I muttered. But then, as Charlotte kept movin' on, I followed once again and said more loudly, "So you agree that blind old woman must be the Oracle?"

I watched the back of Charlotte's head nod, her red hair highlighted by the flickerin' torch light. "Yes. She must be. She fits the sheriff's description of the Oracle well enough."

"Sure. 'Cept the sheriff never said nothin' about the Oracle bein' blind."

"True. But everything else seems to fit. Including her little band of followers."

I snorted. "I wouldn't exactly call it a *little* band of followers…"

"Do you think what she says is true?" Charlotte asked abruptly. She stopped and turned to face me, and I'd been followin' so close I nearly ran into her. I drew up short, looked down into her upturned face with its white-painted designs. "About you?" She put her free hand on my chest. "And me?"

"No." I answered immediately, without hesitation. "I think she's a sick individual who enjoys playin' a part. I think she enjoys scarin' people and prescribin' futures to gullible souls."

Gullible souls like my pa, it seemed.

Charlotte's gaze drifted away from mine, and her fingers on my chest tightened, catchin' a fistful of my borrowed shirt.

The action, simple as it was, stirred thoughts in me I had no business thinkin' right now. I swallowed. Standin' here like this just the two of us, surrounded by darkness and silence, was really not helpin' quiet those sudden thoughts, neither.

"Did you see things last night?" Charlotte asked quietly. "After … after she made that smoke?"

Her eyes came back to my face and I tried to banish all my wanderin' thoughts at once, as if she could see 'em all somehow by lookin' at me. "Yeah," I managed. "I did. You too?"

She nodded. "Bad things," she whispered.

My own nightmares from last night came back to me. So vivid and clear. That bullet goin' into me, right at the place where Charlotte's hand was now. Ethelyn and Mama and Pa, all starin' down at me. Judgin' me.

I cleared my throat and closed a hand around Charlotte's. "Yeah. Me too. But it ain't real, Charlotte." I squeezed her palm. "All of that were only nightmares. Just that old woman tryin' to amplify our fears. Usin' 'em against us to complete the role she likes to play. That's all."

Charlotte was quiet fer another minute, chewin' at her bottom lip. But at last she nodded again, and squeezed my hand in return. "You're right. Of course you're right."

It was nice to hear someone say that now and then.

She released my hand and pulled away, takin' in a deep breath and then lettin' it out in a heavy sigh. "Well. Let's not let her do that to us anymore."

"Oh, I don't plan to." In truth, I was still entertainin' the idea of shootin' the old woman soon as I got my guns back.

"Good. All right. Guess we'd better get back to looking around, huh? Before this torch goes out."

"Probably a good idea."

"Right." She turned around smartly and headed off, and I trailed after her again.

I hoped we'd find somethin' soon. I really needed somethin' to distract me from thinkin' of how much I'd liked wakin' up in her lap earlier, or of how much I already missed the feel of her palm pressed against my chest.

"There's got to be another chamber around here somewhere," Charlotte said. Her words echoed softly back to us from the darkness. "This may not look like your version of a temple … but it also doesn't seem to fit with even a very primitive definition of a temple, either. And it doesn't really look like any of the ruins I saw in—"

She yelped and jumped backwards, crashin' into me.

Instinctively I groped fer guns that weren't there, then scowled and in their absence, brandished my unlit torch like a club.

Charlotte leaned into me, but she held her flame out forward far enough I could just barely make out what had startled her.

My heart wedged into my throat.

People.

Faceless people. Or … some semblance of peo-ple. Two of 'em, standin' at stiff attention to either side of a yawnin' black entrance to another cavern. They were tall, sleek, motionless … and completely made outta metal.

TRESPASSIN'

Fer a good long minute Charlotte and I just stood there starin' at those things.

Then Charlotte moved into a defensive stance, holdin' her torch same as me, ready to swing it at any attackers. And the both of us stood there side-by-side, ready to fight … only nothin' happened.

Those faceless metal people didn't move.

…maybe they were just statues.

Feelin' foolish now, I lowered my torch and tried to slow my racin' heart. Stepped cautiously closer to 'em. Looked 'em over good.

I'd never seen anything like 'em before. Not even in Blessing.

Charlotte approached slowly as well, and held her torch out close to one, sweepin' the light over its unnatural body. They were made of metal plates that had been shaped and polished to resemble the form of a human, and fitted tightly together at the joints. Except where a human face would be, these statues had only another smooth metal plate, oval-shaped.

Both held swords, the tips buried into the ground at their toes and the grips wrapped in their exquisitely crafted metal hands.

Unlike the other iron pieces we'd found earlier … these statues weren't rusted at all. All their metal was still new-lookin', like they'd been oiled and pol-ished on the regular.

I frowned, and my gaze stuck on the nearest one's leg. It looked kinda like my own metal leg. It looked real, real similar, in fact.

I took a step backward, my leg suddenly feelin' awful heavy and sluggish. And it ached, down in the half-bone of my thigh, and the place where metal met flesh ached, too.

"Incredible," Charlotte murmured. She was leanin' real close to one of the metal monuments, her nose almost touchin' it as she squinted at an elbow joint. "The engineering here is incredible. I've never seen anything like it."

"Me neither." I glanced into the utter blackness of the openin' beyond these two metal soldiers and wondered what they might be guardin'. My heart quickened again. I hardly dared hope what I wanted might be through the next stretch of dark.

But then I realized what Charlotte had just said, and I pulled my gaze back to her. "Wait. You ain't seen nothin' like this before? Not even at Whittaker's place? Down in his ruins, I mean?"

She shook her head. "No. They've been mining those Blessing ruins for years … those families don't want anyone to know, but they're about all cleaned out. Not much left there anymore. And certainly nothing even close to this. Certainly nothing in such good condition. I mean look at them! They look newly built, don't they?" She ran her free hand over one smooth, shiny arm.

"Yeah … maybe don't touch them."

Charlotte tossed me a look that was both skeptical and disapprovin' at the same time. "Oh come on, now. Touching them won't hurt anything. Do you *know* how much Old World stuff I've touched?

Even smuggled out a few tiny pieces from Whittaker, when I could manage. It can look scary sometimes ... but in the end, it's all just a heap of old metal."

A sick feelin' squirmed in my gut, memories of those little metal bugs down in Charles Miller's dungeon flashin' through my mind. And that electrical rod of his that bit so much worse than any hotshot. And ... and my leg ... transformed into so many blades...

I cleared my throat. "Uh huh." I figured she didn't know about any of that stuff. Baron Whittaker surely wouldn't have shared the truth about such discoveries with his slaves. I stepped forward quick and grabbed her wrist, pullin' her hand away from the thing.

She whipped a glare at me, but I held tight even as she tried to yank away from my grip.

"Please, Charlotte. Trust me on this."

Somethin' in my voice musta convinced her, 'cause she stopped tryin' to twist her arm free. But her glare remained hard and bright.

"I've had ... experiences," I told her. "Where they weren't just heaps of old metal, after all. Some of those scars you saw earlier ... they weren't made by bullets."

Her glare softened at that, but her eyes narrowed, too. I could fair near *see* all the questions crowdin' her features.

So I let go of her wrist before she could ask any of 'em and turned to study the sword in the hands of the right-most statue.

"All right," she said softly. "Fine. No touching. I'd just like to know when and where you had your *experiences* … I didn't think you were very familiar with Old World artifacts?"

"I ain't," I admitted. "Only had a few run-ins with the stuff. But none of those run-ins have been particularly pleasant. Let's just leave it at that fer now."

She made a noise like that answer weren't satisfactory at all, but I occupied myself with tryin' to work the grip of that sword from delicately jointed metal fingers.

The arrival of more light over my shoulder preceded Charlotte's sharp scoldin'. "Hey. I thought you *just said* we shouldn't be touching these things!"

"I ain't touchin' it." But I was. Though just a little. Just enough to pry the fingers off the sword grip. They moved easier than I'd thought they would. "Just tryin' to get us some kind of real weapon, is all."

"That's still touching it."

"As little as possible," I insisted. "And just to get this sword. I ain't goin' around strokin' the thing like it's a prize thoroughbred!"

Charlotte scoffed. "I was not *stroking* it—"

The sword came free at last. Satisfied, I hefted it in my right hand, keepin' our extra torch in my left. It was quite a bit heavier than I'd anticipated. Difficult to wield in one hand. And probably not all that sharp, given its age and the fact it'd been made fer decoration rather than combat.

Still, it'd be better than a stick, if we ran into any trouble.

"Happy now?" Charlotte asked.

I looked to her, found her glarin' at me again

with her torch in one hand and the other hand fisted on her hip. I nodded. "Yeah."

She sighed. "Good. Let's go, then. See what's through here." She nodded to the near darkness. "And no more *touching*, right?"

"Right."

And so we went, steppin' through the yawnin' mouth of another passageway, this one blessedly wide and open. Charlotte led with her torch held high, and I followed close behind her with the sword at the ready.

We didn't go far before runnin' across more statues, only these seemed more sophisticated than their metal counterparts. They wore clothes, fer one thing. Elaborate costumes the likes of which I'd never seen … not even in travelin' troupes or circuses. Some looked kinda familiar though. Almost resembled those religious sisters I'd seen a time or two. Even had heavy golden crosses danglin' against their breasts. But these had been outfitted with a kind of crown, also made of gold, that framed their head with thin spikes. Almost looked like a sun risin' behind 'em as we passed, or a halo, maybe, Charlotte's torchlight makin' 'em glimmer.

Their heads were bowed, their black-gloved hands folded in somethin' like prayer.

Maybe this really *was* some kind of religious temple…

After those were some dressed in red gowns, embroidered with gold thread and with high, stiff collars. The sisters had had only black cloth beneath their hoods … but these dressed in red were somehow more disturbin'. They still had no faces, only bulbous heads painted in the same red and gold patterns as the rest of 'em. They wore gold gloves, and the ends of their fingers were tipped with golden claws.

And then there were some that I thought at first were more like regular statues, bein' mostly naked men and women in dramatic poses, carved outta smooth white marble. But as we got closer to 'em, I realized they weren't marble, after all. They were porcelain, instead. And they weren't one solid piece like regular statues, neither. Like all the rest we'd passed up till now, they had joints in all the right places. Except the joints of these shone with gold.

And these ... these had faces.

Beautiful faces.

Except the last one. Well, no ... she was still beautiful, in truth, but also terrifyin' in a way that made the hairs on the back of my neck stand up, and I stepped even closer to Charlotte. Three small human skulls had been shaped atop her brow, and two curvin' horns made of more gold rose from her temples. Half of her shinin' porcelain face was missin', revealin' a golden skeleton beneath, and one empty eye socket.

There was sure a lot of gold down here...

I gaped at that last statue as we hurried past, the bright reflection of the torch off porcelain and gold fadin' as we moved away, and the half-demon woman gradually sinkin' back into blackness, until she was entirely lost again from sight.

Then there were no more statues ... just a deep and endless darkness, all around us.

I bumped into Charlotte as she slowed.

"What ... what is this place?" My voice echoed

softly into nothingness. I hadn't really meant to ask that question out loud.

Charlotte shook her head. "Seems like some kind of collection." She whispered it, though we were the only ones in this place, and I was pretty sure the statues didn't care about our conversation. She swept her torch out to either side as far as she could reach, but the only thing we could see in its little circle of light was the rocky floor. "I think we're in another big chamber," she added. "Maybe it's best to proceed forward first? See what's directly ahead? And if it's only a dead end, we'll follow the walls until we make a full exploration of this particular cavern. Agreed?"

"Sure…" I thought I heard somethin' behind us. I turned quick, heart leapin', brandishin' my sword. The sound came again, outta the dark.

Clink. Clink. Clink.

"Charlotte," I breathed. "You hear that?"

She turned to face it, too, stepped up beside me and held the torch forward. "Yes."

Fer a second there was nothin', and I only held my breath and waited. The sword was makin' my arm burn and tremble with the effort of keepin' it aloft, so I dropped our extra torch with a clatter to the ground and gripped it two-handed.

Much better.

Nevermind I hadn't the faintest idea how to use a sword. Except to try and stick the enemy with the pointy end.

Clink. Clink. Clink.

Charlotte and I both sucked in a breath. It was closer now.

There was movement, just at the edge of the torchlight, and Charlotte let out a squeak of alarm.

Myself, I let out a streak of profanity, not carin' a whit whose company I was in.

'Cause the thing makin' that noise, the thing currently walkin' right at us, was that demon-woman statue. She was *movin'*, and she moved as fluid and natural as any flesh-and-blood person, and the profanity kept on comin' outta my mouth even as Charlotte and I hastily backed away from her.

But she kept on comin' at us. Delicate porcelain feet with toes all jointed in gold makin' that *clink, clink, clink* sound against the cave's rock floor as she walked.

"Ch-Charlotte." I finally managed to form a regular word. "You ever seen one of these before?"

She only shook her head stiffly. Struck dumb, I guess. I felt near the same. Thought my heart might burst right on out through my mouth, and the rushin' in my ears now almost drowned the sound of those porcelain feet. I didn't understand what this thing was, or how it was movin' like that, or what it might want from us, or what its purpose here could possibly be.

"*Non intrabis.*"

It ... it *spoke.* The mouth didn't move, but the words had come from it, unmistakably.

Its tone was female, smooth and lyrical, as it repeated the phrase again. "*Non intrabis.*"

The exposed golden half of the statue's skull and those long, curvin' horns shone brighter and brighter in our torchlight as she advanced, faster now, until Charlotte and I could hardly retreat quick enough without trippin' over ourselves or this uneven ground.

"You … you shall not enter," Charlotte blurted suddenly.

I could hardly spare a glance at her as we scrambled backwards. "Huh?"

"That's what it's saying. *Non intrabis.* 'You shall not enter.' It doesn't want us here."

I snorted incredulously. "Oh great. Well it's a little late for that. And anyway … it's blockin' the exit! Maybe you can tell it that?"

"Tibi malevo—"

We did trip, then, both of us, over stuff strewn all over the ground, interruptin' Charlotte's attempts to talk to the thing, and we fell back into a heap of … somethin'.

Parts. It was a heap of parts. Metal plates and springs and rods and gears of all sorts, but I only barely got a look at it before pushin' myself up standin' again and heftin' that sword, readyin' fer a good strong swing.

"Tibi malevolentiam non habemus!" Charlotte shouted, just as the demon-woman statue had pulled back an arm and spread long, golden claws, presumably aimin' a strike at me, herself.

But she paused at Charlotte's words.

Fer a heartbeat there was silence, stillness.

And then I brought that sword down hard, choppin' into the place where the statue's porcelain neck met her porcelain shoulder. The fragile ceramic shattered, pieces flyin', cracks splinterin' all down her chest and shoulder from where the blade had buried.

Sparks lit the gloom, and her horned head fell sideways.

I'd severed half her neck, exposin' a tangle of wires.

"Van!" Charlotte sprang up off the heap of scraps herself. "What are you *doing*!?"

"Savin' us," I grumbled. And that Oracle woman had said we wouldn't need our weapons here. Yeah, sure. I yanked the sword out.

"I just told her we meant her no harm!"

Oh. I let the sword fall so the tip of it rested against the ground. "Well how was I supposed to know that! I don't even know what language that is —and I certainly can't understand it! I thought you were tellin' her to get outta the way!"

"First I was going to tell her we weren't here to cause any trouble—and then you go and do that!" She gestured at the almost-severed head.

"It was gonna attack me," I insisted. And it was. Why else would it have spread its claws like that?

More sparks shot from the wires I'd chopped through, and then the statue lurched forward, causin' Charlotte and I to jump back.

I landed in the pile of metal scraps and fell again, goddamnit. There were too many loose pieces, and they all just kept rollin' out from underneath me even as I attempted once more to get to my feet.

Charlotte had been more self-aware this time and smartly avoided the scrap-heap, but it seemed the demon-woman statue was more intent on me, anyway. She came right at me, her danglin' head not seemin' to slow her down none.

Well shit.

"*Periculum deprehenet!*" she said, loud enough this time that her words echoed off the rocky walls around us. Her smooth and lyrical voice weren't quite right now, thanks to the blow from my sword, I imagined. It was rougher and a little deeper. "*Periculum deprehenet!*" she repeated. "*Periculum deprehenet!*"

"Now what's she sayin'?" I shouted over at Charlotte as the statue closed in on me, and I was still tryin' to untangle myself from junk.

I caught the sword grip in both hands and raised the blade just in time to block the swing from those long, golden claws.

The porcelain along its forearm cracked where it hit steel.

"She says you're a threat," Charlotte offered. "Probably because you tried to chop her head off."

"She was gonna attack me first!" I blocked another swing from its other arm, and that porcelain cracked, too. Well, if it kept this up long enough, there wouldn't be nothin' of it left.

"*Periculum deprehenet!*" it shouted again.

Charlotte picked her way over toward us, careful not to fall herself. I was still pinned against all that scrap and doin' my best to ward off those claws. At such close range I couldn't do much with such a giant sword except block 'em.

"Hey!" Charlotte shouted. She waved the torch around, tryin' to get the statue's attention. "Prohibere! State! Disiungere!"

"*Now* what are you tellin' it?" The next blow jarred my arm as I blocked it. Either the livin' statue was tryin' harder now, or I was tirin' out. Or maybe both. Most of the ceramic along its arms had fallen off now, and I decided I'd liked it more with it on. Beneath the porcelain was a thin metal frame in the shape of a human limb, and that frame was all fulla wires and gears and pistons.

Like my leg.

"I'm telling her to stop," Charlotte said.

"I don't think she's getting the point," I grunted. The tips of her claws came awful close to my face with the next swing, and this time, instead of just drawin' back and swipin' again, her long fingers gripped my blade.

Uh oh.

Without real flesh and blood, the sharp edges of the steel weren't no consequence at all.

She yanked, and the sword came outta my grip with shockin' ease. She tossed it away.

Fuck.

I rolled, only barely missin' a good rake of her claws.

Pieces of discarded scrap sprayed out over me as she struck the pile of junk instead of me. And then I was up on my feet again, and I dodged around behind her to make fer the sword she'd thrown away.

Except the light from our single torch didn't reach that far, so I only had a vague notion of where the weapon mighta landed. I dropped to my hands and knees, gropin' blindly along the ground.

"Van—" Charlotte started, but her warnin' was drowned by the statue lettin' out a long, mechanical hiss.

It spun, and lunged at me.

OUR END

"Charlotte!" I barked, just before throwin' myself sideways. Golden claws sparked off empty rock. "I need light!"

I didn't have much time to register what Charlotte was doin' over there with our only torch … all I knew was that fer some reason she weren't bringin' it any closer, and I sorely needed it right about now.

The statue kept lungin' at me, and I kept barely dodgin' it, but it was also drivin' me back deeper and deeper into darkness, and I was pretty sure now I was movin' further and further away from that sword, too.

"Charlotte!" I tried again.

"Van," she finally answered. "We … we have a serious problem here."

"That so?" I growled. "I hadn't noticed." But even despite the obviousness of her statement, the dread in her tone made my stomach clench. I ducked another swing from the demon-woman statue and risked a sprint through the black, back in Charlotte's direction, back toward our second discarded torch, back toward the sword.

"No," Charlotte snapped, voice echoin' out over the noise of the statue skitterin' after me. "*Look.*"

I chanced a glance even as I ran, and my steps slowed as I realized the true depths of her declaration.

There were other statues movin' now, too, emergin' slowly from the gloom and closin' in all around us. Others made of porcelain and gold like the one now so intent on murderin' me. And some of those in the red dresses, some of those religious sisters, and even, it seemed, the two metal soldiers we'd first passed, one still holdin' its sword and lookin' like it was ready to use it. And there were some we hadn't seen before, too, and animals, even. Birds, butterflies and some kinda other flyin' insect that moved too fast to see clearly.

Terror prickled over my scalp, wedged my heart into my throat. *Holy fu—*

Somethin' slammed into my right shoulder and knocked me clean off my feet. I hit the rocky ground hard and rolled till I came up against the base of a big stalagmite, and then I just laid there gaspin' and starin' up into blackness, takin' account of all the new bruises pulsin' along my body.

Except then, dim through the darkness, the remains of that demon-woman lurched into view. Much of her porcelain was gone now along her limbs, leavin' only her smooth torso and danglin' head intact. But still she came at me. She just weren't givin' up.

I wondered if she'd been the one to knock me sprawlin'. If so, there was an awful lot of strength in those dainty metal limbs.

"Van!"

Charlotte sounded far off now. I roused myself with a groan, forcin' myself to roll over even as my faithful statuesque pursuer closed the distance between us.

But I was too slow this time.

Her cold fingers caught me around the throat just as I stood, and they certainly didn't seem so delicate now. They clutched in an iron grip, hard and unyieldin', and then my feet were kickin' air.

She slammed me back into one of the cave's rough walls, metal grip squeezin' till I thought she might sever my head off my shoulders like I almost did to her.

My hands clawed at her arm and fingers, my boots kicked her in the chest and face; desperate, instinctive measures, but I knew it was all useless.

The black closed in quick this time, but there was one last thing I had to do. I struggled hard to suck down a thread of air. "Charlotte," I strangled out, and I hoped to God she could hear me from wherever she was now. "Get ... get out. *Run.* No ... no weapons."

Then I gagged as those metal fingers tightened, and my struggles weakened.

Maybe that Oracle had been right. Maybe I shouldn't have taken that sword.

Maybe that's why this statue had come after me and not Charlotte.

Maybe those others had only been after me, too. Maybe she could still get out...

A sharp crunch and crack sounded from somewhere near, and a sizzlin' noise, and then the pressure around my throat abruptly let go, and I crumpled in a heap to the cave floor.

Fer a minute all I could do was gag and wretch and drink air in great, heavin' gulps, tryin' to remember how to breathe. A circle of pain pulsed around my neck where hard metal had dug into my flesh, but the black in my vision finally cleared, and I blinked as I realized the light of Charlotte's torch was nearer now.

I pushed myself up to sit against the wall … and saw Charlotte and the demon statue right in front of me, circlin' each other. The torch was on the ground between 'em, and Charlotte had the sword in both hands. The statue had a big hole in the ceramic of its torso now, right through its chest, and more sparks lit inside as it moved. Golden claws glinted in the flickerin' torchlight as it made multiple grabs for the sword blade, but each time Charlotte danced back outta reach.

Damn it all. I'd told her to *run*. I'd told her *no weapons*! Now she was just as much a target as me. And the rest of those mechanical monstrosities were still comin' our way, the big one with the sword out front and leadin' the way.

"Charlotte," I rasped, then coughed. It hurt to talk. "Charlotte … we gotta get outta here."

She dodged in fast at the statue's next grab and swung the sword at the thing's left knee. The lower half of that leg snapped clean off, and the statue crashed to the ground.

She hacked its head off with another strong swing, finally finishin' the job I'd started. And then, fer good measure I figured, she stabbed the sword point down into its chest one final time, right into the place its heart woulda been, had it been made of flesh.

Its metal body jerked and twitched, then went still.

But all those others were comin', so much closer now. Already the fast flyin' insects had found us, buzzin' around our heads like bees as Charlotte ran over to me, planted the sword tip onto the ground, and held out her free hand.

I scowled up at her and swatted one of the bees away. "I said … I said *no* weapons."

She shrugged and shook her head. "And I told *you* I wasn't going to let you get out of my sight, didn't I? Good thing, too."

I growled but took her hand, and she helped haul me to my feet. I wavered there fer a minute as the room spun and my head pounded. Then I nodded toward the sword. "You…" I winced. My voice sounded like I'd been chewin' gravel and every word made my throat ache fresh. "You know how to use that thing?"

She glanced down to the massive blade. "Well enough, I guess. I suppose this is quite different than a saber, in truth, but the fundamentals are generally the same."

"Fundamentals? The fundamentals of what?"

"Sword combat. My brother and I … we used to fence together."

I'd never heard of fencin' combat before, but I also didn't have no more time to be askin' more questions. All those other statues were gettin' far too close fer comfort. I went to grab up the torch, gutterin' lower than I'd like now, then caught Charlotte's arm with my other hand and pulled her after me. "Come on, let's go. Quick! 'Fore those other things catch up to us."

She came after me, but slower than I'd like. "What about finding your ruins?"

I laughed, then winced again and put a hand to my bruised throat. "In case you hadn't noticed, those things want to kill us. You think we can fight through all of 'em and live?"

The answer was no, no way in Hell, not with just the two of us and one old sword, but Charlotte took the time to pause and take account of the metal beasts clamberin' our way like maybe we might have a chance at it, if she could do the math right.

I stopped, went back to her and took her arm again, pullin' her onward. "*No*, the answer is no," I hissed. "Whatever these things are, they're good enough. If we can get outta here alive, I'll give 'em all to Nan. There's enough gold and machinery in here to make anyone happy. And maybe they'll murder that old hag fer me, too, once she gets here."

"All right. Good plan."

Charlotte matched my pace then, to my relief, but we didn't get far before slowin' again. I swept the fadin' torch out in front of us, but all the rock looked all the same. In the dark and havin' been pre-occupied with not bein' murdered, I'd completely lost my bearings. Panic welled, sharp and urgent. I tried to swallow it back. "I … I don't remember which way is out."

"Me neither," Charlotte whispered. She turned to stand back-to-back with me, liftin' that ridiculous sword like she was gonna take on the whole metal army all by herself. "Find a wall and follow it," she suggested. "We'll find the exit eventually."

But not fast enough. And then we'd corner ourselves nice and neat for those guardians, too. I swatted away another of the buzzin' bees and turned to face the same direction as she. We couldn't see most of the things comin' fer us now, only hear 'em. A constant din of metal against rock, rusty gears turnin' fer the first time in a long time, the whir of mechanical wings, and voices. Voices murmurin' that same phrase over and over again: *"Periculum deprehenet!"*

Through the black, they sounded like people. Flesh and blood people.

Gooseflesh crawled up my arms and made the hairs on the back of my neck prickle. They'd already surrounded us.

There was no way out.

The other sword came outta the dark first, followed by the gleamin' outline of one of those metal soldiers. Charlotte lifted her sword to meet it and the blades sparked as they crashed together with teeth-jarrin' force.

I ducked instinctively, and Charlotte staggered under the power of the soldier's blow. I dropped the torch, straightenin' to put both hands around Charlotte's on the sword's hilt. We strained to push the abomination back, but even together could only make incremental progress.

"Van ... get back!" Charlotte ground through her teeth. "Get out of the way!"

"You can't hold it by yourself!" It was almost too strong fer both of us.

"If you would get out of the way I could maneuver correctly!"

"If I let go it's gonna cut you in half!"

"I told you I know how to use this thing ... so let me use it!"

"It's too strong fer you! Let me have the sword and I'll hold it off long enough fer you to make a run fer it!"

"Why do you keep trying so hard to get yourself killed? I thought you wanted to save your sister!"

Before I could explain to her there weren't no way in Hell I was gonna let her die down here, the sword we pushed against abruptly withdrew. I nearly fell on my face, and Charlotte staggered forward a few steps.

The next strike came almost immediately, skimmin' over my head close enough to knock off my hat, but again Charlotte met it blade fer blade, sparks lightin' the dark once more.

The bees swarmed around us, and every time one brushed against my skin I cringed away like it stung even though it hadn't. The memory of those metal insects Charles Miller had kept in jars in his dungeon—and what they were capable of—was still much too fresh in mind.

I swatted one off my arm and crushed it under my boot when it hit the ground.

Charlotte danced with the metal soldier … it looked all the world like dancin' … not like they were tryin' to hack each other into pieces, and I was left absolutely fuckin' helpless. I had no weapons. Not a goddamned thing.

The second metal soldier stepped into view and I grabbed up the only thing I had—our torch. This soldier didn't have a sword, at least, but I only registered what it *did* have in-hand when it leveled it at me.

A pistol.

Fer a heartbeat I froze.

It weren't the weapon itself that had caught me so off-guard, it was the leg holster that stuck outta the thing's right thigh.

It looked … it looked just like the holster in *my* metal thigh.

Nausea hit me like a fist in the gut, a cold sweat racin' over my skin as I stared down the barrel of that gun.

And then it fired.

I woulda been dead. Shoulda been. The bullet shoulda hit me right between the eyes, but fer once, time was on my side. Time had corroded whatever ancient bullets had been in that chamber, and when the pin hit the primer, the whole thing exploded.

I flinched away from the mini-fireball and turned toward Charlotte.

The metal man she'd been fightin' had momentarily paused, distracted by the noise and light of its companion's misfortune.

Charlotte brought her blade down hard across its elbows, and its own sword clattered to the ground.

I dropped the torch quick and dove fer it, grabbed it up and rolled to my feet, only vaguely notin' the way my left bicep throbbed. If I'd re-injured that damn thing again…

But there was no time to worry about that. I swung at the nearest metal soldier's neck, the one whose sword I'd just stolen, and took its head off.

Seemed these swords were made fer combat, after all.

To my dismay, that didn't stop it. But it did slow it down some, and its arms didn't seem to be workin' right no more, neither. Charlotte and I both moved fer the second one now, who seemed awful confused by its weapon malfunction.

Its right hand was missin' now, and in the absence of a blade or a firearm, and with Charlotte and

I both descendin' on it with a vengeance, it adopted the same strategy as the demon-woman.

It swung its remainin' fist hard, right at Charlotte's head.

She parried it with her sword, and I drove the point of mine through a thin gap in the metal plates of its side.

It jerked, straightened, and went rigid. Like it went from somethin' livin' back into a lifeless statue. And then it fell over, topplin' like some great tree to land with a crash.

Well. Maybe this might actually be—

A flash of red and gold surged into my peripheral vision and I spun quick, barely blockin' a blow from one of those statues with the domed faces and the elaborate red gowns. She took another swipe with her other hand and I yelled out as her claws raked across my right forearm. I shifted my weight to my right foot and gave her a good solid kick with my left foot, much like I'd done to Duster the bounty hunter, and like him, this thing went reelin' backward.

A cry from Charlotte made me whip around toward her just in time to see her go to her knees. Four bloody gashes had been ripped in the back of her shirt, and one of the red and gold things stepped up behind her, wrappin' a golden-gloved hand around her throat like that demon had done to me earlier.

I lunged forward, swingin' my blade in a flat arc with all the strength I could muster. I caught the thing good in the back of the head and its neck bent forward all unnatural-like, its face now pressed against its own breast. It let go of Charlotte, twisted toward me. And I drove my sword right through its elaborate gown and into its metal torso hard as I could.

But I didn't hit a gap in its plates this time like I had fer the other one.

The hilt jarred in my hands as the blade bounced right off. Least the force of my stab knocked it back a few steps, though it righted itself quickly enough and came at me again.

To my left, from the corner of my eye, I saw Charlotte on her feet again, sword back in-hand and tryin' her damnedest to hold off more of the metal bastards.

God damn. There were just too many of 'em. And we couldn't even tell which way was out anymore…

My attention went abruptly back to the thing in the red gown and golden gloves. I tried to do like I'd seen Charlotte do, dartin' in quick fer a stab or a swing and then leapin' back again, only barely keepin' its claws away from me. And on my left, Charlotte did the same, and fer what seemed like eternity we hacked at those things, reducin' some of 'em to scrap, but not enough.

My arms and shoulders ached, sweat ran into my eyes, and those goddamned bees swarmed everywhere, fillin' my ears with their endless dronin', constantly tryin' to land on me and do who knew what. I kept havin' to shake 'em off in-between all the fightin'.

Our torch had nearly gone out now … it was gettin' harder and harder to see where the things were comin' from. Soon, it'd go out entirely.

And that would be our end. These metal abominations would rip us apart.

Part of me wished I'd just give up already. There weren't no way outta here alive. Why did I keep fightin'?

Why couldn't I just put down this sword and let 'em take me?

And yet, despite such thoughts … I just kept on tryin', battlin' fer every last minute I had left, I guess. Musta been that Delano stubbornness.

It just wouldn't let me quit. Even when I shoulda.

Charlotte and I stood back-to-back now, pressed close by the crowd of things intent on killin' us. Her fight hadn't waned in all this time, neither. No matter she musta been plum exhausted same as me. No matter those gashes across her back musta hurt like hell, just as much and more as those I had across my right forearm, and that bullet-hole in my left bicep.

And yet she'd never slowed, never wavered.

Her steady presence against my back hardened my resolve.

If I was gonna die down here today … at least I weren't gonna die alone.

Except then … well … all those things tryin' to kill us just *stopped*.

THE CACHE

The metal statues all froze, wherever they happened to be, right in the middle of whatever they happened to be doin'. The birds, butterflies, and bees dropped like rocks to the cave floor, as abruptly unanimated as they had become animated. Some of 'em broke as they landed, and their pieces scattered.

Charlotte and I stood there in the middle of 'em all, and the only sound in the sudden ringin' silence was our harsh breathin'. We kept our swords raised and ready in what dim, sputterin' light of the torch was left, but nothin' moved.

Then another, different kinda sound filled the gloom. A deep, electrical kinda buzzin' noise. And one by one, all around us, lightbulbs flared to life. They were bare and threw out only weak yellow light, strung along on wire nailed high on the walls, but they illuminated the place well enough. Certainly better than our one torch had.

I blinked as they revealed the chamber we stood in, and all the carnage we had caused.

This particular cavern was a big one, all right. Wide and roughly circular, with a high, arched ceilin'. We'd been closer to the exit tunnel than I'd thought—it was over to my left only maybe twenty yards or so. To my right, over against the far back wall, was that heap of scrap parts Charlotte and I had stumbled into. Another tunnel, also strung with lightbulbs, opened up next to it. We were surrounded now by several more of the statues that had come alive … but there were plenty more of 'em still standin' lined up in various places. And some other animals, too. All metal, like their human-ish counterparts. A few dogs, looked like. And a cat and a horse.

We stood ready fer another long minute, but when things remained quiet and still, I let out a long breath and lowered my sword. My arms burned with the effort of wieldin' it fer so long, the muscles tremblin'. I weren't in the habit of thankin' Divine Providence … but I mighta muttered some words of gratitude just then.

"Van…" Charlotte whispered.

"I think we're in the clear."

"No. I can't … something's … something's wrong…"

I turned to face her in time to see her sword drop, the steel clangin' against rock. Her eyes had gone all glassy. She swooned.

I abandoned my own sword to catch her as she fell, then lowered her gently to the ground. She stared up past me at the cavern's ceilin', unfocused and unblinkin'. Fear shoved up my throat. "Charlotte? Charlotte!" I shook her shoulders. Smoothed messy waves of red hair away from her face and patted her cheek. Gently at first, then harder.

She didn't respond. Didn't so much as blink. She was limp and lifeless. Far too much like that poor nameless girl I'd watched die up in the Bone Spur Mountains.

"Charlotte! Can you hear me? What's wrong? Tell me what's wrong!"

But she didn't. My own heart beat too hard, too fast, as I felt fer a pulse. Her chest weren't risin' and fallin' … there weren't no warm puffs of air comin' from her nose or mouth. She weren't breathin' at all.

She looked dead already.

I hissed curses between my teeth and tried to get my hands to stop shakin', tried to focus on seperatin' the throb of my own heart pulsin' through me from the beat of Charlotte's I was frantically tryin' to find.

And all the while my mind was racin'. Tryin' to sort how I might get her outta here, tryin' to figure if there was any chance in Hell I could get her medical attention in a timely manner, or if it was already too late.

Then I felt somethin' beneath my fingers. A pulse, all right.

I choked on the swell of relief, but it was short-lived. She may have had a pulse fer now … but she still weren't breathin'. *Why ain't she breathin'?*

If she didn't start breathin' soon, she was gonna suffocate. Suffocate fer no good goddamned reason at all….

"Mr. Delano!"

The voice, out of nowhere and suddenly so close, made me spring up to my feet and startle so badly I tripped, fallin' back into one of the frozen metal statues. It and myself both went down to the floor in a tangle, but I rolled free of it quick, grabbed one of the swords and came up to my feet again ready to use it.

The other statues around us still didn't move, but

there was another person here now, an actual flesh and blood human bein', though I couldn't see much of him under all the equipment he was wearin'. He had a tall, thin build, and a leather apron covered him from chest to knees. The apron itself had a multitude of pockets and loops sewn onto its front, and every one of the pockets and loops had somethin' stuck into it: tools, vials, flasks, rolled-up papers…

His left arm had leather on it too, a cuff around his bicep and one on his forearm, and both were just as fulla stuff as his apron. Pipes and vials and even a —a lightbulb? And on his wrist was somethin' that looked like a clock or a gauge of some sort, and somethin' like a little leather-bound book he had opened, but instead of pages, it had a row of little buttons inside it.

I could only gape at him, takin' in his ridiculous appearance and half-believin' he weren't even real.

"Well I certainly did not expect to see *you* here!" Half his face was covered by an enormous eyepatch equipped with telescopin' lenses similar to those cat's eye glasses of Sally's.

But even so, I recognized the voice, the heavy accent. The wiry build and the finely groomed mustache.

"Doc—Doctor—Doctor Balogh?" I finally spluttered.

Vaguely, I remembered that blind old woman had mentioned "my friend" was already down here. I'd thought her crazy, of course. She couldn't have known who I was lookin' fer … I'd never told her outright.

And yet … here he was. Dr. Balogh. The man I'd been searchin' fer all along.

Before I could blurt out what had happened to Charlotte—or any of the many, *many* questions I had fer him—he spotted her, sprawled out there on the ground beside me, and his one visible eye widened.

"Goodness gracious!" He rushed forward, duckin' beneath the outstretched arms of statues, and knelt at her side, immediately feelin' fer a pulse like I had just done. "What's wrong with her? Is she hurt?"

A swell of anger clogged my throat at such an absurd question. "Well she ain't just takin' a nap," I snapped.

"I *mean* did you see what happened to her to put her in this state?" The doc pulled a thing from his apron and clicked a button on it, and a little beam of light came out one end of it, which he proceeded to shine in Charlotte's eyes, one after the other.

I stepped closer to watch what he was doin', lettin' the sword lower again. That little thing he had … it was like Charlotte's big spotlight, only so small. I'd never seen one that small before. "No," I said. "I didn't see nothin'. She got scratched by one of the red things, but so did I." I glanced to my right forearm, where blood had crusted at the edges of the tears in my shirt sleeve.

"There is still a pulse, that is good," he murmured. "But no pupillary constriction in response to light stimulus."

"Err. She ain't breathin'," I offered, havin' no idea the implications of what he'd just said.

"Was she hit by any of the flying creatures? A bee, bird, or butterfly, by chance?"

"I … I dunno. She never said nothin' if she was. The bees kept landin' all over me but I kept swattin' 'em off. I didn't have much time to be watchin' her too, ya know. These things were tryin' to kill us." I gestured at 'em all, still circled around us and reachin' with claws outstretched.

"They were reacting to your weapons." He managed to sound rather accusatory as he replaced the tiny spotlight into its appropriate apron loop and then removed a small vial and a syringe from other loops.

I scoffed. "Well I ain't gonna walk into the pitch-black depths of some strange cave without any kinda weapon! Who knows what coulda been in here … and it was a good thing I grabbed somethin', too. Else these things woulda ended us quick."

The doc let out a long hiss of a breath. "If you would have left the swords where they belonged, none of these would have activated. You would not have been attacked at all." He jabbed the needle into the top of his selected vial and drew some of the liquid up into the syringe.

I shifted on my feet. "Yeah, well … what if there'd been a bear in here? Or some deranged flesh-and-blood person?"

"There isn't," Dr. Balogh said crisply. He took Charlotte's left arm and pushed the needle into the crook of her elbow.

I glanced away as it pierced her skin, stomach rollin'. My mind flashed back to Miller's dungeon yet again, and the needles he'd used on me there, and bile rose in the back of my throat. I fought against the sudden rush of memories, the waves of ghostly pain that rippled along my body with 'em, and swallowed hard, turnin' away from Charlotte and the doc entirely.

But then I was lookin' at those terrifyin' metal statues, made all the more terrifyin' by the fact I could see 'em so much more clearly now. So I raised my eyes upward, focused on one of the bare light-bulbs hangin' on the wall, and tried to distract my-self. "What … what're you doin'?"

"Administering an antidote."

I spun back toward him. "Antidote? She was poisoned?!"

"Seems that way, yes. Her symptoms indicate she was likely stung by one of the bees. They carry a par-alytic mixture the ancients often used for hunting in certain locales, and then in later centuries, it was often used for covert assassinations. If left untreated, the victim will die by suffocation."

Bile soured in my mouth again, this time fer a whole different reason. "But … but she ain't gonna die, right? You gave her the antidote, so she ain't gonna die. Right?"

He turned to look over his shoulder at me, lips pressed into a hard line. He pulled his absurd tele-scope eyepatch down to hang around his neck so he could fix both eyes on me square, and he glared in a way he'd never done when I'd been stayin' at his homestead, not even when I'd been so angry about my missin' leg and lashed out. "The antidote will work against the paralysis, allow her to breathe again. Eventually she will have full muscle control again, probably within a few minutes. But her full recovery depends on how long she was in a paralyzed state. How long was she like this before I arrived?"

"Not … not long. Maybe a minute or so."

He gave a nod. "Then I think she will suffer no permanent effects." He turned back toward her and pressed his fingers to the side of her neck again. "But I will need to perform resuscitation procedures to mimic breathing until she regains control. Come. Quick." He stood and gestured at me. "Leave that sword and carry her. Follow me. We need to get her back to my laboratory so I can keep a proper eye on her recovery."

Laboratory? But he was already duckin' underneath the statues' arms again and headin' out across the cavern, so I hurried to do as he said. I laid the sword down, grabbed up my hat from where it'd fallen durin' the fight and shoved it back onto my head, and went to Charlotte to scoop her up. It weren't as easy as it shoulda been, given my arms were already exhausted from all the fightin' with a blade, and I had both my wounds and Charlotte's to be careful of.

But I managed to get one arm under her shoulders and one in the crook of her knees and lifted her with only a grimace. That old bullet wound in my left arm didn't like this much, but I pushed on, followin' the doc across the big open space to the lighted tunnel near the scrap pile.

And I couldn't help but notice as we walked that there were human bones in here, too. Few and far between, but unmistakable nonetheless. And Charlotte and I had nearly joined 'em.

We passed through the mouth of the lighted tunnel, where some old rails started along the floor, bolted into the rock. A handcar waited at the near end of 'em, and they stretched on through the tunnel far as I could see. And so did those lights.

By the time we reached the rail car, after our brisk walk across the cavern's expanse and my limp more pronounced under an extra person to carry, I was winded again. That fight with those metal abominations had taken more outta me than I'd realized.

Doctor Balogh motioned toward the cart. "Set her there. Gently now."

I gave him a look. What did he think I was gonna do? Throw her down like a sack of grain? "What is this place, anyway?" I got Charlotte situated comfortable as I could, stretched out flat on her back along the hard wooden platform.

The doc hopped up onto the hand car. "A cache."

I grunted and climbed up after him. "A cache? Of what? Murderous statues?"

He grunted and took a knee next to Charlotte again. "Of some of the finest examples of engineering the Old World ever had to offer. Of course, you managed to destroy some of the most exquisite pieces in your rampage. Hundreds of years they rested here, safe, only to be reduced to ruin within a matter of minutes after your arrival."

A multitude of thoughts shot through my mind at his accusation, at his tone. My neck still ached where the one of those "exquisite pieces" had nearly squeezed my head right off my body. "Well I weren't gonna let 'em just murder me."

"Now I understand the reason for these caches in the first place," Balogh murmured, dismissin' my protest. Then, louder, he said, "You know how to work one of these things?"

"Course I do."

"Good. Get going then. Fast as you can manage. I've set the junctions already; this track will take us straight to my lab. Meantime, I'll work on keeping oxygen flowing to the young lady's brain."

"All right." I swallowed, not likin' the mention of oxygen and brains too awful much, and stepped around to the side of the car that would allow me to both see down the track in the direction we were headed and keep an eye on the doc and Charlotte both.

Then I grabbed the handle and set about pumpin' it, fast as I could manage, just as he'd said. It was slow buildin' momentum at first, but once I got us goin' along those rails, we picked up speed right quick. The wheels on this car and even the track itself were awful well-oiled. I wondered if they'd been around down here as long as those statues, or if they were a newer addition.

Beside me, Doctor Balogh went about his medical business with Charlotte, alternatin' pushin' on her chest with the flat of his palms and usin' a little bellows pulled from his apron to shove air into her mouth.

It was all I could do to let him do it. It sure didn't look like he was tryin' to save her. It looked like he was tryin' to kill her. A minute stretched by of him workin', and me keepin' our car movin', the string of lightbulbs flashin' by along the wall to my right. Occasionally I caught glimpses of more scrap piled into dead-end alcoves, or bizarre-lookin' machinery built into the rock itself, or other railway offshoots that looked to have collapsed in on themselves with so much time neglected.

The rattle of our car slidin' down the tracks filled

the silence, till I couldn't take it no more. "You *sure* that's meant to keep her alive?"

"Oh, absolutely."

"All right. But … yer sure? Positively certain?"

He paused his work and sat back on his heels, twistin' to face me. "Son, I've been a doctor for almost longer than you've been alive. I know what I'm doing."

I scowled at his use of that term "son" again and focused back on the track ahead of us. "Yeah. Fine."

"If you were really so concerned for her safety," he muttered, barely audible over the dull rumble of our cart sailin' down those rails, "you should have left those swords alone."

"I told you," I snapped back at him, "I ain't wanderin' into an unknown place unarmed. And anyway, how was I supposed to know takin' one of those swords would wake up all those monsters?"

He shook his head and turned his attention back to Charlotte. "For you to have found your way in here at all means the Oracle must have granted you passage. You've got her markings all over you, too. That's what happened, isn't it? You went through her Judgement?"

I growled, givin' my handle another few good, strong pumps, wishin' I could get my hands around that old woman's throat. "We got attacked and drugged, that's what. And robbed. That woman ain't no Oracle. She's a thief who hides behind magic tricks. And maybe she's a would-be murderer, too."

"But she told you that you would not need your weapons in here, did she not?"

I dropped my glare back down to him, found him starin' steadily at me. "She failed to mention bringing a weapon would anger the murderin' statues," I hissed.

"But she told you no weapons?"

"Sure. She mentioned it. I just ain't inclined to listen to a woman who's just drugged and robbed me, is all."

Doctor Balogh sighed and turned away from me. "She did not rob you. She will return your things to you upon your exit."

"How do you know that?"

"Because I have been out myself. Several times. And each time she is there waiting for me … *with* my belongings."

I peered at his back, lookin' over all the strange things stashed in his arm cuffs again. Remembered that the old woman had also said somethin' about "my friend" doin' a particular kind of work down here, and all those questions I'd had upon first seein' him show up out in that cavern of statues came back to me. "What are you doin' down here anyway, Doc?"

"I could ask you the same thing."

"Yeah, well, I asked you first."

Charlotte gasped and choked, and Dr. Balogh sat back at the same time I stepped forward to get a better look at her, relief springin' through me. Color had returned to her face, and she blinked slowly, heavily. Her fingers twitched. But she was breathin' now. Breathin' on her own.

"There we are," Dr. Balogh said. He tucked his little bellows into its appropriate apron pocket, then picked up one of her hands and massaged it. "Take it easy. Take it slow. Feeling will return to normal for you soon. You are lucky I found you when I did."

Then he turned to me, and his gentle, soothin' tone went sharp. "What are you doing? Man the controls, would you? We've almost reached the lab now, be ready to brake. Unless you want to wreck the cart, too?"

"No," I grumbled, but heat stung my face despite myself. I stepped quick back to the pump handle; located the brake lever and got ready to ease it back.

Up ahead not too far now our tunnel opened out into another chamber, and the tracks terminated there in a big wooden board painted with fat black and yellow diagonal stripes. The paint looked new.

Perplexed, I pulled the brake nonetheless as we approached, and our hand car eased to a halt before the big painted board with only some mild screechin'.

Dr. Balogh dismounted the platform and waved at me to follow. "Come now. Bring her. Follow me."

I climbed down myself, went around to gently lift Charlotte again, though at least this time she weren't entirely limp. She was awake and aware now, and I muttered apologies when I saw her wince as my arm passed under her back. But I managed to lift her, and she leaned her head against my shoulder, one hand loosely clutchin' a fistful of my shirt.

I followed the doc into another big chamber … even bigger than the one we'd just left, and this one more brightly lit and outfitted with a great deal more machinery. The dull thunder of rushin' water echoed from somewhere, but my gawkin' gaze came to a full stop as it fell upon a familiar figure.

Someone I'd hoped I wouldn't have to face again.

Someone I'd planned to actively avoid, preferably fer the rest of my life.

But there was no avoidin' her now. She stood there starin' right at me—and lookin' more sour at the sight than probably any other person who had ever laid eyes on me.

Mrs. Hannah Balogh.

EVERYONE DIES

I looked away from her quick as her mouth opened; practically ran after the doc as he headed fer the left side of the chamber.

To my great relief, his wife did not follow. Nor did she yell out whatever it was she mighta been intent on first sayin' at the sight of me. I didn't think I could put off that conversation fer as long as I would have liked … but I'd surely try my best to put it off as long as I could possibly manage.

There was a circle of bed rolls over in this area, and an old wooden table set with four stools. Dr. Balogh reached down to pull a blanket from one of the beds and spread it out over the table, then motioned fer me to put Charlotte there.

I set her on the edge of it, and with proppin' one hand against my shoulder, she was able to sit on her own, though she still seemed awful woozy.

"My heavens!" the doc spat as he noted the slashes along her back. His bright gaze lifted to glare at me again over her shoulder. "Why did you not tell me about these?!"

I glared right back. "I was a little more concerned over the fact she weren't breathin'! And then if I recall correctly, you were orderin' me around and tellin' me to act all quick-like. Didn't have much of a chance to mention 'em, did I?"

He shook his head and muttered somethin' I couldn't make out, then proceeded to fuss over Charlotte fer a minute while I helped to steady her, askin' her to blink and turn her head and move her arms and legs. She was able to comply with all his requests, so he shined that little light into her eyes again, and then nodded and moved around to look at the gashes on her back.

She sucked in a breath as he tried to pluck her shirt away from the torn edges of skin.

I winced myself. Hers were worse than the ones I'd gotten on my arm.

Dr. Balogh clucked his tongue as he studied 'em. "Well, young lady, you seem to be recovering from the poison well enough. But these are going to need to be cleaned and stitched, I'm afraid."

"Charlotte," she mumbled. She lifted a hand to rub it over her face. "My name is Charlotte."

The doc straightened and came around the table to stand in front of her. He held out a hand. "And I am Doctor Henri Balogh. Pleased to make your acquaintance, Charlotte."

She shook his proffered hand. "Likewise, Doctor."

"If you'll just lie down on the table on your stomach, I can take a better look at your back. Get those wounds fixed up. My wife Hannah will have a fresh blouse you can borrow."

Charlotte nodded wearily, shiftin' carefully to lie down.

I tried to help her best I could. "You all right? You scared the daylights outta me. Thought you were dead."

"Oh, sure. I'm fine." But she sounded tired, as exhausted as I felt myself. "Just thought I'd give you a little taste of your own medicine."

I frowned. "A taste of my own—"

"Yes. You're always giving me a fright, trying to get yourself killed. Making me worry. Now you know what it's like."

I didn't exactly know what to say to that, except I didn't like that worryin'. Not at all. Before I could manage to reply, Dr. Balogh caught my attention, ordered me to bring over some old pipes stacked against the wall. So we could form a make-shift partition, he said, to give Charlotte some privacy while he stitched her up.

While I worked on that, he called his wife over, tellin' her they needed to prepare a suitable "medical environment". She went off to fetch other things, but I kept my focus solely on those pipes and didn't dare even glance at her.

Soon enough I'd tied some tall pipes to the legs on one long-side of the table at the doc's instruction, and tied another pipe across the top of those, and then we draped some blankets over it to create a kind of blind.

Mrs. Balogh had brought over a whole kit of medical supplies, and then the doc shooed me away.

"Go on now," he said. "I must get to work. She will be just fine. My daughter Fanni will see to your arm. She's quite good at doctoring herself, you know."

"Fanni?"

"That's right. Go on. I'll let you know when I'm done here."

"I'll be all right," Charlotte murmured. She reached out fer my hand and squeezed it.

I hesitated, though not 'cause of any worry over Charlotte. I had no fear Dr. Balogh would chop off any of her limbs to replace 'em with machine parts. And aside from that affinity fer Old World tech, I had no doubts he were a good doctor. More it were the fact I'd forgotten the doc had brought his children with him, and I was as reluctant to face them as I was to face Mrs. Balogh.

But it was her glare that finally moved me. I could feel it burnin' holes in me, and when I finally glanced up to confirm it, she was givin' me a hard stare, all right.

So I nodded and gave Charlotte's hand a quick squeeze in return before hastily movin' off, around the makeshift wall of blankets and back toward the center of the chamber, where a small portable stove had been set up with a stew pot atop it.

I wondered how they'd gotten all this stuff down here. Surely that pot hadn't been left in here all this time … or if it had, they wouldn't be eatin' out of it. Surely it woulda been rusted through by now. They had to have brought it with 'em, or purchased it in town, along with a whole lot of other stuff I noted spread around this chamber now.

But they couldn't have taken all that through that little tunnel Charlotte and I had crawled through. No way. There musta been some other entrance somewhere…

I slowed as I spotted the children, both of 'em, and both starin' at me just about as hard as their mother had been. They stood near a big workbench littered with tools and … machine parts.

I recalled Nan had said she'd found Dr. Balogh's workshop, back at his homestead near Bravebank. Maybe he'd just come here to continue whatever work he'd started there. My left leg twinged and I scowled, then made my way over toward the stove.

Maybe the doc thought his daughter could fix up my arm, but I weren't gonna impose on her. Not after what I'd done to their family last time … and not with the way the girl was lookin' at me now.

So I just went and took a seat in the middle of the place, starin' at the cold stove and tryin' to decipher what murmurin' was goin' on behind those blankets.

Didn't take long fer the kids to come to me, though.

I had a strong urge to get up and leave as they approached, but it woulda been a futile endeavor, in the end. Where was I gonna go? I didn't know my way around this place, whatever it was. And I surely didn't want to get trapped in another dark chamber with more murderous statues. Nor could I have left Charlotte here, anyway.

So I stayed put, cross-legged on the cool, flat rock of the chamber floor, and stared into nothin' with enough determination you mighta thought I was contemplatin' the mysteries of the universe instead of just how much I didn't wanna face the kindhearted family I'd once stole from.

The boy Radley sat cross-legged beside me to my left, while Fanni moved a different direction, and then I heard her rustlin' around somewhere behind me, and the sound of water bein' poured.

There was silence between me and the boy fer a

space, and then he said, simply and without preamble, "Your leg seems a lot better now."

I only nodded. There was a lot I wanted to say to him. A lot I wanted to apologize fer, even, but none of the things I could think to say just then seemed right. None of 'em seemed like enough.

Then Fanni reappeared to my right, holdin' a bowl of water, a roll of bandages, and a small jar of what suspiciously looked like some of Blackbird's moonshine. A clean rag was draped over her arm. She settled herself on my other side, and again I was overcome with the urge to get up and leave.

To escape the situation all together.

"Let me see your arm," she ordered.

It was the first thing she'd said to me since I'd first laid eyes on her upon wakin' up in her house months ago. All that time I'd spent with her family, and she hadn't said a word to me. Now, I swallowed at her cool tone. "I can clean it up myself. No need fer you to do it." I reached fer the water bowl, but she pulled it away from me, eyes flashin'.

"You want it to get infected? Want father to chop off your arm, too?"

"No…"

"Then I will do it."

"Ya know, I've done plenty of doctorin' myself, Missus. And I ain't died yet."

Her gaze narrowed. "But you would have. Before, when my father pulled you out of the desert. You would have died right then if not for him. And it was your kind of doctoring that gave you that infection in the first place—that killed the flesh of your leg so there was no other choice but to amputate it."

I looked away from her and back to the stove at that, knowin' damn well it were true, but not willin' to admit it out loud.

"And just now, too, if father had not ordered off the attack, you would have been killed for certain."

Ordered off the attack? Wait, did that mean Dr. Balogh could … could *control* those things?

"She's right," Radley put in from my other side.

I scowled, not needin' his input here.

"So give me your arm," Fanni said again, but she didn't wait fer me to comply. She grabbed my right wrist and yanked it toward her, and then I winced as she pushed my sleeve up to my elbow, bein' none too gentle about it. "And I'll make sure it is all done *properly*."

So maybe that's why she really wanted to do it herself. Maybe this was her way of makin' me pay fer betrayin' her family's trust, in whatever small way she could. She'd fix me up, sure. But not without makin' it hurt some.

I inhaled sharply and clenched my teeth against spittin' out a curse as she slapped the rag—now soaked in water—onto my forearm and started scrubbin' at the crusted blood and torn skin.

Reflexively, I attempted to jerk my wrist outta her grip, but she held onto me with fingers nearly as strong as that statue's, I swear. "Not sure such vigorous scrubbin' is really necessary," I managed to grit out. "Those cuts ain't that deep."

"Oh, I see," she replied smoothly. But she did not ease up on her scrubbin'. "Then you've dealt with these automatons before?"

"These … these what?"

"Automatons." She dunked the bloodied rag into

the water bowl, rinsed it, squeezed it out, and scrubbed some more. "Those things that attacked you?"

It was all I could do to sit still under her rough administrations. "No … nope. Can't say I have."

"Well then. Why don't you just leave the doctoring to me, being as you don't know anything about them, or what kind of wounds they can inflict."

I nodded, hopin' if maybe I agreed with her, she'd gentle up some. "Yeah, all right. All right, sure."

She finally stopped scrubbin' and tossed the rag back into the bowl. My arm throbbed a whole lot worse now than it had when she'd started. She didn't let go of my wrist, but reached fer the little jar of moonshine next. She propped it between her knees and twisted off the top, and I tried to yank my arm away from her again, anticipatin' her dumpin' it over those cuts.

She flashed me a glare, pullin' my arm back into her lap, and instead offered the jar out to me.

Oh. I took it from her with my left hand with a little sheepish nod and downed a good third of it, this time welcomin' that searin' burn all down my gullet.

"Which kind was it?" she asked.

I blinked back the eye-waterin' fire of the 'shine to squint at her and coughed. "What kind was what?"

"The automaton that scratched you," Radley said. "What'd it look like?"

"Oh. It was red and gold. Had a fancy dress and a domed face." I took another swig of the 'shine.

"A Siren then," Fanni said, and she snatched the moonshine jar away from me and dumped the rest of it over my arm.

My yell echoed out across the chamber, and I managed to wrench my arm full away from her this time, bringin' it across my body to cradle it protectively. Though there weren't nothin' I could do now about that alcohol seepin' down into those cuts. Just had to grit my teeth and wait fer the white-hot burnin' to fade.

"Everything all right out there?" Dr. Balogh called from behind his wall of blankets.

"Just fine," Fanni answered, fixin' me with a hard look. "Our *guest* is being a baby, that's all." She threw the roll of bandages at me and scooped up the bowl of dirty water and the rag, then stood. "Wrap it up," she spat. "You'll be fine."

Then she turned and marched back over to that workbench, tossin' the bowl to grab up some parts, goin' back to whatever she was doin' before I arrived, I supposed.

"You'll be fine, Mr. Delano," Dr. Balogh's disembodied voice said. "You're very lucky it wasn't much worse."

"Fer fuck's sake," I hissed. "I think it was better before." The 'shine's fire still ate into the flesh of my arm, though it was finally startin' to ease off. I picked up the roll of bandages with my left hand and started to unwind a length of it.

"I'll get you something to cut it with," Radley said quietly, and he stood and wandered off, then returned shortly with a small knife and handed it over.

"Thanks," I muttered. Well, *he* didn't seem to

have too many hard feelin's toward me, at least. If he was bein' so helpful, maybe his mama had never found out he'd been the one to aid me in my escape that night. Or the one to bring me my guns.

Maybe he'd never got whooped fer it.

I hoped he hadn't. I cut what I needed off the gauze roll and started to wrap it around the freshly oozin' slashes across my forearm, though awful clumsily given I only had one hand to work with.

Radley sighed and knelt in front of me. "Here, let me help."

I did. He was far gentler than his sister, windin' the length of bandage at just the right snugness from my wrist to my elbow, then tyin' it off.

"Yer … yer pa get the money I left fer him?" I croaked. "Fer the mule and the saddle I took?"

"Yeah." He sat back, admirin' his work.

"Yer ma and yer sister know about that?" I glanced up to Fanni's back, but she ignored me now. I'd done this family wrong, sure, but I'd tried to make it right later, too.

"Yeah." Radley followed my gaze toward his sister, then looked toward the wall of blankets his parents worked behind. "Otherwise I think Mama might have shot you on sight when you walked in here. Or turned you over to Sheriff Reeves for being a horse thief."

Sheriff Reeves. What would she have thought of that, I wondered? Her newly appointed deputy, turned out to be a horse thief.

A horse thief and a whole lot more worse than that.

I grunted and gave a nod, suddenly wishin' fer more of that 'shine. It would have numbed things up right quick. And not just the lingerin' pain in my arm.

"Why didn't you come back?" Radley asked suddenly, quietly, so the rest of his family wouldn't hear. He settled himself cross-legged again, right in front of me, and looked at me with that plainly open, innocently curious look only children could manage. "You said you were gonna come back. Bring back our mule and all, and then you didn't. You *promised*, Mister."

I dropped my gaze away from that look, studied my hands in my lap and those strange painted designs scrawled all over the backs of 'em, and wet my lips. Nodded again. "I … I, uh … ran into some trouble. Didn't want to lead it back to you and yer family. I'm sorry."

That weren't entirely untrue.

The boy frowned, and his eyes flicked over my person. "We heard there was a shoot-out in town the day after you left. Three men killed. Was that you?"

At last, I didn't have to lie. I shook my head. "No. No that wasn't me."

He seemed to relax a little at that, and I decided not to mention the fact the man who *had* killed those gents was my long-time partner, and he was waitin' fer me somewhere out in the forest above us even now.

"What about your guns?" Radley gestured at my empty hips, where my weapons shoulda been. "Thought you didn't like to go nowhere without them?"

"Yeah. I don't." I sighed and rubbed my left hand over my face, exhaustion hittin' me full force again. "Didn't have a choice this time. Crazy old lady took 'em from me. Wouldn't give 'em back."

"The Oracle?"

"So she calls herself."

"Well why were you attacked then? The machines are only supposed to attack anyone coming in with weapons."

I lowered my hand and peered at him. "Only *supposed* to attack…? Now what the hell does that mean?"

Radley winced and looked over his shoulder again, toward the wall of blankets. "Shhh," he hissed. "Mind your language, Mister. Mama's already mighty sore at you. I wouldn't give her any more reason to dislike you."

I snorted. "Kid, I think your mama is gonna dislike me no matter what I do."

"Well don't let her hear you talking like that. She'll send you right back to those machines to finish you off."

I rolled my eyes, rememberin' those rules she'd listed out to me the night I'd woken to find her sittin' next to my bed with a big ol' knife in her hand. "Yeah. I'll try my best. So those machines. You say they're only supposed to attack people bringin' in weapons?"

He nodded. "That's right."

"How many people find their way down here, exactly?" I couldn't imagine it was very many, given that little burrow we'd had to crawl through to find this place. But then again, it was possible others had found a different way in. A larger, more obvious entrance, maybe; the same entrance the Balogh's musta brought all this stuff in through.

Radley shrugged. "Not many. Most don't pass the Oracle's Judgement, I guess. And if they don't pass, she doesn't let them in. And if they *do* get in, they always bring weapons, seems like. The machines end up killing them. Except for us. We listened to the Oracle. Pa didn't bring a single weapon when he came in here." The boy spread his hands and smiled. "Now we've been living here for weeks, safe as can be."

I thought of all the people crowdin' into Blackbird right now, and all the people frantically searchin' up at surface level fer just this kinda place, and shook my head. "I think it's likely that someday, and probably someday soon, that Oracle is gonna find someone who won't take no fer an answer. She's gonna get herself killed. Her and all her followers, too."

Radley gave me a strange look. "She can't be killed, Mister. She's the Oracle."

I let out another laugh. "Oh, anyone can be killed, kid. Sorry to break the news to you … but everyone dies."

His lips pursed, brows lowerin' over his eyes. "Not her. Her magic protects her."

"Oh fer the love of…" I sighed heavily and scrubbed at my eyes. "She tell you that?"

"Uh huh."

"'Course she did. All right. So she can't be killed. Fine. Yer tellin' me no one has found their way in here without her showin' 'em the way?"

"Not yet. That's why she's there, you know. Her and her followers, they're the protectors of this place. Pa told me they've been here for generations, guarding it."

All of this nonsense was worsenin' my headache. "And what about you? You face that so-called Oracle's Judgement, too?"

He nodded stoically.

I hoped he hadn't seen the kinda things I'd seen. Hoped he'd had far more pleasant visions. I shifted some on that hard rock ground and cleared my throat. "So if you don't got any weapons on your person, those statues … what? Just stand there?"

He nodded again. "They only activate in response to a threat."

I frowned. Well. I guess me stealin' one of their swords and almost hackin' off that horned statue's head *would* count as a threat. To them, anyway. Those strange words they'd been chantin' made sense now, in that respect. "They … are they … are they Old World?"

I almost couldn't get myself to ask. Memories of the metal soldier's all-too-familiar leg holster flashed through my mind, and that sick feelin' churned in my stomach afresh.

But Radley brightened at the question, eyes agleam with sudden enthusiasm. "Oh yes! All of them. Father says it's the most impressive collection of whole, operational Old World relics he's ever seen. You should have seen him when we first arrived … I thought he might burst he was so excited."

"Uh huh." Just what I needed. Yet another person seemingly obsessed with a civilization dead and gone a long, long time ago. "Thought your pa was a doctor," I commented. "What's he want with a bunch of old machines?"

The boy gave a snort. "Machines are the future, Mister. Don't you know that?"

"No." All the old stories started comin' back to me. The ones Mama had used to tell me and Ethelyn before bed. The ones Ethelyn had loved so very much, she'd daydreamed about 'em far more often than Mama had cared fer. "Ain't that what they say caused the Great Fall in the first place? Machines? Sounds to me like they're the past, not the future."

Radley's expression darkened. "Father says those are just stories."

"Ah. Well. What does he say caused the Great Fall, then?"

"People. People like you and me. Same as every other disaster in history."

I chuckled. He had a point there. But was most certainly only parrotin' what he'd heard his pa say before. I wondered if he had any real good understandin' of what that really meant. "Suppose that's true enough," I admitted. "So … yer pa … he can control those things?"

Radley sat up a little straighter, almost puffed out his chest, even. "Sure he can. Worked on it for weeks. Ever since we got here, really."

"Huh." I rubbed absently at my bruised throat. That changed things, certainly. Machines that could murder—or not—upon command. Had Nan suspected somethin' of the sort was down here? Was that why she'd been so intent on findin' ruins in this area?

The thugs in her employ were bad enough.

But *these* kind of things in the hands of Nine-Fingered Nan would be … truly terrifyin'. Deadly. Unstoppable.

And handin' her such weapons just might be the price fer Ethelyn's freedom.

I swallowed, winced as my throat ached, and sighed again. "So the other people who pass the Oracle's Judgement, who come on in here … where are they now?"

The boy sobered quick. But before he could make a reply, a woman's voice answered from behind me.

"They are all dead."

NO TIME FOR TOMORROWS

I startled, twisted around to see Mrs. Balogh standin' there. I hadn't heard her approach. I wondered how long she'd been there; how much of our conversation she'd heard.

"They are all dead," she said again. "Just as you should be. All bringing weapons when they should not, just as you did. And they paid the price."

Reflexively, I scrambled to my feet and pulled off my hat to clutch it to my chest; long-dormant memories of manners springin' to the front of mind again suddenly. Probably 'cause of that look she was givin' me now.

"If your companion had not spoken the language of the Engineers and caught my husband's attention, and had my husband not been so keen to preserve the rare Mortiferum Wraith you were single-handedly destroying, he might not have stopped the machines in time to save you, either."

I'd always found the re-discovery of impeccable manners to smooth my own mama's ire … maybe it'd work on Radley's mama, too. I cleared my throat again and offered her a nod. "Ma'am. Mrs. Balogh. Hannah."

She crossed her arms. "Mrs. Balogh."

"Mrs. Balogh. I don't exactly know what a Mortifer … uh, Mortifera-whatsit Wraith is—"

"It is the automaton you ruined. The one with

golden horns. *Very* rare. We have never found one intact, in fact, let alone one that could still operate. But I suppose you put an end to that, didn't you?"

Damn. She really didn't like me much. I resisted the urge to put a hand back up to my bruised throat. Rare or not, that thing had most definitely tried to kill me. And rare or not, I weren't just gonna let it end me without some kinda fight. "Er, well … I didn't realize … I guess I didn't take much time to consider its value, bein' as it was surely intent on killin' us. But if it was somehow important to you and your family … then I'm sorry fer it bein' destroyed. I do appreciate your husband sparin' us, though. Even if at the cost of that … that Wraith. And thank you kindly fer your hospitality." I shifted awkwardly on my feet. "Uh, again."

Her eyes narrowed. "You planning to steal from us again?"

I shook my head vigorously. "No, no ma'am. Course not. And, uh, well … well I didn't exactly *steal* … I paid fer the mule, didn't I? And the saddle, too."

"A week later," she stated flatly. "That is a week we had to go without our wagon. And I had already sold off some of our furniture, some of my husband's equipment, to have enough to afford another mule before we received your payment."

I winced. Turned my hat round and round in my hands. "I'm … I'm very sorry, ma'am. To have put you and your family at such an inconvenience. I had urgent business that could not wait. And then … as I told your son here … I ran into some trouble. *Not* the shootin' in town," I put in quick, as I saw the question formin' on her face. "That weren't me." I surely weren't gonna tell her that was still the trouble I'd had, even if I hadn't been the one doin' the actual shootin'. "But I had trouble nonetheless. And I … I didn't want to bring it back on you or your children. That's all."

That weren't all. Not even close. But that was all I was ever gonna tell her, and I'd insist that was all of it till my dyin' day if I had to, hand on the Good Book, itself.

Her rigid stance softened a bit. "Perhaps you have gained some wisdom since last I saw you."

I scoffed. "I, uh, I don't know about that, ma'am." More like I'd just gained more guilt. Guilt over flat-out stealin' from the first people to show me real kindness in years. Well, I'd done what I could in the end to make it right … I only had to hope it'd be enough. Fer me and them both.

"Well then, what are you doing down here? Come seeking to be rich like all the other fools?"

The question took me off-guard, and I realized I weren't exactly sure how I should answer that.

Beside me, Radley got to his feet as well, lookin' up at me just as expectantly as his ma. "Yeah, Mister. What're you doing here, anyway?"

"We were looking for you," came a weak, unsteady voice, and I looked toward my left to see Charlotte walkin' stiffly in our direction. She grimaced with the movement and wore an unfamiliar light-blue blouse with her borrowed rough-spun trousers, but at least she was movin' around on her own now.

Dr. Balogh followed her, lookin' none too pleased. "Miss Charlotte, you really should try to rest. At least until I can be sure that poison has fully cleared your system!"

She shook her head. "I'm fine, Doctor. Feeling much better now, thank you."

But I went to her anyway, puttin' my hat back on before I took her arm and helped her to sit on a stool on the other side of the stove.

Dr. Balogh frowned, shinin' that little light into her eyes again. "Fine. You just take it easy, young lady. I'm going to keep an eye on you for the next few hours though, understand?"

Charlotte nodded.

"Looking for us?" Radley repeated. He grabbed another nearby stool and dragged it over next to Charlotte, perchin' atop it eagerly to face her. "Really? How come?"

"Because, er…" I paused again, glanced from his bright gaze over to the highly suspicious stare of his ma. I didn't exactly want to mention Nine-Fingered Nan's involvement in any of this, so I decided to stick with the original reason I'd been seekin' out the good doctor. "Because my leg … the false one … it did somethin' strange a few weeks back."

That caught Dr. Balogh's attention. He stopped fussin' over Charlotte and turned to face me, eyebrows archin'. He'd put that telescopin' eyepatch back over his right eye and looked just as ridiculous now as he had upon first appearin' in the cavern. "Oh? Something strange, you say?"

"Yeah."

Charlotte gave me a puzzled look, and I realized all at once I'd never mentioned to her anythin' about that leg doin' strange things, or that I'd like to ask the doc about it if I did ever manage to find him.

I hoped she wouldn't bring up any of the other reasons we'd been lookin' fer this family…

The doc shooed his son off the stool next to Charlotte and then patted the top of it. "Well come here, then. Have a seat. Let's take a look at it."

I did as he instructed.

"Take off your shoe and lift your pants' leg, please."

I did that, too, rollin' the leg of my trousers so that my left knee and everythin' below it was exposed.

Radley crept in at his father's elbow, starin' at the metal, and the doctor bent down to peer at the thing through his eyepatch contraption.

"Hrmm," he murmured. "Everything appears normal here. What did it do, exactly?"

"It *opened*," I said flatly. "It opened, and there were blades all over it." I waved at the shin of it. "Blades all along here, from ankle to knee. And here," I pointed to the half of my thigh that was metal, currently still covered by my pants, "there was a holster that came out. Carried a pistol and a knife."

Dr. Balogh straightened, then sighed. He pulled the eyepatch down to hang around his neck again. "Son, that is nothing strange at all. That is what it is *supposed* to do."

I glared at him. "You never thought to maybe tell me I was carryin' around an arsenal *inside my damned leg*?!"

Radley gasped at the same time I caught the sharp look from Mrs. Balogh from the corner of my eye.

"Sorry," I muttered. "But you gotta understand what a shock that was, to find out all that stuff had been in there this whole time. And then it all came out … and I didn't know how I'd activated it, or how to use it … or how to close it all back up."

The doc pursed his lips. "Mmmhmm. I had planned to send you with a schematic for the leg, remember? And to teach you how to deploy those weapons, and how to sheath them again. But you left … prematurely." He crossed his arms. "Didn't you?"

I growled, droppin' my glare back to the ground.

"Remember I told you this false leg has advantages?"

"Yeah, I remember."

"Well, *those* are your advantages."

"Yeah. I figured as much. But they don't do me much good if I don't know they exist, do they? Or if I don't know how to work 'em."

"I suppose it is a good thing you came back to me, then." The doc leaned forward and slid his fingers along the side of my left thigh, makin' me yelp in surprise and jump sideways. But then his fingers reached the metal part, so I didn't feel 'em no more, and suddenly all those blades popped outta my shin again.

I gave another yelp of alarm and sprang off the chair.

Radley, Mrs. Balogh, and Charlotte gasped in unison, and even Fanni over at the workbench was watchin' me now, her eyes real wide.

"There, you see?" Dr. Balogh offered. "Easy enough to deploy, yes? And," he reached down to grip the flat of one blade between thumb and forefinger, "if you press inward on any blade, it comes free." He demonstrated with the blade currently in his fingers, and held it up triumphantly. "Therefore, each knife has multiple uses." He whipped around abruptly and hurled the knife toward the wooden table Charlotte had been stitched on. The blade sank deep into one of the thick wooden legs.

I stared at it, then turned to stare at the doc, and I realized my mouth was hangin' open.

I shut it with a click. Glanced to Charlotte. She looked as bewildered as I felt.

I was beginnin' to think Dr. Balogh might be a lot more than just a doctor.

He grinned at me, then reached fer my left thigh again, but I side-stepped outta his reach.

"Now, now, hold still. You want to learn how to deploy that holster or not?"

"I—I don't even know how you managed to deploy the knives…"

"Right here," he said. He stepped closer, took my left hand and guided it to the metal side of my thigh. "There are buttons. High one for the knives. Low one for the holster. Go on. Give the holster a try."

My mouth was too dry, my heart pulsin' in my throat fer reasons I weren't entirely sure of. All I knew was that seein' this leg open up like this, and seein' all those knives again, reminded me too much of the night I'd planted three of 'em into Charles Miller's gut.

I tried to breathe through it, focusin' on the feel of the metal leg's little irregularities through the trouser fabric. I rolled them up further to reveal the place that holster had extended, and then I pushed on the place Dr. Balogh had indicated.

A compartment slid open with a soft whir and

the holster folded outta it, offerin' up its pistol and the fat blade of the huntin' knife.

"Oh my goodness," Charlotte breathed. She leaned so far forward on her stool I thought she might just fall right off of it. But her dark blue eyes shone bright with curiosity, and I didn't think her face had ever lit up the way it was now. "I've … I've never seen anything like that before…"

"I have," I growled. "On one of those metal soldiers. Just now. When we were fightin' 'em. One of 'em was gonna shoot me. This leg…" I had to stop fer a second, an unexpected surge of that sick feelin' pushin' up my throat again. "This leg looks an awful lot like one of theirs. Doc." I looked him square in the face. "Did you attach the leg of one of those *things* to me?"

Mrs. Balogh went quickly to her husband's side at my question, catchin' hold of his arm. "*Henri!* You said you were not performing those surgeries anymore. Not with the Old World relics! The programming—"

"It's all right, Hannah, it's all right." He cut her off, turnin' to face her and takin' her hands in his, givin' 'em a squeeze.

I watched 'em both warily, not likin' the implications of her reaction.

But the doctor himself seemed wholly unconcerned. He granted her a soft, patient smile. "It is not Old World, my dear. It is my own design."

His wife didn't seem all that much more pleased with that news, but it eased the tightness in my own belly somewhat. He turned to me.

"No, son. That leg of yours is not from one of the Paladins—the metal soldiers, as you called them.

I constructed it myself." He squared his shoulders and lifted his chin a little, like such a thing were quite an accomplishment. Which I supposed it were. "I *did* model it off the Paladin construction, yes, I admit. And perhaps a few of the internal pieces were borrowed from defunct Paladin models ... but this is cutting-edge medicine and science we are dealing with here ... I had to have *some* sort of reference to start with!"

"*Henri!*" Hannah hissed again toward his ear. And then she switched to their native language, and whatever else she said to him was lost on me.

He said somethin' back to her, soundin' defensive. And then he looked to me again. "I thought a man found shot, bleeding, and near death in the desert might have need of such further advantages someday. But of course you would not use such weapons against me or my family."

It weren't a question, and he looked me hard in the eyes as he said it.

I shook my head immediately. And not just 'cause Charlotte was sittin' right there. "No. No I wouldn't, you got my word. You've saved my life twice over now, Doc. I, uh ... well to be honest, I figure I still owe you."

I owed a lot of people a lot of things right now, seemed like.

Hannah grunted and crossed her arms again. "Indeed you do."

"Well then," Dr. Balogh said, and his momentary severity vanished quick as it had come. "We have that settled. Now, as for how you put the weapons away ... simply press each button again."

I frowned. Were it really that easy? Had I really

wandered naked all the way into Blessing when I coulda done somethin' as simple as push a few buttons? Grumblin', I did as he said. And then I grumbled some more as the blades folded quick back outta sight, sure enough, and the holster folded and slid inward, too, and the compartment closed.

Fuckin' hell. It *was* that easy.

I let my pants leg drop, rollin' it back down to my ankle and then steppin' back into my left boot. "Good to know," I muttered.

Only I hadn't used those buttons down in Miller's dungeon, when the leg had opened the first time. Was that *supposed* to happen?

Suddenly I didn't wanna know the answer to that question. After the doc's mention of how he'd taken *inspiration* fer my leg from those metal monsters, it was somethin' I couldn't bring myself to ask. Didn't wanna think of it doin' things on its own … even if those things had ended up savin' my life.

It hadn't opened on its own since then, anyway. Was probably just a malfunction.

"That's incredible!" Charlotte blurted. She looked to Dr. Balogh. "You said you constructed that yourself?"

"Indeed I did, young lady."

"Would you … would you mind showing me how?"

Dr. Balogh chuckled at the question, but Radley sprang forward before his father could make an answer, practically jumpin' up and down in excitement. "Oh yes! He can show you! He's teaching me, too, and Fanni! I built a rabbit all by myself—it even hops! You wanna see it?"

"Radley," Mrs. Balogh began.

"I'd love to," Charlotte said.

"Yes," Dr. Balogh said, "I can show you if you'd like, Miss Charlotte, but it is not a simple matter. It will take some time. And is a bit too much for so soon after your recent exertions, I think. Why don't we eat something first, and then you can rest, and tomorrow I can give you a tour of the workshop?"

Workshop. Nan had mentioned a workshop back at their Bravebank home, too.

But I didn't have time fer no workshop tours, or fer waitin' on any more tomorrows.

I cleared my throat loudly, breakin' up their disturbin' enthusiasm over machines.

They all fell quiet, and all eyes turned to me. Includin' Fanni's again from across the cavern. And then I didn't know what I was gonna say to 'em, what possible excuse I could make fer why Charlotte and I might need to leave so quick, and why they needed to leave their so-called treasure trove of automatons so quick, too.

But I was gonna tell Nan about this place … and I didn't want the Balogh family here when she came fer it.

"Yes?" Dr. Balogh prompted when I only stood there starin' back at 'em. "Something to add, son?"

I *really* wished he'd stop callin' me that.

"Oh," Charlotte said softly. "I'm afraid we can't stay long, Doctor."

Relief unknotted in my chest, and I exhaled quietly. Good ol' Charlotte with her proper politeness. She'd think of some good reason to offer for our quick departure, and fer why the family should leave as well, surely.

"No?" Confusion creased the doctor's forehead.

"Why ever not? We have plenty of space here, plenty of food."

"You have a very nice set-up here," Charlotte agreed. "Your family is very resourceful, I can see that clearly enough. And we thank you very kindly for your offer, and for your medical aid. But … Van helped me out of a very bad situation once, and now he's trying to help his sister out of a very bad situation, too, and I've offered to help him. And we don't have much time left to make sure she stays safe."

"My heavens," Dr. Balogh murmured.

Over at the workbench, Fanni stopped what she was workin' on and turned to face us.

Mrs. Balogh's expression morphed from one of stern suspicion to horrified pity, and Radley went to her side and took her hand.

I shifted on my feet, uncomfortable with the honesty, wishin' she hadn't exactly told 'em so much. Here I was, always tryin' to keep other people outta my business, and it seemed they just kept gettin' dragged in, anyway.

"And to make sure she stays safe," Charlotte continued, "Nine-Fingered Nan wants this place for herself. So, Doctor, you and your family should grab what you can and leave, as soon as you can. Go on and head back to your home."

Stricken silence followed her words.

I grimaced. Well. That was certainly *not* how I'd hoped that would go.

TALES OF FLYIN' PIGS

"Absolutely not," Dr. Balogh said finally, breakin' the stretchin' silence. Then, louder and more forcefully, he repeated, "Absolutely not! Nine-Fingered Nan and her type must never find this place, nor any of those metal barons! This place has been preserved, guarded, for generations! Only very few ever find their way in here and live to see its wonders, and even fewer ever get back out ... and there is a good reason why those few have not shared such a great discovery with the rest of the world. Because if they do, it will be torn apart by the greedy. You know that as well as I do."

"Maybe," I conceded. "But Nan knows there's somethin' here. 'Cause of all those birds dyin', I guess. She saw it in the papers. And she's got a strong suspicion already that you know somethin' about it, too, Doc. She..." I hesitated. Sighed and wet my lips, lookin' around to the children and wonderin' how much exactly to tell 'em all. In truth I didn't want to tell 'em any of it, but Charlotte had already opened that can of worms, so there weren't no point in beatin' around the bush now. "She ... she was stakin' out yer home, Doc. She was there when I first went there, lookin' fer you about my leg actin' up. She's the one who told me you'd lit outta town weeks before and came up this way. She was waitin' around fer anyone who came to call on you ... planned to interrogate 'em as to yer whereabouts and why you mighta left so suddenly. Which is how she discovered you went to Blackbird, I suppose."

The good doctor's already pale complexion whitened further at this news. He glanced to his wife in alarm.

I cleared my throat again. "I'm sorry, but she got to yer friend Dr. Wright. I'm afraid he's…" Again, I glanced to the kids. But surely they already knew what I was about to say, anyway. "He's dead. Buried him myself."

Mrs. Balogh muttered somethin' in their native tongue.

Dr. Balogh swallowed visibly. "So you did not just come all this way looking for me about your leg."

I shook my head. "No, sir. I came lookin' fer you in the hopes you'd lead me to this place. But it turned out I found this place myself, and then found you."

Mrs. Balogh straightened at her husband's side, and her eyes glittered as she glared at me. "So you *are* like all the others, then. We should have let the machines take you."

Charlotte stood from her stool, wincin' as she did so. "Now, now, we aren't like those others at all. Those others up there digging around on the surface are just looking for treasure. Trinkets to sell in the hopes of striking it rich. We're here looking to save a young woman's life. I'd say that's nothing alike at all."

Mrs. Balogh took a step forward. "And what do you think Nine-Fingered Nan is after, eh? Do you think she cares about saving anyone's life? What do you think she might do with a place like this, with machines like this, if she were to find it?"

Charlotte held the woman's hard stare evenly, but I saw the uncertainty flicker across her face. She frowned, and then at last she broke eye contact with the older woman to glance at me.

But it were true. I already knew exactly what someone like Nine-Fingered Nan might do with a place like this, with an army of machines like the ones that had attacked us.

But that weren't my problem.

"Look," I said, "if I don't give Nan some Old World ruins … she's gonna sell my sister. Already got a buyer lined up, one willin' to pay more money than I could ever afford in a lifetime, someone overseas. If I don't give Nan somethin', and soon, I'll lose my sister. You understand?"

More silence.

Over by the workbench, Fanni chewed at her lip and turned a wrench round and round in her hands, glancin' from me to her parents and back again. Radley huddled at his mother's side, but it seemed the elder Baloghs were at a loss fer words fer a spell.

Until finally Dr. Balogh stirred, and he shook his head and marched forward. "I don't think you fully understand what this place is, young man." He waved at me to follow him, and then turned smartly toward the right of this large, central atrium, where another smaller tunnel led off into the distance. "Come. Follow me, and I'll show you."

I trailed after him, curious despite myself, and Charlotte followed after me.

And behind her came the rest of the family: Mrs.

Balogh and Radley and even Fanni, bringin' up the rear.

We ducked into this other tunnel, which was also strung with lights, but this one weren't so open. It was narrow, with many twists and turns and crowded with damp, shiny cave formations in all shapes. Columns, ribbons, curtains, and delicate little tubes hangin' off the ceilin' were everywhere.

We dodged 'em best we could, and as we went, the sound of that rushin' water got louder and louder. Until we emerged into another room, this one clearly altered by man, and I stopped abruptly at its entrance and stared, mouth agape.

On the other side of this cavern was a massive water wheel, fed by a crashin' waterfall comin' down outta the ceilin', and churnin' just above a thick stream that meandered along the floor to eventually disappear beneath the left-hand wall. But this water wheel weren't attached to no mill ... instead it were attached to a whole 'nother wall of machinery.

I couldn't make sense outta that wall. It was like nothin' I'd ever seen before. So I only stared at it, speechless, till Charlotte came up on my right and caught my arm, pressin' into my side.

Slowly, I stumbled forward so that she'd have room to pass. But she didn't. She only stayed there with me, holdin' onto my arm and leanin' into me.

The rest of the Balogh family squeezed around us, goin' to join the doctor.

He went to the wall of machinery and then turned on his heel to face the rest of us, like he were maybe a schoolteacher about to give a lesson. "Son, this entire system of caverns and chambers is not only the greatest cache of preserved Old World machinery in existence—as far as I know—but it is one of the most revolutionary discoveries in science."

I scowled and rolled my eyes. Not just because he kept calling me *son*, but also 'cause he was startin' to sound an awful lot like Professor Morton.

"Growing up on this continent, you've surely heard the stories of the ancient walking cities?"

My heart stuttered a little at his mention of those, my mind flashin' back to what the professor had said about that dialed lockbox maybe holdin' a key inside to cross the Valley of Lightning. The legends that surrounded the Valley's origin and the tales of old moving cities were nearly inseparable. Course I'd heard those stories. Along with all the rest.

"Sure," I muttered. "So? I've heard plenty of tales of flyin' pigs, too. Don't mean nothin'."

Dr. Balogh shrugged. "Perhaps you are right. But I've been studying this place for nearly a month now, and as far as I can determine, this," he pointed at the water wheel, "and this," he pointed at the wall of machines, "are the basis of a very large power station."

"A power station?" I repeated.

"Like … a generator of some kind?" Charlotte ventured.

Dr. Balogh nodded. "Similar to that in a way, yes. Or perhaps more like a battery. It seems this wheel generates power, which these devices then store."

"For what purpose?" Charlotte asked. She let go of my arm to wander into the room herself, going to the bank of machines and squintin' at 'em.

"Electricity," Mrs. Balogh supplied, pointin' at

the weak bulbs which illuminated this particular space.

"And much more than that," Dr. Balogh said. "Although admittedly, I do not fully understand this operation or precisely how it works yet. It seems to utilize more than simple electricity—perhaps it even incorporates caerium—but I have been unable to prove that thus far."

"Caerium?" Charlotte asked. "I thought that was all gone?"

Dr. Balogh gave her a nod, but I had no idea what either of 'em were talkin' about. I'd never even heard that word before, though it sounded much too similar to the words those murderous statues had been sayin' fer my comfort.

"As did I," the doc said. "But perhaps that is not true, after all. Further study remains to be done, certainly."

"It runs the cities!" Radley blurted, startlin' me.

"What … what cities?" I couldn't help askin', nevermind that I already knew the answer. I just couldn't believe it.

"The moving ones," Fanni said dryly, fixin' me with a level stare. She walked in front of the various control banks with their numerous levers and gears and buttons and ran her fingers over 'em lightly. "It would take a lot of power to move a whole city. There were once stations like this one, built across the continent, to generate and store power, ready for the next city that needed a recharge to come along."

"The relays that would have transferred the power from these battery banks to the cities' engines would have been at surface level," Dr. Balogh said. "And it appears they have all been destroyed, or buried, perhaps, either by natural or man-made means. But this station still operates as it was designed to, even centuries later, generating and storing electricity."

"Until it overloads," Mrs. Balogh finished flatly. "When it can store no more."

The doctor nodded. "As you know … there is no longer anything for this station to charge. Over so much time, its storage capacity was overtaxed, and it suffered a catastrophic overload."

"But father fixed it!" Radley shouted again.

I could only stand there starin' at all of 'em, and I felt like maybe I might be losin' my mind.

"Not entirely," Dr. Balogh said. "But I did manage to weaken the battery's discharge, at least. I tried to warn the citizens of Blackbird they were in danger … of course they did not listen."

Charlotte glanced back to me, and I knew she must be thinkin' of what that barkeep had said about the good doctor bein' a ravin' lunatic.

"At that point, I knew the only way to save the town would be to try and negate the effects of an overload."

I held up my hand fer a pause while I struggled to sort all this nonsense he was spoutin'. "Hold up. Wait. Yer sayin' you knew about this place and that an overload might happen … *before* you went into Blackbird?"

"Oh yes. I've known about this place for quite some time, Mr. Delano. I have been studying the Engineers of old since before I studied medicine. And it all begins to become clear if you know where and how to look."

He grinned at me, but I didn't like that answer

any more than I woulda liked it if he'd told me he dreamed all this up in some nightmare. If he'd managed to find this place, despite the Oracle and the so-called Guardians, surely that meant that other such interested and learned parties wouldn't be far behind.

And I had a good feelin' none of 'em would be inclined to share.

"So," Charlotte mused, "the birds and other animals that died … was that because these batteries here discharged?"

Now the doc nodded. "That is correct, yes. Unfortunately, the pulse of voltage sent out from this place electrocuted many living things in the area. But it would have been a quick death. Nearly instantaneous. However, if I had not managed to dampen the discharge…" He shook his head. "It would have been much worse. Much, much worse. All of Blackbird would likely be dead. And the forest might have caught on fire and who knows how far that would have spread."

Charlotte's eyes widened. "Does that mean it will happen again, sometime in the future?"

"Yes," Fanni answered. "But we've been working on the system, trying to see if we can rechannel the power somehow to prevent that."

Dr. Balogh shrugged. "It would not happen now for some time. A few grenerations more, at least. But if I am able to do it, then I will do it."

I couldn't think of a single word to say in response to any of this madness.

As if he could sense my state of mind, Dr. Balogh crossed the room and put a hand on my shoulder. "I am sorry, son. But from what I have seen here … those walking cities of old are quite a bit more real than your flying pigs."

I shrugged off his hand. "Unless yer wrong," I growled. "This kinda place coulda been built fer any number of reasons."

He didn't seem angered by my claim. Only adopted a kind of resigned acceptance and sighed. "Perhaps. But why don't I pour you a drink and tell you a little more, and then you can see what you think."

I didn't want to hear no more about battery banks or movin' cities or things bein' electrocuted by that point, but I *did* mightily want that drink, so I followed the doctor back through that twistin', turnin' tunnel to the main chamber, and then I found myself sittin' at the big wooden table Charlotte had been stitched up on, which had now been reverted back to a table meant just fer eatin'.

Mr. and Mrs. Balogh sat too, and Charlotte, but Fanni was charged with takin' Radley off somewhere else, outta sight and outta earshot, and he protested that notion a great deal … at least until his mama got real cross with him and gave him a strong talkin' to in their native language.

Then he sulked off with his older sister at last, though his face was still all pinched up in a petulant scowl.

But it was better this way. He didn't need to hear some of what I might be havin' to tell his parents.

Dr. Balogh had a big jug of that Blackbird 'shine,

and as much as the stuff had seemed undesirable in town, it was now lookin' better and better. I poured myself a generous helpin' … then remembered my manners and offered it to Charlotte first.

She declined.

The elder Baloghs each had themselves a much more conservative pour, and then the doc launched into a story about some fella named Francesco Garavoglia, an Italian sculptor and Engineer who was, accordin' to what few records remained of the time before the Great Fall, quite renowned fer his skill at makin' automatons of the type that had attacked me and Charlotte. And accordin' to this man's journals —which Dr. Balogh brought out fer show and tell right then and there even, two thick leather-bound tomes written in a language I couldn't read—he was still livin' durin' the collapse of everythin'.

In an effort to preserve himself and his creations, he hid away in caverns like the one we sat in now, eventually settlin' into this very one, in fact. And over years, he built a collection. The *cache*, as Dr. Balogh had called it. Until conditions on the surface got too dire, and he gave up on hopin' things might improve durin' his dwindlin' lifetime.

So he blocked off the entrances to this particular power station, programmed all his creations—and those from other builders he'd collected—to "guard and protect" this space, and killed himself.

Charlotte was engrossed in flippin' through the yellowed journal pages scrawled with faded ink at the end of that story, but I only stared down into my tin cup.

Somehow, it'd got empty.

Dr. Balogh went on to tell us where Francesco's

remains could be found—in the deepest cavern, apparently—and how the man's detailed journals had enabled the doc to eventually figure out how the power storage here worked well enough to dampen the overload discharge.

And they had also been what had enabled him to control the automatons well enough to stop 'em before me and Charlotte had been murdered. He held up his left forearm with its leather cuff and beamed. Pointed to the pad embedded into it with all the little buttons.

That's how he did it, he said.

Charlotte looked like she mighta just found a whole heap-load of real treasure, all right. She babbled excitedly to the doc and his missus about the incredibility of findin' a first-hand account of the Great Fall, and how valuable that could be in and of itself, and on and on about this Francesco fella.

As fer me, all their talk muddled together so as to be nonsensical, and my head was spinnin'. Though I didn't think it was 'cause of the 'shine this time.

I stood abruptly, too fast, knockin' my stool over.

The others looked up to me in alarm, but then I just stood there, not knowin' exactly what my plan had been in the first place.

Charlotte reached out to take my hand. "Are you all right?"

Was I? I weren't. But I couldn't explain it, not in the least. "I … I need some air," I said finally. No matter that this atrium we now sat in was bigger than most buildings I'd ever been in. It was startin' to feel too small, and the air too thick. "There another way outta this place, or do I need to go back through all those killer statues?"

The three of 'em all stared at me blankly.

Then Dr. Balogh blinked. "You ... you want to leave?"

What about my question had been unclear, I wondered? Course I wanted to leave. If I had my way, I'd never set foot in this blasted place again. But I managed to keep my frustration, my disgust, in check and only said, "Yeah. Just need some air. Some real air. Sunshine. Trees. That's ... what all you said just now ... that's a lot to take in, you understand?"

The doc sat back on his stool, nodded thoughtfully. "Yes. I understand. Of course. I will ... I will show you the way out."

Mrs. Balogh spat something quickly in their own language, and Dr. Balogh answered her in kind, and I really wished I could understand what the hell they were sayin', especially as I was quite certain they were talkin' about me.

But whatever they had discussed, the doc also stood and moved around the table. He held out an arm toward the back of the chamber. "This way. There is a larger exit toward the back."

I nodded. 'Course there was a larger exit toward the back. 'Course they'd made me crawl through a goddamned burrow to get in here when there was a perfectly good, human-sized entrance somewhere else. I scowled as I followed after him, and we made our way through more of this massive cave without a word. The ground sloped steeply upward, until by the time we slowed again I was fair near outta breath and my hair was damp beneath my hat brim.

I tensed as we passed several more of those

statues lined up along the walls, but these didn't move. There were four of the metal soldiers with swords this time, and two of those with red and gold gowns and golden claws.

The endless string of lightbulbs ended, but not too far ahead I saw sunlight filterin' through a thick wall of brush and vines.

It looked impassable, but there were tracks of wagon wheels in the mud here. Must've been somethin' that could be moved aside easy enough. I frowned, a sudden thought occurin' to me. "Doc?"

"Yes?"

"Where's yer wagon now? And yer mules? I didn't seem 'em inside."

He smiled faintly. "Of course not. Underground is no place for animals. We have left what belongings we did not want beneath the surface in the capable hands of the Oracle, Ms. Higgins."

I snorted. "And you trust her to take care of 'em fer you?"

"Yes, of course."

"You don't think she'd steal 'em, or sell 'em off fer cash?"

He gave me a puzzled look. "She has not done so as of yet. Unlike my present company, mind you."

I winced. Well, point taken. I gave a little cough. "I'll just, uh … take a little walk…"

But Dr. Balogh caught my arm as I moved to step forward, and I drew up short to look at him only to see he'd turned gravely serious again. "Mr. Delano. If you have a mind to return here with Nine-Fingered Nan, or any other unsavory types who might look to take advantage of this place for their own power or gain…" He glanced over his shoulder to the human-like machines all lined up behind us, currently as still as the statues they fully appeared to be. "I will not stop these from destroying you or anyone else you might bring with you. Do I make myself clear?"

Fer a heartbeat I considered goin' back on my word … considered usin' the weapons nestled inside my false leg right now to force him to give me that little leather cuff he used to control those things. Then I considered the fact I probably wouldn't even need to use a weapon … I coulda probably just overpowered him without one to take the thing … but all those thoughts left again just as soon as they came.

Guess I didn't really wanna have to do that. So I only gave a nod myself. "Just wanna take a walk, Doc."

"Very well, then. The Oracle will show you the way back if you become lost."

I laughed and shook my head, certain there must be somethin' in these woods makin' everyone around here crazy. "All right, sure. Sure." And then I shoved my way through all those plants without waitin' fer him to say anythin' else, never so relieved to feel sunshine on my face as I came out the other side.

LOOKIN' FER SOMETHIN'

The sound of a nicker startled me, and I whipped around to find Joe standin' there, tied to a nearby tree. He was saddled and everythin', and my duster was draped over his saddle and my gunbelts looped over the saddle horn.

Fer a good long minute I only stared at him, certain I must be goin' as crazy as everyone else. But then he nickered again, big ears perked straight up, and stomped a hoof.

So … I weren't seein' things.

I glanced around at the woods, but I didn't see that old woman or any of her followers. Musta been past midday now, the sun shinin' bright through all the leaves and bakin' things good and hard beneath its glare, but a soft breeze stirred the muggy air and the branches overhead, makin' the shadows around me shift.

Birds called out to each other here and there, but there was no other noise. No other sign of any other people close by.

A mountin' sense of unease crawled up my neck as I went to the mule and pulled my gunbelts off him first. I kept all my senses on high alert as I strapped 'em round my hips again, checked to be sure both pistols were loaded proper.

If the so-called Oracle had been kind enough to return my things to me … why weren't Charlotte's stallion and all her things here, too? And how long had Joe been tied out here, just waitin' fer me?

Scowlin', but feelin' much better now with my guns back, I grabbed up my duster and shook it out, shrugged into it, checked the inside pocket, and let out a long breath of relief as my fingers found both Ethelyn's folded letter and her necklace I'd taken back from Taggert.

I closed my eyes, just fer a heartbeat, and remembered what the Oracle had said about nothin' of value bein' lost. Maybe she hadn't been lyin'.

But I still didn't trust her none.

I untied Joe and swung up into the saddle, urgin' him off immediately, though I weren't exactly sure where I was goin'. I knew where I *wanted* to go, sure. Right into Blackbird.

Right to the telegram operator.

'Course, I had no idea whereabouts I was currently, so that would have to wait till I got my bearings back.

I noted the landmarks around me, what the curtain of plants looked like that led into that network of caves underground, committin' 'em to memory so I could get back here without the help of that crazy old woman. And then I headed first toward the sound of water, and when I reached the creek, I dismounted again and stripped, and did my best to scrub off all those damned painted marks all over my skin. Though of course I avoided the areas of my most recent injuries: the place that bullet had got me in the left bicep, and the place that statue had got me on my right forearm.

When I'd done my best and my skin was all red and raw from all my scrubbin', I dressed again quickly and mounted back up to follow the creek, suspectin' it would eventually lead me to somewhere I recognized.

It didn't, but eventually it did lead me to another prospector, and I asked him fer directions toward town, which he helpfully provided.

And so it was that as the sun sank low to the west, Joe and I moseyed once more into the town of Blackbird.

It was no less crowded and chaotic than I had left it just the day before, but Joe and I waded through it just the same. I went right fer the post office, all right, bein' as that's where the telegram operator was housed.

I went right fer it … and then I kept Joe walkin' right on by it.

And I cursed myself fer my hesitation. Fer the feelings that lumped in my throat right now and fired anger hot through my limbs. So instead I pointed Joe toward the Ace in the Hole saloon. Goin' back to somethin' at least a little familiar in this mess of a town.

Goin' back to the one thing I knew I could always count on to numb all those feelings … at least fer a time.

I squeezed Joe in-between two tired-lookin' mares at the hitchin' rail; nearly had to climb over the top of 'em to dismount, but I managed. Then I looped his reins and headed inside and went straight fer the bar.

Eaton was there and lookin' even more haggard than he had before. He lifted his brows and came over to me as I wedged myself into a narrow space between elbows. "Deputy DerLynd. Good to see you again."

His use of that title gained me a little more space from the men to either side of me, fer which I was mighty grateful.

"'Fraid I got even less now than I did before," he said.

I slapped several coins to the bartop and shrugged. "Don't care. Just give me somethin'."

"All right." The coins were replaced with a glass, into which he poured a clear liquid.

Guess it was to be more 'shine then.

"Where's your lady friend?" He slid me the glass.

"She's got better places to be than here." I took it, downed it, and signaled fer another.

His brows went up again as he poured a second, and his gaze flicked briefly to the bloody tears in my right shirt sleeve. "No luck findin' your friend, then?"

"Naw." It was better to lie about that than to get into all the specifics, I reckoned. And anyway, I didn't want no one else 'cept Nan knowin' about that particular place.

And Nan only 'cause I had no other choice in the matter.

I threw back the second glass, then slapped down more coin. "Just leave the jug."

Eaton hesitated. "I'm afraid I've had to impose a drink consumption maximum per person, Deputy. Else I'd already be dry—"

"I'll get you more."

That proclamation made the heads on either side of me turn, too.

"You … you got a way to do that?" Eaton asked.

"I'll drive the damn wagon out myself to hunt some down. Just give me the damn jug, would ya?" I pushed my coin toward him.

He hesitated a minute more, glancin' to the men on either side of me before finally givin' a nod, and settin' the whole jug of 'shine down in front of me. "Well, all right. But you just remember what you said about gettin' me more, you understand?"

"Sure thing. I'll ride out first thing in the mornin'." I was gettin' good at makin' promises I had no intention of keepin'.

I threw back a third and a fourth glass of 'shine while Eaton stood there starin' at me and ignorin' his other customers, until he finally said, as I was pourin' the fifth glass, "You all right there, Deputy?"

"Sure," I coughed. "Just fine."

He looked about to say more, but a touch on my elbow then made me start and jump around, only to look straight into the face of Holt.

I squinted at him, sure we'd left him behind yesterday in those woods when we'd gone to investigate Billy Thorn's abandoned claim, grumblin' somethin' about curses.

"The girl all right?" he asked.

I blinked back the blur in my eyes left by the sting of that 'shine, but he was still standin' there afterward, real as Joe had been, it seemed. "Charlotte? Yeah, sure, she's fine."

He nodded, then tilted his chin back toward the main floor of the saloon. "C'mon. I got a table."

A table? He'd been here awhile, then. I glared at his back as he turned away and ambled off through the crowd, wonderin' if he hadn't waited fer us at all after we'd left him in those woods. Wonderin' if he'd come straight back here, instead. Wonderin' if he'd been here drinkin' and gamblin' the whole time Charlotte and I had been dealin' with that old Oracle and fightin' fer our lives underground against killer tin cans.

But I turned to snatch up my glass and my half-emptied jug of 'shine and followed after him anyway, still preferrin' his company to that of a nosy barkeep who looked about to be askin' more questions I didn't wanna answer.

Holt had a small table in the back of the joint, hardly big enough fer two, and there was a tin plate of half-eaten food in front of him.

I took the chair opposite. "How long you been here, then?"

"Awhile. Long enough to see you storm in just now. I waved. You didn't see me?"

"No."

He sighed. "Fer Chrissakes, kid, it's like you got blinders on, sometimes. You gotta learn to look around more."

I only scowled at him and muttered somethin' about lookin' around plenty.

"You want any grub?" He indicated his plate.

I hardly had to look at the stuff to know I didn't. Blackbird musta been runnin' low on supplies, all right. Saloons were servin' up some kinda gruel now, it seemed, thick and pasty and burned in places. My stomach growled anyway, as I hadn't eaten since breakfast, but I fed it more 'shine instead. "Naw," I said.

Besides, the 'shine would work faster without it. And it was already startin' to work.

I could feel it warmin' my insides, loosenin' the

tension in my shoulders, dullin' the sharp edges of the anger and disgust roilin' around in my belly. And the Ace in the Hole saloon was startin' to sway a little, too.

Holt pushed his plate aside and folded his arms on the table, then leaned forward. "What did ya see?"

I paused before throwin' back more 'shine and eyed him. "Whaddaya mean, what did I see?"

"The Oracle," he said, almost whisperin' it like it was some kinda secret. "What did she show ya? I know you found her; her people came and told me they had you. So? What did ya see?"

My gaze narrowed at the question, at his confession that he'd known those Seers had grabbed me and Charlotte, but he'd only come back to town and not bothered to try and rescue us. "What makes you think I saw anything?" I growled.

He pointed one grimy finger toward my glass. "You've been suckin' down that 'shine like water, fer one thing, when before you could hardly stomach the stuff. And fer another thing … yer pa had that same look on his face after he saw her, too."

The mention of my pa stopped me again, this time with the glass halfway to my mouth.

"That's what she does, kid," Holt said. "That's why they call her the Oracle. She shows you yer future. Why you think I'm so keen to avoid the old witch?" He straightened in his chair and shook his head. "I know my own future well enough. Don't need to see it prematurely."

I set my glass back down hard enough to slosh some 'shine onto the table. The anger bubbled up again, but I kept it bottled this time. I'd just saved the old bastard from the noose, after all, and as frustratin' as I found him sometimes, me actin' out against him hadn't ended so well fer me recently.

So I only hissed out an impatient breath. "And why didn't you mention yer run-in with the Oracle before, exactly?"

"I *did*. I told you me and yer pa had had dealin's with those Seer folk, didn't I? And I woulda told you more, but you wouldn't listen. You stormed off into those woods hell-bent on findin' Old World remnants, then you marched right into that cursed place, and you found the Oracle, didn't ya? And somethin' happened. Just like with yer pa. He came out with that same look in his eyes you got now. Like you saw somethin' you didn't wanna see."

I growled some more and gulped down the 'shine, fixin' my eyes somewhere else, anywhere else but on the old man, so maybe he wouldn't talk no more about how I looked like my pa.

The thought of it made my stomach turn. The thought of my pa maybe sittin' here like I was sittin' now, across from Holt—a much younger Holt— maybe hatin' himself and drinkin' himself stupid, too.

The Oracle had mentioned him, somehow. Somehow, she'd known who I was, known who my pa was...

A favor to a loving father who realized he had lost his way too late...

My jaw clenched reflexively at the memory of the Oracle's words. A lovin' father ... a lovin' father who had preached to his son about consequences without, it seemed, takin' into account the consequences of all his own previous sins. And now the rest of us had had to pay the price fer 'em, too.

I wiped a hand across my mouth. "Yeah, well … he ever tell you what he saw?"

Holt shook his head. "Not a word about it. But he weren't never the same, if ya ask me. And after that…" Holt sat back in his chair, liftin' his hands in surrender. "After that he went back to his ranch, back to his wife and his kids, and he … well he told me not to come around no more. Told me if he ever saw me on his doorstep again, he'd shoot me dead."

The 'shine mighta made the silence seem longer than it was, but this was a part of the story I hadn't ever heard before. I eased back in my own chair, thinkin' over all the other things Holt had told me over the years, all the other stories about the things he and pa had done together, all the time they'd spent ridin' together, about how he'd come to think of my pa as a brother, and that was a big part of why he'd come searchin' fer me and my sister in the first place after hearin' our parents had been murdered.

A sudden bitterness rose in my throat.

Holt crossed his arms and shrugged. "So? What'd ya see? You gonna tell me to go get lost now, too?"

I swallowed. Shook my head. And my answer came out as a croak. "Naw. No. No I ain't, Holt."

Another silence stretched out between us, until I poured a sixth full glass of 'shine and then slid it across the table, offerin' it to him, instead.

His brows lifted, but he accepted it without a word. Lifted it as if in toast, and sucked it down with nearly as much gusto as I had been downin' the stuff myself.

I lifted the jug, ready to pour him another, but he shook his head as he pushed the glass back at me. "No thanks, kid. Think you need it more than me."

Well, he was probably right about that. So I helped myself to more. And then I asked the question that wanted to be asked, nevermind the fact I had a feelin' I didn't really wanna know the answer. "Holt … what was Pa doin' here, anyway? When you say he found the Oracle? If he already had the ranch in Kansas and was married and all, why was he all the way down here? And with you?"

The hint of a smile pulled at one corner of the old man's mouth. He shrugged. "He was lookin' fer somethin'. Always seemed to be lookin' fer somethin', long as I rode with him. Yer ma settled him down mostly, far as I could tell fer the time I was allowed to visit, but every now and then he'd get restless again. Always called on me to ride with him, and we went all over the place. Went to see a lot of priests and other religious folk. Anyone yer pa thought could talk to any kinda god, seemed like."

I frowned. None of that seemed to match up to the other stories I'd been told about him, or to how he'd ever acted when I'd known him growin' up. "Why?"

Holt chuckled and pulled off his hat to scratch at his head. "Yer pa … he was an interestin' fella. To be honest, kid, at the time I was convinced he was lookin' fer forgiveness from the Almighty and mercy from the Mother. Maybe some kinda Salvation fer his soul. Somethin' like that."

"Did he ever find it?"

The old man snorted and shoved his hat back on his head. "I dunno. Guess I hope so. All I know is that this place was our last stop. He'd heard tales of that Oracle somewhere, and I guess he wanted to meet her fer himself. Maybe he thought she'd have some kinda answers no one else had given him yet. 'Course I thought it was all nonsense. But when we got here … when he found her … then he came back with that look in his eyes…" He trailed off, blowin' out a long breath. "Kid, I ain't never seen yer pa look scared before that day. Never forget it long as I live."

I grunted, drank more 'shine. My jug was runnin' low now, and I wondered if I might be able to convince good ol' Eaton to spare me another. "Well, I ain't scared," I muttered. And I weren't.

I was angry.

"But you saw her, didn't ya?" Holt pressed, leanin' forward again.

"We found someone who *thinks* she's somethin'. You ask me, she's nothin' more than a thief and a liar."

"So she didn't show you nothin'? You didn't see nothin'?"

The saloon had grown a fair deal more unsteady now, even with me seated. I wrapped both hands around my glass, as if I could anchor myself with it, and flashes of that wakin' nightmare pulsed across my eyes like maybe I was relivin' it right now. I blinked hard to try and clear it, to ignore the feel of my own hands wet with blood, and some of it mine, pourin' from that bullet hole over my heart. "I most certainly didn't see my future."

Holt seemed disappointed. He frowned, leaned back in his chair, then pulled his plate of half-eaten food over to start pokin' at it with his fork. "Well, maybe yer pa didn't see his, neither. But he saw somethin', all right. Somethin' he didn't like at all, I reckon. Like I said, I didn't see him no more after we left here, so I can't say fer certain."

I tossed an agitated glance around the saloon, around at all the bodies pressed close, and the slant of the settin' sun comin' in through the front windows. If I was gonna go send that telegram today, I was runnin' outta daylight to do it in.

"You find anythin' at that fella's abandoned claim besides the Seer folk then?" Holt asked. His gaze went pointedly toward the bloody tears in my shirt sleeve, and his eyebrow quirked. "Seems you were gone a long time."

I turned my glare back to him, the irritation at myself fer my blasted indecision risin' hot again and comin' out as irritation toward him. "How would you know? Did you even wait till we were outta sight before you turned tail and headed back here to yer drink and yer cards?"

He stood fast at my accusation and I pushed my chair back just as fast, leavin' enough room between us that I could draw unhindered.

But he only glowered down at me. "What'd you expect me to do? Wait there till I rotted away? Those Seer people told me you were alive and that they were gonna take you to what ya wanted, so I figured that was good enough. I knew you'd wander back into town eventually, and so you did, didn't ya?"

"I'm certainly glad you were there to back us up if things had gone sideways," I commented flatly.

He scoffed. "I'll back you up in a fight with a fair chance of survival, Van. But not in a fight against creatures like that Oracle. I ain't stupid. I'd think you wouldn't be neither, after all yer past experiences."

I scowled at him. "She ain't no creature, Holt. It's one blind old lady and her band of misguided followers. Most of 'em didn't even have proper clothes to wear, and there was hardly a gun among 'em."

"Yeah?" Holt planted his palms against the table and leaned down toward me. "Well then how'd she manage to get to yer pa, huh? Fastest gun in the Territories—maybe on the whole continent—meanest sonuvabitch since Paul Johnson ... and she got to him good, kid. Like I said, I ain't never seen him scared of nothin' till he met her."

I pursed my lips in disapproval, thinkin' he shoulda known that answer already. "He weren't that man anymore when he found her, Holt. You know that."

Some of the hardness went out of his face at that, and he drew back a bit. "Maybe not. But you think the man you knew as yer pa growin' up woulda been scared of some blind old lady? Huh?"

I looked back down to my empty glass, realized my hands were on my gun grips. I drummed my fingers against 'em. He wouldn't have been.

The realization made my skin prickle.

What *had* he seen? Maybe it hadn't been a vision at all that had spooked him.

Maybe he'd gone down into the ruins themselves, like I had. Maybe he'd seen the metal statues move ... and maybe they'd attacked him, too. Maybe he knew that was all wrong and shouldn't exist in the first place.

"See?" Holt prodded at my silence. "You know

as well as I do he wouldn'ta got spooked like that if she was just some blind old lady out in the woods with a band of misguided followers. That's why I didn't go with ya, Van. Why I didn't stick around. If somethin's gonna spook Lucky Logan Delano like that … well you can bet I ain't goin' anywhere near it. And I tried to tell you not to go, neither, but, well…" He shook his head and sighed, then resumed his seat. "Yer about as bull-headed as your pa, ain't never listened to me, anyway. So. What could I do? Just gotta let you go and make yer own damn fool mistakes. Hope to God you don't end up dead."

I swallowed, still starin' at my empty glass. Maybe he had a point.

My quarrel weren't with him, anyway. Not this time. Slowly, I let myself relax, then pulled my chair back up to the table. "Almost *did* end up dead," I muttered.

Holt hissed through his teeth. "Figures."

"But we found … we found a lot."

He arched an eyebrow. "Oh yeah?"

"Yeah. You don't wanna know. But it should be good enough fer the old hag Nan. More than enough."

"Fer yer sister, you mean?"

I nodded.

"Anythin' we could skim off the top to make a profit on?"

Despite myself, I smiled down into my glass and seriously contemplated pourin' myself another. It'd be my last one. But the drink had nearly done its job. Nearly. I'd just about drowned all that anger and self-loathin', and I'd figured out just what I was gonna tell Nine-Fingered Nan. "Nothin' you'd want," I said. "Trust me."

Holt Haggerty woulda up and plain pissed himself if he woulda seen any of those statues move like I had.

He *harumphed* like he didn't entirely believe me, but I didn't mind if he believed me or not. I went ahead and poured my last glass of 'shine, swallowed it back, and stood, then stumbled before catchin' myself on the back of my chair.

"You got somewhere to be?" Holt asked.

"Yeah. I do. Don't wait up fer me. Though I guess I ain't gotta worry so much about you doin' that, eh?"

His lips pressed into a thin line, but I didn't wait fer him to make a reply. I turned away from him and my empty moonshine jug and my empty glass and shoved through all the millin' bodies toward the saloon's door.

Time was runnin' out, and I had a message to send.

YOU'VE GOT MAIL

I didn't bother retrievin' Joe, bein' as the streets were so crowded I figured I could make faster time on my own two feet along the slightly less-crowded board-walks. And so that's what I did, dartin' and weavin' around all the folk still wrappin' up their daily busi-ness, tryin' to make it to the post office before it closed up shop fer the night.

Dusk had come by the time I reached it, but its front lanterns were still lit, so I stepped quick through the door and shut it behind me.

The mail clerk was there behind his counter, and he looked up and gave me a smile as I crossed the creaky wooden planks of his floor. "Howdy there, Mister. What can I do fer you this fine evening?"

"Just need to send a telegram, is all."

"Ah. That would be Mr. Brown over there."

I followed the direction of his gesture to see a hunch-backed old man with wispy white hair sittin' at a desk in the far corner. He turned at the sound of his name and offered a gap-toothed smile, the thick lenses of his spectacles magnifyin' his eyes. He waved me over. "This way, young man. I can get you fixed up."

"Much obliged. Unless … you don't happen to have a telephone, do ya?"

"'Fraid not. The lines haven't come out this far from Arkopolis yet."

I waved away his apology. "It's all right. Telegram will do just fine."

"Very good, then." He pulled off one of his telegram note sheets, grabbed up his pencil in gnarled fingers, licked the tip of it, and poised to write. "To whom is this message addressed, and where's it going?"

I hesitated. Shifted on my feet and wet my lips. I certainly couldn't tell him this was fer Nine-Fingered Nan. Surely that mail clerk had a weapon behind his counter, and if they thought I ran with her gang, he'd be apt to shoot me dead on the spot. I cleared my throat. "It's going to Bravebank, Arizona Territory. To, uh … address it to Sheriff Jennings."

A flicker of surprise creased the old man's face, but he wrote out the necessary instructions dutifully. "Very well. And what's the message, then?"

"The message … the message is…" It was hard to figure how to phrase it proper under the influence of so much 'shine. All the things I wanted to say were far too forward. These gents here woulda caught on quick, and Nan, if she read such things, would cart my sister off overseas in a heartbeat.

I had to be clever about this. Had to think.

And now I was regrettin' drownin' all my sense in liquor.

God damn, why do I always do that?

"Mister?" the old telegram operator asked. "You got a message you want to send, or…? We're closing up soon, and if you want this received on the other end—"

"Yeah, yeah. Yeah, I got a message." I took off my hat and swiped my fingers through damp, wavy locks before shovin' the hat back on again. "Tell

Sheriff Jennings … I found what his employer was askin' about."

"All right." He started to write.

Behind us, the bell rang as the front door opened again, and bootsteps crossed the creaky floorboards. And then another set of boots. And another.

I looked up to see what kinda party could want business at the post so late in the day, even as I dropped my hands a bit lower, toward my mismatched grips, and turned to face 'em.

Four men sidled in, shut the door behind 'em, and lined up along the front wall blockin' the exit like they were waitin' fer somethin'.

I glanced quick to the mail clerk, but the concern clearly written all over his face now meant he weren't privy to whatever this was. Mr. Brown had also stopped writin' my message, starin' at the newcomers with eyes made all the larger by his spectacles.

I stepped in front of the old man and kept my stance wide, my guns visible. In my experience, men were a lot like dogs: when they traveled in packs, they got dangerous. And the larger the group, the more trouble they liked to stir up. But I kept my tone amicable enough. "Fellas. If you'd like some privacy to conduct yer business, I was just finishin' mine."

The one in front of the door was the broadest of the group, with a black mustache that ran into thick black muttonchops. He crossed his arms as he cracked a smile. "Well now. Just so happens it's *your* business we're interested in."

My heart picked up pace at that statement …

the space was too small and there were too many of 'em at close range to be happy with this arrangement if there was gonna be a fight ... but then, he could have meant a lot of different things by sayin' that. I was currently involved in several "business" ventures, after all, and currently wanted in several different states, or maybe they'd just overheard any number of things. Or been under false impressions entirely. Or had the wrong man entirely.

So I kept my voice calm despite my hummin' nerves. "I see. 'Fraid I don't recognize you gentlemen. Refresh my memory, would you? What business of mine do you hold interest in, exactly?"

The man by the door jutted his chin out toward me, his gray eyes flickin' over my shoulder toward Mr. Brown. "Yer message. Who ya sendin' a message to, huh? Better be to Nine-Fingered Nan, 'cause yer time's just about up, boy."

I gritted my teeth against their use of Nan's name. So much fer my attempt at clever secrecy. Then the implications of his words finally got through the muddle of all the 'shine, and my focus sharpened. I looked 'em all over again, payin' more attention. I was pretty sure the man with the muttonchops had been there at Dr. Balogh's house. The rest of 'em I weren't so certain.

I swallowed, wonderin' what it meant that he was here. That there were others here.

Sheriff Reeves had said she'd heard some of Nan's crew was about in Blackbird ... but that was different than some of that crew knowin' I was here, too, and knowin' that I'd been instructed to send Nan a telegram...

"Yeah…" I answered slowly. "Yeah. I got a message to send her."

"You found it?" The squawked question came from the skinniest one near the mail counter. He weren't young, but the stubble across his chin was all patchy. He stepped forward, brown eyes agleam. "Where is it?"

I scoffed at him, and looked over the rest of the group, too. "You think I'm stupid enough to tell you? After Taggert and whoever it was that told Nan that lockbox was in the wrong coach? Don't think so, fellas. I'll give Nan the location, and no one else."

And I weren't even really gonna give it to Nan, but these thugs didn't need to know that. Least, not yet.

The mail clerk edged back from his counter, puttin' distance between himself and the boys by the door.

The one with muttonchops laughed. "You think yer gettin' some kinda choice in this? That's cute. And yer a fool if you thought Nan didn't know the lockbox weren't in that coach. She knew. She just wanted to watch you jump when she said jump." His laugh got louder, and the other three chuckled along with him. "And, well, I guess you killin' all those men inside fer her was what she really wanted."

My hands balled into fists.

His laughin' finally subsided. "She sent other people after that lockbox, people she trusted more than you. That business at the Haas residence … that was all you then, I reckon, eh?" He shook his head when I didn't answer. "Well I'll give you credit where credit is due, boy. Sure made things difficult fer us there. And took that thing right out from under us. Oh well. Guess Nan still got what she wanted, didn't she?"

That hummin' in my nerves … I was hearin' it in my ears now, too. And this little room had suddenly got too cramped and too hot.

"And she's gonna get what she wants now, too," he said, and he took a long step forward.

I had no room to step back; Mr. Brown and his desk were right behind me.

"You think she'd trust you and you alone fer somethin' this big? You think she don't know you might try and tell her a lie? Try and double-cross her, even? That's why we're here, see? Make sure that don't happen. We've been followin' you all the way from Balogh's place, hopin' you'd lead us right to it."

"Lost you in those woods, though," the skinny one said, "and that bounty hunter shadow of yers was a big pain-in-the-ass, too."

The big guy shot him a glare, then turned back to me.

"But here we are. All together again. Figured you'd have to come by here sometime in the next three days, so we kept our eyes on the place. Even if you were gonna lie, you'd want to tell Nan somethin' before the deadline, wouldn't ya? Make sure yer sister stayed *safe*?"

He leered when he said that last part, and I pulled Duster's shiny gold and ivory pistol smooth from my holster and fired from the hip. Didn't need to aim so much at such close range, but the bullet went right where I wanted it, and that was right up through that man's chin and out the top of his head.

Brains splattered, his fellows gave yells of alarm and jumped away from the gore, and I had time to fire twice more into the man to my right and drop him before the other two recovered their wits and grabbed fer their own weapons.

The two bodies hit the floor at the same time I did, landin' back behind Mr. Brown's desk and pullin' the old man down with me, then kickin' his desk over to use fer cover.

"Hey!" he protested, but I only shoved him back into the corner and motioned fer him to stay put.

A shotgun roared from across the room and I winced as more gore splattered the front window. An answerin' pistol shot punctuated a cry of pain, and I peeked up over the top of the desk to see the skinny man with the patch-work stubble had shot the mail clerk, who staggered back, clutchin' the shotgun, and there was only half of the third thug left, sprawled out across the floor now along with the other two dead.

Nan's last remainin' man was takin' aim again at the mail clerk, but I shot him in the leg. Caught him right in the meat of the back of his right thigh, and he went down to one knee with a yell, grabbin' at it.

I stood from my cover quick and pulled my second pistol too as I advanced on him. "Drop it," I ordered, pointin' my left iron straight at his head. Then I pointed the gold-plated one at the mail clerk. "You too."

He'd been hit in the chest and I weren't sure he was gonna live, but he gripped that shotgun in both white-knuckled hands, and I couldn't take no chances of endin' up like that half of a fella on the floor.

I kept most my attention on Nan's man though, bein' as he was the bigger threat, and from the corner of my eye I saw the mail clerk stumble back into his wall of mail cubbies and then slide slowly to the floor. Well, he mighta still been breathin', but I supposed I didn't have to worry too much about him, after all. So I glared down at Nan's last man, instead.

He hadn't let go his piece, but neither had he tried to shoot me with it.

I aimed both my guns at his head. "Go on, drop it. 'Less you wanna end up like yer friends here."

He grinned up at me. "Go on, then. Whatchu waitin' fer? Think I'm scared of dyin'?" He scoffed and spit, and the wad of phlegm landed on my shirt front. "At this rate I'll see you in Hell real soon, son."

I pistol-whipped him across the face good and hard, and while he was reelin' I holstered my left pistol and pulled his outta his grip, shovin' it into my waistband.

A shotgun cocked to my left and I dove fer the floor just as buckshot peppered the air where I'd just been standin'. If Nan's man had been sittin' up, it woulda taken his head right off. Instead it all buried into the opposite wall, shreddin' a few stacks of waitin' mail.

Swearin', I rolled toward the old telegram operator's overturned desk. "Mr. Brown!" I yelled. "I'd really prefer not to kill you! I just want to send my message, all right? I ain't affiliated with these boys, understand?"

My answer was another cock of the shotgun. "Sounds to me like you are."

I scrambled to my feet and vaulted the edge of the desk just as he fired through it, sendin' splinters flyin'.

He hadn't expected me to come right at him, and I was on top of him before he could swing the shotgun back around toward me. I caught the barrel of it in my left hand as he attempted to do so and gave him a good shove with my right foot in the chest, just enough to yank the gun from his hands and send him sprawlin'.

Hopefully not enough to injure him.

"Well I ain't," I hissed, but I holstered Duster's pistol and leveled the shotgun at him anyway, just to make my point clear. "If I were, I wouldn't be shootin' 'em up now, would I?"

He struggled up off the floor to sit and glared at me.

"And I wouldn't be standin' here talkin' at you … I woulda already killed you. And yer sheriff wouldn'ta made me a deputy neither, now, would she have?"

A flicker of doubt broke through his glower.

I risked a glance toward Nan's man. He looked awful dazed from that blow I'd given him, but he was tryin' to regain his feet, staggerin' and stumblin'.

The mail clerk hadn't yet reappeared from behind his counter, and I feared he mighta already expired.

I turned quick back to Mr. Brown. We'd made a lot of noise here, and there were still bits of guts painted across the front window, and I most likely didn't have a lot of time before someone of the lawful variety showed up to take stock of the situation. "That's right," I told Mr. Brown. "Sheriff Reeves deputized me. Just yesterday. So look … I'm gonna ask this man here some questions. Then I'm gonna need to send that message. Why don't you go and fetch the doc fer yer friend over there? And tell the law you had some of Nan's crew come in here, but Deputy DerLynd dispatched 'em fer you."

The anger and disgust on his face smoothed away some at that. "D-Deputy DerLynd?"

I gave a nod, glanced again over to Nan's man. He was upright now, and hobblin' over toward the mail counter. Likely goin' fer that other shotgun. I had to make this fast.

I pointed my own shotgun toward the ceiling, stepped forward and held down a hand to help the old man to his feet. "That's right. Deputy DerLynd. That's me. You trust Sheriff Reeves, don't ya? Ask her when you see her, she'll have my paperwork. Think she'd deputize me if I was really workin' fer Nine-Fingered Nan?"

He accepted my hand up, but didn't quite look entirely convinced.

"Would I ask you to fetch the law, if that were the case?"

He frowned. "Er … guess probably not."

"All right. So you go and get the doc and tell folk not to worry about the ruckus we caused here, and I'll take care of this last fella."

He considered, and I went ahead and went after the last man, steppin' around the bodies and the gore on the floor.

"Well … all right," Mr. Brown said finally. "But if you still want a message sent, you might have ru-ined my machine when you kicked over my desk."

I winced and muttered curses. "We'll have to address that later." I caught Nan's man just as he was reachin' down fer that other shotgun, all right. I grabbed him by the suspenders and yanked him backwards.

He came around swingin', caught me in the left side of the face and sent me stumblin' into the mail counter. He swiped my left pistol as I went off-balance, then shoved the barrel into my gut.

But I had that shotgun held vertical, so I swept its butt hard left and into his wrist, jarrin' the gun outta his hand before he could fire. And then I brought it up and gave him another good crack across the face.

He went backwards with the force of this one, tripped over the slumped form of the mail clerk and fell, then scrambled away from me as I advanced on him, till he was trapped in the corner. Penned in by two walls and the counter.

I smiled down at him, but from the corner of my eye I saw Mr. Brown still standin' there, starin' at me. "Mr. Brown," I said, "you'd better go and get the doc quick-like. Yer friend don't look like he's doin' too good back here. Don't worry 'bout me. I got this under control."

The old man hesitated, but finally shuffled toward the door. "You … you sure?"

"Sure. I'll be just fine."

Mr. Brown nodded. "All … all right … I'll be back soon as I can."

"Sure." I hoped he wouldn't be back *too* soon.

He changed the sign at the door to read CLOSED, then stepped out quick and shut the door behind him.

I gave Nan's man sittin' at my feet my full attention again. "Ah, alone at last."

He returned my smile, though his was all

bloodied from me crackin' my gun into his face. He was missin' a tooth now, too, I noticed. "You really are as dumb as she thinks you are," he rasped. "You know what she'll do to you once she finds out what you did here? You won't be gettin' yer sister back, I can tell you that. Not ever."

The urge to make his head disappear with this shotgun swelled hot as all that 'shine swimmin' through my blood, but I managed to resist doin' it. He was right. Nan couldn't know I'd just murdered more of her men, especially if they didn't happen to be traitors like Taggert. The three severed fingers from that poor nameless girl still haunted my sleep … and maybe Nan wouldn't disfigure Ethelyn like that, not if that merchant so keenly wanted her … but I had no doubts Nan would be apt to gleefully increase the debt I owed to her at the very least. And who knew what else, besides.

But I kept all that thinkin' to myself, and only fixed the man below me with a cool, hard stare. "Well now, why do you think I left you alive? Think I couldn't have murdered you by now if I'd wanted to? Naw, I got other plans fer you."

His eyes narrowed, and his grin grew wider. "Oh yeah? That so? *Deputy* DerLynd gonna turn me over to the law? Join the crowd of smug, self-satisfied law-abidin' folks to watch me hang so it's all *official?*"

I grunted. Shook my head. Leaned one elbow on the counter next to me. "Naw. Nothin' like that. I was thinkin' more along the lines of … well … you ever hear about what I did to Lloyd Renneker?"

Some of the malicious mockery went outta his expression at that, and his grin faltered.

"Only now, see, I had the pleasure of bein' a

guest of Mr. Charles Miller's in Blessing about a month back, and maybe you don't know about the particular kinda *hospitality* he provides, but lemme tell you, it's one-of-a-kind. Maybe you also heard about what happened to him?"

His grin turned into a frown now, and he looked me over like maybe he was rethinkin' his previous opinion of me. "That was … you?"

"Sure it was. But I gotta admit, I learned a lot durin' my three days with Mr. Miller. Before I killed him, I mean. I bet, if I had Lloyd Renneker here again, to do all that over again, I bet I could do a much better job of it. I bet I could get him to last at least three times as long."

I paused, acted like I'd just got a good idea, and leaned forward a little, like I was gonna tell Nan's man a secret. "Guess it's a good thing I got you now, huh? How about we go test that notion?"

He came up off the floor at me but I dodged him this time, givin' him a good shove as I ducked so that he crashed right back down to the floor. Then I jumped on him, tossin' the shotgun onto the counter so I could put a knee into him and wrestle his arms behind his back. I grabbed the closest thing to me that could work to restrain him, and that was a roll of twine on one of the low shelves. It was awful thin, but I wrapped it thick and tight around his wrists before tyin' it off. He flopped around like a damned fish, cursin' me and makin' all kinds of threats, but I managed to stay on top of him long enough to tie him and shove his bandana in his mouth to shut him up. Then I dumped out a bag of mail next to the mail clerk while mutterin' apologies

—though I was pretty sure he was dead—and put the emptied sack over Nan's man's head.

"There. That's better. Come on, now." I retrieved my left pistol from the floor and put it back where it belonged, set the one I'd grabbed from him and stuck in my waistband next to the shotgun, then hauled him up to his feet. "We've got a *lot* to talk about."

BROKEN PROMISES

I took him out the back door, guidin' him with a hand around his bicep as he limped along, and tried to avoid the thicker knot of folk that had gathered in front of the post office. I kept to the back streets, and anyone we passed who seemed concerned by the sight of me haulin' around a bound man with a sack over his head, I introduced myself to as Deputy Der-Lynd and told 'em I was on the sheriff's business.

Most folk seemed otherwise too preoccupied with their own troubles, or else didn't care enough to question me further, and we reached the back of the Ace in the Hole saloon soon enough.

I kicked the back of his good knee, sendin' him down into the dirt. He rolled, growlin' somethin' I couldn't understand around his bandana, and then I pulled him up sittin'. "You just stay here a minute, yeah? I'm gonna go grab our ride."

I didn't expect him to stay put, of course, but he couldn't go far with a bullet in his leg and without bein' able to see nothin', so I went quick to the front of the saloon to fetch Joe.

Holt was waitin' there already, leaned up against one of the support posts fer the awning, and I drew up short at the sight of him, scowled, then continued my march to my mount. "Can't talk," I said, twitchin' my reins from the hitchin' rail. "Got business."

He appeared unbothered by my brusque declaration. "You hear all that ruckus down by the post office?"

"Sure did."

"You suddenly seem in an awful hurry."

"Sure am." I mounted up, backed Joe out of the tight space.

"You have somethin' to do with that ruckus there?"

"Might have. But fer now, like I said, I got business to tend to." I touched the brim of my hat. "Good luck with yer cards." I turned Joe away just as Holt's face twisted into an awful glower and kicked the mule up into a trot to go around the side of the building into the back.

My catch was tryin' to make a run fer it, all right, but he hadn't got too far at all, havin' run blind right smack into that pile of lumber. I rounded the corner of the saloon just in time to see him stumble over a piece of it and hit the dirt again.

I rode Joe up beside him and reached back to pull my lasso loose from my pack. Didn't need to use it too often … but fer situations like these, it sure came in handy. "Tsk, tsk, Mister. I told you to stay put. I was gonna let you have a ride … but now I think yer gonna have to walk."

He struggled back to his feet, turned away from my voice, and tried to run off again.

I sighed and shook out my rope. Now he was just makin' it easier on me. My loop sailed true, settled neatly around his neck, and I gave it a good yank.

He jerked to a stop with a strangled yelp and hit the ground hard on his back in a cloud of dust.

Holt rounded the saloon's corner atop his black gelding just as I was closin' the distance between myself and my quarry, coilin' up the rope slack as I went to keep it semi-taut. He reined up on the other side of the unfortunate man groanin' in the dirt and let out a low whistle. "Well, well. Got yerself a prize now, did ya?"

"One of Nan's crew," I said. I wrapped what was left of the rope around my horn and pulled, usin' the leverage to drag the skinny man standin' by his neck. He finally got his feet under him well enough to put weight on his own legs—or at least his one good one —and then he stood there wheezin' and gaggin' through his bandana and that sack fer a spell, leanin' against Joe's shoulder. I let him recover his air.

Didn't want him dyin' on me yet.

"Says they've been followin' us since we left Balogh's place," I told Holt. "Says Nan never cared about me sendin' her anything, or tellin' her about anything. She just wanted him and the others to follow me, see if I found what she wanted, and if I did, to tell her about it themselves. She didn't trust me not to lie or double-cross her, apparently."

Holt's face darkened, his bushy brows drawin' down low. "So … yer sister?"

The man at Joe's shoulder coughed a laugh through his gag, so I pulled that rope around his neck tight again till he had to stand up on his tiptoes to get any air at all, and then I left him like that while I answered Holt's question. "That's what I'm gonna find out from this fella here. As well as a whole lot more."

"And the others?"

"He's the only one left."

"So he's the business you got to tend to?"

"Sure enough."

Holt sat quiet in his saddle fer a long moment, and the dark of night deepened around us even as the bustle of Blackbird continued on unbroken, and the gaspin' rasps of the man at the end of my rope filled the space between us.

"This the road you wanna go down?" Holt asked at last. "Well and truly? Yer playin' with fire, ya know, kid. Pokin' the bear. You keep this up and one of these days Nan is gonna come fer you full-force. And that'll be it. Fer you and yer sister."

"Not if I get to her first," I growled. "You don't gotta be part of this, Holt. Like I said, it's my business. You just go on back to yer cards." I nudged Joe onward, only lettin' that rope out a little so that Nan's man had to stagger along beside me or risk bein' dragged by his neck. And I went directly fer the woods that edged the outermost perimeter of Blackbird.

The woods outside the circle of the *incident*. The woods no one seemed bothered with, currently.

Didn't want any accidental witnesses fer what I was gonna do next.

"Fuck you, Van," Holt muttered from behind me, and he rode up next to me on his gelding. "You even know how to conduct a proper interrogation?"

"Sure I do. Done it plenty of times now."

"Not sure I'd call what you did to Renneker an *interrogation*."

"It got me what I wanted."

"Guess so. But there's an art to doin' it proper, ya know."

My gaze dropped down to my left hand on the

reins, where even in the growin' dark the white tips of the bandages around my three middle fingers was visible. Those nails hadn't grown back yet. And all the old pains Miller had inflicted on me durin' those three days came back now, ripplin' ghostly across my skin, and I drew in a deep, quiet breath. "Yeah. I know."

His name was Silas Lowery, the skinny man with the patchy stubble.

And he weren't afraid of dyin', no, but like most men, he didn't prefer to be in a great deal of pain. Holt and I took him far out into those woods, and we laid the hurt on him good.

Took most the night, but I stayed patient. Just like Charles Miller.

We made Silas Lowery hurt, then we doctored him up a bit, let him feel better fer a time before we hurt him again. I didn't have all the tools Miller had had, though admittedly I wished I did just then. And I never woulda thought I'd have ever wished such things on another person. But findin' out Nan had purposefully misled me regardin' that lockbox, and had never intended to let me use my discovery in Blackbird to bargain with, had put me in one hell of a murderous mood.

And if I couldn't take out my frustrations on Nan herself, then her man Silas was gonna have to suffer, instead.

So I made do with what I *did* have: my knife, and rope, and a fire. And I promised Silas I'd kill him quick if he just told me what I wanted to know.

It took some convincin', but eventually he realized that between myself and Holt, we were gonna make his end real, real unpleasant and real, real lengthy unless he cooperated.

And so he did. Finally. Near dawn, I'd squeezed outta him everythin' I was gonna get, it seemed.

I paced under the thick canopy of trees, at the very edge of our little fire's light, and contemplated my new knowledge. I'd hoped fer more … but at least it was somethin'. More than I'd had before.

Silas Lowery didn't know where Nan was keepin' Ethelyn. He'd said only her top lieutenants were trusted with that kinda information. But he *did* know she'd be shipped off via airship, if she was sold, and that they'd leave from that airfield in southern Utah. The one I'd heard about but never seen.

He also didn't exactly know what Nan had been hopin' to find here in Blackbird. Didn't know what she was specifically lookin' fer, but he suspected it had somethin' to do with her plan to cross the Valley of Lightning. She was buildin' a whole special vehicle fer the crossin', even, he'd said, out in the wilds west of Bravebank, and I wondered if that's what Sheriff Jennings had been referrin' to when he'd mentioned her *industry expansion*.

Holt and I had both laughed at this notion, but Mr. Silas Lowery was adamant Nine-Fingered Nan had a good lead on how she might cross that expanse of a death trap. We pressed him fer how exactly she planned on doin' it, but he didn't know the details on that, neither. Claimed that was also information reserved only fer her closest lieutenants.

And when we'd asked why a person like Nan might be interested in the other side of the Valley, Silas had said somethin' about her wantin' Califia fer herself.

Holt and I had another good laugh at that. Califia was somethin' else from all those old stories. The thing Ethelyn had been most enamored with as a child, in fact: a big, gleamin' city. The last one left from the world that had existed before the Great Fall, the stories said. A utopia of humanity, fulla inventions the likes of which we folk on this side of the Valley couldn't even imagine.

It was, of course, all horse shit. More fairy tales.

There'd never been any proof Califia existed, or had ever existed. No one had ever managed to cross the Valley of Lightning ... no one had ever come to our side from the other side, neither. It was a generally accepted fact that the old minefield extended all the way to the western coast. And after hundreds of years of failed attempts to explore it or cross it, it was also a generally accepted fact that the Valley was just there, immutable, impenetrable, and would be there till the end of time, and that was that.

If Nine-Fingered Nan had bought in to the legend of Califia and whatever treasures it might hold, that was all fine by me. If she thought she could manage to get across the Valley in some kinda custom-built vehicle, that was also fine by me. *More* than fine, in fact.

I *wanted* her to try it, even. Wanted her to get fried tryin'. Woulda liked to have been there myself to see it, too. Woulda loved to have seen Nine-Fingered Nan, outlaw queen of the Western Territories, scourge of the Americas, reduced to nothin' more than a blackened, smokin' skeleton.

But first … first I had to find Ethelyn. Make sure she weren't shipped off.

"I could go to the airfield," I murmured aloud, haltin' my pacin'. "Plant myself and stay awhile. Check the manifests. See if anyone shows up with Ethelyn."

Holt leaned back against a tree trunk, crossed his arms and shook his head. "All the way in Utah? It'd take you weeks to cover that distance. Yer sister could be shipped off while yer still en route and you'd never know. Nan ain't stupid. She'd do all that with fewest witnesses possible. Probably wouldn't be anyone not on her payroll around at the time, and you can be sure there'd be no traceable manifests, neither."

I went back to pacin'. He was right. The airfield was too far. Gettin' there would take too long, and the results of such a journey were too uncertain to risk it.

Silas had said somethin' about Nan givin' him and the rest of the group she'd sent after me a code-word to use in their communications back to her, to let her know it was really her crew sendin' word … *Eldorado*, he'd said it was.

Fittin', I supposed, bein' that name had some-thin' to do with lost cities of gold, but also amusin', since it'd long been known that Eldorado didn't ex-ist. And neither did this other city Nan was appar-ently so keen on findin'.

But I could send somethin' back to her myself now, use that codeword, tell her they'd found the motherload and to come on out to collect. Could even give her a false location, and she'd believe it, 'cause she'd think it was her own people givin' her that information.

But if she thought she was comin' to collect … if she thought there was really somethin' here she wanted … would she come in force?

Maybe. And she certainly wouldn't come with Ethelyn to trade, in that case.

I stopped pacin' again abruptly and went to crouch in front of the slumped and bleedin' Silas Lowery. He flinched away from me, but I didn't plan on hurtin' him no more fer the moment. Instead all I asked was, "How bad does Nan hope there's ruins here?"

He shrugged weakly. "I … I dunno. A lot, I guess. She's … she's been after others … but they don't got what she wants. Been … been watchin' this place … long time. But can't … the Oracle…"

I frowned. Leaned a little closer to hear him better. "What about the Oracle?"

He gave a little shake of his head, then winced. Spit blood into the carpet of leaves beneath him. "She … she can't get past. Damn Oracle. None of us … none of us can. Been sendin' … people up this way fer months now. They never come back. That's why … why she sent you. Otherwise…" He choked out a short, painful laugh. "Otherwise she wouldn'ta … wouldn'ta bothered with you."

My frown deepened. Well now. *That* was somethin'.

Somethin' I could use. I stood, turned, and grabbed up my saddle, startlin' Joe out of his doze.

Holt straightened up off his tree. "Where ya goin' now?"

"Back into town. Gonna send Nan a message."

"Please don't tell me yer thinkin' of marchin' off to try and shoot her again? I know you and yer pa have got to be some of the luckiest goddamned bastards I've ever met in my life … but you've said it yerself: yer pa's luck didn't serve him so well in the end, did it? You keep pushin' it, yers is gonna run dry, too."

I threw the saddle up onto Joe's back and pulled my cinch tight, then reached for my bridle, hooked on the nub of a nearby tree. "You didn't seem to have so much of a problem with me doin' that when you came along with yer rifle."

"I think that certainly helped even the odds, yeah," Holt admitted. "You gonna let me do that again? And hope we get the old coot herself this time instead of one of her lackeys?"

I shrugged. "Maybe. Not entirely sure yet." I slipped the bit into Joe's mouth, wrangled the headpiece over his big ears, and then went to retrieve my pack and my bedroll to strap 'em back to my saddle. I hadn't even bothered unpackin' 'em when we'd made camp here, fully expectin' I wouldn't be doin' nothin' but gettin' answers outta Mr. Lowery.

Holt cleared his throat. "So you ain't got a plan at all, then?"

Still preachin' at me about plans, even after all these years. I paused in coilin' up my rope, took in a deep breath and exhaled slowly. "Yeah. I got a plan."

Sorta.

"Let's hear it, then."

I rolled my eyes and stuffed my rope into my pack. "I'm gonna give Nan that codeword our friend

Silas there mentioned … tell her Blackbird has what she wants."

"Yer gonna pretend to be him?" Holt jerked his chin in Silas' direction.

"That's right. And I'm gonna tell her Delano can get past the Oracle … and he'll tell her how just as soon as he has his sister. So if she wants her ruins, she'd better come and get 'em, and bring the girl."

Holt grunted, one hand pullin' at his scraggly beard as he apparently mulled over this plan of mine.

I swung up into my saddle and gathered my reins, heart beatin' too hard, anger rushin' hot in my blood, but Holt snatched the side of Joe's bridle just as I was about to spur him into motion. I glared down at him with a look viler than I'd probably ever given him.

But he held my gaze unflinchin'. "You wanna bring Nine-Fingered Nan into a whole town fulla folk?"

I hesitated, rememberin' tales of how she'd burned whole towns to the ground sometimes, if they didn't comply with her wishes. I swallowed. "I'll … I'll tell her the ruins are somewhere else. Outside of town."

Holt didn't let go of Joe's bridle. "Somewhere we can have high ground. Like last time."

I nodded, knowin' he meant the time we'd murdered Taggert and his band of traitors. He didn't know about the most recent time I'd confronted Nan, when I'd stormed into her viper's nest blind with rage like a goddamned idiot. The thought sobered me a bit, dulled some of the anger that again churned up my insides. He was right. Again.

If I was gonna do this … I had to do it right. No more fuckin' around. No more games. No more expectin' Nan to keep her end of the deal.

I just needed her to bring me Ethelyn. Then I'd grab my sister and get the fuck out, and none of the rest of it mattered.

"Yeah," I muttered. "Somewhere like that."

"All right." Holt stepped up to Joe's shoulder. "There's an old lumber mill, abandoned, fallin' apart, not too far southwest of Blackbird. Paul used to use it sometimes as a base when we were runnin' jobs up here. You tell her that's where you'll meet her. Plenty of spots there fer us to set up with rifles, and it's on the bank of the river and cleared out some. Be better visibility."

I nodded. Swallowed again. My mouth suddenly felt like cotton. "So … if she does come … you'll help me even out the odds?"

Holt sighed heavily and shook his head, finally lettin' go of Joe's bridle to pat the mule on the neck. "Kid, to be honest, I still think it's suicide. But I woulda told you yer hare-brained scheme to free me from the noose was suicide, too. Woulda told you it never woulda worked. Especially with you in that ridiculous dress. But here I am, alive and kickin'. Didn't get my neck stretched after all. So, hell." He shrugged. "Maybe this plan of yers will work, too, and we'll finally be free of Nine-Fingered Nan." He grunted. "Wouldn't that be somethin'?"

"Yeah," I muttered. "Sure would be."

"Long as," he said, and he held up a finger, "you stay smart about it. And that luck of yers holds out. And I'm there with my long rifle. Then maybe … *maybe* you got a chance."

"Guess I'll have to take that chance."

"If this is really the hill you wanna die on…"

I glanced down to him at that, found him lookin' up at me again. Joe nosed at his pockets, but he ignored the mule. And I said nothin'.

He sighed again, nodded as if in resignation, and stepped away from my mount. "Right. Sure, then. Sure. Guess this is the best chance yer probably gonna get, all right."

"Then I'm gonna go set the bait."

Holt pulled his right pistol. "Fine. I'll take care of our friend here, if yer done with him."

"No."

Holt stopped short on his way toward Silas Lowery and turned back toward me with a frown. "You ain't done with him?"

That old familiar anger came back, seeped deep through my bones as I glared toward what was left of Nan's man. "No, I'm done with him. But leave him. Let the wolves take care of him."

Holt straightened, blinked. Pulled off his hat and scratched at his head with his thumb before puttin' it back on. "Van. He gave us what we wanted. We got what we needed outta him. Let's just put him outta his misery—"

"No, Holt."

"Van—"

"*No.*" I walked Joe closer, closer to Holt and closer to Silas. "You leave him to die slow, understand? To rot. Fer the wolves and the crows to eat on … hopefully while he's still alive to feel it."

Silas made a choked noise from where he knelt, tied to a tree with plenty of bones broken and things peeled off him. "But … but you promised…"

"Yeah," I snarled at him, "I did. And yer boss promised she'd give me my sister if I brought her that lockbox. Well I took her that goddamned lockbox, and do you see my sister?" I didn't wait fer an answer. "You didn't seem to have a problem with broken promises before, when it was *me* gettin' played, did ya? I seem to recall you findin' it awful amusin', in fact. Guess it ain't so funny anymore, is it?"

I didn't wait fer him to answer, but switched my glare to Holt, instead. "Let him know what it feels like to have the terms of the deal changed after he already delivered his end of it."

Holt shook his head. "Fer Chrissakes, Van. You don't gotta be like her."

"Don't I? Thought you said bein' a thief and a murderer was in my nature?"

"Not this. This is low, even fer the likes of us. And especially fer you."

I stepped Joe a little closer to him, slidin' my right hand over toward Duster's smooth ivory grip. "After everythin' Nan has done to me … what she's taken from me … this is what she gets. What anyone workin' fer her gets. Leave him, Holt."

The old man stared up at me fer another long minute, then blew out a long breath through his teeth and holstered his pistol. "All right. All right, fine. But this is on you, understand?"

"Sure. Don't bother me none."

Holt muttered somethin' as he went fer his own saddle. "I'm goin' to town then, too. Gonna find a stiff drink and a heavy whore. Ain't stayin' around here fer this."

"You do that. I'll find you after I send the message."

"Sure."

Silas whimpered and twitched. "C'mon, please. Please, you promised…"

I reined Joe away from him, not even givin' him a backward glance. His end wouldn't be no fun, certainly. We'd done things to him that surely hurt, but wouldn't kill him quick. And there was a lot of blood. Predators would be here sniffin' around before too long, happy to pull him apart bit by bit, to finish the job we'd started.

The thought brought me great satisfaction as I kicked Joe into a trot and left Holt saddlin' up behind me, and soon enough even the desperate, broken pleas of Silas Lowery were lost to the fresh peacefulness of a new dawn.

A SPECIFIC KIND OF LOST

I reached the Blackbird post office before it opened fer the day and waited uneasily in the back, tryin' to stay as out-of-sight from anyone and everyone as possible, till I saw Mr. Brown headin' down the boardwalk at last.

I waited a bit to give him time to unlock the place and get settled in, but then I risked goin' around to the front, tied Joe, and strode on in.

He startled at the sound of the bell and turned in his chair, hands already on his shotgun. He'd left it atop his desk now; no longer hidden away. But he let go of it as he recognized me and slowly stood.

His desk had been righted again, and his telegraph machine was all set up again, but there was a big hole in the desktop next to it. And there was still a sizable bloodstain on the floor, too.

I stepped around it as I crossed the room toward him.

His hands lifted. "Now look, Deputy, I don't want no more trouble in here today, all right? Don't think anyone will be in here for weeks after yesterday. You scared 'em all off!"

"I don't plan on any more trouble here, Mr. Brown."

He eyed me dubiously but resumed his seat. "Well that's good. Because Sheriff Reeves wants to talk to you. Said if I happened to see you again, to tell you to go check in at her office."

Check in? I weren't certain whether that might mean she wanted to question me about the specifics of yesterday's murders or put me behind bars for 'em. Either way, it didn't matter. I had no intention of checkin' in at her office. But I nodded to Mr. Brown. "Sure. Soon as I get that message sent. Afraid it's rather urgent."

"All right. The machine seems to still be in working order, at least. Hey, what happened to that other fella?"

I frowned. "What other fella?"

"The one you said you were going take in for questioning. Sheriff Reeves said you never showed up with him at the jailhouse."

"Uh, yeah." I shifted on my feet, restlessness prickin' at my nerves. "Ran into some … complications. He tried to escape. Had to put him down."

"Ah." Mr. Brown nodded thoughtfully, then swiveled his chair around back to his desk, to my relief. "Well, good riddance. The more of that filth gone from this world the better, if you ask me."

"I wholeheartedly agree, Mr. Brown."

"Okay then, Deputy." I gritted my teeth at his use of that title again. He took up one of his sheets of paper and his pencil. "What's that message of yours?"

I went up to his desk and laid a hand over the top of his shotgun. "Now look, Mr. Brown. I'm gonna tell you this message, and you might find it rather alarmin'. But you should know … I'm workin' with the … with the marshal service from the Republic in attempts to end Nine-Fingered Nan's reign of terror out here." Boy, my lies were sure gettin' elaborate these days. But then, Charlotte *had* said her Senator father was lobbyin' fer some kinda big lawful force to send out here, so maybe it weren't as far from the truth as it sounded.

Mr. Brown turned his chair around to look at me, skepticism and concern written all over his wrinkled and deeply tanned face. His gaze flicked down to the hand I had over his shotgun. "That a fact?"

"That's right, sir. So if you don't want Nan herself to come up here with her whole outfit and raze this town to the ground, I suggest you send out exactly what I tell you to send out, and don't ask no questions." I picked up the shotgun. "And I'm gonna hang onto this fer you, too, till my message is sent."

His eyes narrowed behind his spectacles. His expression hardened, but after another long, silent minute of glarin' at me, he only swiveled back to face his machine and lifted his pencil again. "Well then. Let's hear it."

"All right. Address it to Nine-Fingered Nan herself. Goin' to Bravebank, Arizona Territory."

He looked sideways at me, and I could tell he weren't very confident in the tale I'd just spun. But it didn't matter whether he believed me or not. All that mattered was that he sent my message.

So I instructed him to tell her that Blackbird had what she wanted, out in a place several miles southwest of town by an old, abandoned lumber mill, and that Delano had managed to find a way past the Oracle, even—I'd seen it with my own eyes—and that he was more than willin' to share this secret once he had his sister physically in-hand.

Told her we were keepin' Delano safe fer her, that we'd all be waitin' at that mill fer her arrival, and she should get here just as soon as she could so we could proceed.

Then I included the word *Eldorado*, and signed it *Silas*.

Mr. Brown seemed continually more perplexed as I recounted these things, but recorded all of it dutifully, and then he tapped it all out on his machine. When that was done, he tore up his little note paper and tossed it into the trash. "There we are. All set. I suppose … you don't plan to pay?"

I snorted. "On the contrary, Mr. Brown." I fished out some coin with the hand that weren't holdin' his shotgun and set it on the corner of his desk. Gave him a little extra, too. "I appreciate yer services very much. And anyway, what kinda law-abidin' deputy would I be if I went around not payin' folk?"

He took the money, but squinted up at me with high suspicion. "Appreciate it. You can come by later and I'll have any response I receive in the meantime ready for you."

I settled myself back against one edge of his desk and cradled that shotgun. "I'll wait."

He blinked at me from behind his thick spectacles. "Er … but that could take hours. Maybe even days. Depends on the person receiving the message, you know. When they receive it and when they feel like replying—"

"I know how it works, Mr. Brown."

"And you just figure you'll wait around here all that time?"

I shrugged. "Sure. All that I just told you is sensitive information, Mr. Brown. Wouldn't want you goin' off to share it around."

He pursed his lips. Clearly that's exactly what he'd been hopin' to do. Probably hopin' he could go straight to the sheriff so she could come sort out which parts of my story were true or not. "Why don't you at least go see Sheriff Reeves?" he suggested. "She seemed real keen to talk to you."

I bet she is. "After I get a reply, Mr. Brown. Like I said, this is urgent business. I need to hear the response just as soon as it comes in."

He looked none too happy about this, but in the end couldn't seem to muster a way to dissuade me, so he gave up, grumblin'. "So you aim to bring her *here*, huh? Nine-Fingered Nan, right to our town?"

"Not to town directly."

"Close enough," he growled. "I don't know what you're really on about, Mister, but I sure as hell hope you know what you're doing." He went on about his daily business after a few more mumbled complaints, and I stayed there leanin' against his desk and holdin' on to that shotgun, ruminatin' on the chances of this plan workin'.

The hours passed, and the day slipped into late mornin'. But things inside the post office stayed quiet. I took to helpin' Mr. Brown sort mail, bein' as I had nothin' else to do and he'd said his mail clerk friend was still at the doc's and weren't expected to live. Though I still made sure to keep that shotgun well outta his reach.

And he still weren't happy with me, or happy in general, so I tried to console him by remindin' him those who had shot his friend had already got the justice they deserved, at least. And that it had mostly been me who'd given it to 'em.

He only nodded silently, and we went back to sortin' mail.

My stomach growled, wantin' food, and the churnin' restlessness jumpin' around in the rest of my insides wanted some drink to calm it, but I resisted both.

I suspected it would be Nine-Fingered Nan herself who would answer me, and if that were the case, I couldn't risk Mr. Brown interpretin' that when I weren't around. He'd take it straight to Sheriff Reeves, I imagined.

Finally, near midday, his machine started whirrin', and I jumped up from my piles of mail and grabbed up the shotgun, too.

Mr. Brown eyed me, but crossed to it slow. He took his chair, picked up the end of the tape, and started writin' down what it said.

I came to stand next to him and peered over his shoulder, readin' his scrawl as he put it down. It was addressed back to Silas, all right.

From *her*.

My hands tightened around the shotgun till my fingers ached, and my breathin' turned all harsh and ragged.

TELL DELANO I'LL BRING THE GIRL. HOLD HIM. GET HAGGERTY TOO. WILL ARRIVE IN TEN DAYS. KEEP THEM COHERENT.

And that was all.

She signed it *Eldorado* herself, but no name.

Didn't matter, though. I knew who it was from.

She was comin'.

I snatched up the telegram tape and the paper Mr. Brown had written the message on and shoved them both into my pocket. But I couldn't risk the old man tellin' anyone else about this meetin' of mine or gettin' any kind of law involved. Ten days was too long to chance him keepin' quiet about any of this.

Too long…

I gritted my teeth. *Shit.*

I laid the shotgun down across his desk and put my other hand on his shoulder. "Thank you fer yer help, Mr. Brown." Then I put a bullet through his forehead quick, before he could register anythin' was wrong.

He jerked and sagged in his chair, head lollin' back, and I slipped my pistol back into its holster still smokin' and made fer the door. There was another mess splattered all over the inside of this post office now, and I had no stomach fer it.

I stepped out onto the boardwalk in front and kept my hat brim lowered, not even checkin' to see if anyone outside had taken notice of the gunfire this time. Surely they would eventually, given yesterday's events here; I needed to be gone—long gone—quick as I could manage.

So I mounted up in a hurry and pointed Joe off in search of Holt.

Checked a few of the brothels first, then checked the Ace in the Hole saloon and tried to avoid the notice of Eaton, bein' as I didn't have the fresh stock of liquor I'd promised him.

I found Holt there though, sure enough, at one end of the bar, and pulled my hat down even lower as I approached.

He saw me anyway, turned toward me casually and lifted those bushy brows of his. "Well?"

"Time to go," I said.

"Again?"

"That's right. You get what you needed?"

Disappointment clouded his features. "Sorta. Could use more drink, though."

"Yeah. Me too."

"Hey Deputy!"

I flinched at Eaton's call. *Shit.* So he'd seen me after all. I hooked a hand around Holt's arm and pulled him away from the bar. "Come on, we gotta go."

He growled at me, but threw back what little drink he had left and then flipped a few coins to the bartop before pullin' his arm free to follow me.

We made fast fer the door.

"Deputy!" Eaton called out again behind us. "Hey now, don't you forget your promise!"

Shit. I lifted a hand in a little wave and tossed him a backward glance. "Sure thing, friend, workin' on it now."

That seemed to satisfy him somewhat. He nodded, then opened his mouth again just as I reached the door to his establishment.

"Oh yeah, and Sheriff Reeves wants to talk to ya! Stop by her office on your way out, would you?"

I winced again. "Yeah, sure, will do." I shouldered through the door before he could add anything else and wasted no time in climbin' aboard Joe.

Holt followed suite and swung up onto his gelding. "What's all that about?"

"Nothin' important. Deputy business."

Holt snorted a laugh but I ignored him, my

eyes already focused down the street on another crowd gatherin' in front of the post office. So my latest deed had been discovered, then. Well, that's the way we needed to go, but we could go around. Outside town. Through all the trees to stay out of sight.

I reined Joe in the opposite direction, pushed on through the throngs of folk that flowed down Main Street.

Holt caught sight of that growin' crowd now, too, and his amusement turned into a scowl. He hissed a curse as he followed after me. "God damnit, Van, what did you do now?"

"Didn't have a choice," I said.

"Anyone see you?"

"Maybe."

He muttered more curses. "And the message? You send it?"

"Yeah, I sent it." I slowed Joe up a bit to let Holt catch up with me, and my heart still beat too hard as I tried to tell him about Nan's answer. "She's comin'," I finally strangled out. "She's gonna come. With Ethelyn. To the mill."

Surprise smoothed the discontent on the old man's face. "No shit? When?"

"Ten days from now."

He grunted, looked over his shoulder to the commotion growin' at the post office. "Seems you've stirred up this place an awful lot fer us havin' to stay here another ten days."

"We ain't gonna stay here," I said, and I kicked Joe up into a trot as we neared the end of Main Street and the mobs of folk thinned out a bit.

Holt matched my pace. "Oh no?"

"Naw. I've got a place we can lay low fer awhile, should be safe enough. Just follow me."

I intended to take him back to the cave where I'd left Charlotte and the Balogh family. Back to that rear entrance where we wouldn't have to crawl through a blasted burrow or get past so many of those murderous statues.

He mighta taken issue with just those few bodies made outta metal anyway, but as long as the doc kept 'em all quiet, surely Holt would find their company more pleasant than bein' chased outta Blackbird by an angry mob or bein' strung up by Blackbird's sheriff.

So we went around the town through the woods and eventually ambled west along the same path we'd taken only days before, till we reached the place I'd rejoined that road from the north after leavin' the cave myself.

I led us off the road at that point, goin' by memory and followin' the landmarks I'd taken note of on my way back into town. Except ... except it seemed we kept goin' in circles.

I reined Joe up in front of the old dead oak with a split trunk we'd passed at least twice now, and a ripple of dread fluttered in my gut.

Holt reined up beside me. "Yer lost, ain't ya?"

I swore under my breath, lookin' around at all the trees that surrounded us. The afternoon was growin' late, the shadows stretchin' long. Things seemed too quiet; the call of two near crows yellin' at each other too loud. I swallowed. "I ain't lost…"

I'd come by this tree before, I was sure of it. It even had the clusters of small animal skulls hangin' from its low branches, just like the one I'd passed before. I'd been goin' south at the time, which meant we needed to go north now. And that's where we'd headed, just an hour or so ago. We'd gone north. I could still see where our mounts had disturbed the underbrush and mats of old leaves.

And yet somehow we'd ended up back here again.

Holt sighed, droppin' both hands to his saddle horn. "We're goin' in circles, Van."

"That … that don't make no sense…"

"Sure it does. Happens sometimes when you get lost."

"I ain't lost," I snapped. "I came this way before. We should go north from here."

"All right, so let's go north then."

"We did. Before. And now we're back here again."

"Well that don't make no sense."

I glared at him. "That's what I just said."

He shrugged. "We musta got turned around at some point. These woods are tricky like that. Everythin' looks so similar. So many trees you can't orient yerself proper."

"I ain't a child no more, Holt. I know how to check my direction and check landmarks. I'm tellin' you, I've been followin' the landmarks all this time."

He sat quiet fer a time, then nodded. "All right. Well. Let's try again. Talk me through 'em as we go."

It was the same thing he'd used to tell me when

he'd first been helpin' me hone my directional skills, and it raised my hackles that he was talkin' at me like that again now. But I clenched my teeth against snappin' at him fer it.

Either we *were* really lost … or I was losin' my mind. Maybe he could help me figure out which.

I prodded Joe into motion again, headin' north. "North from this tree," I muttered.

And so we went. Again.

And some time later … we were right back at that goddamned tree, split trunk and hangin' skulls and all.

Holt twisted in his saddle to squint out at all the woods that surrounded us. "What in the hell…"

The dread that had stirred in my gut before now sharpened into a real kinda fear. We shouldn't be lost. Not both of us. Not like this. And we both couldn't be losin' our minds … could we? "I told you," I whispered. "Told you I was followin' the landmarks…"

The sound of rustlin' leaves and underbrush nearby had both of us with guns in-hand and ready, watchin' the trees. Eventually, people emerged. Came toward us on all sides, slow and unhurried. They had weapons, but didn't seem intent on usin' 'em.

My heart sank as I recognized their patch-work clothes. It was those goddamned Seers again. I sighed and holstered my pistols.

"Van…" Holt prompted.

I shook my head, not havin' the energy to explain it all, and remembered then what Dr. Balogh had said about the Oracle showin' me the way back if I got lost. He'd failed to mention it might be a very *specific* kind of lost.

I heard Holt's hammers click back and looked to him sharply, only to realize the Oracle had appeared right in front of us, and I hadn't even noticed. I reached over to push his arms down, forcin' his guns to lower.

"Stop," I hissed. "She's gonna show us the way out." I straightened and looked to the old woman. "Ain't you? Yer gonna take us back to the Temple?"

She folded her hands in front of her. "You, yes."

"What Temple?" Holt asked.

I swept my hands back to my own grips again. "I ain't goin' nowhere without him. Yer gonna have to take us both."

"You will follow us," was all she said in reply, and then she turned and made her way off through the trees, and her band of disciples closed in around Holt and me, and the old man glared at me with a look that broadcast his displeasure and suspicion loud and clear.

But so long as she was gonna escort the both of us without argument, I weren't gonna begrudge the guidance. Even if havin' all her people surround us like this made me real uneasy. And even if the implications of 'em all meldin' outta nowhere after Holt and I had been wanderin' in circles fer hours made the hairs on the back of my neck stand up.

Long as we made it back to that cave, I could sort out the rest of it later.

DEVIL ON THE DOORSTEP

The sun had sunk low to the western horizon again by the time we reached the place. We'd followed all the same landmarks Holt and I had followed before … only this time, somehow, we didn't go in circles.

That uneasy feelin' jumped around in my gut now somethin' awful, but at least we'd finally gotten where I'd been tryin' to go all day.

The Oracle's loyal band loosened their knot around me and Holt and moved off into the trees. The old blind woman herself turned to face us again, and Holt looked about as unhappy as I'd ever seen him.

"Here we are," the Oracle said. "You may re-enter," she nodded toward me. Then she looked to Holt as if she could see. "If you will submit to Judgement, and should you pass, you may enter as well."

"And like I told you before," Holt snarled, "you can go fuck yerself."

"Holt."

He turned his burnin' glare toward me. "I ain't doin' it, Van. I seen what she does to enough people … heard enough stories … I ain't doin' it."

I sighed, my shoulders saggin'. Maybe I could have shot down the old woman and many of her followers and gotten inside with Holt, but with their numbers, they could have easily overtaken us soon as I had to reload. Not to mention I didn't want the

Baloghs findin' out later that I'd done somethin' like that.

And I didn't think I believed what Radley had said about the Oracle havin' magic, exactly … but there was surely somethin' about these Seer folks that didn't quite add up. And frankly, I was too tired to bother testin' any of that tonight.

So I only rubbed at my eyes and shrugged. "Fine. Fine, sure. Have it yer way." My hand dropped back to my saddle horn. "In that case, look, there's a big ol' cave underground here. Bigger than any I've ever seen before. And it's Old World, all right, through and through."

Holt's anger faltered. He looked around the woods again, like he might be able to see such a thing up here on the surface somehow.

I filled him in on only the most important aspects of what was below: the fact it used to be a power station, could still function as a power station even after all this time, and that it had overloaded, and the discharge had been what had killed so many animals in the area. Then I told him about the doc and his family bein' holed up in there fer awhile now, studyin' the thing, and that I'd left Charlotte there fer safe keepin' while I saw to other business in town.

I didn't mention the movin', murderin' statues. Or Francesco Whats-His-Name.

And then I was kinda glad he kept refusin' to face that so-called *Judgement*.

Was probably better he never knew about those things, anyway.

By the time I was done with my story, Holt stared at me like I'd gone stark ravin' mad.

Well, I wouldn'ta believed any of it myself if I hadn't seen it with my own two eyes.

"Should be safe enough here," I said as I dismounted, ignorin' his look. "If you wanna make camp nearby." Then I stopped with reins in-hand. "You ain't gonna leave again, are ya? If I go inside that cave fer awhile … I ain't gonna come back out later and find you gone?"

That seemed to knock him outta his stupor somewhat, 'cause he scowled down at me. "Where would I go now, huh? You've got Blackbird all in a fuss thanks to that business at the post office. And Sheriff Reeves knows I ride with you. If she finds me in town, she'd surely ask me as to yer whereabouts. And I don't feel much inclined to be talkin' to no sheriff on yer behalf, I can tell you that."

"So you'll stay, then?"

A mighty frown crossed his face, and he glanced toward the Oracle. Then muttered curses. But he gave a nod. "I told ya I'd help with this damn fool plan," he snapped. "And so I will. Though if I'd known you were gonna lead me to a place fulla these folk," he jerked his chin out toward the blind woman, "I woulda elected to camp somewhere else."

I tossed a glance to the Oracle myself, then stepped up close to Holt and dropped my voice. "Look, these people are strange, I'll give you that—"

"More than strange," he growled.

"—and I'm not sure they're entirely right in the head—"

"Most certainly ain't."

"—but they *did* lead us back here. This is the right location. The cave entrance is there." I nodded in the direction of the tangle of vines and brush. "They coulda ambushed us back there. Killed us easy and left us to rot. But they didn't. I think ... I think if we just keep playin' by their rules, at least fer now, things'll be all right."

Holt tore his accusatory glare away from the Oracle to plant it on me, instead, then leaned over in his saddle to murmur, "Thought you said she was a liar and a thief?"

Well. I shifted on my feet. I *had* said that. I still thought that.

Maybe. Mostly.

But she *had* given my things back. And she *had* brought me back here. I shrugged. "Yeah, well. So are we."

He straightened in his saddle at that.

"It's only fer a few days, Holt. While we get ready fer Nan's arrival. Right?"

"Yeah," he grumbled. "Right. Guess I don't got anywhere else I can go now, anyway. But don't you be in there too long. We got to go over the plan."

I sighed and tied Joe's reins to the nearest tree. "Sure. Won't be long. Never liked those deep caves much, anyway."

Holt snorted. "Right."

I unbuckled my gunbelts and looped them over my saddle horn like they'd been when I'd first come outta the cave, and Holt nudged his gelding up beside me.

"What the hell are ya doin'?"

"No weapons inside. Long story."

"Longer than the one you just told me about everythin' else?"

"Much longer."

He squinted at me. "You sure that's such a wise idea?"

I scoffed and gave a nod. "Yeah. Yeah I'm sure."

He surely thought I must be mad now, but he made no other comment as I headed toward the cave's back entrance, the bigger, roomier entrance, to my relief. If I had my way, I'd never shimmy through another hole as tight as the one we'd first entered from in my life. I watched the Oracle warily as I went, half-expectin' her to stop me, or to claim I needed a second Judgement, or some other such nonsense.

But she only stood there quietly, hands folded, and the twilight sounds of the forest filled the space.

Honestly, her silence was almost more unnervin' than her babblin'.

But at last, just as I was searchin' fer a suitable place to pull aside all those plants, she spoke. Guess she didn't want to disappoint.

"It is not too late for you, Van Delano."

I paused with my left hand wrapped around a particularly thick stalk of grapevine and turned back toward her. "What the hell is that supposed to mean?"

She regarded me calmly. "It is as I said before. You face a great darkness. Already you court its arrival … welcome it, even. But that is how your father lost his way. The deeper you go, the steeper the price. He would not want you to make the same mistakes as he."

I ground my teeth as fresh anger surged. I *really* didn't like her talkin' about Pa. "Maybe you don't know nothin' about my father."

"Just remember," she said. "It was too late for

him. It is too late for your friend, here." She looked to Holt. "That is why he resists Judgement so strongly. He knows it."

A flicker of alarm lanced into me as I looked to Holt, too, even if I didn't prescribe to all this preachin' of hers.

But Holt only shook his head and reined his gelding around. "I'll make camp over yonder," he spat. "I've had enough of this. You come find me when yer done in there, got it, kid?"

"Yeah. I will."

He rode off, and I shot a final glare toward the Oracle before turnin' my attention back to the wall of plants.

"Just remember," she said again, but I weren't gonna entertain her notions no more, so I ignored her and shoved my way through the tangle of leaves and stems till I stumbled free on the other side.

They'd left the lights on fer me.

Or at least the lights along a certain path were still lit, so I followed those, and sure enough I ended up back at that main atrium.

Just in time fer dinner, it seemed.

Everyone looked up from their food as I entered, and Charlotte's eyebrows lifted at the sight of me. "Ah," she said matter-of-factly. "You're back. Must have been some walk."

"Yeah…" I muttered, ignorin' the twinge of guilt. "Sorry. Went to find Holt." I wandered toward the table as the smell of cooked meat made my stomach twist somethin' awful, and I realized I was much missin' bein' able to have a proper hot meal.

The doc and his wife stood as I approached, and he went off to retrieve another stool while his wife went about puttin' together another plate.

And suddenly I felt like an intruder here, interruptin' the family dinner, marchin' in unannounced after a lengthy absence. Reflexively, I took off my hat again, despite the fact this weren't no real house. "Oh, uh, you don't have to trouble yerself fer me," I said. "Didn't mean to disturb yer dinner … you go on ahead and finish up."

But Fanni and Radley had already moved to one side of the table, and Dr. Balogh had put the extra stool in beside Charlotte on the other side, and Mrs. Balogh had a plateful of food set there.

"Nonsense," Hannah said. "It is no trouble to fix you a plate of food compared to what other trouble you have already caused us. Now sit and eat."

I swallowed, nodded. "All … all right. Thank you." And so I did, takin' the stool and settin' my hat in my lap so I could dig into roasted bird, potatoes and carrots with much enthusiasm—until I noted the looks the Baloghs were all givin' me and paused.

Charlotte cleared her throat.

I had the distinct impression she was tryin' to tell me somethin', but I couldn't figure out what.

The doc and his wife took their seats again, one at each head of the table, and then Mrs. Balogh leaned forward, clearly addressin' me. "It is customary to say Grace before partaking of a meal at this table, Mr. Delano. Have you forgotten this already?"

I currently had a mouth full of food, so I gulped it down and sat back on my stool. Hell. I *had* forgotten. "Uh, right. Sorry. Uh…"

Shit. There'd been plenty of awkward, silent dinners durin' those three weeks I'd been laid up at their homestead, and I did remember now that there'd always been a prayer beforehand, but I'd never had to say one myself. I'd just bowed my head and gone along with whatever she had happened to say.

Now, they were all lookin' at me. Waitin'.

I folded my hands and bowed my head, mind racin' back to all the things I'd heard her say before those dinners, back to the prayers my own family had used to say durin' those quiet evenings that almost seemed more like dreams now than somethin' that had once been real. "Uh…" I closed my eyes to block out their starin' and cleared my throat. "Heavenly Father, bless this food and the hands that made it … and, er, bring prosperity to this kind family for their sharin' of it. Thanks be also to the Holy Mother for providin' such sustenance, and may She keep us all safe. Amen."

The family echoed my *amen* and I tried to hide the grimace as I shifted on the stool. Well, that was surely another thing I hoped I'd never have to do again.

But Mrs. Balogh seemed satisfied with my effort, and they all went back to eatin' again, so I deemed it safe to resume eatin', myself.

Maybe it would have been better to not have come back here at all.

Now that I took the time to think about it … I weren't really sure why I *had* come back here. I'd wanted a safe place to wait fer Nan's arrival, sure …

but I coulda done that out in the woods on the surface, makin' camp with Holt…

"So," Dr. Balogh began, pullin' me away from my ruminations. "Did you manage to find your friend? Holt, is it? Miss Charlotte told us he has been your traveling companion for quite some time."

"Uh, yeah. Yeah, I found him." I glanced to Charlotte, worried then about what else she might have been tellin' this family in my absence.

But she only nodded, then focused her attention back on her meal. Her hair was a mess and she still had those white painted markings all over her … and I suddenly wondered how she'd been while I was gone. How were those wounds across her back? Had she been comfortable down here? Had the Baloghs been tendin' to her needs adequately? And then I felt an awful guilt fer leavin' her so abruptly with no explanation, and fer stayin' gone as long as I had.

I didn't owe her an explanation, I supposed, didn't owe her nothin', really. I'd never wanted her to come along on this journey, after all, even if she had certainly saved my life when that demon statue had been tryin' to strangle me. I'd repaid her fer that already anyway, keepin' another of those statues from doin' the same to her. But that guilt settled nice and heavy across my shoulders, regardless, and I wished I knew exactly why.

"Would he also like some supper?" Dr. Balogh was askin'.

"Uh … what?"

"Your friend, Holt," Dr. Balogh repeated. "Would he like some supper as well? We could take some out to him if he is nearby."

I blinked, finally movin' my attention back to the doc, a less pleasant sight than watchin' Charlotte, though at least he'd shed that strange leather apron now. He wore that leather cuff around his left fore-arm, though. "Oh. Right. Sure, he's nearby. Camped up top. Don't like these deep caves much. I'm sure he'd appreciate a bite though … if you've got enough to spare. Otherwise I'm sure he'll manage. He's a resourceful ol' bast—errr." At least I'd caught myself that time. I tried again, studiously avoidin' Mrs. Balogh's stare. "He's … very resourceful. I'm sure he'll be just fine without. Wouldn't want to deplete yer stores. I know huntin' is scarce around these parts."

"That's certainly true," Dr. Balogh agreed. "But the blackbirds are numerous enough. There are so many of them here. They may be small, but … snare enough of them and you can make a decent meal. I'm sure we can spare another plate or two. When we are finished here, I will gather some dinner for your friend as well."

That'd probably make Holt's night, I figured. Didn't think he'd had nothin' to eat except that half-burned gruel since we'd reached Blackbird. "Well … thank you. That's … that's mighty kind of you."

"Our pleasure, Mr. Delano," Dr. Balogh said, and he resumed his meal lookin' quite pleased with himself, indeed.

That awkward silence fell again, and I shoveled food into my mouth quick as I could so I could shortly be done with it.

But Mrs. Balogh spoke again before I could quite make my escape. "You may take the west chamber for the night, if you like. It is a bit damp, but it will suffice."

The offer took me by surprise. "Oh, uh, I ain't stayin', ma'am."

Everyone stopped eatin', Radley with his mouth fulla food.

"No?" Mrs. Balogh asked.

"No." I could feel Charlotte lookin' at me then, but I resisted meetin' her gaze like I'd avoided Mrs. Balogh's just before. And I realized at that moment I couldn't tell her—or the Baloghs—about my plan to meet Nan at that abandoned mill. They'd all insist it was suicide, just as Holt was inclined to do, or worse, attempt to come along and get themselves killed. But all eyes were on me now again, expectant, relieved, suspicious, offended … a whole mix of things, and I shifted on my stool. "I mean, I do plan on stayin' around the area fer awhile, and thank you fer the offer and all, but like my friend, I don't much like livin' underground. I'll just camp up on the surface fer the night. It's what I'm used to, anyway."

"Are you certain?" Dr. Balogh pressed. "There is plenty of room here if you'd prefer a roof … even if it is a damp roof."

I shook my head. "No thanks. But I do appreciate the offer."

"Very well, then. But if you should change your mind, the offer is still there, understand? You and Miss Charlotte—and your friend Holt—are all welcome to stay here as long as you need."

"Sure."

Mrs. Balogh sat back in her chair. "So, Mr. Delano." She wiped at her mouth with a napkin. "Have you brought back with you any unsavory individuals wishing to take this cave for themselves? Are they outside now, waiting?"

Again, everyone paused their eatin' and watched me, and the rushin' of that distant waterfall sounded like thunder in the quiet.

I swallowed my food and met her even stare square this time. "No ma'am, I did not. And the only one waitin' outside is Holt."

Her eyes narrowed. "Is that so?"

"Yes," I hissed, frustration wellin' despite my best efforts to restrain it.

Dr. Balogh cleared his throat loudly, probably in attempts to head off the argument he sensed brewin' between me and his wife. "Miss Charlotte has told us a little about your sister's terrible predicament. If you are willing to tell us more ... perhaps we can help you retrieve her. Without putting such a valuable asset as this power station into the hands of a terrorist."

I dropped my eyes back down to my nearly empty plate, and suddenly had no more appetite. An offer to help my sister from people who didn't even know her. Who'd already saved my life ... twice. Who'd kept me well-fed and comfortably sheltered all the time I'd spent in their company. And even despite all I'd taken from 'em last time.

That's why I'd come back here. Seekin' all those comforts again, like a goddamned moth to a flame. Same reason I'd lamented havin' to leave Sally's place so much, too.

But nothin' good ever came outta gettin' too comfortable. "Yeah. Maybe," I managed to choke out, and there was a sour taste in my mouth.

Dr. Wright came to mind, tied to that chair and

beaten to a pulp, and then there was bile in the back of my throat.

Nine-Fingered Nan and her crew would destroy this family. Just like she'd destroyed so many others. Here they were, gathered around a dinin' table in the middle of the greatest Old World find I figured there'd ever been, actin' like all of this were normal. Actin' like this was their own house. Actin' like they had not a care in the world, like there weren't no other greater dangers out there.

And I was sittin' right there among 'em, actin' like I belonged.

A thief and a liar and a murderer—fresh from the murder of an innocent, no less, killed by my own hand this time—who'd just invited Nine-Fingered Nan herself to bring her crew up here from the west. I was bringin' the Devil right to their doorstep.

I pushed my stool back, feelin' ill. I couldn't let Nan get anywhere near this cave. Anywhere near this family. And the longer I stayed here, the greater the chance they'd get pulled into my maelstrom, too. I caught up my hat, then stood and cleared my throat. "If you'll excuse me, I'd best be goin'. I'd like to set up camp before it gets full-on dark. But thank you ... thank you very much fer the meal."

Dr. Balogh stood again. "Let me get a plate for your friend."

I pushed my hat back on and waited restlessly while he did so, well aware of all the eyes still watchin' me, Charlotte's most of all. There were a lot of questions on her face, and I didn't wanna have to answer any of 'em. I didn't wanna have to lie to her. So as soon as the doc had handed me that plate fer Holt, I tipped my hat to the family, thanked 'em again fer the food, bid 'em all good night, and tried to leave in a hurry.

"Oh, Mr. Delano?"

I gritted my teeth and tried to keep my frustration in check as I drew up short and turned to face the table again. "Yeah, Doc?"

"Come on by again in the morning, would you? I have further instructions you might find useful for that leg of yours."

Further instructions? Beyond how to deploy a whole damned arsenal from the thing? What more could he possibly have to tell me? But I nodded. "Sure thing, Doc."

"Very good. Good night, Mr. Delano."

"Good night." I all but fled the cave.

TROUBLIN' THOUGHTS

I grabbed up Joe's reins once I was in daylight again and followed the thin trail of smoke in the distance to where Holt had made his camp. It was near dark by then, and Holt was mighty happy indeed to receive that plate of real food.

"From the Baloghs," I said as I handed it over.

"Well I'll be damned." His eyes got nearly as big as saucers as he accepted it. "I see why you were so keen to return here now, Oracle or not. Real cookin', huh?"

"Yeah. Real cookin'." I pulled my pack from Joe and started layin' out my things, then unsaddled him, gave him a quick brush, and put him on the picket line with Holt's horse fer the night.

By the time I was done with that, Holt had cleaned his plate. He set it aside and wiped greasy hands on his pants. "That family ain't sore about the stuff you stole from 'em?"

I shrugged. "I paid 'em back fer all that, remember? With some of the money we—you—got from that bank."

"Oh right. More of my share you took without askin'."

I ignored his jab. "Otherwise, yeah, think they would have been awful sore about it." I didn't bother to mention what Radley had said about their mama otherwise turnin' me in to Sheriff Reeves fer bein' a horse thief. I sat down cross-legged on my bedroll, starin' into Holt's small fire. "Think they're still a little put out by it, though."

"But not put out enough not to feed you."

"Seems that way."

Holt grunted. "So they think we're … what? Just drifters, then? Mostly honest and law-abidin', but down on our luck?"

"That's right."

"Uh-huh." There was silence fer a minute as he joined me in starin' into the fire. Then he glanced up at me over the flames. "You tell 'em about Nan?"

I shook my head. "No. Hell no. They've already offered to help without knowin' the full nature of things, and that's bad enough. I don't want 'em involved. Not any of 'em."

"And Charlotte?"

"Especially not her."

"So you didn't tell her, neither."

"No."

Another stretch of silence passed between us, and Holt picked up a nearby stick and poked at the fire's logs with it. Then he gave a heavy sigh and shook his head. "Ya know, kid, that old blind woman was right. It's too late fer me."

I glanced up at him sharply, but he kept his gaze on the burnin' logs he poked at.

"This family, the Baloghs, I mean, and Charlotte … they could be yer chance to start over again, ya know. You ever think about that? Startin' over? Settlin' down, tryin' to live proper, like yer pa did?"

My jaw clenched as his eyes came up at last, but then it was me who looked away, shiftin' my sights to my mule, who lazily snuffled around the dead leaves underfoot. I pulled at a few random tufts of grass stickin' out from under my bedroll myself, then tore 'em up into little pieces as I moved my glare back to Holt again. "No," I lied. "I started that way, Holt. Would still be livin' that life if no one had come along and taken it from me. But now, no." I shook my head, tossed the pieces of grass into the fire. "No. It'd all be a lie, anyway. Just like what Pa was livin'."

Holt frowned at me, and the flames made shadows dance across his face. "You think yer pa was livin' a lie?"

"On the ranch? With me and Ethelyn and Mama? Yeah." My voice cracked. I'd never said these things aloud before. But now, as I said 'em, the truth of it solidified. And all of it one big brick of bitterness wedged in my throat. "Yeah. Or it wouldn't have ended the way it did, would it have?"

Holt's frown deepened, and I could tell he'd never considered it that way before.

It didn't matter. Like most things that plagued my sleep these days, it was all in the past. Nothin' to be done fer it now except to regret it all. And keep movin' forward, toward the hope of givin' Ethelyn a future she wouldn't someday regret.

"So," I prompted when Holt remained in contemplative quiet. "You got some kinda plan fer how to deal with Nan or what?"

He hissed a breath through his teeth and threw his stick into the fire. "Sure. Hell with it. Life was gettin' borin', anyway."

By the time Holt had laid out his ideas, and I had added a few of my own, night had descended over the forest we sat in, and the wanin' crescent moon shone high in the sky. And I was feelin' pretty confident about our chances by then, too.

We didn't know how many Nan would be bringin' with her, but we'd planned fer a lot, just in case. If she happened to bring fewer along, well, that would just make our job easier.

Even still, fer a long time after Holt had fallen asleep and lay there across the fire softly snorin', I laid on my own pallet and just stared up into those trees. It'd been a long time since I'd been around trees of this size and number. The canopy of leaves above me fluttered, shivered in the gentle night breeze, highlighted dim orange on the underside from our dwindlin' fire and flashin' pale silver on their topsides from the moonlight.

All around me, the forest hummed with insect life. Seemed they had been spared from the power station's discharge, unfortunately. I had to swat off mosquitos more than once. Well, I hadn't missed them none, fer certain. In the distance I heard coyotes, and that made me think of Silas Lowery.

I hoped he was gettin' devoured right about now.

Only then I thought of Mr. Brown, and that made me sit up and rub my hands over my face. I hadn't wanted to have to kill that old man, damnit.

I gave up on sleep with a heavy sigh and stood, grabbin' up my gunbelts to put 'em back on. Just in case. Then I grabbed up my hat and put it back on, too. Just a habit.

Joe perked his ears at my standin' and nickered.

I scowled at him. "Shush, you."

He nickered again and I whispered curses, but Holt didn't so much as twitch. Rollin' my eyes and shakin' my head, I left Joe and Holt and our little camp and wandered toward the stream I'd scrubbed myself in earlier. I could hear it, just barely beneath the chorus of insects, and I went carefully in that direction, followin' faint, dappled moonlight and tryin' not to make too much noise as I pushed through all that underbrush. Though truth be told, it was hard to hear much over the deafenin' cacophony of insects out here.

I was just passin' by the entrance to the cave on my way to the creek when a rustle of somethin' and flicker of movement in that direction made me whip around with both guns drawn.

Only to face the shadow of another person, and the glint of their own outstretched pistol.

"Van?" she hissed.

I let out an explosive breath. "Charlotte? What the hell! Yer gonna get shot sneakin' around the woods like that."

She holstered her gun and waded her way through the brush toward me, pullin' at her skirts as they were continually snagged. "I could say the same for you, you know. Thought you might have been a bear. Didn't expect you to be up and roaming about."

I grunted and shoved my own guns back into their holsters. "I didn't expect you to be up and roaming about, neither. What's wrong? You okay?"

"I'm just fine. Couldn't sleep, is all."

I growled and crossed my arms as she finally reached me. "So you think it's smart to come out here and wander around the woods in the middle of the night? All by yourself?"

She crossed her arms to mirror me, cockin' her head. "Why not? That's what *you're* doing. And anyway, I'm armed. I was coming to look for you, matter of fact. Where's Holt?" She pulled her gaze away from me to look around at the darkened forest.

I nodded back in the direction I'd come from. "Over there a ways. Sleepin'."

She turned back to me. "Where are you going, then?"

I shrugged. "I couldn't sleep, neither. Was goin' to the creek to sit fer a spell. Maybe splash some cold water on my face. Not used to this humidity no more."

"I'll come with you, then."

I peered down at her in the dark, all kinds of mixed feelin's risin' up in me at that statement. "You sure yer all right? The Baloghs treatin' you okay and all?"

She nodded. "Oh yes. Yes, they are a very pleasant family, aren't they? Very generous."

"Yeah. Very generous." And lucky. Lucky their kindnesses thus far hadn't got 'em murdered.

"And quite intelligent, too. All of them. Even the children. Makes me think … makes me wonder … how different my life might have been if I'd have been born to parents more like Mr. and Mrs. Balogh."

I lifted my brows. "Instead of to parents like your senator father? I dunno, you keep throwin' his name around out here, and it's at least made that bounty hunter Duster hesitate a time or two. He mighta been able to take me in if not fer that."

She sighed, and her crossed arms looked more like she was huggin' herself. "It didn't do any good at all. It's never done any good at all … only made life more miserable." She stared off into the distance as she said it, and again I got the sense that maybe there was somethin' botherin' her she weren't tellin' me about. I cleared my throat. "Charlotte. What's wrong?"

She hesitated fer a long minute, but then spat it out. "You're planning something. You're planning something, and you want to leave me out of it."

I was glad of the dark then, so she couldn't see me wince at that accusation. Goddamnit. I should have known there weren't no way in Hell I could come back here without havin' to answer her questions at some point.

But she didn't wait fer me to confirm or deny her statement. "Are you going to tell Nan about this place? Because if you are, we need to make sure the Baloghs are out of there, even if we have to hogtie them and carry them out ourselves."

The thought of doin' such a thing made me snort in amusement. "You'd … you'd help me do somethin' like that?"

"If we had to. I know they don't want Nan to have this place … but they don't understand. They don't understand what it's like to be kidnapped and held captive and sold off. And I'm not…" Her voice broke and she paused, took a breath. "I'm not going to let that happen to your sister if I can help it. Even if it means letting Nan take this place." Another pause. "I'd make sure to take the most valuable things out first, though. Like those journals. And Dr. Balogh's controls for the automatons. And anyway, I think those things would take care of Nan and her crew, don't you? There's so many of them … if Nan and her gang went in there with all their weapons … they'd get destroyed by those things. Don't you think?"

I nodded. "Probably. If the Oracle let them through."

"The Oracle? You think she'd stand up to Nine-Fingered Nan, even?"

"Something tells me she would." I wasn't goin' to mention what Radley had said about that crazy old woman havin' magic, nor what Silas Lowry had said about her holdin' off Nan's people so far.

"She'd be killed," Charlotte whispered. "And all her followers too, probably."

"Most likely."

A stretch of silence passed between us then, as we stood awkwardly beneath all those trees, and I gritted my teeth as the urge welled in me to go ahead and tell her my plan. To save her the frettin' over the Baloghs and a crazy old witch woman and her misguided disciples. "I'm … I'm not gonna tell Nan about the cave," I blurted finally.

Charlotte looked to me sharply. "But … your sister…"

"Just so happens another opportunity came up," I said reluctantly, tryin' to stay as vague as I could about just *how* that opportunity had come up. "I'm settin' a trap, instead. A trap fer Nan."

"A trap? And Holt knows about this?"

"Yes."

She straightened, her hands droppin' back to her sides. "But you didn't see fit to tell *me*."

I shifted, able to feel her glare even if I couldn't

see it. "Charlotte … we don't know how many Nan might bring with her."

"Which is why you should have *more* people on your side, not fewer."

I sighed and scrubbed my hands over my face. "You've been through enough, all right? I'm not gonna ask you to take part in somethin' like that—"

"You don't have to ask. I'm *telling* you, that's why I'm here. That's why I went all the way back to Grave Gulch in the first place. I want to help, Van. What else am I going to do?"

"Stay in that cave with the Baloghs," I muttered. "Stay safe."

"And yet you don't seem concerned for your partner Holt's safety," she shot back.

I snorted. "Holt? He's a mean old bastard who's been livin' on the run almost since he was born. No, guess I ain't that worried fer his safety." Though even as I said it, I recalled that Nan had specifically mentioned him in her telegram. She'd instructed her men to bring Haggerty to the mill, as well. And I suddenly wondered why.

"You were happy enough to bring me along when we went to Baron Whittaker's place," Charlotte hissed, pullin' my attention back to her. "You sure didn't seem so concerned for my safety then. Did you even really care about my situation at all? Did you actually want to *help* me … or were you just using me to get what *you* wanted?"

I winced again. "Charlotte…"

"Now that I'm no longer *useful*, it's better to hide me away I suppose, is it? I suppose I have no real value to you unless I can directly get you something you want, huh?"

"That's not what I—"

"Baron Whittaker would have killed you if not for me. And that thing in there," she pointed back toward the cave, "it would have killed you, too, if not for me. Maybe you don't think I'm all that useful anymore … but it seems like you *need* my help a great deal, Van Delano."

I hooked my thumbs into my belts and wet my lips, shiftin' my gaze out into the stretchin' darkness. Heat stung my face, her angry claim about me usin' her at the Whittakers' place hittin' a little too close to home. But it weren't like that … not *all* like that … I mighta used her to an extent, sure. But I had also wanted to help her … I really had…

The sounds of all the insects thundered in my skull as I pondered her points. They were so goddamned loud out here. But all I could think of was her bein' stung by that mechanical bee, and droppin' limp in my arms, and starin' up at the cavern roof with a glassy, unfocused gaze, and I swallowed hard. "Charlotte," I finally said. "I weren't … I weren't just usin' you. Before. And I ain't discountin' what you've done, or that you've saved my life—"

"More than once."

"More than once. But this … this is Nine-Fingered Nan. She's already got my sister, and she's been usin' that against me fer months. Just fuckin' with me. Just fer fun, I think. And this might finally be my chance to get Ethelyn back, sure, but I also can't risk Nan gettin' ahold of anyone else—" I stopped before I could say it.

Anyone else I care about.

I swallowed again, cleared my throat. "Anyone

else she could use against me. Or kill just to spite me. Understand?"

"You don't think I could hold my own against Nan?"

"You know you can't."

"But you can?"

I laughed despite myself. "Naw. Naw, Charlotte, I sure can't. She's the reason I have this metal leg in the first place. That's why we're settin' a trap. So we don't have to face her directly, 'cause none of us would live through that."

Charlotte crossed her arms again and lifted her chin. "Then it sounds like you have nothing to worry about if I come along, doesn't it?"

Now she was just makin' me angry. I stepped toward her and pulled my thumbs from my belts so I could point a finger in her face. "*No.* You ain't comin', Charlotte. All right? And neither are the Baloghs. I don't need yer help, and I don't need their help. Yer gonna stay here, stay in that cave, stay with the Baloghs, and yer all gonna stay out of the way, got it?"

She glared at me somethin' fierce. I was close enough now I could see her face clear enough, and her eyes blazed like they had when she'd shot down the baron from the back of one of his own horses. Her fists clenched and her breath came harsh and fast through gritted teeth.

Fer a second I thought she was gonna slap me …
or maybe worse.

Maybe I shoulda disarmed her first.

"I thought you were different," she spat at last. "Thought you were different from all those arrogant, useless men of the Republic, from the cruel, self-absorbed barons of the Territories ... all they ever saw me as was something to possess, something pretty to put on a shelf, to collect, to *keep safe* ... but I guess you aren't so different from them after all, are you?"

I opened my mouth, affronted by such a comparison, but she didn't give me a chance to speak.

"Fine. If that's the way you want it ... goodbye then, Mr. Delano." She spun on her heel and marched back toward the cave, and I watched her go with the protest still stuck in my throat.

But I swallowed it all back. I wanted to argue her point, sure. *She* probably wanted me to argue her point, too. She probably wanted me to come after her, to take back what I'd said and invite her to come along on this damn fool venture of mine, after all.

But part of what she'd said had been right enough ... this *was* the way I wanted it.

Well, maybe not *entirely* the way I wanted it. I didn't want her mad at me. And I didn't want her thinkin' I was anythin' like the barons of Blessing. But mostly I didn't want her tryin' to come along with me and Holt when we went to take on Nan. So if her bein' mad at me was the only way to achieve that ... then I'd let her be mad at me.

I'd let her think I was somethin' like those barons of Blessing, I guess.

Long as she stayed safe.

I watched her stalk up to the overgrowth that covered the cave entrance and angrily shove some of it aside to disappear inside, and then I let out a breath and growled, turnin' away to resume my walk toward the creek.

When I reached it, I knelt on the bank and splashed the water over my face and the back of my neck. I took off my hat and ran some through my sweat-damp hair, too. It was cool against the muggy night. Felt good.

And I tried to focus on that, the simple pleasure of the cool water runnin' over my skin, instead of on all the troublesome thoughts tumblin' over and over in my mind.

Instead of on the sudden realization that Nan had surely asked fer Holt to be brought to the mill too because she knew I cared.

She knew I cared, and she planned to kill him once she got there. Or worse.

And I was no longer certain at all she'd bring my sister along with her.

But even if she didn't … I couldn't take Holt there. I couldn't take Charlotte, and I couldn't bring Holt.

Both of 'em would only be liabilities. Tools fer Nan to use.

I was gonna have to go alone.

FAREWELLS

The next day brought an overcast sky and rain, but Holt and I went about readyin' our plan despite the weather. All but the dynamite, anyway. That would have to wait till things dried up again.

We gathered all the guns and ammo we had on us, and we rode down to the abandoned mill to scope things out. We took stock of what else we'd need, and then Holt grumbled a great deal about havin' to go back into town to purchase yet more weapons and ammunition.

But I certainly couldn't go. Not after what I'd done at the post office, and with the sheriff already on the look-out fer me. So he left to go acquire those things while I set up what we already had.

And I didn't say a word to him about the fact I weren't gonna let him help me on the day Nan finally arrived. I knew better. I'd have to just leave without him when the time came, and figure out some way to keep him from followin' once he realized I'd gone.

But fer now, I only focused on settin' up. Plantin' trip lines, mappin' out the interior of the rottin' building, already half-collapsed. I checked the sturdiness of its upper floor, noted the places that would still hold my weight … and the places that wouldn't.

I leaned my rifle in one corner near an upper window, stacked a few boxes of bullets next to it.

Left a few boxes of pistol rounds in other strategic places, put the dynamite in a place it'd stay dry till the rain stopped.

Holt returned in the early evenin' with two more rifles, one more pistol, another bundle of rope, and less ammo than I would have liked. And even grumpier than he'd been before, claimin' Blackbird's overpopulated status was havin' a toll on their supply of weapons same as the supply of everything else.

But it was somethin', at least, and it'd have to do.

We camped at the mill fer the night, not wantin' to ride back in these woods in the dark, and finished our set-up of what we had the next day. I wanted more dynamite, but Holt said Blackbird was all out, on account of so many people suddenly becomin' prospectors around these parts.

So I told him I'd just steal it. And so all that next day, I took Joe around the woods that surrounded Blackbird, searchin' fer treasure-seekers, and when I found a few that looked suitable to rob, I robbed 'em. Took their dynamite and their shovels and pickaxes and knives, and the two pistols they had and all their bullets, even their whiskey, and loaded it all up on Joe. Then left 'em bound and gagged at their dig site and headed back to Holt.

The third day was spent mostly diggin'. Plantin' the dynamite and makin' pits. The sun had come out again by then, but the rain had at least taken some of the humidity away with it, and it weren't quite so stifflin' warm anymore.

By the fourth day, we'd done all we could. We double-checked our work, strategized our positions, worked out the order of which perch and gun we'd use and when.

And all the while I wondered if this was really gonna work. And if I should let Holt come, after all. And if I didn't, how was I gonna get him to stay behind?

And then, in the absence of anythin' else to prepare, thoughts of Charlotte came back unbidden, and the weight of that look she'd given me settled heavy on my shoulders. Angry.

No, *furious*.

Betrayed.

That's what it was. She'd looked at me like maybe I really *were* one of those barons.

Disgusted.

I *really* didn't like her lookin' at me like that.

And I hardly slept at all on that fourth night.

On the fifth day we headed back toward the underground power station, though most everything in me was fully against doin' so. Weren't no reason fer me to go back, really, except to show the Baloghs—and maybe Charlotte—that I weren't as bad a man as Mrs. Balogh feared I was.

I wanted to tell 'em I weren't gonna lead Nan to their discovery. And then I was gonna tell 'em I was leavin' the area. So they wouldn't question me further on how I planned to get my sister back, and hopefully wouldn't mention again their offer to help me do so. And I was gonna give 'em some money, too, although Holt didn't know about that part yet.

Seemed the least I could do fer 'em, given all they'd done fer me of late, and fer Charlotte.

This time I weren't surprised at all when the Oracle stepped out from behind a big oak to block our way. Holt didn't say nothin' this time, neither. Only sat there in his saddle glowerin' at her, a hand on his pistol grip.

I didn't bother reachin' fer my weapons. Just stared her down, and she stared back at me with her sightless eyes. Then she turned without a word, and we followed her back to the cave again.

She merged back into the forest once we reached it with no partin' wisdom fer once, seemingly meltin' clean away, and Holt whispered a curse as I dismounted and started to unbuckle my gunbelts.

"I really don't like her," he muttered. "Somethin' ain't right about her. About any of this." He gestured toward the cave.

"Yeah." It was hard to disagree with him on that count. Every time I saw that old woman, my skin prickled. But there was nothin' fer it. Magic or not, she seemed to be the only way anyone could find this damned place. Good thing she favored the Baloghs ... and seemed to favor us. At least fer the time bein'. "But we're leavin' soon, remember? And then we ain't never comin' back here."

Holt grunted. "I think that's about the smartest thing I've heard you say in years."

I scowled at him and tossed my belts over my saddle horn. "I'll be back soon. Don't go nowhere."

"Yeah, yeah. Sure."

I reached the main atrium to find it empty. Curious and slightly concerned, I decided to check that chamber the Baloghs had shown me as the main battery room next. The one with the big water wheel.

Sure enough, Dr. Balogh was in there fussin' about by the wall of machinery. He had that telescopin' eyepatch on again, and when I cleared my throat loudly, he startled and whipped around.

"My goodness! You mustn't sneak up on people like that." He pulled the eyepatch down to look at me square. "Nice of you to decide to drop by again … did you forget I'd asked you to come by so I could talk to you more about that leg of yours? Thought perhaps you had run off for good this time."

"Oh." I glanced down reflexively to my left leg, my fingers brushin' against the metal part of my thigh. "Sorry. Yes, uh … I did forget. I've had … other things on my mind lately."

The doctor frowned at me. "I see. Well, would you like to know how to operate that leg properly or not?"

"I … er, didn't you show me before? With the knives and the gun and all that?" Mentionin' that hidden pistol reminded me to make sure it was loaded. And ideally, I needed a way to be sure it was easily accessible, too. Couldn't always be rollin' up my pants—or takin' 'em off entirely—to get at that thing if I wanted it.

Dr. Balogh barked a little laugh at my question. "Goodness, no. There is a great deal more to it than that, son. Come here, I'll show you." He waved me to the right side of the chamber, the side opposite the big wheel and the underground stream. There was a small table and stool set up there; looked new. The wood still fresh. But the surface of the table was already covered with tools and gadgets, some of 'em modern and some of 'em Old World.

The doc patted the top of the stool. "Go on. Have a seat."

I did so reluctantly, unsure of whether or not I really wanted to learn anything else about this leg of mine. I leaned an elbow against the edge of the table, sweepin' my gaze across all the trinkets strewn there. Then I pulled my arm away again in a hurry as I spotted some of those little metal centipedes like Mr. Miller had used.

These weren't movin', but I weren't gonna take any chances.

I stood, pulled the stool further away from the table, and then sat once more as Dr. Balogh found what he'd been lookin' fer in those pockets of his apron and held it up triumphantly. "Ah ha. Here we are."

It was a little turnscrew.

Frownin' now, I watched as he pulled that ridiculous eyepatch back up onto his eye and leaned over me. "Well? Let's see it."

I sighed and rolled up that trouser leg, far as I could.

"There we are. Now, you've been keeping it clean, yes?"

"Uhhh…"

There was a rubber cuff at the top of the metal part of my leg, the part nearest what was left of my actual thigh. It cupped around the natural end of my leg, so that the mergin' of flesh and metal looked more natural. That part could be removed, I knew; I'd seen the doc do it several times while I'd been stayin' with him the first time, and when he'd shown me how to wash it up good and proper.

But I didn't like to take that part off much myself. Removin' it exposed the metal rod underneath, showin' it clear as day stickin' directly outta my flesh, like a metal bone with all the meat carved off. And then there was that scar plainly visible, too. A big, dark one, runnin' down both sides of my thigh toward the place where my skin puckered around the rod, and lookin' at it too much made my stomach turn.

So I didn't look at it. And I didn't usually take that rubber part off. Not anymore. Not since leavin' his homestead, mostly. Mostly I just tried to forget that leg was metal entirely. If I never looked at it, these days I could almost forget, sometimes.

Except fer the part that the feelin' there was all numb. And it didn't always work quite right.

But Dr. Balogh pressed the release on the rubber cuff now, makin' it loosen from around my thigh, and I opened my mouth to protest as he pulled the edges of it downward.

Only he reeled backwards before I could say anythin'. "Goodness gracious, man! Don't you ever bathe?"

"Sure I do," I growled. "It's just that I—"

"I told you to keep it clean, did I not?" He marched over to grab a wooden bucket from near the chamber's entrance and then filled it with water from the stream.

"Well sure, but I—"

"Told you that if you did not clean it properly, you might get another infection?"

I glared at him as he marched back in my direction, pullin' a handkerchief from one front pocket of his apron. Truth be told I didn't really remember him sayin' that, but I hadn't much listened to anythin' he'd told me durin' those three weeks. I'd been preoccupied by the general horror of havin' a missin' leg, and the nearly overwhelmin' urgency to get to Bravebank to make the deal fer my sister.

He put the bucket down at my feet and tossed the handkerchief into it. "Here. Please clean that up. The cuff as well. It's a wonder you don't have an infection already. The place where that rod exits your flesh never entirely heals, you know. If you do not clean it properly, it is a direct route for sickness to invade your body."

I grumbled as I soaked the handkerchief and then started wipin' carefully around the end of my stump of a thigh, suckin' a breath through my teeth as the cold water hit my skin. That seemed like a pretty important detail he maybe should have made more clear durin' my first stay at his place. But then, maybe he *had* made it clear, and I just hadn't wanted to hear it. "I didn't ask you to put this leg on me, Doc. I never wanted it in the first place."

He was back over at the table, rummagin' through all those various devices, but he turned back to face me at my statement and raised his eyebrows. "Oh no? I suppose that's true. Would you like me to take it back, then? Since it seems clear you are incapable of taking care of it properly in the first place…"

He stepped toward me with that turnscrew in one hand and several very small pouches of some kind of liquid in his other hand, but I lifted my own hands as he approached.

"No. No, no need fer that. I'm just sayin' … I'm just sayin' I don't understand all of it, is all."

"That is why you are here now, is it not? I'll explain it to you, so you can understand, and then take care of it, yes?"

That weren't at all why I'd come here, or what I'd planned to be doin' right now, but I supposed it *would* be good to understand the thing better if I was gonna be stuck with it. "Sure," I muttered.

"Good." He knelt down in front of my stool and started messin' about with the rubber cuff as I finished washin' it up. There were little pockets along the inside of it, turned out, and he removed some empty pouches from those pockets and then slipped the full pouches down into them, instead. "Medicine," he explained as he caught my confused look. "I see the original store I supplied you with was used. Not surprising, considering you were out and about walking and riding much earlier than you should have been."

I remembered clear enough how rough those first weeks away from his homestead had been, how much the place where my leg had been cut off hurt. The fevers and chills, and the feel of little needles prickin' my skin. Damn. So all of that had been true, as well. The leg *had* had medicines in it to help me heal.

If it hadn't, maybe I woulda come down with another infection, just like he'd said.

I finished cleanin' up the grimy, sweat-crusted skin that had been beneath that cuff and dropped the handkerchief back into the bucket.

Dr. Balogh finished his work refillin' those medicines. "Those should last you awhile." He glanced up at me. "Perhaps. If you are smart about it. Should only deploy if absolutely necessary. But if it should deploy, there are very few doctors in this country who could supply you with more."

"Why don't that surprise me?"

"So I suppose if you should need more, go east. Or come see me again, yes?"

"You mean if your obsession with puttin' metal limbs on people don't get you killed before then? Sure."

He gave me a flat stare, clearly not appreciatin' my quip. "And if your habit for not listening to people wiser than yourself does not get *you* killed before then. Yes."

"Fine. Where you gonna be by then, though? Plannin' to stay here fer a spell? After what happened to yer friend Dr. Wright … I don't think you should go back to Bravebank. Not unless you hear Nine-Fingered Nan and her nest of vipers has been burned out, anyway. And you'd better be damn sure it's actually true, and not just a rumor. I think she's gunnin' fer you, Doc."

"That could be true," he admitted. "But no, I do not think we will return to Bravebank any time soon. The work to be done here is too important. We will likely stay here 'for a spell,' yes."

"All right then." But I had no plans to come back here. Just like I'd told Holt. I'd done without the doc's strange kind of medicine fer plenty of years before now. If it ran out, so be it. I weren't gonna face that Oracle no more, nor risk runnin' into Blackbird's sheriff again.

"Now this," he said, and he held up the turn-screw, "this is for you. It is very important, so do not lose it, understand?"

I took it from him with a frown and turned it

around in my hand. It looked almost like a regular turnscrew, worn wooden handle and all, 'cept the head of it looked kinda like a star. "Oh yeah? What's so important about it?"

"That is how you take the leg off, should you ever want to."

I blinked at the tool in my hand, then looked back down to my leg. "Take … take the leg *off*? Why would I ever want to do that?"

Dr. Balogh shrugged, then moved back toward his table. "There may be times in which you want to detach it for various reasons. Or, like you just said, you never wanted that leg in the first place. Now you have a way to be free of it, I suppose."

I peered at his back as he rummaged some more, gettin' the distinct impression he found my dislike of this leg somehow akin to a personal insult. I sighed. "Doc…"

"It is all right," he said as he turned from the table and made his way back to me. "I understand. As I said before, losing a limb is difficult. For any-one. It is understandable you would be upset. I had hoped you would grow accustomed to that one over time, however."

"I have," I admitted. "Mostly. And havin' some kinda leg is surely better than havin' no leg at all."

"My thoughts exactly."

"But it's caused quite a fuss, too, you know," I told him as he stopped in front of my stool again. "In certain circles. Got people thinkin' I'm a demon and all kinds of crazy things. And some people … some people wantin' to cut it off me and all."

He arched an eyebrow above his eyepatch. "Really?"

"Yes."

"Oh dear. Seems the Territories are even more uncivilized than I had guessed. Perhaps Hannah was right, and we never should have settled there in the first place."

I squinted up at him. "I believe I told you that the first day I woke up in your house."

He pursed his lips. "I suppose you did, didn't you? Well, I am dreadfully sorry for any trouble that leg has caused you to that effect. I did not think the general public here would be quite so prejudiced against the mechanical limbs."

"Ain't exactly all fer 'em myself," I muttered, and then, as the doctor opened his mouth, elaborated. "But I'm grateful fer yer help, anyway. Then and recently. You saved my life, Doc … twice. And Charlotte's, too. And I do appreciate that. Even if … even if I still ain't too sure about this leg."

He closed his mouth, then nodded. "Of course. Of course, son. You are most welcome. I hope you are able to make good use of the rest of your life … now that it has been rescued twice."

I grunted, sure he was tryin' to imply somethin'. Maybe that I should quit my drifter ways and settle down. Stop carryin' around two guns while lookin' fer trouble. But in truth my life had been rescued more than twice. There were plenty of other people who'd been good enough to step in when I'd most needed 'em lately. The thought sobered me, and I dropped my gaze toward the doctor's cluttered table. Maybe, if anythin', those people had granted me another chance to free Ethelyn. Or at the very least, a chance to rid the Territories of Nine-Fingered Nan.

I could only hope.

Hope. That soul killer.

"Here," Dr. Balogh said suddenly, startlin' me outta my ruminations.

I looked up to see him holdin' out another turnscrew. "Another one?"

He nodded. "I told you, it is very important. Now you have two. Surely you will not misplace both of them."

I rolled my eyes, but it probably *was* better to have two. I reached out fer the second one, but he pulled it away and then knelt in front of my stool again.

"Let me show you how it works. You paying attention?"

"Yeah," I growled.

"Very good. Now, you must use this type of turnscrew, understand? There are screws here," he touched a finger to the left side of my metal knee, "and here." He touched the right side. "And here and here." He tapped both the bottom and top of it, too. "All four must be loosened, and then this part will come free." He indicated the leg from the knee downward. "To put it back on, then, you will simply realign the leg with here," he tapped the end of the rod that stuck out from my flesh, "and the screwholes, and replace all four screws again. Understand?"

"Seems easy enough."

"It is." Dr. Balogh placed the head of the turnscrew into one of the screws and gave it a few turns to demonstrate how it loosened, then tightened it back up again. "Although it will take some time to loosen or tighten all four screws, so do keep that in mind. Also." He put a hand on my metal knee and then looked up to lock eyes with me, his face gravely serious. "If you do take it off, be certain you fully tighten all four screws before you go walking around on it again, understand? Or else the lower leg will not be secure, and you might risk it becoming detached mid-stride."

"Uh, sure. Got it, Doc." That didn't sound particularly pleasant. I didn't think I was gonna bother takin' it off much, though. But maybe … maybe it might be nice to have it off for a good long bath now and then…

"*And*," he kept on, "if you remove the lower half, **do not lose the screws**! Be sure you put them someplace special for safekeeping. They are another thing you will not easily find just anywhere."

"Right." Not bein' able to attach the thing again didn't sound particularly pleasant, neither. Guess if I was gonna take those good long baths, I was gonna have to be real careful about it.

"So, here you are." He handed me the second turnscrew and then stood, liftin' his hands triumphantly. "And there you have it. All the basics of your leg. I also have a schematic for it, should you wish to have that … let me see where I put it…" He turned once more and went to a basket set near one leg of his table. It was stuffed with long rolled papers that looked somethin' like maps, and he pulled several out one after the other, unrollin' 'em to glance at their contents before tossin' 'em to the tabletop.

While he was doin' that, I fished a folded stack of currency outta my shirt pocket and tucked both turnscrews into it, instead.

"Ah! Yes, here it is." He brought one of the rolled tubes of paper over to me and unfurled it to reveal a pencil-sketched mechanical map of some kind. "This. This is your leg. Is it not beautiful?"

I squinted at that drawin', but couldn't make heads nor tails of it. It made no sense to me at all. "Uh … sure. Whatever you say, Doc."

"Would you like to take this, also?" He rolled it back up and offered it to me.

"Er, you know … I don't think I've got much use fer somethin' like that, Doc. Wouldn't be able to make sense outta it if I tried. You should probably go ahead and keep it."

"Are you certain?"

"Yeah. Yeah I'm certain. You keep it. Fer … reference fer yer future work, or somethin'."

"Well, all right." He shrugged. "I suppose I could use it to model another such leg off of…"

"Yeah. You do that." Then maybe I wouldn't be the only demon wanderin' the Territories…

"I have also left room in the leg for the addition of more … *advantages*, should you want them."

"*More?*"

"Certainly." He tapped the end of the rolled schematic against the open palm of his opposite hand as he grinned down at me. "That is the most exciting thing about the merging of flesh and metal, Mr. Delano. The possibilities! Endless possibilities!"

"I … I think what I've got is good enough fer now, Doc. Already havin' a hard enough time keepin' up with all of this, you understand."

"Oh." His enthusiasm dampened considerably. "Yes, of course. Of course I understand. But if you should change your mind later, you can always come back. Same as for the refilling of those medicines."

"Sure. Sure thing, Doc." I couldn't imagine

what else he might want to put in this leg. It seemed full enough as it was. "And, uh … I have this. Fer you." I held out the stack of cash. It was a good part of what Holt and I had stolen from that young couple in Redemption, and just about all we had left now after our supply shoppin' in Blackbird.

He stared at it fer a good full minute, felt like. Then he pulled down his eyepatch and looked from it to me and back again. "For me?"

"Fer you and yer family, yeah." I waggled the money in front of him. "Go on. Take it, would ya?"

He did so, but slowly. "My goodness. Whatever is this for?"

I snorted a laugh. "You serious? Fer all the things we was just talkin' about, Doc. Fer savin' my life—twice. Fer savin' Charlotte. Fer givin' me a leg, even if it is a lot of trouble. And fer takin' us in here, me and Charlotte. And fer the food, too. And … and to help make things right from before. When I stole—er, *borrowed* yer mule and all."

"That is … very generous of you, son."

I ground my teeth. "Can you *please* stop callin' me that?"

"You did not have to do this, however. We require no payment for our aid."

"I know. But take it anyway. Would make me feel better."

He stared down at it fer another minute, then nodded and tucked it away into another apron pocket as he said, "So you are leaving now."

I blinked at the statement, then sighed and went about pullin' that rubber cuff back up over my stump of a thigh. "Yeah. I'm leavin' now."

"And you are certain you do not want our help in your attempts to retrieve your sister?"

I grimaced and braced myself fer an argument. "No. Most certainly not. Nan is already lookin' fer you, Doc. And it ain't gonna be pretty if she finds you. You don't want to risk that. Don't want to risk yer family, neither. I'll handle gettin' my sister back. You all just look out fer yerselves, ya hear?"

To my surprise, he *didn't* argue. Only watched thoughtfully as I smoothed that rubber up along my stump and then rolled down my pants leg. "Very well then," he said at last. "That's where you are going now? To get your sister?"

"That's right."

"And you will not bring Nan to this place?"

I shook my head. "No. I ain't doin' that no more."

He smiled a little at that, and I'm sure he thought me not bringin' Nan here was a demonstration of my good nature, some kinda proof against what his wife thought of me.

And I was happy to let him go on believin' that.

"Good then. You are a very resourceful man, Mr. Delano. I was convinced you were as good as dead when you prematurely left our homestead those months ago. And yet here you are. Alive, in this place, and having passed the Oracle's Judgement, as well."

Even the mention of that old woman made me squirmy, and I stood from the stool.

Dr. Balogh held out a hand. "Good luck to you, s—" He caught himself this time, smiled. "Good luck to you, sir. I have no doubt you will find a way to free your sister."

Felt like a whole knot of things came loose in my chest hearin' him say that.

I didn't think anyone had ever said that to me since I'd first started off on my journey to find her. Swallowin' against a sudden well of emotion, I could only nod as I gripped his hand and shook it. I took a breath, cleared my throat. "Thank you. Thank you, Doctor. Could you possibly do one other thing fer me?"

"If I am able, certainly."

"Could you be sure Charlotte stays here, with you? She has a mind to accompany me, but I'd prefer she stay outta danger, too. And I know she enjoys the company of yer family."

Dr. Balogh considered my request, puttin' the schematic of my leg back in its basket. "I could try to keep her preoccupied, yes. But I will not hold anyone here against their will."

"Of course not, no. I understand. I would never ask you to." Even if that *would* make things easier, fer certain. "But sure, if you could … keep her preoccupied, I'd be much obliged."

The doc leaned back against the edge of the table and nodded. "I will try my best. She seems to have taken a liking to the engineering side of things. It is quite complicated. Could occupy her for years if she fully applied herself."

"Sure. That would be awful helpful."

"Will you send her down then, on your way out?"

I paused in my walk toward the chamber's exit and turned back to face him. "Huh?"

"Will you send her down on your way out?"

"I ... I thought she was already down here? Somewhere."

Dr. Balogh frowned and straightened up off the table. "She is not. I have not seen her for a few days now ... I assumed she had rejoined you on the surface. Did she not?"

Panic lit through my limbs, mind racin' with all manner of things that could have happened to her, thinkin' of where she could have possibly gone and why, and my whole body went hot with it. Anger came next, anger and frustration and exasperation. Why couldn't she just *stay put*? Why couldn't she *understand*? And why did she have to do this to me *now*?

"No," I managed to snarl out. "She did not."

THE STORIES ARE ALMOST NEVER TRUE

I stormed from the cave in a fury, startlin' both my mule and Holt's gelding and even the old man himself, who'd been checkin' the cylinder of one of his pistols till I came burstin' through that curtain of vines. Then he spat a curse and had that gun up and aimed at me in the blink of an eye.

Only he lowered it again as he realized who it was comin' outta there. "What's the matter?" he asked as I reached him.

I shook my head, grabbin' down my belts from my saddle to put 'em back on. "Charlotte is gone."

His shoulders relaxed as he released a breath. "That's all? By the way you stormed outta there, I thought somethin' was real, real wrong."

"Somethin' *is* real, real wrong, Holt," I snapped.

"But I thought you didn't want her goin' with us, anyway?"

"I don't."

Holt rolled his eyes and shoved his gun into his holster. "Well then why the hell are you so worked up? Ain't it better this way? Now you don't gotta fight with her about stayin' put."

"I already fought with her," I grumbled as I gathered Joe's reins and swung up onto him.

"Huh?"

"The other night … we had a … disagreement. I think that's why she left."

Holt shrugged. "All right. I fail to see why that's such a bad thing. Makes our job easier, don't it?"

"It's the same as before, Holt." I reined Joe around to face him. "She shouldn't be out here at all, much less out here wanderin' around alone. Who knows where she went, or what mighta happened to her now, goddamnit."

Holt put his hands atop his saddle horn and leaned forward a little. "Seems to me she's a grown woman and can take care of herself, kid. Don't you remember what she yelled at us fer on our way to Redemption? She said herself—she ain't no fragile flower. And she's got a point. Six months in the Whittaker mines … I reckon most women from her kinda background couldn't have lasted a week in those conditions, much less six months."

"But she still got grabbed the first time, didn't she? I'm gonna go look fer her."

"Look fer—kid, we ain't got time fer that! Nan's gonna be here in five days, maybe less!"

"Then that gives me at least three days to try and track her down." I prodded Joe into motion, headin' out into the woods.

Holt rode up beside me quick and reached out to grab my reins, pullin' Joe to a stop.

I whipped a glare at him, but he spoke before I could demand he let go.

"And just how do you propose to find her, anyway, huh? She could be anywhere by now. Take a minute and *think*, would ya? You ain't responsible fer her, Van. She's made her own choices. She chose to come back out here despite what happened to her last time. She chose to ride with us to Blackbird. And then she chose to leave again. She's a free woman ... she can do what she wants. Even if her choices ain't smart ones. Hell, when has that ever stopped *you*, eh? You know how many times I've had to let you ride off into doin' somethin' stupid?"

"And yet who was the one with their neck in the noose just a few weeks back?" I growled.

"I ain't sayin' I'm much smarter," Holt admitted, "but you know of the two of us, I'm the one better at stoppin' to think first, and that's what you need to do now. Somehow you've got me talked into this other damn fool plan of yers to ambush Nine-Fingered Nan herself, and if we're gonna do that I need you focused. And we need to be ready long before she's scheduled to arrive, too, and you know that."

I kept on glarin' at him, but he was right, damn it all.

"Long as I've known you, all you've wanted was to find yer sister," he said quietly. "Despite me tellin' you most those years she must be dead. You kept on tryin', anyway, only givin' it a pause when weather stopped you, or when you thought that avalanche had got her. More stubborn and bull-headed than yer pa even, you are, and trust me, he's a hard man to beat. But I guess you were right ... all this time, and you were right about her still livin'. You want to chance fuckin' up this opportunity, everythin' we've been workin' on the last few days—everythin' you've been through up till now—just to try and find another woman who likely don't need yer help anyway?"

I ground my teeth, fingers clenched around my reins.

Holt let go of 'em, sittin' back in his own saddle. "I know yer infatuated with that girl—"

"I ain't *infatuated*—"

"—but if you ain't got a notion to stop tryin' to get yerself killed and settle down with her, well … well, Van, then frankly, she deserves someone better. Guess you gotta make yer own choices too, kid. But tell me now what yer gonna do, cuz if yer goin' off on another wild goose chase, I'm just gonna head on back toward Grave Gulch. I sure as hell ain't goin' up against Nan without you."

I sat fer another long minute in silence, glarin' out at the woods around us, watchin' the leaves rustle softly in the breeze, listenin' to the birds and the insects. Joe snorted and shook his head, chewin' the bit like he was waitin' to hear my answer, too.

I weren't infatuated with Charlotte…

But I remembered how nice it had felt bein' cradled on her lap, the silky feel of her hair in my fist, the things that had stirred inside me when she'd clutched at my shirt, and that terrible, chokin' terror when she'd swooned in the cave, and I'd thought fer sure she was dead.

I swallowed hard. Fuckin' hell. I *was* infatuated with Charlotte.

But she *did* deserve someone better. Even had I not been plannin' to head into a maelstrom of a gunfight in the next few days, even had I wanted to settle down with her, as Holt had suggested … she deserved someone better. Someone far better than me.

"Fine," I spat finally. "Fine. Yer right. Yer right … we can't abandon our plan. Can't risk Nan beatin' us to the mill. Charlotte … Charlotte will be fine. She can take care of herself, sure."

I almost believed it. I wanted to believe it. She'd done well enough against those murderous metal statues. Well enough … until one had nearly strangled her. Until one had poisoned her.

Please let her be all right. Let her be safe…

I didn't even know who I was talkin' to. God wouldn't be doin' me no favors after what I'd done with my life. The Holy Mother, neither. But maybe they'd take mercy on Charlotte fer her own sake.

Swearin' under my breath, I reined Joe back around toward the same campsite Holt and I had made in the area days ago. "But let's camp here awhile, anyway. See if she comes back."

"Van…"

"We can plan well enough from here, too. We'll leave enough time to get back to mill early."

The old man let out an exaggerated sigh and several mumbled complaints about not wantin' to settle so close to the Oracle's territory again, but followed after me on his gelding anyway.

The Oracle. Had she had Charlotte's stallion ready and waitin' fer her when she'd come out of the cave wantin' to leave, like Joe had been ready fer me? Or had Charlotte simply left on foot, with no supplies? Surely not. She was too smart fer that. She must've taken her mount, and all her gear.

Fer some reason that thought only made me angrier.

The Oracle. Somehow, I was gonna have to find her again, and ask her just what she happened to know about Charlotte Harrison's recent disappearance.

We set up camp again, nearish to the cave, and tried to work out what other strategy we could fer our ambush, but my thoughts kept driftin' now and then to Charlotte, and then that anger and anxiety would rise again, and I'd struggle to redirect it.

If Holt noted my continued distracted state, he didn't mention it.

But he was right. I had to let it go. I had to let Charlotte go. I couldn't afford this kind of fractured concentration. Not if I was gonna face Nan again.

I waited till after dark, till Holt was asleep, to mess with that pistol tucked away inside my leg. Kept the fire goin' strong so I'd have enough light to find that button and do my work, and then I pressed it, and jumped despite myself when the holster extended. I pulled that sixgun free and loaded it quick, replaced it, pressed the button again and watched with a strange fascination as it all folded back inside. Then I pulled my pack close, grabbed up my knife, and went about fashionin' a way to get at it easy, just in case.

I cut a flap in the left thigh of my pants, over the place where that holster would come out. Then picked out a needle and thread—the kind meant fer mendin' clothes instead of flesh—and two of the spare buttons I kept around fer repairin' shirts, and sewed 'em to the two bottom corners of the flap. When that was done, I improvised some buttonholes and tested it a few times to make sure I could open it all right and get to that release trigger quick.

It still weren't ideal, but it were a great deal more

convenient than shuckin' my pants entirely, or havin' to pause to roll up the leg. A few seconds now was all I needed to get to that gun easy enough.

Satisfied with that fer the time bein', I put all my supplies away and then sighed, starin' into the fire and lettin' it die down a little. Well, this was gonna be another night I didn't sleep, seemed like, so I didn't bother. I stood again and paced, and Joe watched me sleepily from his picket line at the edge of the fire's glow.

I glared at him. "Why'd she leave, huh?"

His big head lifted at the sound of my voice, long ears swivelin'.

"Don't she know that's a stupid idea? She's smarter than that…"

He nickered softly.

"Damnit." I walked to my pack, dug out an apple, and went to offer it to him, pattin' his neck absently as he bit it in half, smearin' my hand with drool. Only then I caught Holt's gelding starin' at me and sighed. Joe took the rest of the apple from my palm, so I retrieved my last apple and gave it to Holt's horse, givin' him a pat too, then wiped my slimy hand on my shirt.

"I'm gonna take a walk," I told the horses. And I shook my head as I started off into the dark. Talkin' to the horses. Maybe I really *was* just losin' my mind entirely…

I looked fer the Oracle that night. And over the next few days and nights, too, but she never appeared.

Didn't sleep much those last few nights, neither, though I managed a few hours of naps throughout most days when the exhaustion finally caught up to me.

Holt and I ate sparingly, considerin' there weren't much game about still, and little to nothin' available in Blackbird, and I didn't wanna impose on the Baloghs no more. We shifted our camp further away from the cave, so that if the family happened to come out fer supplies or a try at huntin', they wouldn't catch sight of us and start askin' questions.

And I kept my eye out fer Charlotte's return, but she never showed, neither.

I'd asked Dr. Balogh to watch fer her while he continued his business here, for however long he stayed here, and he'd agreed, of course. He'd also agreed to take care of her, shelter her, if she did happen to come back. But I really woulda felt better about it if she'd come back while I was still around. Sooner rather than later. I really woulda liked to have made my peace with her, if I could have, before ridin' off to whatever was gonna come next.

But I guess it weren't meant to be.

By the night before we were set to leave fer the mill, to really put our plan into motion, Holt and I were both wound real tight. We could hardly sit still, neither of us, continually makin' rounds through our meager camp to check that everything was in order, to make sure we hadn't forgotten nothin'. Which, we hadn't. 'Cause we'd already checked and rechecked it all at least fifteen times before.

When at last we were weary of repeatin' the same tasks over and over again, dusk had fallen once more. At dawn, we'd make our way southwest to the road that passed closest to that old mill, and we'd wait fer Nan. And then lead her right into our trap.

Or, *I* would.

I was gonna leave Holt here. And not give Nan the chance to murder him.

But fer now, we both retrieved our last remainin' bottles of whiskey—some I'd stolen off those unfortunate prospectors in the area days ago—and we set about drinkin' and reminiscin'. Hopin' the alcohol would soothe our nerves, let us eventually fall asleep so we could then wake up and finally get this done with.

Holt was gettin' real drunk, and so was I, though I tried to keep my wits about me better than he, if only 'cause I was gonna need to sneak off here in a little while after he passed out.

He pulled a sixshooter from his pack all of a sudden and held it up in the firelight, and my stomach turned as I recognized it. He shouldn't have had that here. And most certainly should not have had that here ***unwrapped***.

It was bright and shiny, even in the dark, reflectin' the dancin' flames along its cylinder and barrel almost perfect as a mirror. Pa might've kept it hidden away at the ranch, but he'd clearly still taken care of it. And then so had Holt.

And now here it was, in the open again. Unburied. Unwrapped. In the hand of a killer again. Its silver platin' etched in elegant scrollwork and crude tally marks.

So many tally marks.

I hissed a breath through my teeth. "Goddamnit, Holt. I thought I told you to put that thing back where it belonged?"

He shrugged. "Well, I did. But then I changed my mind. I still think you oughta take it, especially now." He turned it around to offer me the well-worn ivory grip.

I shook my head. "And my answer is still no."

"If you wanna end Nine-Fingered Nan, you should do it with this. Only right."

I snorted. "You don't even know that it was Pa who shot off her finger. Or that he did it with that gun."

Holt gave a slow nod. "True. But that's the way the story goes. And I'm almost sure it's mostly true."

"You know as well as I do the stories are almost never true."

"'Cept those about Lucky Logan," he countered. "Or me. Or Kill 'Em All Paul."

I sighed, leaned back against my saddle to regard him across the fire. "I ain't takin' a strange gun into a fight as important as this one, Holt. And it's a long barrel; it'll add time to my draw. Time I can't afford. I ain't gonna chance it. You wanna use it, you go on ahead. I'm perfectly happy with what I got here." I patted at my own two pistols.

Nevermind that one of 'em had been a strange gun itself not too long ago. Duster's pistol sat tucked nice and neat into my right holster. I was gettin' used to it just fine by now.

"It ain't mine to use," Holt said.

"Well it ain't mine, neither."

Holt dropped his arm, pullin' the offered pistol back into his lap. "More yours than mine," he muttered.

I straightened up off my saddle, sat cross-legged and leaned forward toward him. "Holt. Pa thought of you like a brother. And you thought the same of him. You've told me this more times than I can count, old man. And you came lookin' fer me and Ethelyn when you heard he and Mama had been killed, took care of me best you could … Pa woulda wanted you to have it. It's as much yers as it is mine, understand?"

He stared down at the sixgun's shiny surface fer another long minute. "I dunno, kid…"

"Well I ain't takin' it. So you have it. And that's that."

And that *was* that. We didn't talk about it no more the rest of the evenin', and eventually Holt did pass out, snorin' somethin' awful and still in his boots, his hat knocked askew from where he'd fallen sideways sittin' up.

I fell asleep sittin' up myself fer awhile, chin drooped against my chest, till I jolted awake again sometime in the middle of the night swearin', and then scrambled to gather all my things to leave before Holt woke up again.

I stumbled around in the dark, our fire now burnin' low and only a young moon in the sky, but I managed to get my pack together and Joe saddled up without too much trouble. The world was gently swayin' as I grabbed Holt's horse from the picket line, too.

If I lived through facin' down Nan again, Holt might very well kill me himself fer what I was about to do. Fer real this time. But I'd take that chance. Long as he stayed safe.

Like Charlotte. I really hoped Charlotte was still safe.

I left him most his things, includin' his pistols

and Pa's old gun, but took both his huntin' rifle and his long rifle, and then I saddled up his gelding and ponied him behind me as I headed off into the night.

The trees shrouded the sky from sight, made it hard to navigate. Made it especially hard to see, given the bare sliver of a moon hardly lit anything in the first place. But I went slow and let Joe find his own way, and when I reached the occasional clearin', I'd stop to check the stars and orient myself, and I kept headin' in generally the right direction.

By dawn, I was well on my way toward that mill, and the effects of all the whiskey were startin' to wear off. I kept a look-out for the Oracle or any of her people the whole way, and yet they remained out of sight. Didn't even see any of their strange, decorated skulls hung up in the trees this time.

I hoped me takin' Holt's horse and saddle would delay him long enough fer me to take care of Nan and her crew before he could manage to find another way there ... which I had no doubt he *would* find another way there, eventually.

And he'd be spittin' mad by then, too, probably.

But one problem at a time.

By mid-mornin', I reached the road that ran north past the mill, and I checked the rutted path fer fresh tracks. My heart picked up pace at the state of it. There were an awful lot of new tracks, looked like. Of course, there'd been an awful lot of people headin' this way from all over of late, on account of the *incident* at Blackbird and rumors of Old World association with it.

These could have been left by Nan's crew ... or someone else entirely.

Surely Nan couldn't have got here quite that fast. I didn't think.

Even still, as I prodded Joe on down the over-grown lane that branched off from that road, the lane that would lead directly to the mill, I kept my hand light on the grip of my right pistol, and my eyes and ears on full alert.

My apprehension eased somewhat as I went; the brush and old leaves that now choked the lane looked to be mostly undisturbed. Whoever had gone by on the main road hadn't turned off here. Meanin' my surprises fer Nan and her crew shoulda been safe.

I guided Joe and Holt's gelding around our traps to the main grounds of the mill itself, then dismounted and tied Joe to a nearby sapling so I could check over the place, just to be sure. But everythin' was in place and the old building still empty.

Only then did I let myself relax, exhalin' slow and even. I took the horses off a ways to the west of the mill, deep into the woods where they'd hopefully stay outta the way of bullets, and got 'em settled to wait there awhile. I ate the last of my food, forcin' it down, and drank the last of my whiskey.

Then I took Holt's two rifles and walked back to the mill to place 'em somewhere good, and once that was done, I walked back up the lane to the main road. There was a hedge tree there at the side of it, a big, old one with gnarled bark and twisted, tangled branches, some of which came all the way to the ground.

I climbed my way up into the thing, swearin' as some of its thorns caught on my clothes, and settled myself in the crook of its main fork, pullin' Duster's pistol to be ready. I could see glimpses of the road below through the canopy of leaves. I'd be able to see anyone comin' up this way long before they ever saw me.

And I had a decent enough shot at the two bundles of dynamite we'd planted along the sides of the road from here, too.

Now all I had to do was wait.

AMBUSH

I woke to the sound of voices with a start and almost dropped the pistol that had been in my lap, then almost fell out of the damn tree. I caught myself just in time, bracin' a hand and a boot against the branches and grittin' my teeth against the burn where the rough bark had chafed at my skin.

Slowly, carefully, I wedged myself back into my seat at the fork, then took a breath and scooped up the loose gun. I scrubbed my left hand vigorously over my face and blinked away the grogginess to peer down at the road below. It was late in the day now, the sun anglin' sharply west and all the trees throwin' out long shadows, but through the dappled light I saw two riders come into view, amblin' at an easy walk.

But they were kitted up real good, armed to the teeth, and I sat up straighter in my treeside perch, strainin' to get a good look at 'em between all the leaves.

They were awful grimy, their faces shinin' with sweat and shirts nearly soaked through. Their horses were damp, too, and tired. One man had shoulder-length, dirty blond hair and a short blonde beard, and the other short brown hair and a goatee streaked with gray. They both wore hats, old beat-up ones stained with sweat around their hat brims.

They were talkin' amongst themselves, and as

they got closer I could finally make out what they were sayin'.

"—this is all a waste of time," the blond one said. "Don't know why she keeps playin' with this fool. Don't understand why she hasn't strung him up or flayed him alive by now." He spit off to one side of his horse.

The other man, clearly the elder of the two, only shook his head. "And why does a cat fuck around with a mouse before bitin' its head off?" He shrugged. "It's entertainment, that's all. When she's bored of 'em, she'll kill 'em."

"Well ain't none of this entertainin' to me," the blond one scowled. "All this way, fer what? So she can bat him around some more?"

"Naw," the one with the goatee drawled. "Think this might be it. Especially if Lowery really got that information out of him."

I tensed at the mention of Lowery, my heart jumpin'. They were right below me now, and they reined to a halt. I held perfectly still up in my perch, though my heart was thunderin' blood in my ears somethin' fierce so I could hardly hear 'em.

These were Nine-Fingered Nan's men.

The blond one gave a snort. "You know Lowery. Wouldn't surprise me at all if he didn't even have Delano when he sent that wire."

My throat closed up at the mention of my name. These were *definitely* Nan's men…

The elder one grunted. "Then he'd better have him by now. Else *he'll* be the one the boss flays alive instead of Delano."

Well, they didn't have to worry about that. I'd

already flayed Lowery good enough. He'd be long dead by now.

The man below me fished in his shirt pocket, then held up a compass and peered at it fer a second before lookin' around at the woods.

I held my breath.

"Looks like this is it. I think."

The blond one made a show of lookin' around, too. "*What* is it? We're in the middle of nowhere."

"Yeah. That's the point. Should be a road goin' west, boss said. Think this is it, see there?" He pointed to the overgrown lane that led to the mill, and my hand tightened around my pistol grip. "See some fresh tracks goin' that way, too. That's gotta be it."

The blond one shrugged. "If you say so."

"I say so. C'mon, let's go give it a look. Tell Lowery to lay out the red carpet. Tell him he better damn well have what he said he had."

"Yeah, all right."

They ambled down the lane toward the mill in no more hurry than they'd been amblin' down the road, and I only watched after 'em with my mind all in a jumble.

Why were there only two of 'em? Where the hell was Nan?

Where the hell was Ethelyn?

I looked off down the road to the south from my vantage point, far as I could see with all the other trees blockin' my view, but I didn't see no other riders comin' this way, nor no cloud of dust risin' in the distance to signal the approach of any.

She couldn't have sent just two of her lackeys. No way. Not fer somethin' this big, surely.

I looked back after the two men who'd gone on down the lane. I could hear their horses pushin' through the underbrush. If they set off any of those traps Holt and I had worked so hard on settin' up … if they found any of my stashed weapons…

Damn it all to Hell … I couldn't decide if I should follow after 'em to make sure they didn't do neither of those things or stay in my tree in case more of 'em showed up.

My first urge was to drop down and go after 'em, end both of 'em before they had a chance to do either.

But somethin' made me hesitate. Pause and think fer a second. Holt woulda been proud. Maybe all those years of his naggin' was finally payin' off.

Lay out the red carpet, the older one had said. Which meant someone important must be comin'.

Nan. It's gotta be Nan. She musta been comin' after all. Perhaps these two were just her scouts, her recon men, sent ahead to clear the road of trouble and flush out any attempted ambushes. If they did find any of my traps or my stashed weapons, I'd have to make sure they didn't get the word back to her.

Of course, then I wondered… would she be expectin' 'em to come back with word of what lay ahead? When would she expect 'em to report? If they didn't come back with news by a certain time, would she arrive expectin' a fight? Or maybe she wouldn't come at all…

My heart quickened again and I ground my teeth against the war of frantic thoughts, the twist of conflictin' emotions roilin' in my gut, the agony of indecision.

But in the end, I stayed put. I stayed hidden in

the branches of that tree, and I listened for yells or shouts or the snap of small branches bein' broken, but no unusual sounds broke the late afternoon hush of the forest. The air had grown uncomfortably still, everything around me seemin' to hold its breath just as much as I was doin'.

Finally, I forced myself to breathe out. Wished fer a breeze of some kind. My shirt had started stickin' to me and sweat made trails down my temples and the back of my neck. It was unusually warm fer this time of year, seemed like. Summer shoulda started fadin' by now in this part of the country, givin' way to the cooler days of autumn. Alas, such was not my luck.

I held my breath again as the sound of horses reached my ears, comin' back this way from the mill. How much time had it been? A half hour or so, at least. It was the two gents who'd gone down the lane before. They hadn't set off any of our traps, then. I couldn't be sure if they'd found my other weapons or not, but it looked like they hadn't acquired any new ones on their persons. If they had, they'd apparently decided to let 'em be.

But they both wore studious frowns now, their brows furrowed. They rode beneath me without a word to each other, and then turned back the way they'd come and trotted off out of sight.

I sat there frownin' after 'em, wonderin' if I'd just made a big mistake.

But surely an empty mill, even in the event of Lowery's absence, and even if they'd seen the left ammunitions, surely that wouldn't be nearly enough to frighten off Nine-Fingered Nan. Stashed weapons without no one around to fire 'em were just more loot fer her and her crew to steal.

So I resisted the nearly overwhelmin' urge to follow after 'em and instead stayed still in my tree once again. I'd wait a little longer. See who else might come on up the road. Nan had to be comin'.

She had to be....

It was another two hours at least and my legs had all but gone numb and a cramp had started to smart in my back before the sounds of more riders comin' from the south jolted me back into high alert. There was a dust trail this time, a brown haze hangin' low over the tops of the trees in the distance, and I cursed myself fer not notin' it earlier.

This was a big group. A real big group.

The sound of a whole lotta hooves grew closer, and the creak of a whole lotta leather. Low murmured voices, and the soft rumble and groan of a loaded wagon or two.

The sun had dipped into early evenin', the shadows deepenin', the heat of the afternoon finally easin'. But the air was still and breathless, thick and heavy like a storm might be comin' soon.

The first riders of the group trotted into view and I gulped at that soupy air, tryin' to still nerves that felt suddenly electric.

They were an awful rough-lookin' bunch. A ragtag spread of individuals rangin' in age from probably fifteen up to mid-sixties or so, mostly men with a handful of women, though the two sexes were nearly indistinguishable from each other in this particular outfit. They wore mostly dirt-encrusted and threadbare clothin', with a few here and there sportin' fancier fare, and the occasional expensive and high-fashion item that stood out clear as day as not belongin' in a group like theirs. Stolen, most-like.

There were two wagons, loaded up with supplies. One covered over with canvas, and the other a chuck wagon. They moseyed on along in the middle of the road, and all the riders surrounded 'em, front, back, and sides.

I shifted in my hard, awkward seat and squinted, leanin' forward some to try and get a better view. Of all those people comin' up the road, there were only two familiar faces I cared about findin': Nine-Fingered Nan's … and Ethelyn's.

My sweepin', searchin' gaze finally stuck on a figure dressed all in black with a wide-brimmed hat. Silver-white hair fell down around her shoulders, and a bandolier crossed one shoulder. She rode her tall bay horse a few lengths in front of the first wagon, surrounded on all sides by plenty of her gang.

Nine-Fingered Nan.

The two men on either side of her looked familiar. They were the two who had been there flankin' Nan when I'd brought back Taggert's gutted body. Their sharp gazes raked the woods around 'em almost constantly, their hands on their grips already.

Those would be two of her top lieutenants then. Men who would know about Nan's plans to expand west or make a try fer Califia. Men who would know where Ethelyn might be bein' held, or where she was supposed to be shipped off from…

Ethelyn.

I steadied myself in the fork of the hedge and lifted my free left hand to shield my eyes, despite the fact the later hour meant there was no overhead sun to glare down at me. And I started at the beginnin' of the horde of riders and I checked every face, lookin' frantically fer a pale young woman with long, dark hair and jade-colored eyes.

I found the two men who had come by earlier to scout the place … but no Ethelyn.

The first of the gang rode beneath me now, paused fer only a second, and then turned left to go down the brush-choked lane toward the mill.

The blood rushed in my ears loud as thunder, and the knuckles of the hand that clenched my revolver matched its ivory grip. I could feel myself shakin', heat floodin' my insides.

Nan herself had nearly reached me now. She looked straight ahead. Didn't bother scannin' the woods fer threats. Maybe she trusted her men that much. Or maybe she thought herself indestructible. Her pearl grips gleamed in the dappled orange light that speared through the trees.

Ethelyn coulda been hidden away in that canvas-covered wagon.

She coulda been.

Or she coulda been somewhere else. Still held captive. Or already sold.

All the hooves and the weight of the wagons rollin' over that hard-packed dirt road masked the sound of my hammer clickin' back.

I took aim at her horse between the edges of my motionless canopy of leaves, and fired.

The gunshot cracked across the stagnant air, shatterin' the stillness, and I saw Nan go down in a tangle even as I rolled quick from my position to drop from the tree and land with a grunt in the brush below.

Her gang was fast; even faster than I'd suspected they'd be. A hail of bullets shredded the leaves above me, sprayed chunks of bark down over me, and buried into the hedge's thick branches where I'd been sittin' hardly a second ago.

I wasted no time. I sprinted.

Tore through the underbrush along the side of the lane, toward the mill, right past those of her crew who'd already started in that direction, and I left their surprised shouts behind as I dodged around a few of the pits Holt and I had dug.

More bullets followed me, but fewer now that I had all the woods fer cover and kept zig-zaggin' between all those trunks, and most of 'em couldn't see me now, or couldn't fire at me without risk of hittin' one of their own instead. Those closest to me gave chase with more shoutin', their horses plungin' through the brush as recklessly as me.

I led 'em straight fer our traps ... and sure enough, I heard two of 'em go down into those pits with an awful yell of curses and the shriekin' of horses.

But I didn't bother lookin' back. More of 'em were comin' still, the noise of the first pursuers who'd gone down soon replaced by fresh ones. I ran across the lane and freed the rough-hewn stick lever that would release our trip line, then dodged behind another sprawlin' hedge just as more bullets hissed over my right shoulder.

The sound of bodies crashin' into the brush erupted behind me, and more horses squealin'. So I'd downed a few more, then. I ignored the clenchin' in my chest, the burnin' in my lungs, and pushed on, runnin' fast as I could manage.

The remainin' few who chased me now fell back a bit, likely wary of what else I might spring on 'em, not wantin' to end up like their companions. It was just what I needed; some space to work with.

I ducked behind a big oak and then whipped around the other side of it, sightin' back at 'em. Three squeezes of my trigger and I shot two off their horses and caught the third in the shoulder, almost unseatin' him. He righted himself at the last second and spurred his horse straight at me. His pistol leveled, too, and I shot him again. Red bloomed across his chest.

He sagged in the saddle as his horse charged past me and I ran after it till it slowed in confusion, ears flickin' around in all directions and eyes wide at all the commotion. Then I caught the dead rider's sleeve and yanked him off, planted a foot into a stirrup and hauled myself up into the abandoned seat.

I'd hardly settled myself before I spurred the horse back into motion, and we once again tore through the brush toward the mill, the sounds of pursuit growin' louder again. But I was almost there…

I passed one of our planted bundles of dynamite, waited till I figured I was far enough away from it, and then reined my horse around sharply. I fired at the explosives once, twice, and my cylinder clicked empty. Swearin', I jerked my left pistol free of its holster and finally hit the dynamite with the third shot, and the blast shook the trees and took out three more of Nan's crew just as they'd been takin' aim.

My borrowed horse reared and pinned its ears. Pieces of flesh—both human and animal—spattered down into the loam. And as soon as my horse hit all four feet again, I turned him back toward the mill and urged him onward. He ran on in a near panic, barely controllable. We almost went right over another of the pits ourselves, but I managed to yank him to the right at the last second.

My ears were ringin' now, but I could hear what was left of Nan's gang shoutin' at each other in attempts to make a plan, to figure out who the fuck I was, and they were still pushin' through the woods after me, but spreadin' out more now.

I stayed low over my horse's neck to avoid all the sweepin' branches, kept him weavin' through all those trees, heard another rider behind me go into the pit I'd almost fell in myself.

Then I broke out into the open of the riverbank, with the flat of the water on my right and the loomin', overgrown mill building on my left, and I tried to slow my horse's wild dash. He threw up his head and sat back on his haunches, then reared again, sprayin' spittle as he shrieked his displeasure at this whole situation.

I held on till he came down again, but then I slid off quick and gave his rear a slap. He didn't need no other encouragement from me, though. He was off like a shot again in the next second, barely missin' more bullets that came at us outta the trees behind.

I ran fer the building.

A bullet pinged into the calf of my metal leg and I stumbled, then practically fell through the gapin' doorway into the dark interior of the mill's main cuttin' floor. More bullets chewed into the wood of the walls and the door frame.

I scrambled to my feet and went to the bulwark of logs Holt and I had nailed together. It was heavier and harder to move by myself; I had to lean my shoulder into it and push with all my strength to move it … but finally it shifted, leaned … and then fell across the open doorway just as it was supposed to. There were other ways in, of course, but Holt and I had boarded all those up. It would keep 'em out fer at least long enough fer me to get into a good shootin' position…

And that's what I did. I went to the front window, also boarded up, but with cracks left large enough to put a gun barrel through. And I reloaded Duster's pistol, and filled the empty chamber from my left gun so they'd be ready when I needed 'em. Then I grabbed up the fully loaded rifle waitin' fer me and took a knee, took aim through one of those cracks.

Nan's crew was just arrivin', pourin' into the flat open of the riverbank on lathered, blown horses and lookin' real, real angry. Some fired into the front of the building just fer spite, their bullets punchin' little holes into the rotten wood fer spears of dim daylight to filter through into the dark.

Splinters rained down over me, but they were aimin' too high. I didn't bother duckin', didn't flinch away. I counted 'em quick; there were only twelve on horses now. Seemed I'd managed to cut their numbers in half durin' my mad race through the woods, though by my measure I only knew fer sure that six of the missin' were dead.

But I'd take what I could get. I put the closest of

the twelve in my rifle sights as the apparent leader of those remainin' barked at the rest of 'em to stop shootin'. My heart jumped as I realized he was one of Nan's lieutenants. One of those who'd been ridin' at her side.

I didn't see Nan herself in this group, but that weren't surprisin'. I'd taken out her horse, after all. It was a long walk to the mill without a horse.

I gritted my teeth at the thought of the outlaw boss, hoped maybe she'd fall into our last remainin' pit on her way, and then pulled my focus back to these men and women at hand. Ten men. Two women.

The lieutenant was instructin' the rest to fan out, surround the building. Cover the exits and watch the windows. And wait. Fer Nan.

He told one of the men to go back fer her, in fact. Give her a ride so she might reach us in a more timely fashion.

I shook my head. That weren't gonna work fer me at all. So I switched my aim to the man who'd turned his horse back toward the road, breathed out, and fired.

He went clean off his horse in a spray of blood.

That made seven dead fer sure.

The others yelled, and I flattened myself to the floor quick as they opened fire on the building again. The boards across my window cracked and split under their assault. I kept hold of my rifle and crawled to the next window, then cautiously raised onto my knees again to take a peek out from there.

Seemed the lieutenant had lost his tenuous control of the others. They weren't listenin' to his shouted orders now. Some rode fer cover in the trees beyond the mill, others were circlin' on the bank as they emptied their cylinders and then reloaded in turn. And one of the women had fished out a bottle of whiskey from her saddlebag.

Fer a minute I watched her, confused as to what purpose whiskey could currently serve her. Till I saw her soakin' a rag with it, and then stuffin' the end of the rag into the bottle.

Well. Two could play that game. Holt and I had stashed bundles of dynamite all over this place. I took aim at the one closest to the woman and fired again.

This time I only needed one shot.

The explosion blew apart one man and stunned his horse, and knocked both the woman and her horse to the ground. Her animal was quick to roll back to its feet and take off riderless into the woods, but the woman didn't move. Unconscious or dead, least she wouldn't be lightin' anythin' on fire no more.

The others fought to keep their horses from boltin', and I took advantage of their distraction. Four more were dead soon enough.

That left only five.

The lieutenant turned tail and ran, gallopin' away toward the road.

I swore, trackin' him with my rifle, but he was into the trees again before I could get off a good shot, and I had to flatten to the floor again as the four he left behind regained their wits enough to return fire at last.

Their hoofbeats pounded up close, and then a fist punched through the boards across the window just above my head.

I swore some more and jumped to my feet, abandonin' that rifle to make fer the rickety stairs in the back corner of this main room.

Bullets followed after me, and the sound of more splinterin' wood as they cleared out the rest of that window. I jumped up and onto the big log carriage, the contraption that had once fed felled tree trunks to the saws, and yelled as a shot grazed the top of my right shoulder. It stung, spread fire all down my arm, but I ignored it. Jumped down from the carriage and ran behind the saws, duckin' instinctively as more bullets sparked off the blades.

Finally I made the stairs and went up 'em two at a time.

The wood groaned under my boots, but Holt and I had tested 'em several times while settin' up. They'd hold. At least fer long enough.

Bootsteps pounded across the floor beneath me, clomped up the stairs behind me, and I dove fer the floor just as a gunshot cracked close-range. It made my ears ring again, but it also told me just where that fella was. I rolled soon as I hit the worn old floorboards and pulled both pistols, firin' multiple times into … one of the women, turned out.

Her face went slack with shock. Blood trickled from her mouth. Then she staggered backwards and toppled down the stairs, tumblin' right into the two men tryin' to come up.

I holstered my irons and rolled back to my stomach to crawl quick to the second rifle we'd stashed. Picked it up as I pushed my back up against the wall and swung it around toward the stairs in time for the two men to shove the dead woman over the rail. She fell with a sickenin' thump to the lower floor. They looked up just as I fired.

I caught the guy in front right between the eyes. He fell back into the arms of the guy behind. I cocked the rifle again, but the angle was no good. The stair's railin' and the body of the first guy blocked any potentially fatal shot.

I hissed a curse under my breath.

And then I heard a different kind of noise from down below. The shatterin' of glass, and the whoosh of flame. Then the crackle and pop of somethin' far too familiar.

Burnin' wood.

ONE LAST PROBLEM

I clambered up onto my knees and risked a glance through one of the upper windows, which Holt and I had also haphazardly boarded up, although not as solidly as the bottom panes. Though these windows up here were small, there was plenty of space between the planks fer me to look down below to the riverbank and the front of the mill.

Two of Nan's crew stood out there, starin' at the building and their most recent handy work with self-satisfied expressions. Smoke started tricklin' out around that fortress of logs I'd pushed down across the door. One of 'em standin' down there was the woman I'd tried to blow up with dynamite.

Guess she'd only been knocked out, then. Shame.

A grunt and the creak of more old wood brought my attention back to the man left on the stairs behind me quick, and I turned toward him again just in time to see him shove the dead man's body out of his way.

We fired at each other in unison, but I was divin' sideways as I did so.

His bullet punched a hole through an empty wall, and mine went wide over his right shoulder.

Then he was chargin' at me across the floor.

I sprang to my feet, dropped the rifle and went

fer my right gun and my next shot caught him in the left side. But it didn't slow him up at all. He was on me in the next instant, one hand around my right wrist to shove my gun outta his face just as I fired again, and that bullet buried harmlessly into the ceiling.

The barrel of his pistol shoved into my ribs hard enough to bruise, but my left hand swept across my body and knocked off his aim, so his next bullet only barely missed hittin' me in the right hip instead of goin' through my heart. The gunfire was deafenin' at such close-range, the gunsmoke acrid and sharp in my nose, the heat of the discharge warm against my belly.

Too close.

I gave him a good head-butt, makin' him stagger back a few steps, and as he did so I wrenched my wrist outta his grip. Unexpectedly, he twisted away from me even as he stumbled, then turned right back around and cracked a left hook into the side of my face.

Stars burst across my vision and I went reelin' into the wooden railin' that separated this half of a second floor from a long drop to the first floor. I lost my grip on my pistol as I frantically scrabbled fer a hold on the railin' to keep myself from pitchin' head-first over it, then scowled more curses as I watched my weapon fall. It clanged against the edge of one of the rusted saws below and bounced away into smoke and darkness.

I whirled off the rail to face the man, but he'd hurt himself, too, throwin' that punch so hard. He winced and sucked in a breath, one hand goin' to that bullet hole I'd made in his side. His shirt was soaked red there, and the rest of it damp with sweat and grime, and he had the smell of a lot of days in the saddle on him.

Even still, his face split into a grin as he lurched at me.

I went fer my left pistol; he brought his own gun down into my hand as I lifted it and I cried out as the metal smashed into all those little bones. My second gun hit the floorboards, and then he had both hands wrapped around my throat and squeezed till I thought my eyes would bulge from my skull.

"Big mistake, boy," he growled, the words hardly more than a rumble beneath the rushin' and ringin' in my ears. "What, you thought you could bring down Nine-Fingered Nan and her gang ... all by yerself?" He guffawed, squeezed tighter, leaned me hard into the railin' so I was as much hangin' onto his arms to keep from fallin' as I was tryin' to loosen his fingers from my throat.

"Think ... think ... I did a pretty ... pretty fair job," I managed to gasp.

He pushed me backwards a little more, so I was damn near halfway over the rail already. The edge of the top board cut painfully into the small of my back. I abandoned my efforts to loosen his grip and instead clutched at his shirt sleeve. If I was goin' over, he was comin' with me.

"Hardly," he scoffed. "This ain't all of us. And anyway, yer little tricks out there just pissed off more of us than you killed." He smiled again, but even through my darkenin' vision I could see the strain in his features, the sweat that slid down his dirt-streaked face. He was hurtin' same as me. I mighta even killed him with that bullet I'd got in him.

He loosened his death grip around my throat a bit and I sucked air greedily. Some of the black haze that had curtained across my eyes cleared.

He squinted at me. "You that Delano kid the boss came here fer? Shit, you ain't as good as they say you are, are ya? Well, I think she'll be awful happy to see yer still alive after all that business out there in the woods. Guess there's somethin' you got she wants real bad, eh? Maybe I'll take you out to her myself, then. Or … *or…*" He gave me a shove and a strangled noise came outta me as my boots momentarily left the floor. If not fer his hold on my throat and my desperate grab at his arms, I'd have been tumblin' down to break across those saws. "Or maybe I'll just toss ya over now," he said. "Claim you were already dead when I found ya. Would save us all a whole lotta trouble, I think. She'd never know, would she?"

I kept my right hand clamped firmly around his forearm, but slid my left hand down to that flap I'd made in the thigh of my pants and groped at it till I managed to unbutton it. "Guess … guess not," I rasped. I fumbled fer that little button on the side of my metal leg till I felt it, and pressed.

The compartment there whirred open; the holster extendin' with a hiss.

The man contemplatin' murderin' me frowned. Confusion flickered across his face as he glanced down toward the noise.

I pulled that sixgun free and shot him four times in the chest, just fer good measure.

His hold on my throat slackened and I gulped

full breaths at last till my lungs stopped burnin'. But he didn't seem to understand what was happenin'. He just kept starin' down at my smokin' pistol, and then his arms dropped limp to his sides, and his eyes lifted to find my face.

He coughed, blood bubblin' in his mouth.

"What?" I prompted huskily, my voice all rough from bein' strangled. "No one mentioned my demon metal leg?"

He blinked once. And then collapsed forward, right at me.

I barely side-stepped his body, slidin' left along the rail just in time. But his dead weight proved too much fer the old, rotten wood, especially after we'd been pushin' against it fer so long. The boards snapped, and he crashed right through 'em to plummet down to the first floor.

Just enough of my own weight had been leanin' against that railin' fer it to unbalance me as it gave way, and I flailed as I felt myself fallin' too.

I twisted and caught the edge of the second-story floor with my left hand as I dropped, then grabbed on quick with my right hand. I dug my fingers into the cracks between the floorboards; struggled to haul myself back up. The old bullet hole in my left bicep and the new graze in my right shoulder screamed in protest, but it was either that or let go and get cut in half like a log.

My boots kicked empty air, tryin' fer leverage, till I finally hooked my elbows up over the floor above and then pulled the rest of me onto it after. I rolled onto my back gaspin', heart throbbin' wild in my chest, starin' up at a dilapidated ceiling.

I didn't have time to be restin', but fer a space I

just laid there anyway. My temples pulsed in pain, and my forehead where I'd cracked it into that other man's skull, and my right cheek where he'd decked me, and my throat where he'd nearly squeezed the life outta me, and all my other old and new injuries alike had lit with fresh agony.

A tendril of black smoke drifted across my vision, and I became vaguely aware of a roarin' fire now down below.

The fire. Right.

The smoke thickened, fillin' all the mill's open space and crawlin' toward what little cracks Holt and I had left available in the building. The smell of burnin' wood and heated iron reached me, and I had no more time to be layin' around.

With a groan I forced myself to roll over again and then pushed to my hands and knees. I gathered up my two dropped pistols—the left one and the one from my leg—and I loaded both cylinders full again before puttin' 'em both into belt holsters. There was no gettin' back that nice pistol of Duster's now, and I couldn't afford the added time of gettin' the other one outta my leg if I needed it again. So fer now, I put the more familiar gun in my right holster and tucked the smaller sixgun from my leg into the left. Then I folded in the leg holster, closed its compartment, and buttoned the flap over it.

That done, I got painfully to my feet and went to the little window again, scoopin' up the rifle on the way. I sagged against the wall, pantin'. The smoke had made its way up here now, and it was gettin' harder to breathe. I wouldn't be able to stay in this fortress of mine much longer.

The two left of Nan's crew were still down on the

riverbank, pacin' back and forth like caged big cats. The woman I'd almost blown up was limpin'. Only now I saw others too, comin' outta the woods and onto the bank. Most walkin' but a few ridin', and some nursin' injuries. A few broken legs and arms, looked like. And some with cuts across their faces or stainin' their shirts and pants red in places.

Musta been the others I'd felled before with our traps. They were finally catchin' up.

"Come on out here you cowardly dog!"

My gaze went back to the limpin' woman at her yell. I brought the rifle up to my shoulder and sighted down the barrel.

"We've got you surrounded!" Her voice echoed out across the water, into the trees.

Sure enough, the seven newcomers, even with as haggard as they looked, drifted off toward each side of the mill.

"That whole building is goin' up in flames, dog!" she shouted. "You gonna burn up hidin' away like a scared little child or you gonna come out here and fight us like a man?!"

I gave a snort. Nine against one weren't fair odds by any count. And anyway, pride didn't serve a dead man none at all, as Holt liked to say.

"Hoss?" the man in front with her yelled out now. "Murray? Hollingsworth? You all still in there?"

I lifted a brow. Those must have been the three who'd come after me.

He got no answer of course, and that made him growl curses and pace again. One of the men who'd come from the woods cradlin' his right arm spoke up. "Maybe they killed him, too. Maybe they're all dead in there."

I stifled a cough and swung the rifle around to my right, to sight at the fella who was about to go around the mill's far corner. If they did surround the place, I wouldn't be able to pick 'em off one by one anymore. And that wouldn't do.

I squeezed the trigger, and then it was eight against one.

I worked the lever action quick as I could and took down two more before the rest scrambled into places out of my view and I swore.

The woman was shoutin' again, orderin' the others to stay off the bank. Tellin' 'em to cover the doors and windows and wait me out. I'd burn up soon, she said. Or suffocate. Or they'd get me when I tried to come out.

Well, all of that were true enough.

I let myself cough at last and shouldered the rifle. Pulled my bandana up over my nose and mouth and blinked waterin' eyes. The smoke was gettin' real thick up here, and the heat had become almost unbearable. The air shimmered with it as I left my window perch and made fer the office in the corner of this second story. The door had been left open and hung half off its hinges. I moved past the old desk with its stacks of curled, yellowed documents and past the mildewed chair to the side window. We'd boarded this one up pretty good given there was an awning below it, figurin' that might give others on the outside a good opportunity to climb up in here.

Only now I was hopin' to use it to get down from here.

Cursin' our thoroughness, I grabbed at each board and yanked, tearin' 'em free. Sharp, stabbin' pains shot through my bruised left hand and bloodied right shoulder at the effort and as soon as I'd made a hole big enough to crawl through I shook out my hand with a wince.

The crash of some kinda equipment fallin' from the first floor reached me even inside the office, and the walls around me groaned. The floor shifted under my boots.

Shit.

I leapt fer the window, threw myself outta it and landed hard on the awning beyond on my left shoulder. I cried out as the impact jarred my sore arm, but then I was rollin' down the angle of its roof straight fer the ground.

A resonant **whump** I could feel in my bones sounded from behind me, and the roof I was rollin' down suddenly dropped away from under me, and I was fallin'.

The awning hit the ground first, and then I hit the awning on my stomach with a grunt and rolled off into the brush.

"He's here!" a man shouted. "He's here, I got him!"

Shit. I tried to move and fell into a coughin' fit. Blinked more tears outta my eyes. They felt all gritty, and my throat stung somethin' awful. I'd lost my hat somewhere, but at least I still had all my guns on me.

I managed to push up onto my knees, and someone yanked the rifle off my shoulder.

All right, well at least I still had my pistols on me.

I looked up into the barrel of another sixgun and lifted my hands slowly.

The other five left of Nan's gang were runnin' our way.

But this man's hand was shakin'. He was awful roughed up.

A series of explosions soundin' like gunfire popped from behind me and instinctively I dropped back to my belly, coverin' my head with my hands. The man holdin' a pistol at me jumped, liftin' his gun to point at the mill.

Then I remembered all that ammunition Holt and I had left stashed inside there.

Another series of pops came from the other side of the mill, and the fella in front of me jumped again. Those other five whirled to face it, too.

I surged to my knees and pulled my own guns, emptyin' both in a matter of seconds, shootin' down all six remainin' of Nan's crew.

And then it was just me. Kneelin' there in the dirt, my whole body achin', and the old lumber mill hardly more now than a monstrous blaze belchin' black smoke up into the darkenin' sky.

I took a minute to breathe ... to let the fact I was still alive sink in.

More bullets caught in the flames exploded, but I didn't even flinch this time. Instead I dragged myself standin' and retrieved my rifle once more. Slung it over my shoulder. And went about reloadin' my two pistols yet again almost without thinkin'. The actions automatic and mechanical.

There was just one last problem.

Nine-Fingered Nan weren't here.

I hadn't seen that lieutenant of hers since he'd run off up toward the road, neither.

Were they still there even now, waitin'? Maybe

waitin' to see how the rest of the gang fared? Waitin' fer news that it was all clear, that the way was safe, that the threat had been taken care of?

Or maybe they hadn't waited at all. Maybe they'd kept on movin' in search of a suitable hideout. Maybe they were settin' up camp somewhere else. Or maybe … maybe they'd gone straight into the town of Blackbird to take whatever they could take and burn the rest of it down.

My gaze flicked upward in the direction of the town, toward the tree line. Lookin' fer smoke.

But there weren't none I could see on the horizon except what the mill was currently puttin' out.

My stomach turned at such thoughts, and I shoved the pistol I'd finished reloadin' back into its holster with more force than necessary. I'd thought Nan woulda followed her crew. Woulda chased me down same as them fer shootin' her horse out from under her.

If she was back on the road, or had moved on to hide somewhere else in these woods, or had gone into Blackbird…

I clenched my jaw and shook my head, then moved away from the swelterin' heat of the burnin' mill. I spotted my hat a little distance away and swiped it up, shovin' it back down onto my head with a satisfied grunt.

I came out from around the side of the mill and went toward the river next, plannin' to dunk my head into it. Tugged my bandana off my face and took a few good gulps of smoke-free air.

Well, least Nan wouldn't have so many guns around her now. I'd just have to go get Joe and head back to the road myself, see if I could track her down, no matter where she'd gone.

"Mr. Delano."

The voice echoed out from beneath the trees, over the roarin' and cracklin' of the mill fire.

I froze.

The forest shadows had got so deep now I could hardly make out her figure.

But there she was. Across the stretch of open gravel riverbank, standin' beneath the trees and starin' right at me. She stepped forward as my eyes finally found her, into the dusky light of evenin', and the glow of the burnin' mill turned her belt buckle and pearl grips orange.

That lieutenant of hers was a step behind her and to her right, holdin' his rifle leveled at me.

Fuckin' hell.

"I wondered if all this might be your doing." She walked toward me, slow and easy. "That was quite a show, I'll give you that."

I turned nice and slow myself to face her square, and I kept my hands outward at my sides ... away from my guns, but not too far.

She stopped nearly twenty paces from me. Just far enough fer a draw.

I stayed ready, every muscle on alert, and tried to remember to breathe. Tried not to let her see the way my nerves were hummin'. But my heart was runnin' wild again, and I hardly dared blink. The light of day was fadin' quick, and the darker it got, the harder it was to see if she might go fer her guns.

"I suppose you killed Mr. Lowery?" she asked.

I gave a nod. "As slow as I could."

She smiled, but her lieutenant cocked his rifle with a snarl and I tensed.

She lifted a hand to stay his shot, but never took her eyes off me. Instead, she took hold of the man's rifle without lookin' and pushed it downward. He glanced at her in clear disappointment, openin' his mouth to protest, but in the end he said not a word. He only switched his gaze to me and glared somethin' fierce.

"And the rest of 'em, too," I added, fer his benefit. "The others with Lowery. Shot 'em all down like dogs. Like all these fellas." I lifted my hands a little higher to indicate the dead bodies that littered the place.

Nine-Fingered Nan tilted her chin up as she eyed me. "Ya know, yer pa murdered a lot of folk … but he weren't much into torture. He was more of a quick-and-clean-kill kinda man. You, on the other hand, you got no issue with makin' a person hurt to get what you want, do ya? You might be just as slippery and hard to kill as yer pa, just as much a murderer and a thief, but you got a cruel streak in ya he sure didn't have." Her grin widened. "Just my style."

I only glared back at her, but the words brought bile to my throat anyway.

In the heartbeat of resultin' silence I heard a strange, unfamiliar sound, faint and far-off. A steady thrummin' sort of noise, and it seemed to be comin' from the sky. But I couldn't look up; couldn't glance in that direction. If I so much as shifted my eyes away from Nan, she might shoot me.

Her lieutenant heard it, too, though. From the corner of my eye I saw him tense and turn, searchin' fer the source.

But Nan herself ignored it entirely. Keepin' her stare locked on me, unblinkin'. "Just the kinda man I could use in my outfit, if you were so inclined," she said. "Which is lucky fer you, 'cause it means I'll give you one more chance to tell me what you found out here. You see, Mr. Delano, I've just come a real long way. A real long way in search of somethin' real important to me. And you just kilt my horse. A damn good horse. And then you shot up all my men." She waved a hand around at the dead. "Another five of our horses had to be put down back there, too, thanks to those snares of yers. That's an awful lot you owe me now, Mr. Delano. A whole awful lot. So you can start by tellin' me how exactly I get past the Oracle. And you can tell me if you ever managed to find that doctor friend of yers, and if you happened to find any Old World items of any consequence in these parts. We'll start with that. And once you tell me all of that, I'll decide whether or not I'm gonna tan yer hide."

Now it was my turn to smile. I thought it felt natural enough, nevermind the fact my ears were ringin' again, and my heart throbbed so hard in my throat I thought I might choke on it. "Well," I managed to drawl, "see now that's the thing. Turns out I already paid my dues. All this," I spread my hands, "this is what I owed you. Fer all the things you've done to me lately. Fer all yer ... *entertainment*. See this, this was all real entertainin' to *me*. But I'm done fuckin' around now, Nan. All I want is my sister. Tell me where you've got her or I swear ... I swear I'll finish what I started here ... I'll destroy everythin' you've got."

She laughed.

Her man lifted his rifle quick, but just as quick Nan caught the barrel of it and shoved it downward again, her laughter cut short. She motioned fer him to stay put, and then she took a few more steps forward, movin' closer to me.

That thrummin' noise was gettin' louder.

I stood my ground despite a nearly overwhelmin' urge to move away from her. But she stopped again at only ten paces, and she fixed me with a flat, even stare. "Yer pa already did that a long time ago, boy." She scoffed and shook her head. "Ya know, I used to be like you. Passionate and full of rage. The desire for revenge colorin' every moment of every day. But do you know the problem with that, Mr. Delano?"

I said nothin', so she went on, liftin' her right hand to wiggle her fingers—what was left of 'em—in the air.

"It makes ya sloppy," she stated flatly. "And desperate. And that's how I was able to use ya all this time, weren't it?"

"Boss…" her lieutenant spoke up abruptly. "Boss, we got an airship incomin'."

Airship? I almost looked, almost. But Nan was too close. And all the amusement had gone outta her face.

She held up a hand to her man again, curt and forceful this time. Tellin' him to shut up. And never takin' her eyes off me. "You wanna know where I got yer sister right now?" she whispered. "All right, sure." She shrugged like it weren't no big deal, but my breath caught in my throat, my thunderin' heart skipped a beat, and I forgot all about the incomin' airship.

Nan took another step forward. "I sold her off a

long time ago, you damn idiot fool. She's gone. She's gone, you understand? You lost her."

Fer what seemed like an eternity I stood there and stared at her, and the world suddenly felt like it might be underwater. Everythin' muffled and slow, shiftin' and blurred. And then it all snapped back into focus, and I pulled iron.

SALVATION

Pain shocked through my chest even as I pulled the trigger; two reports ripplin' out over the hills nearly overlappin'.

I stumbled, hit my back on the gravel bank and gasped, choked. I couldn't fuckin' breathe. My lungs spasmed, but there didn't seem to be enough air.

I heard more noises now: somethin' big crashin' through the underbrush, the thrummin' of that airship loud, competin' with the roar of the mill fire, and Nan's lieutenant sayin' somethin' frantic to her, and her snappin' somethin' back.

But I couldn't sort the words. The pain drowned 'em all out, my whole chest burnin' white-hot, and all the little rocks of the riverbank diggin' into my back as I laid there gapin' fer breath like a goddamned fish…

My pistol … it was still in my hand. I closed my fingers around it just as Nan's face eclipsed my view of the sky. Her right hand was pressed to her left side. Blood seeped between her fingers.

I coughed a laugh, then cried out and choked again. Tasted blood myself.

Well, least I'd got her. Least I'd shown her Nine-Fingered Nan could bleed.

Nine-Fingered Nan could die.

I shuddered, and a cold sweat prickled across my skin. Fuck, but she'd got me, too. She'd got me good.

Her boot stepped on my right wrist, and then she leaned down and pried the gun outta my hand. "Like I said, Mr. Delano. Sloppy."

I wanted to say somethin', but every inhale was a struggle, and the words wouldn't come. My left hand fumbled fer my second pistol with numb, heavy fingers. I couldn't seem to grasp it … and all the effort sent new hooks of agony tearin' through me till I had to stop tryin'. Till the pain was like a vice, slowly crushin'.

Nan straightened and shook her head. "When ya get to Hell, tell yer pa hello fer me. You tell him I was the one who destroyed his life. Destroyed his family. Took everythin' from him and his children both. Tell him I got my revenge, all right, despite his best efforts." She smiled. "And don't you worry about the Oracle or yer doctor friend. I'll find 'em both soon enough. I always get what I want in the end. The benefit of patience, Mr. Delano."

She touched the brim of her hat with her bloodied fingers, turned, and walked away.

I shifted, wantin' to sit, wantin' to pull my other pistol and fill her back with bullets, but all I succeeded in doin' was to make my heart seize up and black spots scatter across my vision so I thought I might die right then and there.

But I didn't. I only fell back into the gravel and blinked the blur outta my eyes, tried to breathe around the blood wellin' in my throat.

Gunfire cracked suddenly from the edge of the woods on the tail of thunderin' hooves, and answerin' fire sounded from off to my left. There was too much smoke and fire and pain to see what was happenin', but I heard boots runnin' off and a set of hooves chargin', and shots goin' back and forth.

And then there was the belly of that airship. Right above me. Huge and dark and floatin' soft as a butterfly. Part of me wondered if it was even real. Maybe I was hallucinatin'. My last dyin' wish … gettin' to the ship that took Ethelyn…

"Attention, outlaws," a voice boomed from the sky. "By the authority of the East Republic, you are hereby under arrest. Cease fire and surrender your weapons or we *will* shoot to kill. We have you in our sights and I repeat, we *will* shoot to kill."

The airship … the airship was talkin'. But the shootin' on the ground didn't stop. Not surprisin'. No one out here cared anythin' about the Republic's laws. We weren't even in the Republic; they had no jurisdiction here. The hell were they doin' so far out from their own borders, anyway?

"This is your last warning," the boomin' voice said again. "Cease fire and surrender your weapons—"

The gunfire went silent all at once. The horse skidded to a stop beside me, sprayin' gravel.

Boots hit the bank, and I saw … Holt? He dropped to his knees at my side, and from the look on his face I knew I weren't gonna make it. He spat the worst string of curses I'd heard him utter in a long time, and then he unknotted his bandana and pressed it up against the hole in my chest.

"*Goddamnit*," he hissed. "Goddamnit, Van. Look what you did this time you stupid sonuvabitch."

I managed to get my left hand over the top of

his. There was a lot I wanted to tell him, like the fact his horse was safe and sound, tied up a distance away. And that I was sorry I'd lost his long rifle; it'd have been burned up in that fire by now, nothin' more than melted slag. And there was a lot I wanted to ask him, too, like had he managed to shoot down Nine-Fingered Nan and her lieutenant, and why the hell was there an airship from the Republic hoverin' over us ... but every time I tried to talk I only choked, and then shuddered and gasped.

Holt worked his left arm under my shoulders and propped me up a little, and some of the blood ran out my mouth and then it was a little easier to breathe. The evenin' had turned to twilight, but even the glow of the mill's remains seemed dark now.

Guess I'd find out if pa had ever found that salvation of his soon enough.

"*Van?*" Another voice rang out from above, but this one didn't boom. Instead, it was high and thin, carried from far away. "*Van!* Hang on, we're coming down!"

It sounded like Charlotte. But that didn't make no sense...

Holt glanced up to the airship, then gave a snort. "It's the girl. Where in the hell you think she found a whole airship, eh?"

I shook my head, then winced. He pressed harder on that bandana. I couldn't imagine how she mighta found an airship, or why she might be on one in the first place, but I guessed it didn't much matter now.

"If those Republic bastards coulda got here earlier ... think they were the ones to scare off Nan more than me." Holt looked around at the other bodies strewn across the bank, then twisted to give the burnin' mill a good look, and he shook his head again and whistled low. "You do all this yerself, kid?"

I gave the slightest inclination of my chin, not wantin' to risk a full nod.

"Damn." His left hand squeezed my shoulder. "But *damn*. We had a plan, Van. And a damned good one fer once. Why couldn't you just stick to the goddamned plan? Why'd you have to take my horse, huh? Took me *ages* to track down another one I could steal ... coulda been here *hours* ago otherwise!"

But he hadn't been. And that's how I'd wanted it.

Couldn't let Nan take anyone else from me.

Not Holt, and not Charlotte.

Least the two of 'em were still alive, and still free. Least I had that.

Holt was still talkin', but I couldn't understand him no more. I closed my eyes and let his voice lull me into the dark.

Fer a long while, I drifted.

Through darkness and light, comfort and pain, occasionally aware of other sensations and sounds, and sometimes lost in somethin' like fever dreams. There was the crow-headed Oracle with her huge black wings, tellin' me it weren't too late. But she was burned up by the fire at the old lumber mill.

No, it weren't the mill. It was our house.

Our house in Kansas, lightin' up the night.

And Nan was there, watchin' it burn with a grin on her face, the flames dancin' in those pale eyes of hers.

And I was stuck in the middle of it. In the middle of the fire lookin' out at her while my skin boiled and fell off my flesh. I think I screamed. Or, I wanted to scream. I tried to.

Blackness swallowed the fire all at once, and fer a time I had peace. Until an airship appeared, floatin' across my vision. On the promenade deck stood Ethelyn as a child, and she was reachin' fer me.

I reached back fer her, and a hand met mine. But it weren't Ethelyn's.

My sister was still out of reach.

I blinked, opened my eyes. They felt dry and gritty.

There weren't no airship, and there weren't no Ethelyn. Instead there was … Holt.

Holt?

He grinned as my bleary gaze landed on him and sprang up to his feet, clappin' me on the shoulder hard enough that pain spiked all through my chest and I grimaced, lettin' out a choked cry.

He sobered at my yell, his hearty shoulder-clap softenin' abruptly to a gentle pat. "Damn, sorry, kid. Sorry. Just so surprised to see ya awake … praise the Holy Mother herself, I ain't seen nothin' like it as I live and breathe!" He caught my face in his hands abruptly. "Yer *alive* you fuckin' *lucky sonuvabitch*!"

I winced as his exuberance jostled me again, and when he sat back I managed a slow, relieved exhale.

Fuckin' hell. That's right. I'd been shot.

I shoulda been dead.

Shoulda been dead and not layin' here in … where the hell was I, anyway? Holt was here, sure, but I didn't recognize the surroundings. It was dark, only lit here and there with lanterns hung on walls or set on empty stools, and there was a small fire glowin' in a stone hearth.

The walls, what little I could see of 'em, looked like … logs? A log cabin of some kind, maybe. And I weren't layin' on no bed. Though I had a pillow and blankets, and there was somethin' soft under the bare skin of my back, it was too tall fer a bed. And too hard, despite whatever paddin' had been attempted over the top of it.

I worked my mouth till some semblance of a voice came out, though it was hardly more than a croak after so long—how long?—of disuse. "Wh— where are we? What happened?"

Holt whistled and shook his head. "Ha! Well, it was a ride, I'll tell ya." He resumed his seat next to me. "As fer the where … you won't believe it, kid. We are currently, right now, in the home of that crazy witch the Oracle, herself."

I didn't much like that idea. A strange mix of feelin's stirred through me and I glanced around at what I could see of the little house again. But fer all her strangeness and unexplained abilities, her home seemed regular enough. At least fer the time bein'. I remembered the way she'd loomed over me in my dreams though, crow-headed and dark, and shuddered.

"Hey, hey, take it easy," Holt prompted. "I don't like it neither … you know how much I dislike that creepy old woman. But she's got a whole little village out here, and it seems they do pretty well fer themselves. And to be honest, kid ... well, she's been almost downright hospitable lately. Keeps preachin' about undergoin' Judgement fer anyone who wants to enter *the temple*, of course, and she's mentioned you takin' part in somethin' called a Great Awakenin' a time or two now, whatever that means ... so she's certainly still crazy. But she did offer us a place to stay while you heal, and she's been feedin' us decent, and none of her followers has murdered us yet, so ... so I guess in a way they're all right."

I let out a little groan, not so certain about any of that.

"And as fer *what happened*," Holt continued, "*you* thought you could take on Nine-Fingered Nan and her whole crew all by yerself, it seems."

"Yeah," I husked. "I remember that part."

"I gotta admit, you put the hurt on 'em pretty good. Coroner counted twenty-two bodies, the paper said. They're callin' it the Massacre at the Mill."

"Twenty-five," I said.

"Huh?"

"I got ... got twenty-five of 'em. Three ... three got burned up. In the fire."

Holt lifted his eyebrows. "Well. Anyway. Massacre at the Mill, that's what they call it. Think those Republic fellas see ya as some kinda hero. They came all the way out here to try and dispatch Nine-Fingered Nan fer good only to find you'd already laid waste to a good part of her crew."

I frowned, vaguely rememberin' somethin' about Republic folk, and wonderin' why they were so far outside their own borders.

"But you know how it ended?" Holt asked.

I closed my eyes, not wantin' to say it out loud.

I'd lost. Those twenty-five of her gang I'd managed to gun down didn't matter in the least. There was still no Ethelyn. Ethelyn was gone. I'd managed to hit Nan this time … but her shot should have killed me. And not indirectly by leavin' me stranded and bleedin' out in the desert.

No, this time she'd been about as direct as a person could get. Straight fer the heart.

"Nine-Fingered Nan gunned ya down," Holt said, unnecessarily. "Put a bullet into ya and shoulda fuckin' killed ya. Four inches lower, Van, and you'd be six feet under right now instead of here talkin' to me. Hell, even where she got ya shoulda killed ya."

I tried to wet dry lips. "Nan … I got her, too. I got her, Holt."

He grunted. "Yeah. You did. And yeah, that's somethin', kid. Ain't heard of anyone gettin' a shot on Nan fer a long, *long* time now. But she still walked away, didn't she? And you didn't."

I cracked my eyes open again. "Coulda still killed her."

He shrugged. "Maybe. I dunno. She was runnin' pretty good when I got there. Took some shots at her myself … I mighta snagged her some but it was hard to tell. Think I got her man good once. But they both high-tailed it when that airship got there. Those Republic gents are still out there lookin' fer her."

"The hell they doin' all the way out here, anyway?"

Holt gave a snort and twisted on his stool to look over his shoulder briefly, though there weren't nothin' or no one there fer the moment. Then he turned back to me. "Yer girl," he said lowly.

"Huh?"

"Charlotte. Charlotte Harrison, daughter of Senator John Henry Harrison from the east, you remember her sayin' all that back in Copperwell?"

I frowned more, not seein' how any of this related to that airship. "Sure."

Holt leaned forward on his stool, closer to me. "Yeah, well, when she ran off, turns out she went to Blackbird. While we were settin' up the mill, she sent a wire to her senator father. Told him Nine-Fingered Nan was comin' to this area and to send the calvary. And I guess he did."

My mind felt disoriented, sluggish, and I had a hard time figurin' how Charlotte would have known where or when Nan might be comin'. I'd never told her. Hadn't told her on purpose.

"But remember how she also said her pa didn't know where she'd gone, back when we first found her lurkin' around at Grave Gulch?"

"Yeah…"

"When she sent the wire about Nan, her pa figured out where she must be, of course. He was real sore about her runnin' off, apparently. Ordered some of those men he sent after Nan to escort her home immediately. On that airship, no less."

My heart picked up pace at this news, pulsin' a heavy ache through the left side of my chest, and I took deep, slow breaths to try and ease it off. "Did … did they…?"

Holt scoffed. "What do you think? Hell no, kid. She don't want to go home. Fer all that wealth she's got, her home must be an awful place with as certain as she is about not goin' back. They had her all loaded up on that airship already when they went to the mill to go after Nan, but when she saw you bleedin' out on the riverbank, she told her pa's men you were the one who'd helped rescue her from Whittaker, convinced 'em to take you aboard and bring you to yer doctor friend." He paused, and his shinin' blue gaze went distant fer a spell, his expression goin' slack before he blinked and snapped outta it. "Gotta tell ya, kid, yer doctor friend is somethin' else. I ain't never seen no doctor do the things he can do. Not in my life."

I glanced down to the shape of my metal leg beneath the blankets and twitched the metal toes. They moved just like I wanted 'em to. Just like natural toes. Maybe me and that leg were finally gettin' used to each other. "Yeah," I croaked. "Me neither."

"'Course, bein' that yer doctor friend was in that cave of yers—the *temple*, she calls it—and none of those Republic fellas had passed her Judgement, the Oracle made all that quite an affair. Thought you were a goner fer sure by the time Charlotte herself went in alone and brought out the doc … thought we might have ourselves another massacre, but eventually Dr. Balogh got everyone calmed down and got to work on ya. And that's why we're here now, and not in that cave. Cuz of the Oracle's blasted *Judgement* and no one wantin' to partake of it. Which is just fine with me, mind you. Never wanted to go into that place myself, anyway. Not after all the things you told me about it. And the senator's hired guns are far more interested in findin' Nan than in the ravings of a crazy old woman."

I struggled to make sense of it all, tryin' to sort

through everything he'd just said. But it was a lot. And I couldn't get my words to keep up with all my questions.

Holt kept on goin' before I could manage to speak, anyway. "'Course that means those Republic bastards are gonna stick around fer awhile, I guess. Till they find Nan, find her body, or are satisfied in some other way before headin' back east to report to Senator Harrison. I think a few of 'em mighta gone ahead and taken Charlotte home already though, 'cept their airship seems to be havin' some kind of mechanical difficulties." He glanced around the empty house again and then dropped his voice. "If ya ask me, I think the girl sabotaged it on purpose. But that means we got 'em millin' around here fer awhile, waitin' to drag Charlotte back home and … well, I'm not entirely sure what they wanna do with you and me, kid."

I closed my eyes again. "How much do they know?"

I heard Holt shift on his stool. "Dunno. Don't think too much beyond what Charlotte's told 'em about us so far, which ain't much considerin'. So far I believe it's all been positive. And like I said, they seem to regard you as some kinda hero fer takin' out so many of Nan's gang. Guess they consider murder all right long as yer murderin' people they want murdered. If they don't do too much diggin', they shouldn't wanna hang us right off, at least. Although … although there *was* mention of Sheriff Reeves sayin' somethin' to 'em back in Blackbird about you bein' wanted fer questionin'. Somethin' about the murder of Blackbird's long-time telegram operator Mr. Brown."

I grimaced.

Holt grunted. "So it *was* you."

I opened one eye just to be doubly sure there weren't no one else around besides Holt. But we were still alone. So I let out a breath and closed that eye again. "He saw the return wire from Nan. He woulda told Sheriff Reeves."

"Well maybe you shoulda let him. Then maybe you wouldn't be here now layin' on that table almost dead."

"She woulda got other people involved."

There was a heartbeat of silence, and then a creak as Holt shifted forward on his stool, his voice soundin' closer when he spoke again. "Yeah. That's the point. *Then maybe you wouldn't be here almost dead.*"

"Or maybe all of 'em woulda ended up like me," I countered. "Or ... or worse. Or maybe they woulda screwed up our ambush, or never ... never let us plan it like we wanted in the first place. Not ... worth the risk, Holt."

He grunted. "But it was worth the risk to take on a whole crew like that yerself, was it?"

I pulled my eyes open again, though with some difficulty now. All this talkin' and thinkin' was downright exhaustin', but I managed to hold his incredulous gaze. "Yeah. She was gonna ... she was gonna kill you. And Charlotte, if she woulda been there, too. She woulda done it outta spite. To get at me."

That look she'd given me at the end, when she'd been standin' over me as I was dyin' ... it chilled me to the bone. That carefully measured mask of hers had gone entirely, leavin' behind only raw, wild hatred.

That's when I'd known I'd done the right thing in goin' to that mill alone. No matter how it had ended … if Holt or Charlotte or both had been there, she woulda taken them, too. No doubt about it.

"Tell him I was the one who destroyed his life. Destroyed his family. Took everythin' from him and his children both."

But not everything. Not quite.

Holt let out a heavy sigh and shook his head. "*Or* … I coulda been there to take the long shot at Nan while she was distracted with you, and those Republic gents wouldn't have to be out there wanderin' the woods tryin' to find her right now."

"Maybe," I croaked. "But maybe she's already dead. Maybe we both got her, after all."

Holt shrugged. "Maybe. A mean ol' coot like her, though? Wouldn't bet on it."

A moment of silence passed between us as I pondered Nan's chances of bein' alive, and Holt dropped his eyes to his lap. "So. You … happen to get any word on yer sister durin' all this mess, bein' that's the whole reason we set this trap in the first place?"

The mention of Ethelyn went through me hot and sharp as that bullet had and my fists clenched around handfuls of the blanket that covered me. I squeezed my eyes shut even as the rest of me blazed in a sudden swell of rage. But that only served to send a new burst of agony radiatin' outward from my wound, makin' me gasp and cry out again.

Holt stood fast from his stool. "Van? You all right?"

I ground my teeth and waited fer the pain to pass, clutchin' at the blankets fer all I was worth. Cold sweat broke out across my skin.

"Hey, take it easy." Holt reached over behind my head to grab a damp washcloth. He dabbed it at my face. "Doc says you shouldn't be gettin' yerself worked up. I'm sorry, I shouldn'ta asked—shoulda known better—"

I reached up to snatch his wrist with my right hand, makin' him stop pattin' at my face. "She's … she's gone. Sold off."

His face fell and he lowered his arm, though I didn't release his wrist. "Fer sure? You don't think Nan was just fuckin' with ya again?"

I shook my head. It'd been hard to tell one way or another most times … but not this time. There'd been a cruel certainty in her tone this time that hadn't been there before. Not even when she'd told me at first Ethelyn was dead. "Not this time." My voice was all gruff and I cleared it. I was gonna say more, but then suddenly I couldn't.

So I only laid there and tried to breathe through all the little hooks pullin' at my ribs, and all that rage still circulatin' in my blood. I let go of Holt's wrist, and he dropped that hand back to his side. "No mention of where? Or when?"

I shook my head again. "It's why … why I … why I shot her."

Holt looked to me sharply. "*You* pulled first?"

I nodded.

He hissed a breath through his teeth. "The hell were you thinkin', Van? Goin' up against Nine-Fingered Nan direct like that? No wonder you ended up on yer back with a hole almost right through yer heart…"

I glared at him. "I was thinkin' she kidnapped and sold my sister and deserved a bullet 'tween the eyes, that's what." I coughed, grimaced … the pain worsened again, blood rushin' in my ears. I tried to calm down, tried to will myself into that patience Nan loved to preach about so much, but then that only made me angrier.

Holt motioned at me to settle down like maybe I were some riled-up, rabid dog. Even backed away slow, toward the vague outline of a door I supposed was the entrance to this particular little cabin currently servin' as my bedroom. "All right," he said soothingly. "All right, kid. Just take it easy. Don't get yerself excited, remember?"

He *really* weren't helpin' any here.

He opened the house's front door and leaned out into the darkness beyond, then yelled. "Doc? Hey, doc!" His voice echoed away into the night outside. "Think I might need some help here!"

Dr. Balogh appeared almost immediately, and he looked both surprised and dismayed at seein' me awake. He sent a pointed glare in Holt's direction. "You were supposed to alert me when he regained consciousness."

Holt shrugged. "It weren't too long ago he woke up. And anyway, I told ya just now, didn't I?"

The doc rolled his eyes and came to the left side of my makeshift bed. "He seems quite agitated … did you upset him?"

Holt took a step back at the accusation, spreadin' his arms. "What? Naw, it weren't me—Nan's the one that's got him all upset."

Them talkin' about me like I weren't layin' right there was upsettin' me. "I can speak fer myself," I spat. Although in truth, speakin' was gettin' more and more difficult. Seemed to be takin' more and more effort.

"You should not be speaking," Dr. Balogh said dryly. "Or at least, only speaking at a minimum. You just went through a lot, young man. Came to me in an even worse state this time than the last time I found you almost dead. You certainly seem to have a greater affinity for death than anyone else I've ever met."

I only grunted.

"You got no idea, Doc," Holt offered.

I sent him another glare. Half the times I'd almost died durin' the last eight years were *his* fault.

"Well, Mr. Delano," Dr. Balogh said. "I suppose we meet again much sooner than either of us expected, eh?" He gently lifted the blanket from my chest and checked the bandage there. It'd been wrapped thick around my torso under my arms, and then up over my left shoulder. There was a little circle of blood leakin' through it high on the left side above my heart, but nothin' compared to what it'd been bleedin' like before.

The doc murmured somethin' and let the blanket down, then smoothed it over me gently. "I've managed to stabilize you … for now. If Ms. Harrison had not thought to bring you to me immediately, it would have been a very different story. You required extensive surgery, and it will take you several weeks to recover, but you should be all right. *As long as* you do exactly as I say, Mr. Delano, do you understand? *Absolutely no* sneaking off before you are fully healed this time, do you hear?"

I grumbled, fixed my glare on the old wooden door across the room. I didn't like the thought of layin' here in this uncomfortable makeshift bed in the house of an old woman I didn't trust fer weeks, but I also didn't think I coulda sat up right now without blackin' out. Figured I didn't have much choice in the matter.

"I've arranged for someone to stay with you at all times, mind you," Dr. Balogh went on, movin' now across the tiny house to shuffle through various vials lined up on a roughly hewn wooden shelf. "Just to make sure you stay put. But for now, you need to rest. Minimize your movement, and your speaking. We will take it one day at a time and keep a close eye on that wound to be sure it does not catch infection."

He came back to my bedside with a bottle of laudanum. Poured me a spoonful and offered it out to me. "Here. Take this. It will help with the pain, and help you rest."

I turned my head away. "No thanks." But already it was feelin' like a weight was crushin' my chest again, and I was cold.

"I am afraid I must insist, Mr. Delano."

Holt reached down near the stool he'd been sittin' on and brought up a half-empty bottle of whiskey. "I got this."

Dr. Balogh sighed. "Mr. Haggerty, would you go and fetch another blanket please?"

Holt squinted at the doctor, but then shrugged. "All right. Sure." He glanced to me. "Do as the doc says, kid. He's a goddamn miracle worker far as I can tell."

Dr. Balogh pursed his lips and raised his eyebrows. "Not a miracle worker, Mr. Haggerty. Just very practiced at what I do."

"Seems like the same thing to me," Holt muttered on his way to the door. Then he pushed out of it and shut it behind him, and I was left alone with the doc.

NOT EVERYTHING

In the end, I took the medicine. Mostly 'cause I didn't have enough strength left to offer any more resistance to it. And admittedly, I was awful keen to have the growin' pain dulled again. Then the doc took my temperature; seemed satisfied with the result and went about lightin' a few candles that put out a gentle, pleasant scent. Lavender and maybe chamomile, I think.

Despite everything, and all the questions I had crowdin' around in my head, I started to relax. Started to get sleepy. I drowsed as Dr. Balogh kept shufflin' about the single room. Didn't have a clue what he was doin', but somethin' about the quiet activity was calmin' in and of itself. I was only vaguely aware of Holt returnin', and they laid another blanket atop me, but then I couldn't keep my eyes open any more, and I slipped into a heavy sleep.

Next time I woke, the house was still mostly dark. Fewer lamps and candles were lit now, but the fire in the hearth burned brighter, givin' the place a soft, warm glow. The little table to my right had a plate and cup on it, leftovers from a recent meal.

The sound of a page turnin' caught my attention and I glanced to my left to see Charlotte herself sittin' there now. She wore a white blouse with ruffles down the front and at the end of the sleeves and a simple pink skirt, and had one leg crossed over the other. Atop her knee was one of that ancient dead fella's journals. She was skimmin' the yellowed pages by candlelight, and now and then she'd absently tuck a strand of hair that had escaped her loose braid behind her ear.

Fer a minute or two, I just watched her. Remembered what she'd said to me last time we'd seen each other proper. And swallowed.

She glanced toward me, then did a double-take as she realized I was awake and shut the journal.

I blinked, shiftin' my eyes somewhere else. Hoped she didn't think I'd been starin'.

"Oh," she said, standin' from her stool. "How long have you been awake?"

"Not long."

"Would you like something to eat? Dr. Balogh gave us the recipe for a good soup. Said you should eat something tonight if you're up for it."

I considered. "Sure. Sure ... that sounds ... nice."

"All right then." She moved to the hearth and took the lid from a small pot that sat near it. Dished some soup into a bowl, fetched a spoon, and brought it to me. "Here."

I took the bowl from her, usin' my right hand so as to not have to move my left arm. "Thank you."

"Let me help you sit up just a bit." There were more straw and down-filled pillows on the floor, and she managed to both help me sit slightly and wedge them one after the other under my shoulders till I was at an appropriate angle to eat without chokin'.

"Thank you," I said again. There was a lot more I

wanted to say, too, but I was havin' a hard time gettin' it out.

"You're welcome," was all she said in return. Then she put a cup of water atop a stool to my right so I could reach it and resumed her seat on the stool to my left. She flipped open the journal again and went back to readin'.

The sounds of the forest at night had quieted since the last time I'd been conscious fer an evenin', and I found myself wishin' fer that thunderous chorus of insects again to fill the sudden void of silence.

I sat fer a minute waitin' to see if she might say anythin' else, but she didn't. I finally tried the soup, and it was good, and as soon as it hit my belly I realized how hungry I was, and I drank the rest of it down quick. And then gulped the water.

But Charlotte just kept on readin'.

Shit. Well, I weren't gonna sit here the whole night like this … and I wouldn't be able to rest none, neither, till the air was cleared between us. So at last I took a deep, slow breath and exhaled quietly. The doc had told me not to talk too much, but some things had to be said. Or asked. "How … how did you know where we were?"

She paused her readin'. Then she snapped the book closed and turned on her stool to face me. "You mean because you never saw fit to include me in your plan?"

I met her angry blue glare evenly. "I didn't include Holt neither, in the end. If that makes you feel any better."

Her gaze narrowed. "No it does not, Van. That's

why you're here, like this. That's why you almost died. If you'd had Holt, and me, and my father's hired guns, we could have arrested all those people—could have had Nan, even—and brought them all to justice."

"I already brought 'em to justice," I growled.

"Except Nan."

Anger spiked, bringin' pain again. I tried to swallow it all back. "They ain't found her yet?"

Charlotte shook her head.

Goddamnit. Though I supposed there was still a chance she was out there dyin' miserable and slow and alone like her man Lowery had done. I could only hope. Though I woulda preferred a body to confirm it, certainly. "She had wagons with her," I offered. "Two of 'em. Those'll be … slow and harder to hide. Maybe those hired guns of yer pa's should … should start lookin' fer those. Find the wagons, and I bet they'll find Nan, too."

"Good idea," Charlotte admitted. "I will tell Mr. Eckerton in the morning. He's the one in charge, apparently."

"Still don't explain how you knew where we were," I said.

Charlotte straightened her shoulders and clasped the journal in her lap. "I followed you. You and Holt. Watched till you rode off from the Temple … the power station, I mean, and then I followed you at a distance. It was rather easy, to be honest."

I scowled. Despite her intense displeasure at me orderin' her to stay put at that cave, it'd never occurred to me she might try somethin' as simple as just followin' us. "Yeah well we weren't expectin' to have a tail," I growled. "And you shouldn'ta done that … shouldn'ta been ridin' around so soon after gettin' those stitches."

She pursed her lips. "Like *you* should be one to lecture *me* about what to do and not to do after getting injured. It wasn't exactly comfortable, true. But I managed just fine, thank you. And once I realized you were fortifying that old lumber mill, I decided you must be planning some kind of a stand there. That's where you wanted Nan and anyone else she might bring with her to go. That's where the fight would happen. Or else you and Holt wouldn't have put so much effort into readying the area. Then I calculated travel time between Bravebank and there, since Nan was reported as being seen in Bravebank most recently, and assuming she would want to take the fastest route to the mill as possible. As soon as I was sure of that, I traveled back into Blackbird and sent a wire to my father informing him that I knew where Nine-Fingered Nan would be in seven days' time, and that he should send whatever men he'd managed to recruit immediately so they could apprehend her."

I dropped my gaze to my hands, which had clutched at the blankets. All of that sounded awful logical. And yet … she had no idea how the arrival of all those law-abidin' guns coulda fucked everythin' up if the timin' had been different. Not to mention that accordin' to them, in most cases, I'd be just as much an outlaw as any of Nan's crew.

I lifted my eyes back up to Charlotte and gave a careful sigh. "I didn't want the law involved on purpose. Or any hired guns, neither. They don't know Nan like I do. What if … what if they'd spooked her before I could spring the ambush? What if she'd brought Ethelyn along and my sister got caught in the crossfire? What if they'd gunned Nan down before I got any of my questions answered ... or worse, decided she needed a proper trial and denied me my own justice? Bringin' in more people just brings in more unknowns, Charlotte. And in a situation like that ... you can't afford more unknowns."

She looked at me evenly fer a long minute, and then her shoulders softened, and she slumped on the stool a little. "Why couldn't you have just told me all that before?"

I blinked, the question unexpected in its simplicity. "I ... I don't know." I suppose I'd been too wrapped up in my plan, in doin' things my way, and still unused to workin' with much of anyone outside of Holt.

Unused to fully trustin' much of anyone ... even Holt.

"I ... should have. I'm ... I'm sorry."

Charlotte turned to set the dead fella's journal on the shelf behind her, then smoothed her skirts over her lap and sighed heavily. "I thought I was helping. Thought I might prevent you from being killed and help end Nine-Fingered Nan too in the process. Though I did fail to consider that doing so would alert my father to exactly where I was, and that he would then demand my immediate return back home." One of her eyebrows arched. "I also did not realize that Sheriff Reeves wished to speak with you so keenly."

My heart jumped at the mention of the sheriff, and I clenched my jaw against the fresh ache in my chest. I was really gonna have to work on stayin' calm, at this rate...

"I had planned to return to the mill," Charlotte said, "had planned to even let you know I had figured out what you were doing and had help on the way. But I suppose the sheriff had put out word around town that I was an acquaintance of yours, and someone must have spotted me and informed her, because she found me soon enough. And ... *apprehended* me. For questioning."

That fresh ache deepened as my heart picked up pace again, afraid of what she might tell me next.

"Mostly about *your* whereabouts. Your history and tendency toward violence." She shifted on the stool. "I didn't exactly like her line of questioning, so I didn't tell her much. But she insisted on holding me at the sheriff's station until she managed to track you down. I think she thought you'd eventually come looking for me. Only my father's men arrived a few days later, of course, and they confirmed my identity and had orders directly from my father that I was to be escorted back home."

I frowned. "But this ain't the Republic. Sheriff Reeves don't have to listen to yer father."

Charlotte scoffed. "No, but my father has been working with the Commune's Council to form that new organization of his ... and since his hired guns came here to specifically apprehend Nine-Fingered Nan if they could, he had the Council's full blessing. And Sheriff Reeves *does* have to listen to the Council. Especially if she wants their aid in handling the current supply shortage."

"Huh."

"My father also took the liberty of voiding your bounty for Baron Whittaker's murder."

"*What?*" I was quite sure I'd heard her wrong. I

struggled to sit up further on my pillows, but gave up quick when the motion only served to make everything hurt worse. I grimaced and sank back into 'em as Charlotte stood again and shook her head.

"No, no, stop moving around. Lay still. There you are." She adjusted the blankets over me. "He got some lawyers to plead your case. Given the baron purchased me illegally, and given your help in my escape, they said you were acting in self-defense when 'you' murdered him. Of course the Territories have no centralized ruling body, so it's really only void in the Commune and the Republic … but it does mean any licensed bounty hunter won't be able to legally collect that bounty anymore."

"Legally," I grunted.

Charlotte pursed her lips. "If they were going to do it illegally, they wouldn't bother getting a license in the first place. At least that means that Duster fellow should leave you alone now."

I snorted. If her pa coulda done such a thing weeks ago, then maybe I wouldn'ta had to throw the man off a train. But Charlotte still didn't know I had done that. So all I said was, "Sure. Yeah, I suppose." Now if only her pa could void the rest of my bounties everywhere else, too…

"It only applies to that one specific bounty, though," Charlotte said, almost like she could read my thoughts. And then she fixed me with a very pointed look that made me highly uncomfortable, and I wished again I could manage to get up off this bed and leave. "What did you do in Blackbird, Van? Sheriff Reeves *deputized* us. And then I go back and she's holding me in a *jail cell* and asking me questions about how well I know you and about what kind of man you are. Why?"

I tried to hold her stare but couldn't bear it. So instead I closed my eyes and focused on takin' slow, deep breaths. Fer a second I considered tellin' her the truth. Opened my mouth to say it, even. To tell her I'd killed that helpful old man Mr. Brown, and that Sheriff Reeves had likely heard from witnesses about a fella lookin' somethin' like me comin' outta there right before he'd been found slumped in his chair with a bullet between the eyes. But when I spoke, it was a different truth that came out. "Some of Nan's men found me at the post office when I went to send a wire to her about findin' those Old World ruins."

"You said you weren't going to tell her about that!"

"I … I wasn't. I didn't. I mean I was gonna tell her I found somethin', just to get her out here. But some of her crew had been followin' us all the way from near Bravebank turns out, and I … well I ended up murderin' 'em all. And I suppose there were probably witnesses to all that. And I'm sure the sheriff had some questions about it."

There was a moment of silence. "I see."

I kept silent, kept my eyes closed. Didn't want to volunteer anythin' else about any of that business.

"That settles that then, I suppose." She breathed a soft sigh. "Perhaps I'll see if Mr. Eckerton can go speak to her on your behalf and explain the situation."

I winced, pretty sure that was a bad idea. "Does she know where I am now?"

"No. None of us have been back to town since departing for the mill three days ago. She sent a water wagon and some men to try and contain the mill fire after it was reported … but no, she doesn't know where any of us are right now."

"Should probably … probably stay that way fer awhile. She may not take kindly to murder inside her town, even if all those murdered were no good bastards. May not … may not want her talkin' to Mr. Eckterton, anyway."

I heard Charlotte shift on her stool. "Why not?"

"What if she tells him she suspects me a murderer?" Maybe he'd passed off her first mention of it, but if the two of 'em happened to get into some kinda involved, deep discussion about me and what I had or hadn't done … I was fair sure one of 'em would end up doin' that diggin' Holt and me both surely didn't want 'em doin'. "Didn't yer pa organize those men to clean up the Territories? Ain't … ain't that their whole purpose here? And in the eyes of the law, a murder is a murder. What if they decide I'm no better than Nan or any of her gang? What if they wanna take me to trial … or just hang me right off?"

Charlotte was silent fer a long minute. She must not have ever considered that side of it before. In the interest of my own neck, I was happy to enlighten her.

She shifted on the stool again. "Well. Perhaps I will not send Mr. Eckerton to speak to her, then."

"Wise … wise decision." Words were becomin' difficult again, and I felt short of breath.

"You should rest," Charlotte said abruptly. "You're looking a little pale. I'm sorry, we've probably talked too much. Would you like any more soup, or water?"

I shook my head.

"I believe you are due for another dose of medicine. Let me get that for you." She bustled about briefly gettin' it ready, and I took it obediently, mostly 'cause I just wanted to sink back into that hole of nothin'ness again.

No more talkin', no more questions, no more thinkin' of Mr. Brown, murdered so I'd have a chance at gettin' Ethelyn and endin' Nan, only I hadn't done either. And how many others had been murdered along the way fer the same purpose? All to get me here, layin' in some makeshift cabin in the middle of the woods, almost dead.

"Get some rest," Charlotte said quietly. "I'll just be here reading for awhile longer if you need me."

I heard the scrape of leather bindin' against wood as she pulled that journal off the shelf, the whisper of paper as she opened it again, and then came the flick as she turned a page. And then another.

The laudanum sank in and warmed my limbs, took the edge off the pain, and then it was easier to breathe again. And I just laid there and listened to all the muted night sounds, and the soft crackle of the fire, and to the sounds of Charlotte readin'.

And I remembered layin' there dyin', chokin' on my own blood next to the river, and the thought I'd had then came back to me now, too.

Nine-Fingered Nan hadn't taken everything from me.

And she hadn't killed me neither. I was still livin', and so was Charlotte, and so was Holt. Fer all the folk I'd murdered, and all that had happened to me, least I'd done that. Least I'd managed to keep those two safe.

I reached my left hand out weakly, carefully, gropin' till my fingers brushed Charlotte's sleeve.

She caught my hand, and I wrapped my fingers around her palm and gave it a squeeze.

She squeezed back.

LIVE SO THAT YOU MAY LIVE

It took a good few weeks to heal, all right. Just like Dr. Balogh had said.

By the time I was able to get up and around without swoonin' or collapsin' into a mess of hurt, autumn had come and nearly gone in Akansa, and winter was drawin' nearer than I liked. The hired guns from the east had finally given up on bringin' Charlotte back to her father and departed on their mended airship two weeks past, though not without quite a fuss.

They'd been furious and appalled when they'd learned Charlotte had watched over me at the beginnin' of my healin' without a *chaperone*, as they said, and had thereafter insisted one of 'em stay with her at all times if she were ever gonna be sittin' with me.

It was the most ridiculous thing I'd ever seen, them watchin' over her carefully as a nanny might a child, and most times glarin' at me through narrowed eyes, too. No matter that I was mostly hardly conscious and couldn't get off the bed without feelin' like I'd got shot all over again.

And when she'd still refused to accompany 'em back to Pennsylvania later, I thought there might be another gunfight. I'd been half-healed at that point, able to hobble around fer brief periods, and all the shoutin' and arguin' had roused me enough to open the door of my temporary housin' and check on things.

In the end, Charlotte had hidden away in the power station's cave, and none of her father's men could find her. Neither Dr. Balogh nor the Seers nor myself would help 'em locate her, and their resultin' threats were not taken kindly. They were driven back to their airship under a whole lot of arrows, a few warnin' shots from pistols, and a flock of mechanical birds Dr. Balogh had been tinkerin' with. I'd been hopin' the doc had had some of those poisonous bees to use on 'em by that point … but no such luck.

They assured Dr. Balogh—and anyone else nearby enough in the forest to hear their shoutin'— that Senator Harrison had promised to disown his daughter if she did not return with 'em, and that meant no more future estate and no more money.

Apparently, Charlotte cared not one bit.

I was beginnin' to see why she'd come back west now.

It was only later, after Charlotte had been informed that they'd finally departed and she'd rejoined us in the Oracle's little village, she told us she'd taken enough jewelry and other small valuables from her home on her way out here to provide her a decent livin' for a good long while, anyway.

I imagined that was probably another reason her father had been so put out about her abrupt departure.

Holt had missed the commotion surroundin' the departure of the hired guns, bein' as he remained mighty uncomfortable with the Oracle and her people and spent most his time roamin' the woods in search of game and supplies, but he was there to hear Charlotte admit to stealin' from her own family, and he gave me a pointed look from across the fire.

Told you so, it said. *Told you she could be useful.*

I only pursed my lips and gave a little shake of my head.

I still didn't want Charlotte goin' with us anywhere, to do any of the usual things we did. I'd worked this hard to keep her outta any real danger again … I weren't gonna willingly put her right back into it.

To my relief, Dr. Balogh and his family invited her to stay with them, and she was more than happy to accept their invitation. I didn't think she'd stopped porin' over those old journals since I'd woke up after thinkin' I was dead. And her eyes lit up any time the doc mentioned any of those metal contraptions he'd been workin' on. Given her upbringin', she already spoke what the doc called "the language of the Engineers", which was the language most of those movin' statues had been programmed to respond to. Apparently it was somethin' wealthy folk in the east often learned as children, though more as an academic curiosity than fer any practical use, but I'd never heard it used before. That's how she'd been able to talk to the demon-woman thing when it had first been comin' after us, and why Dr. Balogh had taken note of what was happenin' in that chamber in the first place.

She'd fit right in with the Balogh family. Would be happy stayin' with them. Happier than she ever musta been in the east.

Happier than she woulda been if she'd stayed to ride on with me and Holt.

I ignored the tightness in my throat at the thought. Tried to concentrate instead on figurin' out just what the hell I was gonna do now. I'd probably enjoyed these last few weeks a little too much, in truth. Despite all the pain, the frustratin' helplessness, the lengthy recovery, and the disturbingly close presence of the strange Oracle woman most times ... there was also almost a hypnotic, soothin' calm to the whole routine.

I usually didn't like stayin' in one place fer so long. Those three weeks waitin' on Nan in Bravebank had nearly driven me mad. But here ... this place was different. Tucked away far in the woods, away from outside pryin' ears and eyes, there weren't much chance of any law happenin' across us. Or any others who might be wantin' to collect on any of our bounties.

And despite the intense unpleasantness of her so-called *Judgement*, the Oracle and her people had been relatively benign and helpful durin' our stay with 'em. Holt remained highly suspicious, but I'd found myself beginnin' to relax.

Beginnin' to almost even trust 'em.

This place felt ... safe.

And that was a feelin' I didn't often have these days. Hadn't felt like I could afford to relax much ever since Mama and Pa had been murdered. There'd always been somethin' to concern myself with since: where the next meal was comin' from, where to find shelter, where to find work so I could earn some money fer travelin', who might be comin' to rob or murder me ... where was the next word about a girl named Ethelyn Delano.

And that was the worst part.

The fact I was feelin' safe at all. The fact I was here bein' tended to and patched up and fed … and I'd even let myself enjoy it. I'd let that old sense of languid contentment slip in some days, especially lately when I was hurtin' less and wrapped in a fur blanket and set in front of the hearth to keep off the chill of the oncomin' winter. I'd let myself wallow in that feelin' some days.

But I didn't deserve it. None of it.

By all accounts, I shoulda died on that riverbank. That's what I deserved. Not to be resurrected to heal in relative comfort while Ethelyn was still a captive somewhere.

The news that she'd already left this continent had killed that obsessive, burnin' urgency once like a livin' thing inside me … but now in its wake was only a cold vacancy. A feelin' of bein' completely lost. Overwhelmed at the notion of her bein' in a completely different country, at the number of possible countries she could have gone to, at how the hell I'd ever find out exactly where she might have gone, how I'd ever get there, how I'd ever find her if I did get there...

Senator Harrison's hired guns had never found Nine-Fingered Nan, either of her wagons, or her last remainin' lieutenant. There were accounts of more murders in the woods … dead prospectors and travelers, and more robberies along the roads in the area as well. And Sheriff Reeves started sendin' out patrols and posses, but they were spread thin and nothin' much ever came outta 'em.

Coulda been Nan and her skeleton crew doin' the robbin' and murderin' … or it coulda just been some desperate folk fightin' fer their chance at survival out here like all the rest of us.

Holt kept his eye on the papers when he could sneak up to the outskirts of Blackbird and snatch away a discarded one, but there was no mention of Nan appearin' in any nearby town. Or any town at all, fer that matter. In fact, after a few weeks, the **Blackbird Daily** started speculatin' that Nan's long-standin' reign of terror in the west might have even been collapsin'.

Seemed a few groups of her gang she'd left behind in various other footholds of hers were gettin' restless at her absence; had started fightin' amongst themselves and made the job of what law there was in the Territories a lot easier.

Maybe I'd killed her, after all.

Maybe she was nothin' more than bones even now, scattered by the wildlife and indiscernible from any of the other bones left behind by the *incident*.

I considered the notion as I helped gather firewood fer the village one chill mornin', all the dead leaves underfoot havin' a thin layer of frost atop 'em —the first frost of the year—and my breath cloudin' in the air. I was only gatherin' small stuff, no big logs and certainly no choppin' yet, doctor's orders, but it was a rhythmic chore that left plenty of time fer thinkin'.

And I was thinkin' it was time fer me to move on, whether Nine-Fingered Nan was dead or not. No matter what contentment I'd managed to find in this little cluster of haphazard log shacks populated by unstable, forest-dwellin' folk. No matter how safe it seemed.

That itch had started to come back now that I

was feelin' more myself. The pervasive rot that always seemed to be eatin' away at me, no matter where I was or what I was doin'.

Guilt.

I shouldn't be here just livin' a simple life. I needed to be *out there*, doin' what I'd said I'd do nine years ago. Or at the very least, fulfillin' my promise to Nine-Fingered Nan.

I'd told her I'd destroy everythin' she had if she didn't give me my sister.

Seemed far past time to start deliverin' on that promise ... even if she weren't around to know about it.

A week later and I was saddlin' Joe up in the cold of pre-dawn, a lantern set on a nearby tree stump makin' just enough light fer me to see by. After almost a decade in the desert, I'd also forgotten how cold a winter could get. And it had only just begun.

I hadn't had any suitable warm clothes no more, so Dr. Balogh and the Oracle's flock had generously donated a coat to me and Holt both so we wouldn't freeze in the swiftly coolin' weather.

I pulled the wool-lined collar up to shield my neck and retrieved Joe's bridle, warmin' the bit in my hand before slidin' it into his mouth. The saddle had been a bit tricky to work with; throwin' it up onto his back had stretched muscles in my chest that were still tender and reluctant to work that hard just yet. But there were no more stitches, and the scars were only faint now, and there weren't generally any more pain unless it came from the nightmares.

Once Joe was ready, I re-checked everything to be sure it was all in order. It'd been a spell since I'd ridden out, and I almost felt outta practice already. Satisfied as I could be fer the moment, I caught up Joe's reins and grabbed the lantern, and turned to see a person standin' there.

He caught me so much by surprise I jumped backward and fell right into Joe's shoulder, blurtin' a few good curses under my breath. The mule blew a snort and then nickered softly, and I raised the lantern to better illuminate the man's face.

Holt squinted in the light. "Think sittin' around here so long has dulled yer senses some, kid. I weren't even tryin' to be all that quiet."

I gave a grunt, steppin' away from the mule to blow out a breath of my own and resume my walk toward the edge of the Oracle's small settlement. Holt had been campin' outside of the village, even despite the worsenin' weather, but he was suspiciously fully clothed and kitted up already, boots and guns and all. "Why are you even awake?"

He fell into step beside me. "Had to take a piss. Saw the light and figured no one who was up to any good should be up this early. Then I saw you saddlin' up, figured you thought you could sneak off without havin' to say any goodbyes."

I shrugged. "That … that was the plan, yeah."

"Uh huh. Well come on, then. We'd better get goin' 'fore you wake up anyone else."

"*We?*"

"You think I wanna stay here with that crazy old woman any longer? Hell no."

I stopped walkin', considerin', then turned to face him. "I don't even know where I'm goin' or what I'm doin' yet, Holt."

He shrugged, a cloud of breath foggin' around his head. "And when exactly has that ever mattered? C'mon, I'm freezin'. I wanna get movin'." He turned to trudge back toward his camp, and I followed more outta habit than anythin' else. As we got closer, I saw he'd already packed up and saddled his gelding.

I frowned as he mounted up. "You were gonna leave today, too?"

He reined around to face me with a snort. "Naw. I just saw you fixin' to leave and packed up myself." A wry smile parted his scraggly gray beard. "Think sittin' around here so long has slowed you up some, too. Got myself ready to go in about half the time it took you to saddle the mule."

I scowled at him. "Yeah, well … I almost got shot through the heart, ya know. That takes its toll on a fella."

"So I've heard." He sobered some and sighed, glancin' toward the ramshackle village we'd just left behind. "Look, kid. You seem awful happy here … 'specially when you started feelin' better. Don't think I've ever seen you lookin' so peaceful. I know this ain't much of a life, but it's more than I could ever give ya. It's more like what you grew up with, ain't it? And I think … I think it's more of what you really want. Seein' Death up close and personal like that tends to let a man know real fast what he really wants." He grunted and shook his head. "Trust me, I know. Seen it myself. So what I'm tryin' to say is … maybe you should stay. Maybe this time … maybe this time you don't need to ride off."

Maybe you don't need to ride off…

Fer an instant, the pull to stay put fer once was so strong it brought a sour taste to my mouth. To have a home, even if borrowed, and many more days around a roarin' hearth listenin' to the quiet sounds of Charlotte readin'…

But then I swallowed. Pushed through it. Shook my head. "I … I can't. I can't stay."

Holt sat quiet fer a minute, and Joe nosed at my elbow, wonderin' why we were just standin' around. "You sure?" Holt asked. "I had to watch yer pa search fer his salvation, remember. He searched fer it awful hard … but in the end I think he found it with yer ma, and with you kids. Think that's why he left everythin' else behind. And I was sore about it, sure … but he was happy there. Just 'cause I ain't found my place yet don't mean he didn't find his. And don't mean you ain't found yers. If you wanna stay…"

"No," I said, quick before the temptation could rise again. I put out the lantern and set it over at the base of a nearby tree. Someone would find it later. Then I swung up onto Joe and gathered my reins. "I ain't stayin'."

Holt lifted one bushy eyebrow. "Still ain't pun-ished yerself enough, eh? Fer Chrissakes, kid, ya al-most took a bullet to the heart! You sure it's worth it? Sure it's worth leavin' all this behind?"

I glared at him steadily, then took one last look over my shoulder before nudgin' Joe forward. "It's a crazy old woman and her lot of backwoods folk. Ain't nothin' I can't do without."

Holt prodded his gelding after me. "*And* the doctor who saved yer life—twice."

Three times, in truth. There was the time in the cave he'd stopped the automatons from tearin' me and Charlotte apart. But Holt hadn't yet heard all of that story, and I didn't mention it now, neither.

"*And* the pretty girl you like. And I think she likes you, too."

That sour taste rose in my mouth again. "She deserves a lot better than me," I muttered.

Holt scoffed. "And yer ma deserved a lot better than yer pa, believe you me. But that didn't stop *him*, did it?"

I clenched my jaw and said nothin', dislikin' the route of this discussion.

Holt came to ride beside me, but at my continued silence got the hint, and finally let it go with a heavy sigh. "Fine. Fine. Well then, the least you can do is take this."

I glanced at him to see him holdin' out pa's sixshooter again. The silver platin' was impossibly bright even in the muted light of early dawn. I rolled my eyes, but he pushed on.

"I tried shootin' it, Van. It's what I used when I managed to track you down at the mill. Emptied it at Nan and her man … but it just don't feel right. It ain't mine. It's supposed to be yers." He extended his arm, so the thing was nearly in my lap.

I pulled Joe to a halt and Holt did the same, and then I sat there starin' down at the pistol. There was a phrase elegantly scrolled along the barrel that I hadn't noticed before: *Vive ut vivas*. I had no idea what that meant, but I knew sure enough what all the tally marks over the rest of it meant.

My right holster currently held the gun meant fer my left, and the left was empty. I'd put the smaller sixgun meant fer my leg holster back into its hidden compartment, and the doc had refilled those little bags of medicines again, bein' that they'd deployed when Nan had shot me. The leg was all put together and whole again like the rest of me, but I was still missin' a gun.

I'd planned to run through a town later, once I was far from Blackbird and Sheriff Reeves, and pick up another one.

But then, here was pa's. I swallowed again and lifted it from Holt's palm.

It was hefty, heavier than the pistols I usually preferred. I let my reins drop over my saddle horn and turned it over in my hands, studyin' it. Feelin' all the little grooves of the tally marks beneath my fingertips. There was some empty space along the frame.

Room fer more notches.

"Holt … was it Nan who came after us? Who murdered Mama and Pa and burned everything?"

He shrugged. "I dunno, kid. I weren't there. You didn't see her?"

I shook my head. I hadn't seen the person doin' the murderin'. I'd been in the back room with Mama and Ethelyn. We'd only heard the shot, seen the results of it. "Papers said it was some of Paul's gang," I said.

Holt nodded. "Coulda been. Or it coulda been Nan, too. Like I told you before … she hated him most of all, seemed like."

"She told me at the river she was the one who destroyed his life. Destroyed his family. Took everything from him."

Holt's face went hard. "Then it sure sounds like it was her, all right."

My right hand tightened around the pistol's ivory grip. "She said it was revenge."

"Fer losin' her finger?"

"She didn't specify."

"That's a lotta rage over a finger."

It was. A whole family and their livelihood destroyed. Well, maybe Holt was right. Maybe it was only right I finished takin' down all the rest of what Nan had built, and did it usin' pa's pistol. I pulled mine from the right holster and moved it back where it belonged on the left, then settled the big forty-four at my right hip. "I'm gonna take it all down, Holt."

"Didn't expect anythin' less of ya, kid. I knew what was in yer head just as soon as I saw you saddlin' up."

"Then why'd you try to get me to stay?"

"Ain't I always been here to talk some sense into ya? I had to try, at least."

I grunted. *Sense* is what he called it, huh? I tugged my hat down a little lower. "Right. Sure. All right, then. Let's go." I spurred Joe onward. He leapt into a brisk trot, headin' away into the woods.

Holt followed, and we made a trail through the frost goin' westward, our backs to the risin' sun.

EPILOGUE

THE SHADOW

They had been following her for quite some time. Four of them.

But the dark and the drizzling rain and the hood of the cloak she currently clutched around herself made it impossible to properly identify them. Some of Yamamoto's men, maybe, come to retrieve her despite the old man's claims she was not his property? Despite his assurance that she now had the freedom to roam about the city as she pleased—though he strongly recommended she take along one of his guides, of course.

But no. If they had been some of Yamamoto's, surely they would have caught up to her already and announced themselves. They wouldn't have been lurking around back there, slowly creeping closer and closer like maybe they thought she wouldn't notice they'd been tailing her since she'd reached the city's outskirts.

Ethelyn pulled her cloak tighter around herself and stole another glance at them in the reflection of a shop window. She'd been through enough rough territories in her life to spot when a person was following her; had been attacked and robbed and swindled enough to know when a person meant trouble.

These four meant trouble.

And all she had on her for weapons was a pair of those wooden sticks the people of this country commonly ate with and the single filigree butterfly hairpin currently nestled into the coils of her dark locks.

She cursed her impulsive foolishness. She knew better than this. She knew better than to walk into a potentially dangerous situation unarmed and unprepared. She hadn't been this careless in years. But the invitation of freedom, the chance to leave Yamamoto's manor, the opportunity to test all of his claims that she was not property, not a slave or even a servant, had been too much.

As soon as he'd announced to all of his newest arrivals that they were free to do as they wished, even leave if they wanted—while always having a home at his estate, should they wish to return—she had fled.

And sure enough, none of his black-clad guards with their ever-stoic expressions and double swords at the hip had lifted a finger to stop her. Or to stop any of those who had left along with her.

But they had all gone their separate ways not long after reaching the end of Yamamoto's long drive, and eventually she'd found herself in the depths of a strange and unfamiliar city, completely and utterly lost.

Now night had fallen, and darkness shrouded already unknown streets. There were more buildings and lights and people crowded together here than she'd ever seen before, and the reflections thrown back from rain-slicked edifices and pools in the narrow dirt corridors only made everything more disorienting and confusing.

This city, this place ... there were so many *people*. And so many *machines* ... they rumbled in the sky, growled down the wider roads, and whirred and clanked from the doorways of shops.

It was all nearly overwhelming. Oppressive. Suffocating.

She couldn't read any of the signs, couldn't understand or speak the language, had no idea where she was going or even where she was. She had no money, and hardly a thing to trade. And the more she kept twisting and turning down side streets and back alleys and dodging through the thick presses of people in efforts to lose the men following her, the more lost and turned around she became.

She shouldn't have left Yamamoto's place so soon. She should have stayed longer, even with as stifling as it was ... she should have stayed to *learn*.

Stupid, Ethelyn. You know better than this. Why didn't you think this through?

She'd have to deal with her tail. Better to get them out of the way so she could think clearly and maybe find a safe place to bed down for the night. Better to confront them on her own terms, rather than wait until *they* finally decided to strike.

She stepped abruptly off into another side alley, then threw back the hood of her cloak and turned her face to the sky, closing her eyes as the cold drizzle hit her bared skin like so many tiny, pricking needles. She pressed her back up against the wooden side wall of a shop. Inhaled deeply through her nose, then exhaled explosively through her teeth and pulled the hairpin free, shaking her head as her long locks tumbled free around her shoulders.

Here goes nothing.

She'd die before she let anyone else drag her back into captivity. It would either be her or them bleeding out in the rain tonight. Her right hand tightened around the end of the hairpin, the points of the butterfly's wings digging painfully into her palm.

The first of the four men rounded the corner into the alley's shadows, hooded in a dark cloak, his face hidden.

But it didn't matter. Ethelyn still had a pretty good idea of where his eyes should be. She brought the sharp end of the hairpin up and around in a flat arc, sending a quick stab into the darkness beneath the rim of the hood.

She caught him completely by surprise, and the pin stuck into flesh, all right. The man shrieked and recoiled with a jerk, his hands flying up to cover his shrouded face as he reeled backwards.

The other three men rushed up behind him, drawing weapons that were much more deadly than Ethelyn's meager pin.

Her heart picked up pace at the dim glint of their long knives in the rain, and she took a few steps deeper into the alley as they looked quickly over their injured companion and then lifted glares in her direction.

One snarled something she couldn't understand, then lunged at her.

She ducked away from him, jabbing outward with her pin again. But she only snagged the wide sleeve of his *kimono* this time, and he caught her in the temple with the hilt of his knife.

Stars burst across her vision and Ethelyn stumbled, right into the arms of one of the other men.

She felt strong hands around her arms, fingers digging painfully into her biceps, but she dropped down quickly to her knees and twisted her body violently, managing to wrench herself out of his grip. She rolled, jumped to her feet, and tore off her cloak, heavy and clinging with wet.

The three men encircled her. The fourth was leaning against a wall hunched over, one hand over his face, and in the guttering glow from distant lamps she saw the dark spread of blood all down his cheek.

Good. She pulled the wooden eating sticks from a pocket in her sleeve and circled to face the three remaining in turn, baring her teeth like some feral animal, wielding her makeshift weapons as if they were blades themselves.

The three men, all dressed in dark, simple garb, only laughed. One said something to the others, and though she couldn't decipher his words, his tone was clear enough. Derisive, dismissive, arrogant.

She caught a glimpse of his grin beneath his hood … wanted to stab the haughty expression right off his face.

Only before she could make a move, something darker than a shadow dropped down soundlessly behind him.

He must have seen her expression change. His smirk faded, and he turned to follow the shift of her eyes.

Too late.

Another, much longer blade flashed, and the man's head separated neatly from his body.

Ethelyn jumped back as the other two whirled, and one shouted in alarm. They were dispatched as quickly as the first, spurts of blood staining the rainwater red at her feet as they fell.

The fourth man, still holding his face and woozy near the wall, never got a chance to see his death coming. The sword pierced his back and came out his front, right through his heart.

He sagged and choked on blood, and then the shadow planted a boot against his rear to yank the sword free, and the would-be assailant crumpled to the mud alongside his fellows.

The shadow turned to face her then, and she saw he wasn't really a shadow at all. Just dressed all in black, wearing the traditional garb most people here wore, only with pants instead of a skirt. His smooth black hair was shoulder-length, but half had been pulled back into a knot at the back of his head. And he wore proper boots instead of sandals. If only she could have had some proper boots herself…

In the darkness, his pale face almost seemed to glow, his dark eyes calm and quiet and not at all alarmed by the beheaded bodies at his feet, or by the streams of blood lapping at the soles of his shoes.

Ethelyn had braced herself to run, to turn and flee the alley and lose herself in the crowd of people again, not convinced at all this shadow had come to rescue her, but suspecting instead he was just another who meant her harm. Only then he sheathed his sword, and she realized with a start he had two. Two swords. On his left hip, and dressed all in black … just like Yamamoto's guards…

She narrowed a glare at him. "I knew it. I knew Yamamoto's freedom was just a lie!"

He blinked once. "It is not."

His use of English took her by surprise and she

rocked backwards, blinking herself. Only Yamamoto and very few of his staff knew English. She'd certainly never heard one of his guards speak it. She spluttered for a return retort. "Then … then why are you here? Why are you *following* me?"

In answer, he merely spread his hands, indicating the corpses bleeding out beneath them.

Ethelyn swallowed. "I could have managed."

This time he tilted his head a fraction to the left, and one corner of his full lips twitched. "Certainly not."

She didn't need his skepticism. Or his protection. Or … why-ever else he might be here. She whirled away from him and stalked back out of the alley, tucking both the eating sticks and the hairpin into her sleeve pocket, her sandals sinking and sliding in the muddy street.

She was soaked through now, having discarded her cloak, but she didn't care. It was chilly, especially with the rain, but nothing compared to the winters of Colorado or Kansas. She'd manage just fine till she found some kind of shelter. She only needed a safe, dry place to stay for the night. And in the morning, she'd decide what to do next.

"You should have taken a guide."

Ethelyn jolted to a stop and whirled again at the voice. It was him, the shadow … but when she turned, he wasn't there.

She frowned.

"It is unsafe for you to wander alone."

She whipped back to the front only to see him standing there, so close she recoiled and instinctively reached into her sleeve pocket for her hairpin. But just as quick as she pulled it out, he caught her wrist in a grip like steel, and she gasped despite herself.

"Yamamoto can teach you," he said simply.

Ethelyn tried to yank her wrist free, but to no avail. "If it is unsafe," she finally said through gritted teeth, "then why did he tell us we could go? *Without* a guide if we so wished?"

Now he smiled, and the expression softened the severe lines of his face in a way that almost made him attractive. Almost. He let go of her wrist abruptly. "Yamamoto believes his students should learn their own lessons."

"I am not his student," Ethelyn snarled, and she stepped around him to continue on her way, marching briskly down the road.

"Are you not?" he asked at her shoulder.

She turned to snap at him, but he was gone again. Her steps faltered briefly, but she shook off the unease and kept on going, trying to recover her wits. She still gripped the butterfly pin in her right hand. Kept scanning the crowd for further threats. He *had* been real, hadn't he? Surely she hadn't imagined those other men getting their heads chopped off…

"My name is Takumi."

She yelped and jumped sideways as he appeared at her left elbow. And then, to her irritation, he fell into step beside her, easily keeping pace with her angry march.

"I know what you are feeling," he said quietly. "I remember it well myself. It is hard to know when you can stop running. Hard to know who to fight."

"I'm not running," Ethelyn snapped. "And I know exactly who to fight."

Takumi only let out a little grunt.

There was silence between them for a while, and Ethelyn wished he'd leave her alone already. She had half a mind to dodge off through the crowds and twisting side streets again, like she had before in attempts to lose those other unsavory men who'd been following her, but she had a good idea even her best efforts at losing this particular man would prove futile.

So she just kept walking, staring straight ahead, and decided to ignore him. Maybe if she ignored him for long enough, he would understand she didn't want—or need—his company. Or his opinion. On anything.

But eventually, he cleared his throat and spoke again. "My parents died when I was young. My uncle took me in after that, then sold me when I was ten. I … I did not go to Yamamoto first."

Ethelyn slowed her pace, watching him from the corner of her eye. His jaw clenched, muscles rippling along his cheek. His dark eyes shifted away from her, into the distance. And she felt a pang of grief herself.

Ten. When her own parents had died … when her own brother had abandoned her…

She swallowed back bile.

"Yamamoto saved me. Taught me many things. Gave me the skills to take back my life." Takumi's left hand went to rest atop one of his sword hilts, and his gaze lit with fire as he turned to look at her again. "To deal with men such as those who attacked you in that alley. Would you not like to take back your life?"

Ethelyn squinted at him. She wasn't entirely sure he was being genuine. Not entirely sure this wasn't some kind of elaborate ruse. Some kind of trick to lure her back to Yamamoto's manor, into some kind of captivity disguised as the greater good … she'd seen such things done before to others. Had almost fallen victim to it herself a time or two.

And one of those times had got her cousin killed.

Ethelyn stopped walking and turned to face him. Around them, the rest of the pedestrians continued on their business, flowing like one great river of bodies back and forth and between. Overhead, a pot-bellied machine made of copper whirred by, making her momentarily flinch. But she kept her eyes locked on Takumi. "What do you think I'm doing right now?" she asked.

He arched an eyebrow. "Wandering in circles?"

She scoffed, rolled her eyes, and marched onward.

He followed.

"I'm taking back my life."

"How?"

"By getting out of here."

"How?"

She gritted her teeth, fingers tightening around the hairpin. "I'll find a way. I always do. I'm going home."

"You don't have a home."

The words seared through her like fire. Rage surged hot and sudden, and she struck out quick as a snake with that hairpin, aiming for his chest.

Her wrist struck his forearm instead, her hand going numb, the pin flinging from her fingers. His fist hit her in the sternum in the next instant and crushed the air out of her, and then she was rolling over wet cobblestones, the startled cries of passersby echoing out into the evening's bustle.

She laid there choking for air as the rain pelted her face; struggled up to her hands and knees as Takumi approached, but there were little black spots floating in her vision, and her lungs felt crushed.

She noticed how no one else seemed eager to come to her aid. Noticed how they all passed wide around her—and especially *him*—scurried by with averted eyes and whispers to each other.

She almost expected him to behead her now, too. But instead, he held down a hand.

She only glared up at him.

"This district is not safe for foreigners to wander unescorted," he said gently. "That is why Yamamoto sent me, and my brothers and sisters, to watch after his fleeing flock. But if you do not wish to return to him, he will not make you. And neither will I. You may send me away, continue on as you are, and see how long you last. Or you may come with me, and I will show you the way back. I will show you how to take back your life. I will show you how to walk any street, anywhere, without fear. That is the gift Yamamoto has given me. And I think it is a gift you would very much like as well." He took another step closer, reached his hand a little lower. The rain ran in rivulets down his face and dripped off his fingers. "You have no home," he repeated. "But you could."

Ethelyn eyed his outstretched hand. The tightness in her chest had begun to ease now, and she gulped air hungrily, her fingers digging into the cracks of the cobblestones. Could he possibly be telling the truth?

What if she *could* move like he did? Drop from

the sky … vanish and reappear seemingly at will … wield a sword? She wondered if he might be any good at firearms, too. At least *that* she was fair skilled at already herself.

She had just scolded herself for her impulsive foolishness at leaving Yamamoto's manor too soon. Told herself she should have stayed longer to *learn*. Maybe she could still do that. Learn the language and the customs of this unfamiliar country, and maybe a lot more than that, a lot more *useful* talents, too, if Takumi could be trusted.

At the very least she would have a safe and dry place to stay the night, and more time to develop a smarter, better plan of escape if it turned out he was being less than truthful…

She hesitated for another long moment, but Takumi simply waited.

He watched her, deep brown eyes soft and patient, and made no other demands or arguments.

So at last she sighed, set her jaw, and reached out to take his hand.

THE END

THE ADVENTURE CONTINUES IN

THE LEGACY OF LUCKY LOGAN
BOOK 4

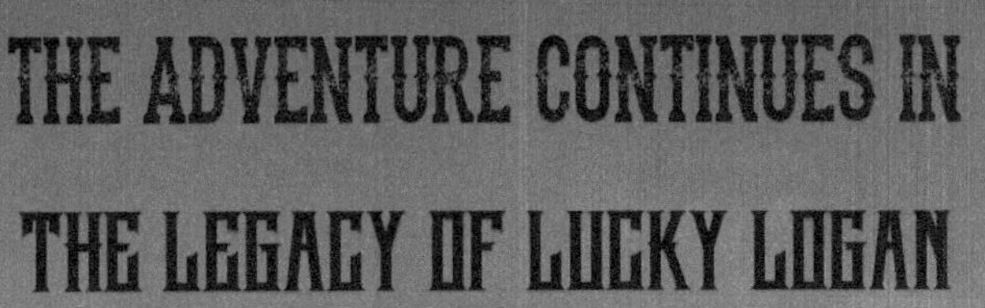

GET YOUR COPY NOW!

Enter this link in your browser to get it today!
https://jrfrontera.com/demon-at-devils-de

Don't forget to check out your free bonuse

Enjoying this series so far and want to g deeper into this world? Then you might w to head to your computer and check this out…
https://jrfrontera.com/the-lost-and-found

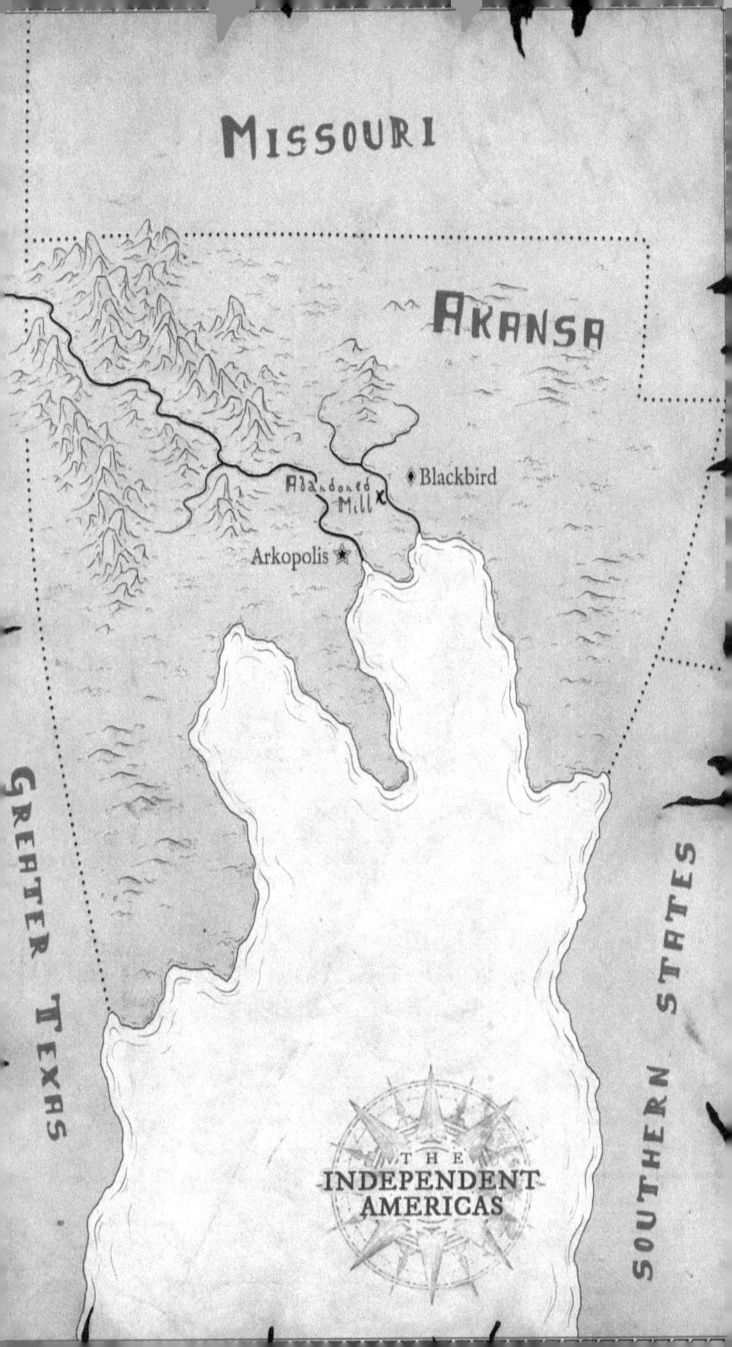

MISSOURI
AKANSA
Blackbird
Abandoned Mill
Arkopolis
GREATER TEXAS
SOUTHERN STATES
THE INDEPENDENT AMERICAS

PROCLAMATION from the WHITTAKER ESTATE OF BLESSING
WANTED!
for capture ALIVE
HAVE YOU
SEEN HIM
HAVE YOU
SEEN HIM
$50,000 REWARD
Name currently UNKNOWN, last seen fleeing Blessing. Wanted for ARSON,
THEFT, AND MURDER. Has a LAME LEFT LEG MADE OF METAL and
walks with a noticeable LIMP. Considered EXTREMELY DANGEROUS.
MR. CHARLES MILLER has offered CASH REWARD PAID
IN FULL UPON RETURN of this criminal ALIVE.

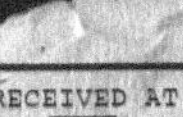

WESTERN UNION
TELEGRAM

DEAREST VAN

AM HOME SAFE. HOPE AND PRAY YOU AND SISTER ARE THE SAME. EVER SO GRATEFUL FOR YOUR AID. PLEASE CALL UPON MYSELF OR MY FAMILY IF YOU NEED ANYTHING. WILL SEND PROPER LETTER VERY SOON. PLEASE WRITE AS SOON AS YOU CAN.

Van, dear brother,

They tell me you are still alive. They tell me they are bringing these letters to you. They tell me you are coming to get me. But it has been weeks now, and I am beginning to fear the worst. I fear they are lying, about all of it. I cannot fathom why they would tell such lies, except to torture me with the hope that it is all true... and brother, it has been torture of the worst kind. Except for that, they have treated me fair decent enough, though I am told daily that is only because the man who wishes to buy me absolutely insists I am given to him unmarked, and that if they should ignore that condition, he will not pay for me, and then that Nine-Fingered Nan would flay them alive. But even that is miserable to endure, as I do not know how much longer I will be here, or how much longer such people can stand to obey orders, even if from someone they fear as much as they clearly fear Nine-Fingered Nan.

Brother, if you are still alive, I pray this letter finds you, and I pray you are able to come for me as they say you are. But please be careful. These people are vicious and cruel, and I could not bear to think of you murdered, too, for my sake.

May the Grace of God and the Holy Mother be with you.

With all of my hope and my heart,
Ethelyn.

THE DAILY NEWS

25c

NOTORIOUS OUTLAW HOLT HAGGERTY TO DIE ON THE GALLOWS

DESTRY, ARIZONA TERRITORY, AUGUST 30 – The dusty streets of our fair town are a-flutter with the thrilling news that the infamous outlaw Holt Haggerty has been sentenced to hang for his myriad of dastardly deeds. The gallows will be erected in the town square and the event is set for a fortnight from now, promising to draw spectators from miles around eager to witness justice served.

Haggerty, a name that strikes fear in the hearts of law-abiding citizens, stands accused of a veritable laundry list of crimes. His nefarious escapades include capital murder, assault, robbery, and arson, as well as more underhanded offenses such as theft, kidnapping, and forgery. Furthermore, the scoundrel has been known to impersonate officers of the law, sell stolen goods, rustle cattle, and steal horses with a callousness that leaves all sensible townsfolk shaking their heads in disbelief.

Captured just a week ago after a daring shootout on the outskirts of town – following Haggerty's failed attempt to rob Destry's bank – Haggerty has been the source of countless tales around campfires, each more exaggerated than the last. Local lawmen expressed relief at his capture, stating, "This ruffian thought himself invincible, but justice has a way of catching up with even the most slippery of snakes."

As the day of reckoning approaches, Sheriff Jacob "Buck" Bell is urging all citizens to come forth and witness the hanging. "It's a sight no decent person should miss," he remarked with grim determination. "Let it serve as a warning to any who dare cross the law. Even out here in the Territories, and especially in my town, there are consequences for outlawry."

Expectations run high as townsfolk prepare for this momentous occasion, eager not only to see Haggerty meet his end but to revel in the communal spirit of justice. The gallows, freshly built and looming, will stand as a stark reminder of the cost of a life lived in crime.

Mark your calendars, folks—September 13th shall be a day etched into the annals of Destry's history; a day when villainy shall be vanquished and the town—nay, the entirety of the Western Territories—will breathe easier knowing that one more outlaw has been sent to meet his Maker.

READ ON

FOR THE AUTHOR'S NOTE WITH BEHIND-THE-SCENES DETAILS AND A SNEAK PEEK AT *DEMON AT DEVIL'S DEEP!* ...

THE BLACKBIRD DAILY

MASSACRE AT THE MILL

BLACKBIRD, ARKANSA, OCTOBER 8 – A scene of unspeakable horror has unfolded at the old saw mill a day's ride out from Blackbird as flames danced against the twilight sky, drawing the attention of lawmen and townsfolk alike. What they discovered upon arrival was a ghastly tableau of death and chaos: twenty-two bodies strewn across the forest floor and the riverbank, with several dead horses nearby, all victims of a violent shootout that sent ripples of fear through the community.

The charred remains of the mill, now but a smoldering ruin, were the site of what appears to be a calculated ambush against the notorious outlaw queen of the Western Territories herself, Nine-Fingered Nan, and her infamous gang. Authorities were left aghast at the brutal scene, with Sheriff Madeleine Reeves stating, "This is a tragedy of unimaginable proportions. We are fortunate the flames did not spread, but the loss of life is beyond reckoning."

Initial investigations suggest that the dead are likely members of Nan's crew, long feared and loathed throughout the region. However, the identity of the assailant – or assailants – remains shrouded in mystery, leaving the law at a loss. How such an audacious attack could be launched against the infamous outlaw Nan and her band of miscreants is a question that looms large. Sheriff Reeves is urging any townsfolk or travelers who may possess knowledge regarding this horrific event to come forth. "We must uncover the truth behind this massacre," she implored. "It is crucial to determine whether this murderer is a friend or foe to the good people of Blackbird." In a bid to gather information, the sheriff has announced a handsome reward for anyone who can provide leads related to the attack. As word of the massacre spreads, tension hangs heavy in the air of this fair town, with many fearing that a new and deadly player may have entered the game... one capable of taking down even the most terrible of outlaws.

As the coroner continues to examine the bodies, the people of Blackbird are left with more questions than answers. The shadow of violence looms ever larger, and the townsfolk can only wait and wonder who will strike next in this perilous game of survival...

Don't forget, if you'd be so kind, to leave a review for this book on your favorite platform! The number of a book's reviews directly influences how visible the retail platform makes it to other readers! And leaving a few sentences about what you loved most about the book will help others decide whether or not this book might be for them, too! Also, you'll have my eternal gratitude!

You can also find *Bones in Blackbird* on audiobook – narrated by none other than the amazingly talented Roger Clark (of Red Dead Redemption II fame)! Visit https://jrfrontera.com/allaudiobooks/ to learn more!

AUTHOR'S NOTE

Caution: Spoilers contained within!

Read only after you've finished *Bones in Blackbird*.
*(Unless, you know, you don't mind being spoiled.
Hey, I write rebel stories for rebel souls, so if you
wanna read this before you read the actual book, I
get it, and I ain't gonna stop you!)*

Oof, Latin!!! Yowza, y'all, that was a mistake. Lol. But I figured, hey, ancient old machines should speak Latin, right? I mean, all the magical and arcane stuff always involves Latin, right!?! That was my thinking, anyway.

And then I pretty much immediately regretted that decision. Do you KNOW how HARD it is to find anyone who actually knows anything about Latin?! Google is certainly no help at all in that regard, either. All my Google Translated translations were WRONG.

Thankfully, I finally managed to track down some knowledgeable folks! (THANK YOU so much to Randy and Audrey Hughey!!!) That being said though, if you are a true Latin Nerd (and if you are, I humbly salute you, because that is no joke right there) and you notice that my translations are still incorrect, or that the automatons are actually screaming nonsense, please don't hesitate to reach out and let me know! Just send me an email at jrfron tera@gmail.com with the subject line YOUR LATIN IS STILL WRONG and I'll be forever grateful if you could then provide corrections! (But also keep in mind you'll likely then become my go-to Latin Expert for all future books, hehe.)

Anyway. So yeah. The Latin. Gotta say I'll never be doing that again. I've already got some tricksy author tricks up my sleeve for how to address all that for the rest of this series. I mean, if those automatons show up again. Which they might. Or might not. I'm not at liberty to say either way, at the moment. Hey, this note has spoilers for the book you just read, not for future books in the series!

But going back to talk about the book you just read … did you catch all the Easter Eggs? All the fun little homages and references and call-outs that were meant to be tongue-in-cheek nods to my fellow nerds out there? There were quite a few in this novel! I tend to throw a handful or two in every book in this series, so someday I'll probably go back to *Bargain at Bravebank* and *Bastard of Blessing* and put in one of these notes for those too, so everyone can be on the same page!

In case you missed any of the Easter Eggs in this book, though, I thought I'd talk a little about some of them here.

Firstly, there were THREE in the very first chapter! Three! Although admittedly, one of them was by accident. Probably a subconscious thing, and then one of my beta readers pointed it out later. Ha! Did you catch all three? Honestly, you probably didn't. So here's what they were:

1. "But if your hand touches metal, I swear by my pretty floral bonnet I will end you." Does that line sound familiar? It should! It was uttered by Cap'n

Tightpants Malcolm Reynolds himself in *Firefly*, when he was all dressed up in a dress (and the aforementioned pretty floral bonnet) disguised as a woman to try and draw out some bandits that had been terrorizing a town. And yes! When I was trying to figure how Van might manage to free Holt from the noose, that scene of Mal dressed like a woman sprang to mind, and then I realized I just could not pass up the chance to dress Van up like a woman, too. And give him a pretty floral bonnet, of course. Most readers do catch this one, but the other two, not so much…

2. The town of Destry. This one came from one of my longtime readers. I needed a name for the town Holt was going to be hanged in, and was really having trouble thinking of a name that seemed to fit. This lovely reader of mine suggested the name of Destry, after one of her own favorite movies, the western *Destry Rides Again*. I looked up the movie myself out of curiosity, and it's now on my list to watch, since it definitely sounds like something I'd enjoy! And so, the town of Destry was born! A fitting name, if I do say so myself, and a fun but subtle reference for any fans of those classic western films to boot.

3. Sheriff Bell. This was the *apparently subconscious* Easter Egg. I needed a name for the guy, and I'm just awful at coming

up with names. At this point I've named so many towns and characters and animals, my brain just blanks when it comes time to name yet another one. So there I was, frantically scrambling for a name for some Redshirter, essentially, and then it hit me: Bell. Sheriff Bell. *Sure, that works*, I thought, and I slapped it down. Only later did one of my beta readers draw the connection to the character Micah Bell from the videogame Red Dead Redemption II, ha! Of course, in the game, Micah is not a good guy, and definitely no lawman. But even still, it's a fun little connection that some people might wonder about. And my subconscious probably dredged up the name from all my time spent playing RDRII. But regardless, the name still fits, and so that's that. Bell is a sheriff now, lol.

Okay, okay, so that covers the first chapter. What about the rest of the book? Am I going to spend another one hundred pages explaining every little thing throughout the entire novel? Oh my, definitely not! I have a life to live (and a LOT more books to write!) and I'm sure you do too! (… have a life to live, I mean. But maybe you have a lot of books to write, as well! In that case, I feel ya, and let's get cracking!)

So in the interest of time and with respect to the rest of your life, I'll just name a few other fun tidbits here for you, with a brief explanation of how they came about!

First up on this list is the train-top chase scene between Van and the bounty hunter Duster. Well, not exactly that. The train-top chase scene is really just a train-top chase scene ... because every western needs a train-top chase scene. (Or at least, that's my opinion on the matter.) Heck, every thriller in general needs a train-top chase scene, if you ask me. But I digress.

The point being, even from the start of that scene, I knew how it would end. Van would kick Duster off the train (not shoot him in the face, because Duster is too cool to be shot in the face, and I wanted to leave him not-postively-dead so that he could come back to haunt Van later if I wanted). And if Van kicked Duster off the train, then there was really only one thing that could come after that, because I am a die-hard fan of the *Indiana Jones* movies. (Except that fourth one ... we won't talk about that one. Okay, maybe we'll talk about that one, but not here.) And if you, too, are a die-hard fan of the *Indiana Jones* movies, and I tell you that someone is going to get kicked off a train, I hope you immediately think of the scene in *The Last Crusade* where Indy throws the Nazi out of the airship's window, and then, since he's also dressed as one of the airship's stewards at the time (albeit in a uniform slightly too small, making him look appropriately ridiculous), and all the other airship passengers are staring at him in horror for what he's just done, he jerks his thumb toward the window and quickly says, "No ticket." And then all the passengers hurriedly fish out their tickets and wave them around for him to see, so that he doesn't presumably toss them out the window, too.

And I LOVE that scene. Even after watching that movie over and over, it gives me a chuckle.

So as soon as I knew that Van was going to kick Duster off the train, I knew the other train passengers were going to see him toss the bounty hunter, and then I knew that the only logical thing for Van to say at that point would be, "No ticket."

And yes, I'll admit, it made me giggle while I was writing it. I hope it made you giggle, too. Or at least snort and roll your eyes. If you didn't catch the reference, or haven't seen any of those original *Indiana Jones* movies yet … um. Well. What are you doing here? GO WATCH THEM!!

At that point in the book, by the way, that train-top chase scene was officially the longest action sequence I'd ever written to date in my entire author career. It was rather exhausting, and I had to break it down into a few days of writing to get it all done. But I was quite happy with the way it turned out. (And I hope you are too?)

A long, long time ago, in a galaxy not so far away, I took a workshop with Writer's Digest where we were supposed to write an entire rough draft in three months. (Hysterically unrealistic for a new writer, btw.) During the three-month-long workshop (in which I in no-way-whatsoever even came close to writing a full rough draft, mind you), we received personal instruction and feedback from a very kind and very accomplished pro author. My instructor happened to be Stephen Mertz. Go ahead and look him up, he's pretty cool. In any event, I will never ever forget that during that workshop, Mr. Mertz highly complimented my writing of "high action".

Of course, by that point in my life, I'd been

writing stories since I could get my child's hands to make letters properly (and actually before that, since I drew picture stories), had been writing my own novels on and off for sixteen years, and had been in the fanfiction trenches for a full decade (which is what really polished my writing, turns out).

Even still, hearing that kind of praise from an accomplished author right at the beginning of my indie author journey was AMAZING. It gave me a MUCH needed boost of confidence, and motivated me to keep on struggling back to the original fiction side of things. (Fanfiction is kind of an addiction, I think. It's hard to get over sometimes.)

It's also something I've prided myself on ever since. Delivering high-quality action-packed scenes has been a personal goal of mine ever since first receiving that feedback from Mr. Mertz. And since then, I've had other people compliment my action scenes, too. Hooray! That means I'm still doing something right! It helps, of course, that I'm an action-junkie myself and REALLY enjoy writing those kind of scenes. So yes, you can absolutely expect a lot more of those big action sequences, like the train-top chase scene, in all of my books!

And also—yes—that ending ambush scene WAS even LONGER than the train-top chase scene. O_o So currently, THAT scene is officially the longest action sequence of my entire author career! And yes, it was also exhausting to write! To be honest, you're probably not going to see something of that magnitude again until the big ending battle in book six. (But oh, that ending battle is going to be EPIC.)

But then, I've learned by now to never say

never… so I guess we'll just have to see what happens, won't we?

Other than these little moments that call back to some of my very favorite movie and tv show scenes, I threw in another *Indiana Jones* Easter Egg … did you catch that one, by chance?

That one pops up when the gang is talking to Sheriff Reeves at the Ace in the Hole saloon in Blackbird. She asks their names after deputizing them, and Van and Holt give her their standard fake names. (I'm hoping you already caught the reference in Van's fake name in the last book? If not, it's just a little Red Dead Redemption II call-out, which I thought would be especially amusing given that Roger Clark narrates the audiobooks, and he played Arthur Morgan, the main character, in RDRII. Van's fake name is Van DerLynd … which is a reference to the Van der Lind gang, the gang Arthur Morgan is a part of in the game. Hah. Works well, dontcha think??? But NO … Van's actual name did not come from the Van der Lind name. That was just a happy accident!) Holt, however, gives his name as Henry Jones.

Yes. THAT Henry Jones. Lol. (OKAY if you're lost, Henry Jones was the name of Indiana Jones' father, and as it turns out, Indiana's real name, as he was named after his father and is therefore technically Henry Jones, Jr. …But seriously why haven't you watched those movies!?)

Remember how I told you I'm terrible at names these days? Yeah. So when Holt was put on the spot and needed a fake name fast, my brain immediately jumped to Henry Jones. I mean Holt is an old guy, too, a father figure to Van, traveling along on this adventure with Van and complicating things, a lot like Henry Jones Sr. in *The Last Crusade. Eh, why not?* I thought. *That would be a fun little joke, and we'll see how many people catch it!* So? How about you? Did you get the little joke there?

And speaking of names ... Sheriff Reeves was named after an actual REAL person: Bass Reeves. If you don't already know about Bass Reeves, you need to look him up. He was a serious badass who worked for thirty-two years as a federal peace officer and made over THREE-THOUSAND arrests of felons (without ever being wounded, to boot). He also mostly worked in Arkansas, where this particular book is set.

So when I created the character of Blackbird's sheriff, and her personality became clear to me, and I needed a name for her ... it only felt right that she should be named after Bass Reeves. I most certainly think he and she would have gotten along quite well, and I even like to imagine that Madelaine is perhaps a distant descendant of his. In any event, she's going to hold down law and order in her town come Hell or high water! And she sure had a challenge on her hands in this book!

I thought perhaps she might show up at the end, during the ambush. I even thought maybe those hired guns from the east would show up sooner, and completely screw up Van's plans. But thankfully for him, neither of those things happened. At least some things were able to go his way this time, for awhile.

But admittedly, I was kinda sad we didn't get to see more of Sheriff Reeves in this book.

I wouldn't count her out, though. These characters of mine keep turning out to be VERY strong-willed. It wouldn't surprise me in the least if she happens to appear in a later book. Or Sheriff Longley, too. Remember him? Do you think he died in that Sonoita jail explosion?

I liked that guy a lot, too. I didn't really want to kill him.

So is he dead? Well, I guess we'll have to see.

For now, I'm sure there is so much more about this book I could talk about here, but I think I've rambled on long enough. Some day I plan to create an audio commentary to go along with each book— basically like the Director's Commentary on any DVD movie you might buy. Only this audio track will be the Author's Commentary on these books. And you can follow along with the audio by flipping through the book, as I'd call out the page numbers when talking about any particular thing regarding Easter Eggs, or funny behind-the-scenes tales, or what crazy thing or another might have inspired that scene or line of dialogue or character, etc.

And in those audio commentaries, I'm sure I will wax poetic about all the other behind-the-scenes scenarios I didn't have time to go into here. I think it will actually be a fun listen, but then, I'll let you be the judge of that! If you'd like to know when those audio commentaries become available, you can follow me at any of my social media spaces, which I will list here shortly, OR, even BETTER, you can come join my very special VIP group known as The Poncho Agenda.

The Poncho Agenda is so awesome, we even have our own logo! Yes, I'm serious. And it is super badass. Much like all the amazing people who currently hang out together in The Poncho Agenda.

Okay, so now that I've got your interest piqued, what exactly IS The Poncho Agenda? Well, it's what we call my Discord server! (And ask me sometime to tell you the story of how that name came about…) What exactly IS a Discord server? Well, it's kind of like an internet forum, like the kind of forum that harkens back to the "good ol' days" of dial-up … only way cooler. And slicker-looking. And with way, way faster load times. If you'd like to come join us, you can find it at https://jrfrontera.com/the-poncho-agenda-invite.

Come on in and say hello! We have a lot of fun there, and who knows … maybe your idea for an Easter Egg will make it into a future book even! You never know! The Poncho Agenda is where I go any time I need some help coming up with character names, or need readers to vote on whether or not a character lives or dies! (I'm looking at you, Sheriff Longley…)

So, if that sounds fun to you, and you'd love to have a hand in creating future books in this series (as well as the fifty-quadrillion other book ideas I currently have), head on over there and join up! I look forward to meeting you!

If, on the other hand, you've never heard of Discord and you hate learning new things, I get that, too. In that case, you can look me up in the same old, same old places, like Facebook and Instagram. I'm gradually phasing out Facebook, but I do still really enjoy Instagram!

I'm on Facebook as Jennifer R Frontera, and on Instagram as jrfrontera. Definitely reach out and say hi if you see me there! And you can always find me on my website, too, at jrfrontera.com, where I'll be posting semi-regular book and author-life updates on my blog. As well as sneak peeks of upcoming books and the occasional free bonus short story!

In the meantime, I genuinely hope you enjoyed this particular tale, and I hope you're looking forward to more. I am honored to have you along on this journey with me, and please know I treasure each and every one of my readers. I will always take care of you to the best of my ability. We're in this together! <3

Now, I'd better get back to the writing! There's a book 4 to get finished, you know! (And a book 3 audiobook to produce! Roger's waiting! Eep!)

Until next time, my dear friend … keep reading, and keep riding!

— J. R. (Jeni) Frontera, November 23rd, 2021

THE LEGACY OF LUCKY LOGAN
BOOK 4

A PICK AND A SPADE

It took a good long while to dig a grave big enough fer a full-grown man … took even longer when you were diggin' it all by yerself and had only a pick and a spade to do it with.

And even longer still when that grave you were diggin' was meant to be yer own.

But I'd always been more stubborn than impatient, and so I'd set myself on a nearby boulder, lit a cigarillo, and watched the man work under the light of the full moon. He could take all night if he wanted. I didn't mind. The grave would be dug and he'd be goin' into it one way or another, whether it took him hours or days.

Although I didn't think his friend was gonna last much longer.

The second man was laid out at my feet, all bloodied up and with wrists and ankles bound. I'd had to beat on him awful hard to get him and the one diggin' to share their secrets … but they'd cracked eventually. Most did, in the end. I'd worked my way up Nine-Fingered Nan's chain of command a long way over the last few years, and these fellas here were some of the last few left.

Lieutenants.

The folks I'd been workin' toward trackin' all this time.

It was sometimes slow work, but it always paid off.

Just like this time.

I took a long draw on the cigarillo, and the end of it flared a bright, burnin' red in the darkness. I savored the taste of it fer a spell, then exhaled a cloud of smoke.

The fella diggin' his own grave kept eyein' me sideways. I had a notion he hadn't yet given up on the idea he might yet best me somehow, or maybe at least get away with his life. So the next time he glanced my way, I bit down on the end of my light and grinned at him, givin' him a little salute before pattin' the silver-plated .44 restin' on my right hip.

He scowled and went quick back to diggin'.

His only escape tonight was gonna be a fast death. I'd promised him at least that much fer all the helpful information he'd given me. And I'd let him have that, sure, long as he kept on diggin' that hole and didn't try nothin' stupid.

A ways off, coyotes yipped and howled, but they'd been gradually gettin' closer and closer all night. They smelled blood.

My mule Joe roused from where he dozed a few yards away and pricked his ears in that direction.

I lifted an eyebrow and shook my head, pluckin' my light from my mouth to cluck my tongue at the fella laborin' at the hole. "Might wanna hurry it up, Mister. You don't get yer friend here six feet under soon, those coyotes just might make off with him." I stuck the cigarillo back between my teeth and chewed on the end of it as I gave him another grin. "Course, if they *do* come fer him, well, I ain't gonna stop 'em. Are you?"

He was down on his hands and knees, scoopin' out handfuls of sandy dirt with the spade, but he paused at my question and sat back on his heels. Even in the moonlight I could see the shine of sweat and streaks of grit on his skin, the damp that soaked his shirtfront, and the glare he fixed me with now coulda flayed a man.

But I only kept smilin' at him.

Then, suddenly, he quirked a smile himself and snorted a laugh. "Look at you … awful proud of yerself, ain't you? Sittin' there smug as a goddamn cat that's got the cream. You think you've accomplished somethin' here? Think you've made a difference?"

"Oh, I've made a difference, all right."

He laughed again. "That so? And what, exactly, have you accomplished then? Huh?"

I pulled my right pistol and he flinched. But I didn't plan to shoot him with it. Yet. Instead I just turned it over in my hands, my fingertips runnin' over the multitude of tally marks etched into it. There had been some empty space along the frame when the gun had first come into my possession, when I'd finally accepted it at Holt's repeated urgin'.

But now … now there weren't no blank space left. "Well, let's see…" I pretended to count those dark etches in the silver, though there weren't no real need fer it. I already knew exactly how many there were. Exactly how many my own pa had put there, and exactly how many I'd added myself.

Fer the benefit of this particular discussion, however, I only counted the new ones.

"Seems I've put thirty-six of Nan's crew in the ground thus far," I commented mildly, liftin' my eyes to the fella by the hole again. "You'll make thirty-seven, and yer friend here thirty-eight." I kicked his boot, but he didn't so much as stir or even grunt. Unconscious … or maybe already dead. "Not sure I got any more room on this here pistol to accommodate yer notches." I held it up fer him to see more clearly, and the silver gleamed in the moon's white light.

I always made sure to keep it polished. Just like pa had done, and then Holt after him.

"But then, I guess that's what I got this one fer, ain't it?" I patted at the pistol on my left hip. I'd sprung fer one to match pa's awhile ago, havin' disliked the imbalance of my old .38 sixgun alongside pa's old .44, so now I had two silver-plated, ivory handled .44s, and I guessed it was about time to start addin' notches to the second one.

The man's jaw clenched, and some of the amusement went outta his face. His throat bobbed as he swallowed. "Guess you're too young to remember how the Territories used to be," he growled. "Before Nine-Fingered Nan came along. You think things were bad under her rule here?" He scoffed. "Boy, you ain't seen nothin'. Boss brought order and structure and *economy* to the Territories, you understand? Things here used to be chaos. Petty thieves and bandits all over the roads. Hardly an honest trade to be made anywhere. Folk bein' murdered on the daily. You want to go back to that? That really what you're tryin' to do?"

I narrowed my glare at him, puffin' at my cigarillo a few more times before stubbin' it out against the side of the boulder I perched upon and then flickin' it at the unconscious fella at my feet. "Look, Mister, I don't give two shits about the Territories, all right? I couldn't care less what happens to 'em. All I know is I made Nan a promise … and I promised her I'd destroy everythin' she'd built. So that's what I'm doin', and I'm gonna continue to do it until it's all gone. All of it. All her order and structure and *economy*—I'm erasin' all of it. You understand?"

He glared at me flatly fer a long, silent moment, and the frantic cries of those coyotes rose to fill the quiet.

"What you're doin' is suicide," he finally said, hardly audible over the coyotes. "You realize that? If Nan don't get you for this, then all the rest who's been waitin' for the Territories to open up again is gonna do it. Maybe the *demon* you pretend to be has had a good run … but you can't fight 'em all."

I gave him another smile and stood from my seat, pa's old gun still gripped loose in my hand. "Now, now, Mister. You've really gotta work on yer threats. I won't *have* to fight 'em all. That's what those fine Eckerton fellas are for, yeah? I'll leave the clean-up of the rest of the Territories in their very capable hands."

The Eckertons. A full-fledged, federally backed organization these days, and very capable, all right. *Too* capable, if you asked me. More than once now they'd gotten in my way, spoiled my plans, hauled off one of Nan's people to face proper justice before I could enact my own kind. Even the thought of 'em now heated my blood, and my fingers tightened around my pistol grip, my left hand ballin' into a fist.

And then came the other thought that always followed my acknowledgement of that particular brand of lawmen: Charlotte.

Charlotte Harrison.

It was her senator father who had lobbied fer the Eckertons' creation in the first place, after all.

But I'd left her … left her behind five years ago when Holt and I had ridden out from that makeshift village of so-called Seers. And I hadn't seen her since.

Had a pile of letters from her, ones she sent every now and then to the Grave Gulch post office, but those had been comin' less and less frequently of late.

And I'd stopped goin' to our camp in those hills a long time ago, too worried I'd show up there one day to find her waitin' fer me, demandin' to know why I'd left without a goodbye all those years ago, demandin' to know why I couldn't even be bothered to send a letter back.

But I couldn't risk it. Couldn't face her. Couldn't afford to have her along with me fer any of this business here, and didn't have the time or the energy to fight with her over it if she insisted. And I had a good idea she would insist.

I swallowed, flooded briefly by memories of my time healin' in that village, rememberin' still much too clearly the periods of comfort and contentment, two things I never shoulda allowed myself … two things I surely hadn't deserved.

Not then, not now.

That sour taste rose in my mouth again and I scowled as I shook myself free of the memories, the regrets … that goddamned *longin'* … and turned the full of my attention back on the man kneelin' by the half-dug grave. "And as fer Nan," I growled. Sayin' her name helped me re-focus. Helped harden over that brief bubble of feelin'. "As fer her, well, I figure it'll be mighty hard fer her to do anything about me wreckin' her business, considerin' she's dead and all."

That grin of his came back, his teeth gleamin' dully in the moonlight. And then he threw back his head and laughed.

I waited fer him to expend his amusement. The higher-ups in Nan's extensive web across the Territories often reacted like this when I told 'em their boss was dead. The lower grunts, the expendables, and those less loyal, on the other hand, they tended to agree with me. Tended to think the once-infamous Nine-Fingered Nan was either dead or had abandoned 'em fer some other enterprise elsewhere, and they were mighty resentful of her fer either. When I'd first started out on this venture, it'd almost been too easy to get 'em to turn on her.

But now ... now it was gettin' more and more difficult.

I'd started findin' all her most loyal dogs now ... and they were loathe to admit the outlaw queen they'd followed all this time, had admired fer so long—worshipped, even, seemed like sometimes—was gone.

But gone she was.

Nearly five years now I'd spent eradicatin' her people, her deals, her trades, her establishments, her businesses ... if she were still alive, if she was anywhere this earthly news could travel to her waitin' ears, she woulda never let me get away with any of that.

She woulda found me after that first night I'd burned down one of her brothels and strung up the people of hers who'd been runnin' it, aimin' to finish what she'd started alongside that abandoned mill down by Blackbird.

But … she hadn't.

Five whole years now, and not a peep from her. Not even so much as a note, or an indirect message from any of her other lackeys.

Nine-Fingered Nan was gone.

As unsatisfyin' as it had been in the end—and ever-lovin' *painful,* considerin' the bullet that'd almost gone right through my heart—it seemed I'd managed to end Nan's reign at the Massacre at the Mill, after all.

I stood a little straighter at the thought. Whatever else I'd done or hadn't done in my life, or couldn't have 'cause of this, or given up fer doin' this, or lost 'cause of that old hag … that fact alone made all of it at least a little more bearable.

The man by the hole meant to be his grave was still laughin', but there was a high edge to it now, makin' him sound almost manic.

I sighed and took a few steps toward him, but he didn't stop laughin'. Now I was startin' to get annoyed. "I suppose yer gonna tell me she ain't dead?"

"She ain't!" he managed to choke.

"Uh huh. And I suppose yer also gonna tell me she's gonna come back someday? Come back with…" I waved my empty left hand in the air, tryin' to remember what the other lieutenants had claimed. "I dunno … somethin' or other that's gonna make all the Independent Americas kneel at her feet?"

"She is!"

I rolled my eyes. "Right. I've heard it all before, fella. But you know what? All this time I've been tearin' down what she built and murderin' all her loyal dogs and she ain't yet raised one finger to stop me. You tell me … if she were alive … you think she ever woulda allowed any of that?"

His snickerin' finally subsided enough fer him manage a complete sentence. "Oh, she's got bigger fish to fry these days, Delano. Everythin' you've done, what you think you've accomplished here … it ain't nothin' compared to what she's got comin'! She'll give ya what's comin' to ya soon enough, don't you worry about that. You'll be squashed under her boot like a bug, just like all the rest! Hell, the only reason you're breathin' even now is 'cause she thought she already killed ya!" His amusement turned into a sneer. "Heard you tried to pull on her, and she plugged you right in the heart. Left you bleedin' out on the riverbank and gapin' like a fish. Lucky Logan's brat, they said, ended just as easy as his pa, even after all the stories we always heard told about the indomitable Lucky Logan Delano."

He had to stop talkin' to laugh again, and I took another step toward him, my finger curlin' around my trigger. If he kept this up, I was gonna take back my promise of a quick death.

"But maybe he just passed all his luck on to you, huh?" he went on, once he caught his breath. "'Cause here you are, still alive despite it all. Guess maybe the boss shoulda blown your head off, instead, like what happened to your pa. Ain't no comin' back from that!"

The crack of my .44 echoed out across the desert, and the man gave a grunt as the bullet punched through his gut, his right hand droppin' the spade quick to cover the sudden bloom of blood.

Well hell. I hadn't really meant to shoot him; it'd just happened. A reflex. I was gettin' better about bein' so impulsive, but I guess sometimes the temptation to shut up a no-good sonuvabitch with a bullet was too much to resist.

"She didn't get me in the heart," I said, slow and quiet, walkin' a little closer, but mindful of the pick he still had at his disposal. "She missed her mark. And maybe you didn't hear, but I got her, too. Got her right in the gut, just like I got you now. And no one ever saw her again. She's dead, Mister. She's dead, and Lucky Logan's **brat** is the one who got her."

He gave another choked chuckle and shook his head. His left hand moved. I took a step back and lifted my pistol again, but he didn't go fer the pick. Instead, his fingers went to the top of his left boot and then emerged holdin' what looked like a small metal ball. I couldn't tell what it was, but he didn't do nothin' with it, only held it loose in his fist.

Except I'd seen enough alarmin' Old World contraptions made of metal to stay wary of it, and I switched my aim toward his hand … just in case.

"We saw her," he panted, his voice now strained. "Me an' Bobby." He nodded toward the bound, unconscious man I'd left near the boulder. "She came back from Akansa, alive and well. Heard Long-Eye Harry managed to open that lockbox you brought her. And inside … oh, inside there was a mighty fine treasure, all right. It was the last piece she needed."

His words made my skin prickle, although I was fair certain he was lyin'.

Mostly certain.

Except fer that little cold snake of fear that

crawled up my throat. Fear that he might *not* be lyin'. Fear that Nine-Fingered Nan had had five whole years now to plan who knew what from God only knew where.

But no. So-called *bigger fish* or not … she still woulda never let me wreck her business like I'd been doin' lately. This fella was lyin'. Tryin' to rile me up; feel like he had some kinda victory in these last moments of his life.

I still had my pistol pointed in his direction, and now I thumbed my hammer back. "I told you once and I'll tell you again: lyin' is only gonna make yer end more miserable."

"Think I'm lyin', huh? How much you willin' to bet on that?"

"Maybe you forgot that deal we made was dependent on you bein' forthcomin' with any information I happen to request outta you."

He glanced down to the blood that soaked his shirtfront and seeped between his fingers. "Maybe you forgot our deal entirely, considerin' you just gut-shot me."

I smiled at him, but even I could tell from the way it felt that it was more of a snarl. "Tell me what was in the lockbox then, and I'll still keep my end of the deal. Put my next bullet through yer skull instead of through yer knee."

The chorus of coyotes rose abruptly again around us. They were startin' to circle. Still out of sight, but real, real close.

Joe whickered nervously from behind me.

I ignored all of it, never breakin' eye contact with the fella on his knees.

He held my stare fer another long minute, then

closed his left fist tight around that little metal ball. Bright blue light flared out between his fingers, but it was his last, lop-sided grin that made me twist away from him and leap fer cover—just as an explosion tore him apart.

AVAILABLE NOW!

https://jrfrontera.com/demon-at-devils-deep

ABOUT THE AUTHOR

J. R. Frontera is an Outlaw Storyteller who dares to write the stories she personally loves most for the readers out there who are looking for something different, and not for the algorithms, sales numbers, or the most recent popular trend. She has been telling stories in some form or another since she could hold a crayon and draw, and her love of science fiction and fantasy originated with her early exposure to the worlds of Star Wars, Star Trek, Lord of the Rings, and Dune. Exploring the potential and pitfalls of humanity in future or fantastical worlds is a temptation she's just never been able to resist. She co-founded a local writing group known as The Wordwraiths in 2013 and is co-owner of their publishing imprint Wordwraith Books and their newly minted entertainment branch Wordwraith Studios, under which she'll be producing her first film in 2025. When she's not writing, filming, momming, or working at her full-time job, she's often horseback riding, playing videogames, or cosplaying. She lives in rural Missouri with her husband, son, and more animals than she'd prefer to disclose. You can find out more about J. R. Frontera, her books, and her films by visiting her website at https://www.jrfrontera.com.